D1576920

A Terrible Kindness

Jo Browning Wroe

A TERRIBLE KINDNESS

faber

First published in 2022
by Faber & Faber Ltd
Bloomsbury House
74–77 Great Russell Street
London WC1B 3DA

Typeset by Faber & Faber Ltd
Printed in the UK by CPI Group (UK) Ltd, Croydon, CR0 4YY

*This is a work of fiction. All of the characters, organisations and events
portrayed in this novel are either products of the author's imagination
or are used fictitiously*

A CIP record for this book
is available from the British Library

ISBN 978–0–571–36829–7

For the embalmers who went to Aberfan
and for the people they went to help

Contents

Part I

ABERFAN

1

OCTOBER 1966

Something dreadful happened in Wales yesterday, but it was William's graduation and so he has been distracted. He left the Thames College of Embalming with outstanding and unprecedented results. Tonight is the annual social highlight for the Midlands Chapter of the Institute of Embalmers; the Ladies' Night Dinner Dance in Nottingham. To celebrate William's success, and equip him for his first social highlight, Uncle Robert has bought him a dinner suit and a bow tie. Aged nineteen, William is a little excited, but mostly terrified by the news from his uncle that their president, David Melling, is going to ensure that a fuss is made of him.

Fifty miles from home in Birmingham, William will spend his first night in a hotel; the Lace Market, along with Uncle Robert and his business partner, Howard. Sharing a table with them are the Strouds, an undertaking family from Solihull, and on William's left, the only other person his age, Gloria Finch, also from an undertaking family, with whom William lodged during his year at college in Stepney. Glorious Gloria, whom William has loved from their first conversation a year ago, drinking cocoa in the Finches' cosy galley kitchen, while her parents watched telly in the lounge. Tonight, she's wearing a tight black dress with sequins, through which her whole body seems to be winking at William.

'Swanky' is how Robert described the event to William, and he wasn't exaggerating. The bright, trussed figures of the women, with sparkling necks, wrists and fingers, are vivid against the men's solid black and white – though Howard's cuff-links are sparkly too. Howard loves an event; loves a fancy do. He helped to choose William's dinner jacket and dicky bow, and stood behind him to demonstrate tying the tie, his broad cheek, brushing occasionally against William's face, making them both giggle.

William takes in the ballroom's high ceiling, the pink and white embellishments, looping and twisting in and out of the alcoves. Giant diamond teardrops and swooping strings of chandelier glass hang imperious and heavy over the tables. There may be more knives and forks on either side of William's plate than in their entire cutlery drawer at home – he must work from the outside in. The knife is heavy, the white linen napkin that he unfolds and puts over his knees surprisingly stiff.

It's been a while since William has seen such dressed-up tables and people. Not since he was a boy chorister in Cambridge and sang at Formal Hall, or one-off special occasions. He quickly pushes the memories away, but not before registering a difference. Even as a ten-year-old, William understood that those seated at high table hadn't *arrived*, they'd always been there, and opulence was no treat. Tonight's excitement is palpable, so too the satisfaction of these embalmers who have earned an evening of opulence, a reward for their dedication to exacting, important work; the work of their grandfathers, their fathers, and for some, their sons.

After the hard graft and study of the last year, William is happy to take his place in a world in which you do a difficult but honourable job to the very best of your ability, most of the time for little reward beyond your own sense of satisfaction. But every now and then, you get to pat each other on the back and go swanky.

4

The fish soup is salty, but delicious eaten with the dainty roll he's daubed with curls of ridged butter. William is using the perfectly round spoon, tipping the bowl away from him when he gets to the bottom. He notices that Gloria is watching him, beaming her warmth through her lively green eyes.

'I'm glad you came,' he says quietly.

'I'm glad you asked me.' She grins, and holds his gaze long enough to let William feel he can gently rest his leg against hers under the table.

The roast pork, crackling and apple sauce move from William's plate, to his mouth, to his stomach easily, and it makes him happy to see Uncle Robert's bright-eyed enjoyment of the evening. But during pudding, he notices David Melling at the top table patting his breast pocket and removing a piece of paper, which he unfolds and looks at over his glasses. The jam roly-poly expands in William's mouth. The weighty cutlery slides in his palms.

Gloria glances at the top table then back at William and slips him a wink. 'Get ready for the fuss,' she whispers, leaning so close he feels her breath on his ear and smells her perfume. They joked earlier about quite what that would mean. Gloria thought they might sing 'For He's a Jolly Good Fellow', and William, desperate to appear nonchalant and funny, said he hoped they'd stand him on a very high pedestal and bow down.

Howard takes a cigarette from the bowl on the table and lights it, as does Gloria. William, who still considers his lungs the most precious part of his body's architecture, even though he hasn't sung for five years, has never considered putting one to his mouth. Yet there's something appealing about the bluish wreaths of smoke winding through the banquet hall – a communal breathing out and relaxing. As coffee is poured from skinny silver pots, people lean back in their seats. William wants it over and done with. He sees Uncle Robert look to the top table and then at William, giving him a small nod.

2

'Ladies and gentlemen, I hope you've enjoyed tonight's feast.'
David Melling smiles. 'And don't you polish up well!' He bran-
dishes a piece of paper. 'I have my dance card here, ladies, though
you may have to form a queue, so please be patient.'

Once the laughter dies down, Mr Melling talks, William
notes, for eight minutes and ten seconds about the continued
high standards of the institute, its charity work, its growing
international reputation. William resists wiping the sweat at
the back of his neck.

'But now,' their president says, putting the card down, clasping his hands in front of him, 'closer to home. In a profession
largely family-run, though it's frowned upon nowadays to put
pressure on the next generation, it is, nevertheless, a heartening
and happy circumstance to hear of a young man not only taking
up the baton, but winning gold.'

Gloria raises her eyebrows at William. 'Bring on the pedestal,' she mouths. Uncle Robert grins at him. His throat catches.
'Our longstanding member, Robert Lavery, of Lavery and Sons,
is, I know, a very proud uncle this week.'

The idea of everyone looking at him is suddenly intolerable.
William wants to run. He can't, for Uncle Robert's sake. Not
again. He must force his mouth into a smile, calm his eyes. The
thud of his heart is so aggressive he's sure if he looks down, his
shirt will be punching outwards.

'Young William Lavery graduated from the Thames College
of Embalming this week, not only making him the youngest

embalmer in the country . . .'

William stares at the floor. Will he have to stand? Should he wave? Bow? Say something? David Melling has stopped talking. William studies the hectic yellow and orange swirls of the carpet, the spiked breadcrumb near Gloria's stiletto. Why has it gone quiet? He forces his head up. A waiter has handed Mr Melling a piece of paper, which he is now reading.

'Thank you,' he says to the man, who is leaving through the tall double doors of the ballroom.

The hush is like a scream. Uncle Robert is frowning. David Melling's moustache glistens under the chandelier as he stares at the pink piece of paper.

'Apologies.' He holds it up briefly. 'This is a telegram from Jimmy Doyle, Northern Ireland Chapter, and I'm afraid it requires our immediate attention.' William's eye is caught by Uncle Robert shuffling in his seat, disgruntled. 'So, many congratulations, William Lavery, for being the first student to achieve full marks for every piece of work, both practice and theory,' continues Mr Melling with a surge of good cheer, propping the telegram against a small vase in front of him. 'Let's give him a big round of applause.' William stares at his crystal glass, smiles, nodding his head a couple of times. Sweat dribbles into his left temple. Gloria pats his knee under the table. 'We expect great things from you, William.' He pauses then reaches for the telegram. 'But sadly, we have another important matter to consider. It concerns the tragedy at Aberfan yesterday, of which you will no doubt have heard.' He reads aloud. '"Please share with gathered institute members."' William sees thin strips of David Melling's scalp shining through his brilliantined comb-over. '"Embalmers needed urgently at Aberfan. Bring equipment and coffins. Police blocks surround village; password

8

Summers."' He lays the telegram down and stares at it for a second. A cold creamy smell wafts up to William; the custard sitting in his bowl. 'I suggest, gentlemen, those who feel able to answer this call for help, have a strong cup of coffee and be on your way. The rest of us will try and enjoy the remainder of the evening on your behalf.'

William knows his uncle expected more of his moment of glory, but he is relieved at the sudden refocusing of attention and feels a steadily building resolve in his chest.

'I want to go,' he says.

Uncle Robert's face shows he wasn't anticipating this. 'I think they'll want experienced men, William.' He glances at Howard. 'Maybe even with a bit of disaster experience.'

'They didn't say that,' William says. Gloria is watching him.

'Maybe *I* should go?' says Uncle Robert.

'Your back wouldn't last,' Howard says immediately. 'No sleep, a long drive and then God knows what.' Howard nods his head at William, but holds Uncle Robert's eye. 'The boy's a wonderful embalmer, he's stronger than you or I. Let him go.'

'With respect,' William hears himself say, 'I don't need permission. I'm going.'

Everyone at the table is looking at him – Uncle Robert, Howard, the Strouds, Gloria – but William doesn't care.

'Good on you, lad.' Mr Stroud pats his hands on the table. 'This says more about you than any exam results. You show 'em!'

Half an hour later, wrapped in his winter coat, William is on the pavement with his uncle. He'll drive himself and two other embalmers back home to Birmingham, where they will get changed and load their cars with all the kit and coffins their hearses can hold.

'You're going to see things you'll never forget.' Uncle Robert glances sideways at William, concern all over his gentle face. He turns back and looks straight ahead. 'You know, your mother's not far from Aberfan.' He slides a piece of paper into William's pocket. 'You could call in on her.'

'I can't. You know that.'

His uncle's mouth turns down as it always does when they mention her. He breathes in and out slowly. 'And *you* know I've never accepted that, and I never will.'

3

It's half past midnight when William leaves Nottingham with his two passengers, heading home along largely deserted roads. Roy Perry, an embalmer from Erdington, reads out reports from the armful of newspapers that the hotel receptionist gave them on their way out.

Just after 9.15 yesterday morning, waste tip number seven on the upper flank of Merthyr Vale colliery, loosened by two days of heavy rain, had slipped and descended the mountainside. Half a million tonnes of coal waste gathered trees, boulders and bricks on its way. It had been sunny on the mountaintop, but foggy down in the small village of Aberfan. So while the tippers had seen the slag start to move, the villagers had no warning that the 40-foot wall of debris was coming their way at over 50 miles an hour. Having laid waste sections of the railway line, a disused canal and a farm, its finale was to rip through Pantglas primary school and two rows of houses.

Frantic parents dug through the rubble with their bare hands. Miraculously, some children were pulled out alive in the first two hours, but since 11.00 that morning, there had been no more cause for celebration. Over 140 bodies needed rescuing.

With water and mud still flowing down the mountain, miners came straight from their shifts armed with shovels. Volunteers flooded the village, clambering over the slurry. Police voiced concern that well-meaning, untrained volunteers were hampering the work of the rescue teams now on site.

The recovered bodies of children were wrapped in blankets

11

and taken to Bethania Chapel, the nearest communal space to the school. The police set about trying to clear off the viscous slurry so the children could be identified, but with no electricity, water or experience, they struggled.

. . .

Once Roy finishes reading, the three men continue their journey in silence, and soon William's passengers have settled deep in their seats to doze while they have the chance. He is wide awake, the blood romping through his veins. The treacly black coffee has done its job. Well, the coffee and Gloria.

Each time he remembers what happened, his body responds afresh, as if it were happening to him right there at the steering wheel. Once it was decided that William was going to Aberfan, Gloria stood up and led him by the hand, out of the ballroom and into the lush hotel gardens where she planted a kiss on his surprised mouth. He wonders now if, after the last year, when his reticence has scuppered so many possible moments of intimacy with Gloria, it was his sudden resolution to volunteer that made her want to kiss him.

'Thank you,' he said, as the liquefying sensation swept his body, and her hands sat in his without him knowing how they'd got there.

'You're welcome.' She laughed, her eyes so glittery and alive, so *hopeful*. 'You daft bugger.'

'Can we do that again?' he said, already leaning down towards her magnificent lips, his whole body alive to the thrill of a future filled with Gloria.

. . .

He reaches Merthyr Vale at 3.35 in the morning, the Lavery and Sons hearse loaded with 30 gallons of formaldehyde, embalming instruments and four child-sized coffins. He's already passed through two police blocks with the password, 'Summers', the largest undertakers in Cardiff. Though his journey has been in the dark, the thick belching chimneys sitting close to the countryside and the narrow lanes tell him he's in a different country.

There's no denying the excitement, even though for the last hour each blink has scratched his tired eyes. He feels noble, heroic even, driving through the night on his own, armed with all the skills he's learned this year. Perhaps disaster embalming is his future. Perhaps the next twenty-four hours will shape his life. When stray thoughts of his mother, physically nearer to him now than for five years, flash through his mind, he bats them away.

For the last half-mile into Aberfan, he's opened his window to stay awake. The spindly paths are periodically washed with yellow light and he has to pull over to let open lorries pass, humpbacked with glistening heaps. A harsher halo of white light shines above the village like a foreboding star. Now, yet another policeman stands shrouded in a rain cloak, waving him down.

'Embalmer?' He glances through the hearse window. Despite himself, William wants to laugh; he sounds *exactly* like Tom Jones.

'Yes. Password Summers.'

'You'll be needed in Bethania Chapel' – the policeman leans in closer – 'where the bodies are being put.' With a dart of surprise, William realises the police officer is crying. Suddenly backlit by the lights of an oncoming truck, his slick mac turns silver-white. 'Pull over a minute.' William edges the hearse onto the verge and the officer waves the lorry on. 'You'll see it on your right.'

'Thank you.' William engages the clutch, starting to feel the urgency, the need to get on with what he's come to do.

Aberfan is floodlit and teeming. Men swarm over a colossal, ungainly mound, some in lines, passing bucket after bucket to man after man, until the last one empties it into the waiting lorry. Others are bending and straightening, plunging shovels into the dark mountain they stand on, faces like blackened granite. When William spots the school roof jutting out of the slurry at unnatural angles, he swears softly.

Driving slowly because of all the people, he sees a flat-faced, dreary-looking building with a line of women standing outside, a few sitting on metal chairs. Another policeman is at his window immediately.

'I've got embalming fluid and equipment to unload,' he says quickly. The policeman stands back and gestures at the piece of pavement directly in front of the chapel and the waiting women. William jumps out of the car, latent energy strong in his limbs. The women stare at him with heavy, dark eyes, and with a flash of heat through his body he realises they are mothers of dead children. He opens the back of the hearse and starts to pull out the formaldehyde, standing the containers side by side. The policeman helps, and a man materialises at his side and does the same. No one speaks.

The chapel door swings open and a man strides out. He looks to William to be in his early thirties, older than him, but much younger than his uncle. He heads straight for the hearse.

'I'm Jimmy. Jimmy Doyle.' He doesn't look at William, but at what he's brought with him. 'Thank God,' he says quietly, when

14

he sees the small coffins. 'We brought a load from Ireland. The airline even took the seats out so we could fit them in, but they weren't nearly enough.'

William doesn't know what to say, so he just keeps pulling the fluid containers from the hearse and placing them onto the pavement.

'As soon as you're unloaded, I need you to help in here with identification.'

4

'Thank you for coming.' Jimmy puts a hand on William's shoulder, walking him a few feet away from the gathered women. William's feet are sticking to the pavement. 'What's your name?'

'William Lavery.'

'Were you at the dinner dance?' William nods. 'It's pretty basic in there.' Jimmy has a thick Belfast accent. He's talking quietly so the women can't hear. 'Electricity and water were cut off when it happened. The fire services are doing their best, but for now it's a hurricane lamp and buckets of water. Doors on trestles for embalming tables.

'Bodies are brought here, wrapped in blankets. Before we arrived, the police were cleaning them to get identification from the parents. We've managed to get the coroner's permission to treat the bodies without post mortems, thank God. We've set up a couple of stations in the vestry and a couple more in the other chapel down the road. We wash them, get them identified, treat and coffin them. Then they're moved to the other chapel.' Jimmy still has his hand on William's shoulder, but he's talking to a spot on the ground a few feet ahead of them. William tries to concentrate; there won't be time for questions later. 'Our biggest challenge is the slurry. It's like tar and all you've got is soap and cold water. Just do the best you can.' Jimmy rakes a hand through his red hair. 'Now listen, William – it is William, isn't it?' William nods again. 'The help we can give these people is not complicated. We do our job. We do it well, we do it quickly and we leave. We're not priests, or friends or family. We're embalmers. Keep your head down and your heart hard. That's your kindness.' He squeezes William's shoulder. 'Got it?'

'Yes, sir.'

'One other thing.'

'Yes, sir?' William wants to get on with it. If he doesn't start soon, the desire to run might overwhelm him.

'There's a concern that more slag might come down. Especially if this rain carries on. If you hear the alarm, you get the hell out. Understand?'

'Yes, sir.'

'Right then, let's go to it.'

They return to the chapel entrance, watched intently by the line of women.

In the chapel gloom, William can just make out cocooned shapes; on the pews, upstairs and downstairs. Compared to the lofty, stained-glassed majesty of his chorister chapel it seems ludicrous that this simple building can even share the same name. They could have as many embalming stations as they wanted in there, and the choir could still practise without getting in the way.

'The bodies recovered first were relatively intact and most of those have been identified, embalmed and coffined,' Jimmy says. 'Now it's getting harder. That forty-foot pile of slag hit the school at one hell of a speed, so they're not just covered in it. You can imagine, with that sort of impact . . .'

William glances round at the blanketed bundles, guessing there must be over fifty. 'How many more to be rescued?'

'Don't know exactly' – Jimmy walks through to the vestry and William follows – 'but there were a hundred and sixteen children missing overall, plus adults.'

A paraffin lamp casts a dim glow round the room with peeling white paint. There are two doors supported by trestles. William's heart jumps at the sight of such small bodies lying on them. During training, he'd looked after one child; a ten-year-old boy hit by a car. At the time, he thought he'd taken it in his stride. Now he thinks the embalmers look as if they're working on dolls. Two men stand over a body, one pumping embalming fluid in with a hand pump, the other attaching a label to a big toe. On the floor is a bucket into which blood flows. There are mounds of black rags at the embalmers' feet.

Another man, at the second station, looks immediately to William and opens his arms slightly in a gesture of relieved welcome.

'Harry, this is William,' says Jimmy, 'your partner for the next few hours. I'll leave him with you, Harry.'

'Thanks, Jimmy,' the man says, then turns to William. 'Ready for this, lad?'

'Ready,' says William, not wanting another speech.

'Right then.' Harry picks up a pair of scissors and hands them to William. 'I've cleaned him up as best I can.'

The boy's brown hair lies flat across his forehead. His face has smears of grey across it, but large smudges of freckles are clear to see on his neat nose, reminding William suddenly of his old chorister friend, Martin. His arms are freckled too and his shorts are rumpled. Then William notices that below the knee, both legs are crushed.

'You saw the parents on the way in?' Harry asks. William nods. 'They're waiting to see if we've got their child.' A tiny muscle twitches under Harry's left eye. 'First, cut the shirt off. Neat as you can.'

'OK,' says William, moving already to the body, noticing one

18

side of the shirt is covered in slurry and the other is strange-
ly fresh. He snips down the clean seam and manoeuvres it off
the boy. One side of it feels light and insubstantial in his hands
while the other is heavy and pulls downwards. 'Where shall I
put it?'

Harry shakes his head slightly. 'You're going to take it out
there' – he nods to the chapel door – 'hold it up, and ask whose
little boy went to school in it on Friday morning. Then bring
them in here.'

5

At nearly 5 a.m. there is a purple tint in the sky; a tired light, as if it's reluctant to break open the third day of Aberfan's suffering. The drone of lorries taking the slag from the village is constant and William feels the air move as one of them moans past.

The waiting parents, mostly women, stand to attention at his appearance. He fights the instinct to crumple the shirt in one fist behind his back. He doesn't like being watched. And never, not even as a soloist in Cambridge, has he felt so scrutinised. But in that second something happens; a peculiar emptying sensation, as if everything that has mattered this far drains away through the soles of his shoes into the slurry-slick pavement. Everything he must do this day is about these people standing before him now; that woman in the tweed coat and torn stockings, that man with the ragged shirt and terrified eyes, and that little boy on the table with smashed legs. William is here now because he has a skill that nobody wants to need. But they do, and he will provide it.

His breath catches as he inhales, his throat suddenly too big. He lifts the shirt aloft and calls on every bit of voice control he's ever learned.

'Whose little boy went to school—'

'*Owen!*'

There is a low thump and crack as the woman's knees hit the pavement. Others gather around her, take her elbows, pull her up. A speck of rain taps William's cheek. One woman turns away from the chapel and shouts, 'Get Evan Thomas!' A series of male voices call out, a vocal chain leading back to the mountain with a school roof poking out of it.

The mother emerges from the throng of parents, like someone coming through a drawn curtain. She approaches William with her arms out and it takes him a moment to realise she is reaching not for him, but the shirt. Long seconds pass as she holds it to her face. A man appears, the whites of his eyes startling against his skin, shirtsleeves rolled up, breathing heavily. He rests his filthy, strong arm across the woman's shoulders. She's stoic now. Blank-faced. Blood on her knee. They both look beyond William to the chapel, not at each other. They want to see their boy.

'Come with me,' William says softly once they are close enough, and opens the door.

It's him. It's their son.

'Owen Elgar Thomas,' the father says in response to Harry's question. The mother is silent and dry-eyed as she gently touches the hand, the head, the chest, of the little boy. Harry tells them they will see their son again once he's been embalmed and put in a coffin.

'Maybe you should try and rest now,' William says, walking them out of the vestry and through the chapel, past the remaining blanketed bodies. He holds the door open for them. 'I promise you, we'll look after Owen.'

'Nicely done, William,' says Harry quietly, when he returns to the table.

■ ■ ■

As the hours pass, the condition of the bodies worsens. At least the fire services have got them electricity in time for the diminishing light. Sometimes, all William has to take outside is a scrap of fabric, a hair bobble, a shoe. Yet it doesn't take much to send a mother's body lurching towards him, saved and destroyed in the same second. These eagle-eyed, hungry-hearted mothers could identify their children by a single fingernail.

When William has to walk onto the street and ask whose little girl has blonde hair, three sets of parents come forward. And possibly, these are the worst moments, when they approach the body with dread and fear that William can taste, and then realise it isn't their daughter after all. He understands, after the last seven hours, the relief and comfort of knowing at last where their child is and that no further harm can come to them. What an appalling world he's in, where the lucky ones are those able to identify their child's dead body.

It's raining again. The road hisses at squelching lorry tyres. Pellets of rain seem flung down on the chapel roof. Nineteen years old, freshly graduated from the Thames College of Embalming, with top marks for every piece of practical and written work, William looks at what's left of the little girl who he's just found out is called Valerie, and realises none of it counts for anything, not a thing, unless here and now he can do his job and prepare this child's broken body for her parents, who are right now standing on the wet pavement outside.

In ordinary times, the room he stands in is a chapel vestry, but this is no ordinary time and William is blind to its details; the sloping pile of black bibles in the corner, the tatty kneelers stacked by the door, the deep smell of the dark wood wrestling with the cool whiff of formaldehyde, or the piles of small coffins against the back wall. Oblivious to it all, William finds himself transfixed by an unbidden memory, sharp as the scalpel in his hand.

Woken from his afternoon nap by the buttery fug of baking thickening the air in their flat, William drags his blanket into the kitchen to snuggle into the old armchair and watch his mother. Warmth washes over his legs as she reaches into the oven, pulling out the wonky old baking tray and laying it on the melamine table. She slides the palette knife under the largest biscuit, puts it on a china saucer and cuts it in half. Together they watch the rising coil of steam. 'For his Lordship.' She gives a deep curtsy, holding the saucer in both hands. The gold leaf on its border glints at him, and his sleep-soft face lifts into a smile as he reaches out to take it. 'Don't burn your mouth,' she whispers.

It is then that William notices Valerie's perfect left hand. Nothing missing or mashed, no blood, no bruise, not even a scratch. No matter the twisted leg, the missing toes or the indent on one side of her skull. It will be her perfect hand that her parents remember when they have to remember this.

Carefully, he lifts the carotid artery from the neat incision in her neck. He rests it flat on the stainless steel separator, noticing the tiny capillaries tracing their delicate path through the blood vessel. He eases the small artery tube into the cut he has made and then repeats the process with the internal jugular vein. After joining the first to the supply of arterial fluid and the second to a tube leading to a bucket by his feet, William picks up the hand pump. *Squeeze release, squeeze release, squeeze release.* The fake heartbeat drives the fluid through the girl's arteries and her blood into the bucket. William's hand aches from all the pumping. His back aches from leaning over small bodies, but he doesn't slow down, or stretch his back, or flex his fingers.

Once the body has been aspirated, treated with fluids and the incisions sutured, William breathes deeply. He takes her

23

left hand in both of his and rubs, bending her knuckles, easing the fluid to the very end of the fingertips, rendering them pink again.

'There we are, Valerie,' he says, 'all done.' He doesn't mind that Harry, busy now at the next table, can hear. While he continues to hold her hand, he finds himself singing, very softly, barely more than a murmur.

> *'I forget all your words of promise*
> *You made to someone, my pretty girl*
> *So give me your hand, my sweet Myfanwy,*
> *For no more but to say "farewell".'*

The last time he'd sung this he was holding another hand. Martin's, his best friend in Cambridge, who would theatrically grab his whenever they sung it together. 'She's *Welsh*, you idiot,' he mutters to himself, 'sing it in Welsh.' He glances up at Harry, but he is suturing, and doesn't seem to have noticed his quiet serenade.

> *'Anghofia'r oll o'th addewidion*
> *A wneist i rywun, 'ngeneth ddel,*
> *A dyro'th law, Myfanwy dirion*
> *I ddim ond dweud y gair "Ffarwél".'*

William walks to the stack of coffins. The top one is white, flown over with the Irish embalmers. He's glad. Valerie would probably prefer white. He lowers her into it, arranges her head to one side, covers her body with one of the donated blankets and rests her hand on top of it.

He carries the coffin into the chapel and lays it down on one of the pews, uneasy that Aberfan seems to have resurrected memories of the two people he's trained himself so rigorously to forget.

The waxy lampshades dip and swing as the door opens. Jimmy's lean figure enters quickly carrying a blanketed body. Another one. And after that will come another. And the later they come, the harder it is. The longer they have been under the slurry, the quicker the decomposition once the air hits them. Now the diggers are moving through, some bodies are hurt a second time. Jimmy takes the bundle through to the vestry.

'I'll tell you what.' Jimmy stands, out of breath, hands on hips, next to Harry's station. 'I'm not religious, but after this, I'll never hear a bad word against the Sally Army.'

'They'd been here twenty-four hours before we even arrived,' says Harry, walking to the back wall for a coffin, 'must have served hundreds of cups of tea and still going strong.'

'You'd expect sandwiches and tea,' Jimmy says, 'but you know what else they've got?'

Harry nods. 'Whisky.'

'And cigarettes.' Jimmy shakes his head.

'Good on 'em.' Harry carefully places the body from his trestle into the coffin. 'Some of those miners came straight from a shift on Friday morning and haven't stopped. And where are we now? Sunday lunchtime!'

William is suddenly ravenous. He hasn't slept and no one has mentioned a break, though Jimmy has brought them sandwiches every so often. On a busy day at work, he might look after three bodies. Valerie was his seventh. There are now five embalming stations around him doing the same. The formaldehyde fumes he usually enjoys are intense, even with all the leaded windows tilted open to the chill day.

'Jimmy?' he asks. 'Can I go and get something to eat?'

'Surely,' says Jimmy. 'At the last count, there are five left to recover.'

On the way through, William glances at Valerie and notices a speck of dirt still in her index fingernail. He reaches in his pocket for his Swiss army knife, flicks open the smallest blade and, holding her hand firmly to get traction, he scrapes hard at it, wiping the black smudge from the knife onto his trousers before going at it again.

In the porch he slides his coat on and ties his scarf over his chest. With the cold air streaming through the gap under the heavy door, William hears Jimmy from the vestry.

'Let's hope this doesn't screw that young man up forever. He's a natural.'

'Got a beautiful voice on him too,' says Harry.

Braced against the cold, he thinks at least there's one good thing about not having spoken to his mother for five years. He can't even be tempted to tell her about any of this. She wouldn't be able to bear it. He decides, with relief, that it wouldn't help either of them to visit her when he is finished here, even if it's the nearest he's been to her since she left.

6

Outside the air is bitter and damp. The light is failing, but it doesn't feel like any particular time of day to William. He tries to imagine Aberfan as an ordinary mining village, with children alive and well, and grown-ups whose world is still intact. He weaves in and out of cordons, police, miners and sand sacks, to get to the Salvation Army station. The soles of his shoes are tacky. The idea of trying to clean them when he gets home is revolting.

Chuck 'em out, William, they're only a pair of bleedin' shoes.

At this, the first conscious thought of Gloria since he's arrived, his stomach flips at the remembered sensation of her confident, full lips on his. The slide of her red lipstick, the brief *tick* of her teeth against his, bone against bone amongst the warm softness of lips, mouth and gum. William considers finding a phone box to call her, but he hasn't seen one yet and hasn't got any change. *Stop it*, he thinks. *Eat, drink, get back to work.*

The smell of tannin and the rising steam from the urn balanced on stuffed brown sacks remind him how physically depleted he is.

'Want something stronger with that?' The tall uniformed man hands him a cup. 'Some like a drop with their tea?'

'Maybe. Yes.' William passes his cup back.

The man unscrews the flat bottle and amber liquid slaps into his tea. 'Take the weight off your feet.' The man points to a fold-up seat a few yards away.

William realises how tired his legs are once he sits.

'You must be one of the embalmers,' the man says, handing him an egg and cress sandwich.

William nods, chewing.

'You look young though.' The man takes the empty cup back from William and pours him another one.

'I qualified this week.' William reaches out for a second sandwich, the white bread heavy and bending under the weight of the filling. His body is so greedy he barely tasted the first.

The man drinks his own cup of tea. 'Family business?'

The cold is starting to affect William. His legs are trembling. He puts the tea on the pile of sacks and flicks up his coat collar. 'Yep. I'm third generation.'

'So you always knew that's what you'd do?'

He shakes his head. 'Dad was keen but Mum was against it.'

Two miners arrive, silent, before the urn. William eats another sandwich while they are served. They nod their thanks and walk away, shovelling the food in just as William had.

'So your dad got his way, then?' The man opens a packet of Kit Kats and hands one to William.

'Not really,' he says, 'he died when I was eight.'

'I'm sorry.' He pauses. 'Your mother must be proud of you now, though?'

'Wouldn't know.' He stands, gulping down the last of his tea and handing the mug back. 'I'd best go. Thanks for the food.' He turns back momentarily, wanting to ask the man to call Uncle Robert and say he's doing just fine, but he simply raises his hand and nods his head.

'All the best, young man, God bless.'

'Thank you.' William waves again before plunging his hands into his pockets and walking as quickly as he can through the people and muck and lorries, back to the chapel, promising himself afresh with every step that he will not shed a tear, not a single one, until he has left this place.

7

William is laying a blanketed body on the table mid-afternoon, when the vestry door whooshes open. William, Jimmy and Harry look up from what they're doing. A policeman stands before them, his hand on the shoulder of a plump, short woman in a red dress swamped by a man's jumper. She's breathing heavily, as if she's just run here. She makes eye contact with each of them, but her gaze rests on William for the longest.

'This is Betty Jones,' the policeman says. 'She's asking—'

'I can't settle,' she interrupts, clasping the thick handle of her bag. 'My home's buried under this murderous filth, so we're staying with family.' She turns to the policeman and then urgently back to them. 'Gentlemen, please let me help. I'll do anything, *anything*. What I *can't* do is spend one more minute at my sister-in-law's and not *do* something!'

Her hair sits in neat, brown curls. The strip of red hem below the green wool is pretty fabric, the sort his mother would wear, but the way she's thrown on that big jumper, and the wellies on her feet, make her look childlike. Her legs are stocky, her body brimming with energy. 'Please,' she continues before Jimmy can answer, 'let me help.' Her face creases.

'Thank you, Betty,' Jimmy says eventually. 'Any job in here is extremely harrowing. Especially if you know any of them.'

'I know *all* of them,' she replies immediately, 'and their parents. If this had happened twenty years ago, it would have been my two on these tables.' Her voice drops. 'I want to do something for those poor parents.'

'William?' Jimmy nods at him. 'Let Betty help you prepare them for identification.'

Betty puts her bag in the corner next to the coffins, then reaches into it for some yellow rubber gloves.

'I've come prepared.' She stands opposite William and looks at him with a brave, business-like smile. 'So, love, tell me what to do.'

Betty is nothing like his mother; she's older, smaller, there is no flow or elegance to her movements, but he recognises a quality in her. She is terrified, traumatised, but she is also courageous and determined.

'This'll be hard,' he says, taking a light hold of the grey wool, wondering how long he should give it before removing the blanket. He finds her direct gaze easy to meet. 'First there's the slurry, and then we're working on the last ones to be recovered. They're in a bad way.' Betty's red lips are a firm, straight line, her eyes on him unwavering. She nods once and swallows, and William notices a pulse at her throat. He needs to show her he knows what he's doing, give her confidence in him. 'We'll take off the clothes. I'll check the state of the body. Then we'll clean it. Together.' Betty's eyes shine suddenly; two sapphires. 'I'll show you how.' She nods again, blinking at him. 'Right then,' William says.

He pulls back the blanket in one swift yet gentle move, letting it fall off the end of the table. Betty's compact body starts, but William doesn't show he noticed. Together, they look. Together they smell blood and tar and the beginning of something putrid.

In the strained, yellowy light from borrowed lamps, Betty groans and rests her hand on the undamaged side of the girl's face. 'All right, Helen,' she whispers, 'Betty's here.'

31

The room is still and silent; William knows the other embalmers are watching. Betty straightens, breathes deeply, so the movement of the cross at her throat catches the light. 'Now, sweetheart,' she says, louder, matter of fact, her rubber fingers resting on the girl's arm, 'your mam and dad are coming to see you, so me and this lovely young man are going to get you ready. It's all over now, sweetheart.'

When Betty's oval face, at once resolute and bewildered, finally turns back to William, he has to fight to keep his own expression impassive, so potent is the rush of intimacy she has brought into the room.

'You cut the clothes' – he hands her the scissors – 'I'll get them off.'

With steady hands, Betty snips through the cotton skirt's waistband and then diagonally across the shirt. Soon, only streaks of yellow shine through the black tar that covers her gloved hands. In a fraction of the time it has been taking him, William drops the fabric onto the pile at the foot of the table. He worries that the left foot will detach itself from the body when they come to clean it.

He takes the freshest bucket of water brought by the volunteers and dunks the sponge in it. 'At least now we've got hot water.' With firm, long strokes he goes to work on the left arm, wiping, pulling at the sludge, soaking and squeezing the sponge again and again. Betty watches.

'You work on the arms, I'll do the legs.' He hands her a sponge and she immediately plunges it into the water. William has never seen anyone concentrate so hard on anything as Betty does on that slender limb. After her initial words to Helen, she is now silent, focusing on nothing but the inches of flesh beneath the grimy rectangle of sponge.

He suddenly feels the need to fill the silence. 'What was she like?' William says as he positions himself near the damaged leg.

She pauses, looks up at him. 'I'd best not.' She starts to rub again.

'Of course, sorry,' says William, embarrassed at himself, cradling the shattered foot as he starts to clean the shin.

The cold swill of air and the sudden blare of a lorry make him look up. It's the navy blue coat and the tall figure of the Salvation Army man who served him, striding in with a black box in both hands.

'Thought you might like a bit of background something,' he says. 'Batteries are fresh in and I've got more if they run out.'

'That's very thoughtful.' Jimmy stops work and points to a window ledge at William's back. 'Could you put it there and tune it in to something? That would be grand.'

'You're welcome.' The man walks to the window, holding the radio out slightly before him. 'There we are.'

His deep voice and roly-poly vowels remind William again of Tom Jones and, as the radio static fills the air, knobs are twisted and voices swoop in and out of clarity, William half hopes to hear 'What's New Pussycat?', or 'It's Not Unusual'.

'I'm guessing music would be the thing,' the man says, peering at the dial.

Orchestral music snaps into focus, purer and louder than William would have expected from a small transistor.

'Marvellous, thank you,' says Jimmy.

'Anything we can do to help. Anything at all,' the man says on his way out.

They finish cleaning the body in half the time it had been taking William. When Helen's parents walk in, the mother

33

clutching the piece of skirt fabric, and see their girl, Betty is there with her strong arms. Over the next two and a half hours, they clean the bodies of two more girls and a boy.

8

'The two of you go and get a bite to eat and a well-deserved cuppa now,' Harry says, once William returns from walking another set of parents back onto the street. 'I'll deal with this one.'

William and Betty fasten their coats and walk out into the night towards the refreshment station at the end of the street. Although it's no longer raining, the October air is sodden. Aberfan is black, white or grey. The lights on the site are harsh and bright again, picking up the stark white stonework, like bared teeth, around the windows of the nearby terraced houses. There's a gaping hole in the row directly in front of the school.

Betty pauses, hooks her arm in his and stares at the glistening rubble.

'That was my home. Twenty-five years we've lived there.'

'I'm sorry,' William says.

She pulls at his arm to move him on. 'We weren't in it, that's something.'

As they walk past houses, he can see dark shadows through the windows; mini mountains of slag in sitting rooms. From one, the top of a chair pokes out alongside a stiletto heel. They pass the school on their left, and a sharp wail turns their heads as a man folds in two at the sight of something being pulled from the debris. He presumes it's the mother behind him, her hand still at her mouth, and there's Jimmy, already lifting the body to get it to the chapel before it starts to decompose.

'If I had a home, I'd have invited you in for a cuppa,' Betty says, tightening her grip on his arm, 'but my sister-in-law's already got a houseful to look after.' She raises a short leg to show William her wellingtons. 'These are hers, they're two sizes too big.'

'That's OK, we can't stay away for long anyway.'

The lorries are still on the move, to and fro, to and fro. The rescuers, fewer in number than when he arrived, work on. The clang of shovel into slurry is quieter and calmer, but persistent. William and Betty stand on the edge for a moment. He imagines the initial adrenaline shot of horror that powered their shovels, stung their muscles into action, must surely have drained from their bodies after two days. There's no hope of finding any life, but they can't stop. Laundry that should have been taken down days ago criss-crosses the alleys in between the house backs; ghostly bedding ripples in the breeze. Shirts and jumpers, skirts and trousers not needed now.

'Thanks, Betty,' William says, as they lean against the sacks with their tea and sandwiches. 'It's a big help, having you there.'

They sip whisky tea, tangy and oily. Betty blows ripples across the top of hers, but William lets his burn his throat.

'She was a naughty little thing.' For a moment William doesn't know what Betty's talking about. She turns and leans her hip into the sacks to face him. 'Helen. She was in trouble last week for pinching a packet of Spangles from the newsagent, and last Christmas, in the chapel nativity, she moved the chair when Mary was about to sit down, and she hit the floor with one hell of a bump. Bruised her coccyx!' All that's left of Betty's lipstick is a faint red line outlining her smile. 'And she was a right little giggler.' Betty stares past William and takes another gulp of tea. 'I hope she's giggling now.' The shine is back in Betty's eyes. 'There can't be anything worse than losing a child.' Her gaze

36

drops to the ground, then she breathes in sharply and looks up at him again. 'How old are you, William?'

'Nineteen.'

'Well, I hope your parents know what a fine son they have.'

William shakes his head and looks down. *God*, he's tired! 'I should get back.' He puts his paper cup down on the sacks. 'You take your time, but I should go.'

'Have I upset you, William?' She stands up straight too.

'No,' he says over his shoulder. 'Come when you're ready.'

9

'Last push,' Jimmy says, back at the chapel, 'I'm assuming you'll need to get back tonight?'

'Not if I'm still needed.' William walks to his station. As he passes the radio, he registers a murmuring voice. The heap of raggedy ripped clothes in the corner is now waist high.

'There's only three left to recover,' Jimmy continues, washing down his table with a vigour that gives no hint of the exhaustion he must be feeling. 'Harry can stay through the night and I'll be here till it's all done.'

'Are you sure?' William feels weak with relief. Soon, he can drive away, to his uncle's calm mortuary, to a life with Gloria in it. Gloria who kissed him.

'I'm sure,' Jimmy says. 'There's one body in the chapel. Look after that, catch a few winks in the car first, and then be on your way.' He turns to Harry. 'Your turn for a break.'

'Won't say no.' Harry walks to the door. 'What have you done with Betty, William?'

The door swings open, nearly hitting Harry.

'Whoops.' Betty smiles at Harry who holds the door for her then leaves. She stands opposite William. He feels he ought to apologise, but her calm gaze lets him know she is not expecting anything from him.

'There's just one more for us to do,' he says. 'Can you get the buckets and sponges ready?'

'Of course.' She immediately turns to the wall against which the buckets are waiting.

Coffins, not blanketed bodies, now fill the pews; some are dirty, smeared with slurry, though they tried not to let that happen. It takes him a moment to spot the brown bundle. Feeling the give of flesh, the bend of a leg, he wonders what lies inside, worries he might not have it in him to go through this again, marvels at Jimmy and Harry's stamina. At least with Betty, he has reason to keep his face calm, tell himself he can do what he has to do.

Two buckets and two sponges are ready. Betty stands as if to attention on one side of the table.

'Thank you,' he says.

'You're welcome.'

He gives them both a moment, time to breathe in and out a few times.

'This is going to be one of three,' Betty says plainly, 'I've seen the parents left outside.'

William pulls back a blanket for the last time. They look. William glances at Betty. She shakes her head, lips pursed. 'Can't be sure.'

Almost in synchronicity, the two of them plunge their sponges in the water and set to work. A peace settles over William, knowing most of this is behind him. He and Betty work well together, intuitively knowing which parts of the body she can clean, and which need his expertise.

Next to them, Jimmy is hand-pumping the embalming fluid through a body. For a few seconds, the only sounds William's aware of are the suck and hiss of the pump and the swill of dirty water squeezed from their sponges. Then, a plummy voice from over his shoulder: '. . . Chapel Choir, Cambridge, singing Allegri's "Miserere".'

William spins round and lunges at the radio, his gloved

fingers grappling with the knobs until the noise stops. He turns, radio in both his hands. Jimmy and Betty are staring at him.

'Sorry.' He exhales quickly to imitate a laugh. 'Can't stand that poncy stuff' – he puts it back on the ledge – 'can I retune it to something else?'

Jimmy nods at William's workstation. 'Best just get on, there are parents waiting.'

■ ■ ■

The child's silky black hair could have been recently combed, but the face is its own disaster zone. Betty rubs with the tired, soft sponge on the left forearm. William is glad that Betty doesn't try to talk. She's taken off her glove to scrape a stubborn patch of slurry with her fingernail. William glances at her every few seconds but she doesn't look up.

When Harry returns from his tea break, the room is moment-arily filled with the familiar thunder of a departing lorry. Jimmy, Betty and William are focused on the work and don't notice Harry casually turn the radio back on. So when the simple plainchant of the tenors can be heard – *Amplius lava me ab iniquitate mea: et a peccato meo munda me*; 'Wash me thoroughly from my wickedness: and cleanse me from my sin' – Betty doesn't notice the change in William. Neither does Jimmy, massaging formaldehyde through a wrist. And even though they are working in such close proximity, no one notices the sponge drop to the floor as William grips the edge of the table. But Betty does look up in time to see him put both hands over his ears, eyes tight shut. He takes a step back from the table. His head hits the wall, his knees crumple, and he slides down until he is squatting on the floor.

40

10

'Apologise once more, William,' Betty says, kneeling before him, 'and I'll hit you over the head with that radio.'

William feels his spine against the cold wall, the floor bearing into his bony backside. He clasps his shins, his body a tight, clutched package, while Harry and Jimmy look down at him. He notices that his shoes are *filthy*.

Betty sits next to William, legs outstretched, prises one hand from his leg and holds it in her lap.

'To be honest,' she says, 'I feel the same when the Beatles come on. I can't *stand* them.' She turns her head to look at him, play in her eyes. 'I'm going to do this next time my husband starts dancing around like an idiot to "Yellow Submarine".'

Harry and Jimmy chuckle. Harry bends to make eye contact with William. 'Sorry, mate, just turned it back on. Didn't realise.'

'You weren't to know,' William says, getting up, letting his hand slide from Betty's, grateful, embarrassed. 'I'm OK now.' He lowers his gaze again, doesn't want to look or be looked at. 'It's just that music.'

■ ■ ■

Uncle Robert is on the driveway before William has turned off the engine. It's after 10 p.m. and he wonders if he can summon the energy to get out of the car. He leans into Robert's embrace, feeling the pat on his back; tenderness disguised as vigour that has characterised his care of William over the last five years. The smell of his aftershave, the neat tie and woolly jumper bring tears to his eyes.

'Hungry?' He takes William's elbow. 'There's a shepherd's pie with your name on it.'

'I'm starving,' William says as they walk into the house. He takes off the shoes that tomorrow he will throw in the bin and leaves them by the door.

Howard is in the kitchen, oven gloves on, lifting out the casserole dish.

William shakes ketchup onto the side of his plate next to the rich mincemeat oozing from under mashed potato. Howard and Robert sit with him at the table but he's grateful they don't ask any questions, because although William is ravenous it's a struggle to talk or eat. He clears his plate but says no to the tinned peaches and evaporated milk that Howard has taken from the fridge.

'I'd best turn in. I haven't slept.'

'Gloria called,' Robert remembers as William is getting up. 'She sends her love and hopes you're OK.'

William stops. Uncle Robert is studying him. Oh, how he wants this to be good news! How he wants that delicious rush of lust and love and certainty he had on the way to Aberfan, set ablaze simply by the thought of her, saturating his future. But all he's left with now under Robert's gaze is despair. He knows exactly what Gloria will want of him at some point in the future and has even spent a lot of the last year imagining just that. But after what he's just experienced, he doubts he will ever feel able to give it to her.

'OK' – he nods at Robert – 'I'll call her, once I've slept.'

'Goodnight, William, rest well. You're home now.'

'That you are,' adds Howard, nodding.

Relieved to be alone, he strips and climbs into bed. The grandfather clock in the hallway strikes eleven. He thought he'd fall asleep immediately, but with the insistent *tock* of the clock, and the quarter-hour chimes that he doesn't normally hear, quarter-hour after quarter-hour after quarter-hour, he finds he is not alone after all. Wrecked bodies, faces of parents entering the mortuary, moans and wails of grief. Aberfan, he learns, staring at the white tasselled lampshade above him, has set up camp in his body; it's behind his eyes, in his ears, his nose, on his hands and running through his blood.

It's just after 1.15 when he gets up to go to the bathroom. Opening his door he expects darkness, but the landing is buttered with a soft light from under Robert's door. Glancing to his left, he notes that Howard's door is open and his bed empty. William freezes at the sound of muted voices.

'. . . she might be a comfort.'

'If you ask me, we'd do better to put our hope in Gloria than his mother.'

William clears his throat and treads his feet heavily across the landing to the bathroom. When he comes out, the hallway is in darkness and Howard's door is shut.

11

Black and silver, bumper to bumper over the bridge, glinting in the grey winter light; every hearse in South Wales, it looks like. From the narrow pavement, he could reach out and place his palm on the polished hearse rolling past, see his own outline imposed on the coffin.

The pavements fill with black-clad figures oozing from doorways. *Keep your head down and your heart hard. That's your kindness.* Earlier, gazing into the purple dawn through the windscreen, William imagined a cup of tea with Betty, hearing about life with her sister-in-law. Now, he tells himself, he mustn't think like that; he should leave these people alone, drawn tight into the folds of their community.

He turns away from the procession of hearses and overtakes the human tide rolling towards the mountain graveyard; black coats and hats, downcast eyes, flower-filled arms. William strides up the lane to the left of the cemetery gates, over tufts of grass and patches of moss blending with the bitumen. He's unsure why, four days later, he's returned, and that's probably why he's told no one. Not Uncle Robert, not Gloria, who he has only spoken to once since he got home anyway.

She was so pleased when he called the day after, her warmth and concern so palpable she may as well have been standing next to him. And he knew, as he answered her questions with lone words, like *yes,* and *no,* and *terrible,* and *unbearable,* that he was building a barricade between them. That when she said she'd love to see him soon, his *maybe* had made it clear to her as well.

William loves Gloria, has done ever since he met her lodging with her family for his embalming training. He's loved her without a moment's wavering through all that happened – things that would have sent other men running. And then, at last, at the dinner dance, with that kiss, he dared to believe they had a future. But Aberfan has scooped out the core of him, stretched it thin and catapulted it into the wild blue yonder. Maybe that's why he's here; to try and get himself back.

The path twists to the right, above the graveyard, on top of the mountain. William climbs quickly, heart thudding. Skinny autumn trees stand sentinel every two feet or so, their lower branches reaching straight out, as if to shield him from what's about to happen. He's glad of the criss-cross limbs, for he too is obscured. Across the valley, on the opposite hillside, are hundreds, maybe thousands of people gathered in stunned solidarity.

The world has been watching Aberfan, and the floral cross dominating the mountainside above the graves shows that it has also sent flowers. Mourners swarm the hillside. Some add their own bouquets to the cross, before heading towards the gaping wound where the coffins are laid. From up here, they look like beige piano keys, occasionally white; the ones Jimmy brought from Ireland. Two or three rows deep, mourners lean towards the open ground. Some drop a flower, some simply touch the earth, as if to be blessed, or to bless. *What boundless capacity for pain*, William thinks, *is expected of such tiny, frail humans.*

A robin lands on a branch to his left at eye level, its twig-legs seeming too delicate to support the plump feathered body. The bird cocks its head at him once, then it's gone. Jimmy was only half right, William is not one of them, but neither is he merely an observer. He wishes Jimmy were here now, so he could tell him how he's afraid that part of him is being buried with those

45

children, that the village's brokenness has broken him.

A violent sawing cuts through the sky, then a *thup-thup-thup* of dashed air, so loud and close that William drops to his knees on the muddy path. When he looks up he sees photographers at the helicopter window, their giant black lenses trained on the hillside.

He's indignant at their intrusion, yet along with its racket, a feeling of liberation steals over him. He imagines the bodies within those coffins, some of which he was the last one to touch. He remembers the girl's hand in his and something in him shifts. His throat clears, his lungs draw in the cold air, as his body prepares to give its best to these shattered families.

> *'Paham mae dicter, O Myfanwy,*
> *Yn llenwi'th lygaid duon di?*
> *A'th ruddiau tirion, O Myfanwy,*
> *Heb wrido wrth fy ngweled i?'*

The memory of Martin's beautiful voice comes to him so clear and complete, it's as if they're singing their favourite duet again right here on this mountaintop. His voice is warm and elastic; his hands unclasp and conduct with smooth, generous sweeps. William sings like he hasn't sung since he was a boy. It doesn't matter that no one hears him. It matters that he's doing it.

> *'Anghofia'r oll o'th addewidion*
> *A wneist i rywun, 'ngeneth ddel,*
> *A dyro'th law, Myfanwy dirion*
> *I ddim ond dweud y gair "Ffarwél".'*

As if rehearsed, at the final verse the helicopter pirouettes and whomps away across the landscape with its loot. The smell of soggy bracken and trampled ferns fuses with a sense of being untethered, of floating free across the mountains.

The gentle patter of dog's claws on the path behind stops just as William registers it. He turns. Ears pricked, head to one side, the Jack Russell looks at him before trotting off, sniffing the road, lifting its leg. William wipes his sleeve across his face. Time to clamp his defences back down before the flotsam and jetsam of his own life is washed up by the tidal wave of Aberfan's grief; his father's death, the abrupt end to his chorister days, the rift with his mother, with Martin. And now, Gloria. The cold hardens around him and the weight of the white sky seems to push down on the hillside. He can tell by the rise and fall of their voices that the villagers are singing 'Jesu, Lover of My Soul'.

Afterwards, they drift down the mountainside and along the pavements towards home. William watches, hands deep in his pockets, his thumbnail catching on the loose lining.

The vivid grass tufting down the middle of the lane is so bright it seems to be singing to him, its pointed blades distinct and intense. And the phone box, the reddest of reds, shouts out to him at the turn of the path. He pulls a threepenny bit from his pocket.

It's colder inside the phone box than out; the air is dank and solid. The *click-click-click-click* of the dial grinding back into position, the distant purr of the dialling tone – all of it particular and sharp in the enclosed space. At the shrill pips, William pushes the coin into the slot.

'William? Is that you? Are you all right?'

William tastes his stale breath bouncing back from the heavy Bakelite. 'I'm fine.'

'We've been out of our minds,' Robert says, 'where are you?'

47

'Aberfan.'

There is a pause. 'The funerals.'

'Yep.'

'You sure you're all right?'

'I think so.' The silence, William knows, is his uncle's wariness of giving advice, being overly parental. 'I sang to them.'

'What did you sing?' The urgent pips cut in between them and William fumbles in his pocket to find another coin, shoving it in with numb fingers. 'Hello?' Robert says.

'Hello.'

'What did you sing to them?'

'"Myfanwy".' The pause is so long William breaks it. 'Uncle Robert?'

'Lucky them,' he says eventually, 'I bet they thought it was beautiful.'

'No one heard, but it doesn't matter.'

Robert laughs softly. 'Come on home, boy.'

'Uncle Robert?'

'Yes?'

'Thank you.'

'What for?'

'Making me an embalmer.'

'You've done that yourself, William.'

'I won't be back till late. I'm going to Swansea.'

'Oh!' Robert says, suddenly louder. 'Good! We'll be here. Waiting.'

■ ■ ■

William drives west, the crumpled paper with an address in Robert's handwriting on the dashboard. When he reaches

Mumbles, he stops to ask in a corner newsagent for directions to Plunch Lane. He's close. The five-minute drive ends with him parking his car opposite a chalet-style house halfway up a steep hill.

He turns off his lights and stares at the illuminated face of his mother's home, lights shining through the curtains of both downstairs windows. He can't quite believe that her life is contained within the walls of this neat little house, with its beige gravel path and privet hedge, that he has not once visited. He imagines sitting down with her and telling her what he's seen, what he's done at Aberfan. He imagines that old feeling of being the centre of her world, the focus of her intense love and attention.

Bone-tired and hungry, he knows it was the raw displays of parental love in the mortuary that have bought him to her house. The dogged blame and judgement that have sustained him for so long started to lose their grip in Aberfan. With the engine off, and the car growing rapidly colder, force of habit takes over. She left him, after all, to come here. None of this was his doing. He taps his head on the steering wheel, the cold creeping into his muscles. He lets the familiar reel play again; her driving away, waving but not looking back at him, the impact just above his sternum, the desolation of watching her leave.

Robert had suggested he invite her to his graduation, telling William that he and Evelyn had exchanged letters over the past few months; friendly, open. 'Maybe we can put all this behind us,' he'd said. William flinches at the memory of the recent – the only – argument he's ever had with Uncle Robert.

'She didn't even want me to be an embalmer! Are you kidding me?'

Howard appeared at the lounge door. 'How are we doing in here?'

'This little *prince* here doesn't like the fact that his mother and I are in touch at long last.'

Little prince! That stung. William's whole life, Robert has only ever said kind things to him.

'Maybe he needs time to adjust to the idea, Robert.'

'She was *hateful* to you.' William ignored Howard altogether. 'She humiliated us.' The momentum of his anger was stronger than his self-control; his face pulled into tears. 'She *left* me!'

Twice he removes the key from the ignition, twice he puts it back. Eventually, he punches the dashboard and starts the engine.

'No, Mum.'

■ ■ ■

Stopping at the first phone box he sees, he scrabbles for change in the glove compartment, gets out. With the coins in a tidy pile on top of the telephone, he rests his forehead on the red ridge of a window pane for a moment before dialling.

'Mr Finch?'

'William!'

'I'm calling from a phone box. Is Gloria there, please?'

'She is! Hang on!' Car headlights fleetingly bleach his legs.

'Hello, you!' Gloria's voice is loud and relieved. 'Robert called, he's beside himself.'

'Don't worry,' he says softly, 'I've spoken to him.'

'Where are you?'

'Wales.'

'Oh God, the funerals.'

'Yes.'

'Are you OK?'

'Yes. No. Kind of. I need to say something, Gloria.'

'All right.'

'Promise not to speak till I'm done.'

'OK . . .' She sounds wary.

'I love you, Gloria. Have done since the day we met.' He pauses; there's absolute silence. 'After the dinner dance, I drove to Aberfan thinking, when I get home, I'm going to ask Gloria to marry me.' The relief of saying it out loud is immense, but he must press on before she misunderstands. 'But after this, I can't. You want to be a mum. You *should* be.' He scrunches his eyes at the memory of the pulpy blood on the Finches' stairs, of Gloria being carried out of the house. 'You'll be wonderful, but I'm not cut out for family life. You need to find someone else.' Utter silence. He waits, just to hear her breathing, but there's nothing. 'Goodbye, Gloria.'

Part II
CAMBRIDGE CHOIR

12

SEPTEMBER 1957

The sky is bruise-blue and the air almost golden with the promise of rain. He is chilly in his grey shorts and green blazer.

His mother, Evelyn, is kneeling down, though the ground is gravelly and she's wearing new stockings. Her face is so close he can see a swirl on her right cheek where her make-up isn't quite rubbed in. Her eyes start to silver. He hopes they won't spill. William glances over her shoulder and sees a tall father with a wide smile slapping his son's back. The mother's make-up is silkier and thicker than Evelyn's, she has a pretty scarf tied under her chin, and she wears pointy sunglasses even though it's not sunny. She's smiling too, but with her eyes behind the slanted black lenses, her face looks blank. There's a hanky in her hand. William wishes his dad could be there to smack his back and make them all smile – and then his mum wouldn't be all alone when she leaves in a few minutes.

'I'm so proud of you,' Evelyn is saying, the tide in her eyes still high. 'And so would your father be. You know that, don't you?'

'Yes.' He puts his hand on her shoulder because he can't bear her to look sad. She stands up so quickly, his hand slaps down onto the grey flannel of his new shorts.

'Don't start being all nice to me, William Lavery, you'll set me off.' She smiles down at him, blinking. 'I'm allowed to come and see how you're getting on in six weeks. It'll come round before we know it. By then you'll have all sorts of lovely music in your head you can sing to me over lunch.'

'I will' – he forces his voice to be big and brave – 'like this.' He puts his hands out theatrically: 'Laaaaaaaaaaaa.' He doesn't want her to go, but he knows she has to and he mustn't make it worse for her.

'And just think,' she says in a whisper, her watery eyes bright, 'one day I might be coming to hear you sing the "Miserere".'

The boy he saw over his mother's shoulder turns away from his parents and is propelled forward by another slap on the back from the father, who looks insanely happy and shouts, 'Bye, Charles,' in a plummy voice that William has only ever heard on the radio. Mother and father loosely link hands and walk towards a grey car with a little statue on the bonnet of a woman with wings. A man in a hat sits at the wheel.

'And you'll be on the front row,' he says, making his face happy and strong, 'and I'll give you a wink.'

William glances at the boy called Charles heading towards the school – this place that somehow is also going to be their home – and notices the boy's red lips stretch suddenly across his open mouth.

'Bye, Mum,' William whispers, kissing the knuckles on Evelyn's left hand, feeling the cool of her wedding ring on his lips. 'I'll go with him, he's upset.'

Evelyn holds his chin with one hand, ruffles his hair and turns. William knows she won't turn back, that she's crying now too and doesn't want him to see it. He's grateful that she managed to keep herself in check. Of the four new choristers – known as probationers – starting this term, William, at ten, will be the oldest. The others will all be seven, the age you're meant to start at. It would be awful to be the oldest and the cry-baby. His mother knows this. It is both a comfort and a torment, this understanding they have, that skips back and forth between them.

William and his mum only found out how special his voice was last year, when he joined the local church choir. The choir-master said he'd never heard anything like it and had his mum ever considered applying for a scholarship at one of the university choir schools? So she did, and here he is now, having to walk away from her.

William slips alongside Charles as they enter the wood-panelled vestibule, and does what he thinks everyone does to comfort someone who is upset. He scoops up the boy's hand. Charles's distorted face jerks towards him, angry and scared as he wrenches his hand away.

'Get off!'

A knuckle cracks, but William can't be sure whose. The boy's jaw is suddenly made of stone, and he marches off into the hall where men in black gowns stand with clipboards.

William waits at the threshold, hoping Evelyn didn't see, determined not to look back, until a much bigger boy bumps his shoulder on their way past and he stumbles into the room.

13

The three other probationers, including Charles, are huddled together in the corner this morning when he wakes. A tight knot of exclusion, they glance at him as he gets up from his skinny mattress for the first time. That hand holding was a *big* mistake.

Last night, curled up in a ball, wondering how he could possibly fall asleep without his mother nearby, William discovered that he could conjure her voice.

My job in life, William, is to love you like no one on earth, and I have to say, I think I'm doing a pretty good job . . . You're special, the college choirmaster said so. You'll be singing solos before you know it.

It was as if he could literally hear her speaking, feel her breath across his face, see the pretty ridges on her white teeth. Now though, watching the three boys leave the dorm together, Evelyn feels so far away, she may as well not exist.

He jumps as a set of soft, large fingers close around his arm. 'Come on. Let's get the dips over with, then I'll take you to breakfast.'

'Dips?' says William, letting himself be led into the corridor by a tall, plump boy with short red hair that has a rigorous wiggle running through it. 'What's that?'

'You'll see,' says the boy, releasing his grip. 'You get used to it. You get used to everything eventually.'

'How long have you been here?' William runs a couple of steps to catch up.

'Three years.' The boy's face is broad and flat with smudgy freckles and wide front teeth with a gap in between them. 'I'm Martin Mussey.' He strides ahead on sturdy legs. 'I've got a good voice, awful attitude. I'll never be head chorister, but I get plenty of solos.'

'Pleased to meet you.' Good manners cost nothing, Evelyn has taught him, but work magic. 'I'm William Lavery. Thank you for inviting me.'

Martin laughs and stops until William is level with him again. 'You might not thank me in a minute. But Matron's not so bad.'

There's a sharp-as-a-needle smell in the bathroom. Everything is pale blue or white. The bright light makes William squint. Following Martin's lead, he takes off his pyjama top and drops it on the floor behind him. They stand adjacent to another boy at the bath and another joins them to William's left. Martin is the only one with any spare flesh on him. He even has boobs.

The woman dressed like a nurse holding a large metal jug must be Matron. The muscles in her arm flex through the saggy flesh as she lifts the pitcher.

'Down!'

The boy leans over and rests his hands on the floor of the bath. His spine curves into a frill of little bumps. As Matron pours the water over his head and body, he exhales quickly as if he's been punched. A couple of drops ricochet onto William. He flinches. It's freezing.

The boy uncurls, scurries to a row of pegs and snatches one of the thin towels. Matron refills the jug from the sink behind her. Martin steps sideways into the vacated space. His belly wobbles slightly as he puts his broad hands flat on the bath and his upside-down face scrunches into a different shape.

59

'Shuffle up!' she snaps at William, once Martin has moved away and started rubbing his body, beaming with relief, or maybe encouragement. But William doesn't move. He waits for what seems a long time for Matron to look up from the bath. When she finally meets his gaze, William smiles politely and shakes his head.

'Not for me, thank you, Matron. It's too cold.'

The boy on his left sniggers, then stifles it. Matron's face is surprised into a moment of softness before she grabs him, her thumb easily meeting her fingers round his upper arm, and pulls him next to her.

'I'm afraid his Lordship doesn't get to choose.'

He hears another laugh from the boy on his left. Then his head is pushed down and a cascade of cold water shoots up his nose, into his eyes, through his ears, and its icy fingers curl around his tummy. The pale lino glitters with water. His gasp is loud and high.

He straightens up, water blurring his vision, and hurries away. He buries his face in a towel for a few seconds before wiping himself down.

■ ■ ■

'If you're on the way to a whacking, nick a handkerchief from here.' Dressed now, they leave the dorm to go for breakfast, and an invigorated Martin points towards a huge cupboard on the landing. 'Mr Atkinson can tell if you've got a towel stuffed down your trousers, but handkerchiefs slide nicely into your underpants.'

'A whacking?' William has only met the headmaster twice, but he hadn't seemed at all violent. 'What do you get that for?'

His body is still smarting from the cold water.

'Last one was for bed hopping.'

'What's that?' William's feet patter lightly down the stair-case behind the rhythmic pound of Martin's two-steps-at-a-time leaps.

'Two minutes before Matron's due to check lights are out, you jump from bed to bed till you're back at your own.'

They are overtaking Charles and the other probationers in the corridor. William concentrates on Martin as they slip into the dining hall ahead of them.

'How many beds?'

'Ten.'

'Crikey.'

'And you do it naked.'

'Pardon?'

'You do the bed hop naked.'

William has never seen a naked body apart from his own and can't quite believe that anyone would do such a thing.

'I got more whacks than anyone last year.' Martin leads the way to a serving hatch. A wide woman with a blue apron taut across her massive bosom is lifting a ladle from a tin pot and dropping porridge into green bowls. Martin takes one without speaking to her. 'If I didn't sing well I'd be out on my ear.'

A milky smell stirs a trace of hunger William didn't know he had as he waits for the woman to ladle a lumpy grey spoonful into his bowl. She glances briefly at him. The edge of the ladle clips the bowl and a spot of porridge lands on the counter.

'Thank you very much,' he says.

She says nothing, but nods her head at him and a coil of dark hair bobs up and down.

William follows Martin to an empty table where he screeches a chair back on the parquet floor. There's an energy to Martin's speech and movement that lifts William's spirit and makes him feel braver. Since his father died two years ago, William has had to tighten up his insides and work hard to cheer his mother up. She does seem to wake up lighter again, and be playful like she used to be, but he feels a relief as Martin's carefree manner slides comfortably over his shoulders.

'Not for me, thank you, Matron,' Martin says, in what William supposes is meant to be a Midlands accent. But the brief weight of Martin's hand on his shoulder, soft and heavy, stops his feelings from being hurt.

'My mum calls me his Lordship' – William swirls his spoon through his gloopy breakfast that smells of salt – 'but it sounds different when she says it.'

Martin's laugh is a gurgle deep in his chest. 'Lavery, you're a gem.'

As William takes in the dining hall, its scrubbed, woody smell, high windows and plain tables, he is relieved that it seems all he needs to do to be liked by Martin is to be himself.

14

When the boys gather in the vestibule after breakfast, bending double to put on outdoor shoes, William is excited for the first time since he arrived, busy putting his shoes on, bracing himself against the knocks and nudges of everyone doing the same. He's not great at tying his laces, so he's had to concentrate hard. It's only when he straightens up that he notices boys putting on black gowns and funny square hats. He doesn't have either of those. He and the unfriendly seven-year-olds, Charles, Edward and Anthony, stand in their blazers and feel the difference.

It was six months ago, in March, that William came here for his voice trial. Since then, he's kept half an eye on the life he was living, but most of his time was spent imagining the future. He imagined entering the vast chapel, stepping across the glimmering black and white tiles that blinked when the light hit them. He imagined the bright beauty of the windows, like coloured diamonds turning ordinary light into something so amazing it almost hurt to look at it. He imagined gazing up at the friendly-looking saints with their arms out as if in welcome. He imagined being dressed in white and purple robes, breathing in to fill his chest with air. He imagined opening his mouth wide for the escape of his voice. He imagined how it would feel like flying.

What he stolidly ignored was the fact that he'd start his time here as a probationer, not a chorister. He won't have the full uniform and he won't be able to sing at evensong, so there'll be no chance of a solo. He isn't sure how long this in-between time will last. At his voice trial, Phillip, the choirmaster, was fuzzy about it.

'The probationary period is usually about a year,' he said, running through details of chorister life, 'but as you're considerably older . . . well, we'll see.'

'Walk with me, William,' says Martin now, cheerful and hearty as the line of boys starts to take shape.

Once they have passed through the gate into the college playing fields, Martin's hand darts out.

'See that hole in the cricket pavilion window? I took it out last term with a cricket ball and no one's fixed it yet. I got whacked for that.'

'Oh.' William keeps his head turned towards the pavilion so Martin knows he's taking it seriously.

'See that tree?' Martin points to the left. 'I fell off it and broke my little finger in my first year. Look!' He waves his large hand before William's face. 'It set crooked.'

William thinks Martin's mother must be very different from Evelyn. He imagines the horror of having to tell her he'd been hit by the headmaster for jumping on other boys' beds without any pants. The other older boys are friendly enough towards Martin, but he seems to float free of any allegiances – unlike Charles, Edward and Anthony, who may as well have melded into one hostile person.

Once through the lofty iron gates of the college, their feet *scrunch-scrunch-scrunch* over the rusty gravel. William spots the chapel spire. Compared to these thick stone walls, he and all the boys are so very small and fragile, even Martin. But walking step by step closer to the chapel, a fluttering starts in his chest. They may be small, but they are *special*. His lungs feel sprung and strong. He imagines that the chapel can hear their footsteps and their chatter and is excited for the singing to start. But at the last minute, the procession bends away from the chapel entrance, off to the left.

'Where are we going?'

'Song room,' says Martin.

'Not the chapel?'

'Choristers go there for evening practice and then evensong, but it's here in the morning.' It's a small, very ordinary room, with cream walls and rows of benches. 'Probationers sit over there.' Martin points to the far corner and gently presses his back.

Even though William knows he'll eventually become a chorister, a pebble of disappointment plummets the length of him. He sits with Charles on his left and wishes yet again he hadn't bothered to try and cheer him up yesterday. Because now, you'd think he'd tried to hold *all* of their hands, or even kiss them on the lips, the way they shuffle away, and whisper and laugh without him. *It's all right for them,* he thinks, *they've got seven years here.* As a ten-year-old latecomer, his time is much shorter.

It is a relief when Phillip Lewis, the choirmaster, walks into the room at last. William no longer has to pretend to be interested in the organ scholar sitting at the piano arranging his music. He chooses to ignore the unfriendly boys for the next hour; he will think only about this man who told his mother he has a special gift. He will listen to what he has to say about the music and how he should sing, and he will do as well as he possibly can.

'Welcome back, everyone. And welcome to our new boys.' Riffling through his papers, Phillip Lewis nods in the probationers' direction but doesn't meet anyone's eye. William recognises the gentle, lilting Welsh accent from summer holidays in Port

Madoc. Tall, stick-thin and quietly spoken, the choirmaster has a bald head with a remaining band of wispy grey hair that almost reaches his collar. 'Let's wander through a few arpeggios, shall we?'

'Right.' Phillip rummages through the music once the warm-ups are done, snatching one piece out. 'Let's take a look at the "Te Deum". Remember' – his eyes flit from one boy to another – '*list*en. I want to hear *one* sound, one voice, not fifteen.' His body looks relaxed, his face isn't pent up with excitement like William's choirmaster at home, and yet he is absolutely in control. 'So, we'll look at the Tallis, five-parter.' His head is down and his large bony hands rest at last with the sought-after pages spread out before him. 'Mussey? You take the first.'

As the singing starts, William challenges himself to distinguish the individual voices from the blend. He watches the back of Martin's big ginger head, dipping and swaying to the music with a freedom no one else is showing, but because William can't see his mouth, he can't make out his particular voice until the solo.

When it happens, William smiles. He can almost feel his own skull vibrate as Martin's voice goes its own way. He's careful to hold his own in check, but he knows it could cut through the others like a knife through warm butter. Like Martin's. Perhaps better. He's pleased though to find his friend is so good, and when at the end of the piece Martin's head twists round to catch William's eye, they grin briefly at each other and William feels known.

15

'What's the matter, Lavery?' Charles is smiling, and William knows straight away that they've done something with his pyjamas. He has looked under his pillow, under the blankets and under his bed. The silence bristles with pent-up laughter. He is exhausted. The choristers are having their post-evensong supper, so William's on his own with the probationers.

Not trusting himself to speak, he sits on his bed in the hope one of them will tell him where they are, but it's as if he's invisible. He goes to the bathroom wearing his vest and trousers to clean his teeth, praying that when he returns his pyjamas will have appeared on his pillow. If so, he'll smile, maybe even laugh, if he can manage it. As he looks in the mirror something catches his eye. He spins round. Dangling over the lip of the toilet bowl is one leg of his pyjamas; the other is submerged. The water is unmistakably yellow. He gags then blinks repeatedly to try and stop the tears. Unable to bring himself to touch the pyjamas, or even look at them any longer, he runs out of the bathroom and bumps into Martin.

'What's up?'

William doesn't want to cry; he points to the toilet and heads back to the dorm, eyes on the floor, where he takes off his trousers and gets into bed in vest and pants.

'Goodnight,' he says with a normal voice. He turns away from them and tries to listen to his own breathing instead of the muffled whispers and giggles. If only his ability to conjure his mother's voice was dependable. Tonight he can magic no comfort from her at all. He hears the spring and bounce of Martin getting into bed, but doesn't open his eyes. When Matron comes to check on them, he pulls the blanket up high over his chin.

A gentle tap on his hand a few minutes later makes him jump. Martin is kneeling at his bedside, looking intently at him.

'Give it ten minutes,' he mouths, holding up his two hands, all digits splayed and white in the dark. William stares back, as Martin returns to his bed and lies still under the covers.

He counts groups of sixty, but he must have drifted off because he's pulled back to himself by a tap on his arm. Martin is at his side again, white-striped pyjamas glowing. Carefully he is folding his blanket into a long thin column.

'Bed crawl revenge,' he whispers.

Like a surfer paddling out into the sea, Martin propels himself forward, under William's bed, his big body positioned neatly along the length of the blanket, not making a sound. William hangs over the bed and watches Martin glide under and out and under and out of the beds to his left, surprisingly graceful. William can no longer see him, so he lies back down and waits in the thick quiet of communal sleep.

A series of sudden, sharp raps make William start, followed by the squeak and groan of bedsprings. Then a creepy, twisted moan: 'Charles. Charles.'

'Who is it? Pack it in.' Charles's voice is high-pitched with false bravery.

'Get William's pyjamas.' Martin's distorted voice is louder now.

'I can't!' Charles snaps. 'We widdled on them.'

'Get them. Put them on.'

'No!'

There's a sudden movement and a cry of pain. 'Ouch! I'll tell Matron.'

'If you're not back in bed wearing William's pyjamas in thirty seconds, *I'll* tell Matron what *you* did.' Martin has given up on the voice.

'I can't! It's disgusting.'

There's another soft thud followed by a yelp. 'Imagine being expelled for pissing on someone's pyjamas. You'd go down in school history. Go! Now!'

Appalled, William lies rigid. Charles jumps up and runs the length of the dorm. The bathroom light pings on; a quiet slap, drips, the rasp of wet fabric pulling against skin, muffled grunting. The room hums with the silence of waiting, listening boys. When Charles scurries past, tiny and scrawny in oversized, drenched pyjamas, William fights the urge to apologise.

'And if you tell anyone about this,' Martin says, emerging easily from under the next bed to William, 'I'll come tomorrow night. And the next.'

William counts to thirty and then whispers to Martin, 'Tell him he can take them off now. Don't make him wear them all night.'

'He's got to learn his lesson,' Martin whispers softly. 'You don't want to have to put up with this for the next four years, do you?'

'But what will Matron say in the morning? It'll look like he's wet himself.'

'Trust me, William, he'll leave you alone now.'

As Martin's breathing quickly deepens, William is horribly aware of Charles's restless shivering six beds away. It is a long time before sleep relieves his mind of the puzzle of how his new friend can be both so kind and so cruel.

16

Dear William,

Thank you for your letter – even though it made me hopping mad. I'm sorry to hear how unkind one of the boys has been, and can't help but be pleased about how thoroughly your friend taught him a lesson, even though it was a tough one. Martin sounds quite a character – I think I'm glad you've got him looking out for you.

You were quite right not to tell your mother. And I'm happy to be the one you turn to when things aren't so good. We all know that after your dear father died, your mother needed you all to herself for a while. We understand, but we've missed you. We might pop up to Cambridge for evensong every now and then, though I'm not sure how your mum would feel about that.

Anyway, I've been racking my brains for a way to make you feel better. I decided to hunt down something of your father's – a good thing about still living in the house we grew up in! I found the shrivelled old conker he beat mine with in 1933 but it doesn't look very impressive nowadays. You came dangerously close to getting a cracked old soap on a rope he once gave me for Christmas. Then I remembered you saying that apart from clothes, a blanket was about the only possession you were allowed. Bingo! Your father's old blanket was ready and waiting in the bottom of the ottoman in his old bedroom. It's stood the test of time better than the conker and soap, that's for sure.

Think of the blanket as a big hug from your dear dad (and me) whenever you need it.

Your loving Uncle Robert

PS Howard says hello in his best Donald Duck voice.

PPS Nice touch to put your tuck rations under Charles's pillow for the last two weeks, though I'm not sure he deserves it and I think you should enjoy them yourself from now on.

On the Monday morning of William's fourth week, he is walking through the playing fields which are shiny and soggy from a night's clattering rain. Apart from singing, this walk with Martin is William's favourite thing. He still can't quite believe how large and soft and friendly Martin is, and when they're walking along side by side, it seems there is nothing to worry about. It astonishes him that Charles doesn't seem to bear Martin any grudge, and, as predicted, he and the other probationers leave him alone.

His father's grey and green blanket, with its fiery red stitching and inky camphor smell, has been a comfort over the last three weeks. The routine is starting to feel, not quite familiar, but not quite so foreign either. Up at six. Dips. Instrument practice (piano for him, clarinet for Martin). Breakfast: egg and tomatoes on Monday, porridge on Tuesday, egg and beans on Wednesday, tomatoes on toast on Thursday, kippers on Friday, variable at weekends. Choir practice. Lessons. Lunch. Lessons. Early tea to keep the choristers going until after evensong. Prep. Supper.

Lessons are hard. The other boys seem to have a bottomless pit of knowledge, general and specific, that he simply doesn't. But he knows that a chorister is expected to excel at everything, so he always tries.

During choir practice, William is alert and alive. The younger

71

probationers yawn, lean heavily on their elbows, sometimes struggle to know what page they're on, come in a little early or late, or fail to *list*en and don't blend their voices as Phillip asks. He wishes he didn't have to stand with them, but as soon as the piano plays, and Phillip's graceful hand invites him to sing, everything but his breath, his voice and the music, is forgotten.

'Blimey, I don't feel so good,' Martin says now, as a thrush flies low across their path. He skims his plump belly with both hands but still manages a smile as he looks at William.

'What's the matter?'

'Just don't feel right.'

Abruptly, Martin pitches forward and is sick on the path. The boys behind make sounds of disgust and skitter away from the steaming puddle, pinching their noses. Martin is bent over, hands on his knees, breathing hard.

'Are you all right?' William says.

'Not finished!' he garbles, and belches up more onto the grass.

The rest of the boys, to William's dismay, have all walked on, and it is only then that he realises his hand is softly patting Martin's back.

'Is that it, do you think?' William puts his hand into his pocket.

Martin straightens and takes a deep breath before puffing out loudly. 'Think so.' He strides off. 'Come on, we'll be late.'

'Shouldn't you go back?' William runs to catch up, feeling a bit sick himself now and relieved at the cool breeze.

'I'm fine. Better out than in!' Martin says, cheerful again and on his way.

As usual, William sits alongside Charles, Edward and Anthony. Occasionally there is a waft of sick, and he suspects it's his shoes.

'Right, boys,' the choirmaster says, 'we're starting with the

Stanford in G from the top. Mussey, you'll be taking the solo.'

There's a sudden movement on the front row and Martin runs with his hand over his mouth out of the song room. They all stand listening to the deep heave and the slap of liquid on the flagstones.

'Oh dear!' Phillip says quietly, looking over his glasses at the empty doorway. He turns to Ian Mills, number two chorister.

'Take him back to the house, Mills, but go via the Porters' Lodge, tell them there's some clearing up to do, would you?'

'Yes, sir,' says Mills, running light-footed out of the door.

'Right,' says Phillip, glancing up from his papers, 'we need a soloist.'

He looks straight at William and it feels as if somewhere deep inside has been pierced by a needle. Their choirmaster will often look over their heads as he talks to them, but William discovers that when he does choose to meet your gaze, it is very direct. He wills himself not to look away.

'Right then, Lavery.' He says it so casually and softly, William wonders if it was his name he heard after all. 'Let's hear what you've got, shall we?'

Charles, to his right, lets out a little gasp and spins round to look at the others. William suspects this won't help with his popularity, but when he is beckoned to the front row, and he goes to stand with the choristers, all he feels is a rock-steady readiness.

Simon Porter, head chorister, points at the music to show him where he should be, but William knows, and anyway, it's a piece his mother has been playing to him his whole life. There is a tricky bit, but its shape and pattern are set deep in his bones. It's what he sang for his sight test at his voice trial and he suspects Phillip remembers this.

'Ready, Lavery?' He glances at William. 'From bar fourteen, everyone.'

Porter points again to the music and William smiles at him briefly. The piano starts. His cheeks burn and buzz. Six bars to go. The swell of the boys' voices lifts and lightens him; it is as if their sound glides between the soles of his shoes and the flagstones, raising him an inch from the ground.

Three bars. Lungs emptying and filling, eyes fixed on Phillip. One bar. A quick glance at the music then back to his choirmaster, who nods, as William catches the breath he needs.

Phillip's mouth turns up slightly and his head dips to the right as William sings his first solo, confident and clear, with a solid thump of joy in his heart.

The organist lifts his hand from the key. Silence. Porter clears his throat. William glances round. Every face is turned to him. He looks down and then quickly back at Phillip.

'Nice work, Lavery,' he says, already leafing through his music for the next piece, 'nice work. That'll do for tonight. Porter? Make sure he's gowned up properly.'

'Yes, sir.' Porter tidies his music.

■ ■ ■

The oily liquid dotted with blobs of vegetable doesn't deserve to be called soup, but William is so hungry he knows he will eat every drop. He heads for Martin who, after a day in sickbay, is now sitting in the corner of the dining room.

'Hello.' William puts his bowl down next to Martin and climbs over the bench seat from behind. 'Are you better?'

'Think so,' Martin says, glancing up and swallowing. 'Matron

74

says I should wait till morning to eat, but stuff that. I haven't eaten since breakfast! We'll see what happens after this.'

'Fingers crossed.'

'So' – Martin wipes his finger round the bowl, all his bread gone – 'anything to tell me?'

William feels his cheeks flame. He concentrates on the greenish lump of something on his spoon. 'I'm glad you're feeling better.'

'Are you?' Martin's skin is even paler than usual; his freckles are livid, scampering over his nose. His spoon hovers above his empty bowl.

Something stirs in William, a resolve. If he can't do this without cringing and apologising, his time here will be ruined.

'I *am* pleased you're feeling better, but I'm pleased I got to sing a solo too and that Phillip liked it. I'd be crackers if I wasn't, wouldn't I?'

Martin puts his spoon down and sits back. 'Porter said you've got a strong solo voice.' William meets his eye, hoping his scarlet cheeks are fading. 'He says we'll have to watch out.'

'I'm only a probationer. You're safe for a while.' William tries to smile. 'You're the best soloist, Martin. Everyone knows that.' William's fingers are crossed under the table. He knows he is at least as good as Martin, if not better, but strictly speaking, he's still not a chorister.

'Good job I am.' Martin grins and looks more himself. 'It's the only thing I *can* do.'

William decides not to write about his solo in his weekly letter to Evelyn; he wants to save it until he sees her in two weeks' time. He'll tell Uncle Robert though. There's no danger he'll spoil the surprise; his mum doesn't even know that they correspond – another of those things his uncle worries might upset her.

17

EXEAT Name: Lavery from 12.30 to 4.45
Date 20th October Signed AG Atkinson

Since receiving his exeat on Wednesday, William has dreamt about Evelyn twice. In the first she was lolling on their settee at home, throwing warm biscuits to him in the next chair, relaxed and smiling as crumbs pattered onto the carpet. In the second, she appeared in his dorm, wearing her mac and a scarf on her head. She looked so pleased to see him, he woke with a start, full of embarrassment, because she was painfully out of place and about to make a big fuss of him.

All he had to do was go into the headmaster's room and take the exeat from Mr Atkinson's hand. Glancing round the wood-panelled study, at the vase of yellow roses on the table, he found it hard to believe this was where Martin had been given all those whacks. He couldn't see a cane anywhere. Coming from such a gentle upbringing, there was a large part of him that couldn't quite accept caning actually happened, that a piece of willow could be kept with the sole purpose of hitting a boy. But his encounter was polite and straightforward. The only challenge was to stop himself jumping up and down, because the little piece of paper in his hand allowed him a whole afternoon with his mother in four days' time.

. . .

And now it's Sunday and after the service he's free to leave. With her! Lined up to process into the chapel, full of those parents who suddenly vanished from their lives six weeks ago, everything feels different. Charles, Edward and Anthony are so busy making each other laugh, they don't seem to have noticed. But then William thinks maybe being silly together, fluttering and chirruping around, is their way of noticing. He doesn't think Charles will cry today when he has to say goodbye; it's as if he has become another boy altogether from the one who walked away from his parents in tears.

William loves the stone and wood smell of the ancient antechapel. Martin breathes in and puffs out heavily as he always does the second before they process. As the organ starts, the purple and white vestments sway and the boys move forward. The ceiling is so high he has to tip his chin as far as it will go to see it. The tiles are hard and beautiful beneath his feet. His favourite saint looks him in the eye, arms outstretched. And when this service is over, the flesh and blood arms of his mother will wrap around him.

There she is. Right next to the choir stalls on the left. Her hair has been set and it's longer than it used to be. She's ramrod-straight, holding her order of service level with her chest. She's spotted him.

When it comes to it, when he's so close they could nudge elbows, William can't bring himself to look at her. He feels the brightness of her smile on him, registers the scarlet fabric of a new dress and smells her L'Air du Temps but can only stare straight ahead. Charles, he notices, turns his head the slightest fraction to the right to meet his mother's eye, and smiles lightly, briefly. Before he has even got to the choir stalls, William is filled with regret and guilt for not having done the same.

'So, Master Lavery, tell me *everything*!'

William is relieved that none of the other probationers has chosen the Copper Kettle on King's Parade for their lunch. He wonders where they have gone. This is the only place he knows about. Martin comes here with his family. On his china plate lies ham, egg and chips; huge, luxurious and shockingly greasy.

There's a hint of lipstick on his mother's front tooth, and where once he would have reached over and rubbed it off, he points at his own teeth and rubs. Instantly she lifts her napkin to her mouth.

Having spent the last six weeks adjusting to the shock of her leaving him at the school, simply walking away and not being there, he now finds it just as strange to be sitting opposite her, with the comfort and the responsibility of being the centre of someone's world again.

'So?' She grins. 'I'm waiting.'

How does he even begin?

'Martin, who did the solo this morning, is my friend. He's my age, been here three years. I like Phillip. I like Mr Atkinson – he gave me this.' He pulls the exeat from his pocket and dangles it over his mother's meal. 'I couldn't have come out with you if he hadn't given me this.'

'I'd have clouted him round the head with my handbag if he hadn't! What about the singing?' Her eyebrows arch in expectation. William notices they are softly coloured in.

'The chapel makes us sound *amazing*.'

'And?' It's the excited look she has when he's about to open a present from her. A waitress squeezes past their table, holding a tray level with her plump face.

'Every morning, I have to line up by the bath,' he says, with

78

a sudden desire to shock her, 'put my hands on the bottom of it and get cold water poured over my back.'

It works. Her brow collapses. 'What on earth do they do that for?'

'Make men of us.' He wants to sound nonchalant.

'When you say cold, do you mean cold, or just not very warm?' The worry on her face for some reason pleases him.

'*Ice* cold,' he says.

She spins her ring on her slender finger and frowns.

'And Mrs Potts, our school cook, smokes over the food.' He doesn't tell her that he's quite fond of Mrs Potts, and if he gets to the kitchen early enough she lets him watch her work.

Evelyn wipes her mouth with a napkin. 'Oh dear,' she murmurs, two worry lines at the bridge of her nose.

The waitress comes and refills Evelyn's teacup. In less than two hours he will be saying goodbye to her until Christmas. His insides soften.

'But she's kind to me,' he adds, 'just not as good a cook as you.' He reaches across his plate to touch her hand. The smell of egg yolk makes him feel full, and if he doesn't keep his elbow high it will drag over his chips.

Her smile is back. 'And?' she says. 'Anything else to tell me?'

He swallows a chip and looks at the length of gristle running through the ham on his plate. So she knows already.

'Who told you?'

'No one important, only your headmaster.' She leans towards him. 'I'm waiting to hear it from *you*.'

The headmaster's always telling them they have to stand on their own feet now, look after themselves, but he's been talking to his mother behind his back all along. His indignation is too weak though, her excitement, directed at him, too strong, and a smile sweeps his face. He gives himself up to the joy of having good news for someone completely on his side, whose happiness depends on nothing more than his own. Evelyn puts her cutlery down.

'Come on, tell your mother how bloody marvellous her son is!'

'Naughty!' He wags his finger at her and she laughs.

The clatter of voices, the chink and scrape of cutlery, the waitresses in their black and white uniforms, all recede. Him and her, back in their bubble. He tells her – even though she already knows – that because Martin was sick, he sang a solo and did so well that Phillip wanted him in the choir by half-term, helped by Porter's voice breaking.

'So from next week, I'll be sitting with the choristers, next to Martin.'

Evelyn has picked up her cutlery and is struggling to chew her food because of the smile splitting her face. William wants to keep her happy.

'At practice yesterday, Phillip asked me to sing on my own and afterwards he said, "That's the sound I want, boys! Sing like that."'

And it is wonderful that those words, the same words that brought a brief but thick silence over the choir, now make his mother clap her hands and laugh. 'I *knew* it! Your Uncle Robert can put *that* in his pipe and smoke it. You're headed for the auditorium, William, not the gloomy funeral business!'

William looks down at his plate, impales a chip with all four tines of his fork, ploughs it through the puddle of egg yolk and taps the end in the ketchup. It's a cold but flavoursome mouthful that he takes his time to chew. He looks up at Evelyn. She winks, her left cheek bulging with food. Happiness always takes the edge off her table manners. Her unkindness towards Robert always takes the edge off William's happiness.

In the two years since his dad died, Uncle Robert has been a flesh and blood link to his father. Memories of him are no longer as sharp and reliable as William would like. He remembers being thrown into the air by him and sitting on his lap, burying his face in a brown wool jumper and breathing in the rich, twiggy smell of pipe smoke. He remembers standing next to him at the newsagent's on a Sunday morning, waiting for their quarter-pound of chocolate caramels to be poured into the bag from the wide metal scoop of the scales. He remembers him chasing Evelyn around the kitchen in a rubber gorilla mask, arms stretched out to reach her, making loud monkey noises, her screaming and laughing and surprising William at how fast she could move while making all that noise.

When he worries about forgetting, Uncle Robert's very existence is a comfort. Because not only were Robert and his father brothers and best friends, they were also identical twins. William can understand how it's hard for his mother to be reminded so much of his father, but it troubles him that sometimes she doesn't even seem to like Robert. Or Howard.

After lunch, they walk left along Trumpington Street and look at the lions guarding the Fitzwilliam Museum. William notices Fitzbillies on the other side of the road as they make their way back towards the school.

'Martin always goes there with his parents for a Chelsea bun. He says they're world famous.'

'I've got biscuits for us today,' Evelyn says, taking his hand, 'but next time we can do it. Oh!' She stumbles into the open gutter, landing with one knee in the water. Her face twists in pain, and William is not fooled by the sudden smile and laugh as she gets up. She's hurt but doesn't want him to worry.

Back on King's Parade, they watch a copper beech leaf scooped upright by the wind and pushed along as if it's running. Once it falls from the kerb into the gutter, Evelyn sits on the low wall and pats the spot to her left. William sits as she reaches into her bag and pulls out a Tupperware box. She holds it up, a playful look in her eye. Through the plastic, he recognises his favourites: butter biscuits. Unexpectedly, his eyes prickle.

She plonks the box on William's lap. Saliva makes his mouth tingle. He wants to pull the lid off, but waits. Evelyn leans down and pulls two napkins from her bag, the brown linen ones that live in the drawer next to the sink. He sniffs the one she hands him and thinks of the wooden spoons and rotary whisk they sit alongside. She nods for him to open the box and the sugar coating glitters on the top biscuit.

Eating them alongside her as they always did at home, the taste floods him with homesickness. He eats one after the other, until his lips and fingers are slick. By the time they get to the school, his new independence has melted away and all he wants is to go back to Sutton Coldfield with his mum. He wraps his arms round her, his cheek against her scarlet dress, and decides he won't let go. Her perfume and the aftertaste of butter in his mouth make him slightly nauseous.

'Come on, Master Lavery, you've got solos to sing.' His mother is pushing him away from her. 'Can't do that hanging on to me, can you?'

He can't speak, but manages a smile. She pats his back, energetic, cheerful, and nudges him towards the gates. He realises there's nothing for it but to walk away. He's through the door and has decided not to turn back when he hears her voice, high-pitched and urgent. He turns. She's leaning in towards him even though she's so far away. He notices a smudge of blood on her knee.

'William! Do you want me to write a letter about that cold water?'

He waves, shaking his head, and goes inside.

18

'It's always worse – after the first exeat.'

William thought he was managing to cry silently. Martin is lying on his side in the next bed, his head propped up in his plate-like hand.

The memory of his mother calling after him, asking if she should write to Mr Atkinson about the dips, with her hurt knee, squeezes his heart so tightly his breathing comes in soft grunts; the urgency of her voice, the folds of her face concentrated so keenly on him.

'Don't worry, you're like me,' whispers Martin, who, for such a raucous person, has the quietest voice when he wants to. 'Once you're back in the chapel you'll feel better.'

Martin's right. In the chapel, it's easy for William to forget his mother. And sooner than he could have hoped, Porter's voice starts to squeak and wobble him out of usefulness, so by the end of October, William is fast-tracked from probationer status. A heavy black cloak to walk to chapel in, a mortarboard with a silky tassel swinging at the edge of his vision, and a purple robe transform him into what he was always meant to be. A chorister.

Daily routines are rigid. Lessons and prep are slow and dull compared to his time in the chapel, but they have to be done, and by the time they are done, minutes and hours have passed and it's time to sing again. Even the rehearsal room, which on William's first day was such a disappointment, pleases him now. Small and plain, it seems the perfect place for introductions between choristers and music. Later, just before evensong, they're ready to present themselves to the mysterious chapel and let it work its acoustic magic on what they've practised.

'Morning, gentlemen,' Phillip says this morning, the usual tentative smile lifting his cheeks.

William spots sheets of pristine music on top of Phillip's folder. Something new. William has noticed new pieces draw something different from Phillip; a lightness, a gentle spirit of adventure. Rehearsing things that have been sung here for two hundred years, William wonders if the chapel ever thinks, *Not this one again!* And with pieces sung for the first time, he imagines the chapel tasting their sounds, harmonies and rhythms for the first time. But this morning, after spending twenty minutes on Bach's 'Herr Gott, nun schleuss den Himmel auf', and then quarter of an hour on Tallis's five-part 'Te Deum', William wonders whether they'll make it to the fresh scores. Then Phillip smiles at them.

'Now, something a little different.' He lifts the smooth white paper and holds it loosely in his hand, so it flops slowly towards them. 'You may have heard that Professor Hughes, Regius Professor of History, died last week. Wonderful old soul. There's a memorial here on Tuesday afternoon.'

'Excuse me, sir.' William finds himself with his hand up and speaking before Phillip has even nodded back at him. 'Is that the same as a funeral?'

Phillip pauses long enough for William to regret calling out, but when he finally answers, his voice is kind.

'No, Lavery, not quite – there's no coffin at a memorial because the funeral has already happened. It's more of an opportunity to remember and give thanks for the person who's died. More of a celebration, really. Of a life.'

'Thank you, sir.' William nods and frowns down at his music.

William was eight when his father died. His mother told him children weren't allowed at funerals, but a year later, a schoolfriend had the afternoon off school to be at his grand-mother's.

'Oh, darling,' his mother said, pulling him into her slim body. He'd come home from school in tears, wanting to know why she'd lied and why he hadn't been invited to his dad's funeral. 'We were so sad and it was so awful, I didn't want to put you through it.'

'It shouldn't be too gloomy,' Phillip continues now. 'Professor Hughes was a ripe old age, so there's a lot to be thankful for.'

What he means, William thinks, *is that when someone dies at an unripe age, like thirty-two, there isn't.*

'So' – Phillip looks round at the boys – 'we're going to do something rather special. Professor Hughes was Welsh and *loved* this piece. It's been in the Welsh popular culture for many, many years.' He hands Bishop, the new head chorister, a pile of papers to give out. As William reaches out for his, he sees there's an English translation too, which is unusual.

This isn't the first time they've sung in Phillip's native tongue. It's a funny language and there's simply no guessing how to pronounce it. Once, Martin asked what the Welsh had against vowels. Phillip, in good humour, said perhaps because the language is so old, vowels hadn't been invented.

'Right, have a quick read of the English so you get a feel of it,' he says now, apparently scanning the words himself. William's eyes skitter down the Welsh before settling on the translation of the last verse.

86

Myfanwy, may your life entirely be
Beneath the midday sun's bright glow,
And may a blushing rose of health
Dance on your cheek a hundred years.
I forget all your words of promise
You made to someone, my pretty girl
So give me your hand, my sweet Myfanwy,
For no more but to say 'farewell'.

'As you see, it's called "Myfanwy",' Phillip says, 'composed by Joseph Parry, first performed around 1875. A sad, noble song. The beloved – Myfanwy – has fallen out of love with the poet, but this is his generous acceptance of the fact, setting her free.' William sees Charles roll his eyes at his friend, but Martin, next to him, who loves a story, is hooked. 'He wants above all her happiness and to hold her hand one last time, to say farewell.' Phillip raises his eyebrows. 'Bit soppy, you may think, but it's terribly affecting when performed well. One of those songs whose music perfectly reflects the sentiment behind the words, thus giving *birth* to those very feelings in the listener.

'There's disagreement over the words' origins, but it was probably written by the poet Hywel ab Einion.' William loves the effortless switch in Phillip's voice to Welsh pronunciation. 'We'll sing in Welsh. No solos. It's often sung by male voice choirs, a giant tap of Welsh nostalgia, and that's not a bad thing for a memorial service, but don't worry, I'll take care not to drown you.' Phillip usually makes jokes with a deadpan delivery and it can take a moment and a look between the boys to confirm they're meant to smile. 'We'll be unaccompanied, so it's vital we get the pronunciation right. We'll start with that.' He waits for them to gather themselves. 'Let's just say the words. Ready?'

Daily, they sing in Latin, or Italian, or German, but with Welsh, the boys feel an added pressure to get it right.

'*Paham mae dicter, O Myfanwy,*' Phillip says with great precision. 'Everybody?'

They say it back to him.

'Right,' Phillip continues, business-like, 'it's important to get the poor girl's name right, don't you think? It's Mu*v*anwuay, Got it? Mu*v*anwuay. Everybody say it. Go.'

'Mu*v*anwuay.'

'Better. Good. Next line, a bit tricky . . .'

19

'That was juicy.' Martin has been humming the melody across the playing fields.

'What colour?' William's foot slides on mud and he grabs Martin's arm to right himself.

'Plum, of course, D flat.'

William always understands Martin's choice – violet for 'Faire is the Heaven', egg-yolk yellow for 'God is Gone Up' – but he could never come up with them himself.

Martin hangs up his coat next to William's before they make their way with four others to maths on the far side of the school. 'Pity there aren't any solos.' Martin bends down to pick up a conker in the middle of the corridor and slides it in his pocket. 'Will singing at the memorial be tough?' Martin keeps his eyes on the ground. 'Because of your dad?'

'Not sure.'

Martin puts his heavy arm round William's shoulders briefly before he opens the classroom door.

It took a few weeks for William to get used to arriving late for the first lesson of the day, but now he quite enjoys walking in once everyone has started and having a quiet few moments with the teacher to catch them up. As they weave through the desks in the room of bent heads, Martin mutters, 'I'm going to learn it in English, and I'll sing it for my party piece at Christmas.'

Mr Shrubs comes to their desks and drops a worksheet before each of them. He crouches down, resting his big index finger on William's purple bander copy. 'Long division. More practice, carrying on from yesterday.'

William can do long division. Fractions and percentages, not so good. As he scans the worksheet, he wonders if he could sing at home this Christmas. Martin's huge sprawl of a family are always performing to each other. He's told William about school holidays when he, his four siblings and nine (nine!) cousins spend all day writing and rehearsing a play; making a stage set, ransacking wardrobes for costumes, and then performing to the adults in the evening after supper. *Imagine that!* William thinks of himself, with just his mum, Uncle Robert and Howard sitting in the lounge together, quiet and tense. Still, they would love to hear him sing.

'Martin?' William mutters after completing three of the sums. 'Can we practise "Myfanwy" together? Then I can sing it at Christmas too.'

By the memorial service four days later, Martin and William have sung the English and Welsh versions so many times they've been asked to be quiet by three masters, everyone in their dorm and the head gardener. William has even sung it in his Donald Duck voice, thrilled at the loud belly laugh it raised from Martin. Always, at the last lines, 'So give me your hand, my sweet Myfanwy, For no more but to say "farewell",' Martin grips William's hand with one of his, the other melodramatically over his heart.

· · ·

Tiny, stick-limbed and hunched, Professor Hughes's widow reminds William so much of a bird, he thinks she could hop right into the showy floral display at the front of the chapel and not be noticed amongst the bright fleshy petals. William stares at the three young children, who he presumes are the professor's grandchildren, squirming between their parents on the front row. The dark army of gowned staff behind the family look too solemn for a celebration. William thinks it's all a bit of a nonsense. Isn't it always just *sad* when someone dies? He starts to picture his mother and uncle at his dad's funeral, but it's time to sing.

They leave the stalls to stand before the altar. William wants to watch the professor's widow, but by now he is too well trained; he keeps his eyes on Phillip, who waits for complete stillness and attention before he lifts his hand.

The sound is rich and mellow with an insistent sadness that scoops deeper and deeper with every line. By the velvet bloom and fade of the last verse, with Phillip pulling the feeling from the music with every fluid move of his right hand, the surf of emotion rolling back to them from the congregation astounds William.

The instant Phillip ties off the final note, William glances at Mrs Hughes, in time to catch the look between her and Phillip. It lasts a fraction of a second, but her gratitude and his kindness bring instant tears to his eyes. Blinking, he bites the soft sides of his mouth, until the physical movement back to the choir stalls rescues him.

In bed that night, he can't stop thinking of the service and all the stories about the professor that made everyone sad and happy at the same time. He wonders what stories would have been told about his father, with him and Evelyn, Robert and Howard sitting on the front row, the smell of lilies sharp and powdery in the air.

Someone, probably some vicar, would definitely say how

much fun he was. How when he came near, William's body would tighten a bit, get ready; to be picked up, thrown in the air, tickled, cuddled. How his dad always had to sit in the middle of the sofa when the three of them watched telly, so he could put his arm round both of them and say he'd got all he needed to be happy right here, tucked under each armpit. But, William wonders, how would a vicar know that? Only he and his mum knew about that. The vicar would probably say how proud his dad was to be an undertaker and to carry on the family business with his brother, and that makes his tummy tight because he knows it would make his mum feel left out and lonely.

The best memories a vicar wouldn't know about, and anyway, William's not sure what a *best* memory is; they're all a muddle of good and bad, warm and cold. There is one of him sharing a private joke with his dad that he loves so much, it's worth enduring the not so nice sequence of events that led up to it.

William was a poor sleeper as a baby, so his dad would leave the house with him on a Saturday morning to let Evelyn sleep. Howard and Robert soon joined them, and the fact that by the time he was two, William slept a solid twelve hours every night, was no reason to stop such an enjoyable routine. The men slipped back into their old camaraderie from school days, with the entertaining bonus of a biddable toddler.

During late spring of William's fifth year, an early heatwave gave Robert the idea of them taking William fishing. No one thought to prepare the animal-loving boy for what was about to happen.

'Stop!' William screamed, when the silver-blue creature appeared, dangling by its mouth, its body flick-flacking. 'You're hurting it!' he bellowed, appalled at the unprecedented cruelty of his uncle.

'Woo-hooo! Halloooo, William! Isssn't thissss fffun?' It was Howard, speaking in a funny, splashy voice. 'Pleassh can I dance on the gwassssy bank before you put me back in?' The voice was happy, and as Howard spoke, he jerked and flicked his own body a bit like the fish.

William watched intently as Robert put it on the bank and gently removed the hook.

'Thank you, Wobert,' the fishy voice said, in time with its flipperty tail, and the horror started to ebb as William dared to believe in the goodwill of it all. His eyes switched from the fish to Howard's impression of it, till they melded into the same thing. Robert, smiling at Howard, took the fish and threw it into the air.

'William, want to come for a sschwim in my world?' He hadn't even noticed Howard taking off his shirt, and his shorts, before diving in. 'Come on in!' the fishy voice called.

'Can I, Dad?'

His dad responded by taking off his own shirt and trousers, then helping William with his.

'Where are you, fish?' William called in his best Donald Duck voice, doggy-paddling towards Howard. And there followed a glorious half-hour of William's Donald Duck talking nonsense to Howard's fish.

On the way home, soggy but warm, exhausted but content, they stopped for petrol and Howard plucked a big bunch of red tulips from a bucket outside the station. When Evelyn answered the door to four bedraggled figures, Howard bowed low and offered them to her in the stupid voice.

'For Madam, fwom Laverwy, Sssons and Gwandsssson.'

She took them from him, trying to smile. 'Goodness, look at you all!' She held her arms out to William. 'What were you

93

thinking, Paul?' – the smile and the words horribly at odds with each other.

Later he saw the tulips lying in the sink while Evelyn cooked tea. 'They need water, Mum.'

'Give it to them then.' She shrugged, still out of sorts. He put them in a mug, but had to lean them against the wall to stop them falling over.

Under the misapprehension that the flowers had been a hit, Howard bought an identical bouquet the next week. William looked at his dad, wondering if they should stop him, but he shook his head and whispered, 'He's being kind.'

This time, once she'd closed the door on Howard and Robert, Evelyn let out a clenched scream.

'Lavery and Sons and Grandson!' She rammed the flowers into the bin and a few petals dropped onto the floor, like thick drops of blood. 'Howard's not even family. *I'm* Mrs Lavery . . .' She paused, on the verge of tears. 'And anyway, why aren't I ever invited?'

'Maybe if you weren't so prickly with Howard,' William's dad said softly. 'He thinks you don't like him. He's just trying, and anyway, the point is to give you some peace and quiet.'

'He's *my* son,' Evelyn said, as if he hadn't spoken, 'don't I get a say in what he does with his life?'

'Of course you do.' His dad kissed the top of her head. 'You're his mother, and you're magnificent.'

'One thing's for sure – if William goes into the family business, that's the end of it. He'll be one of your tight little gang and I'll *always* be on the outside.'

'Oh, Evelyn,' his dad said, pulling her close to him, 'there's enough love to go round, you know?'

'I know,' she said after a moment, leaning on his shoulder.

Then she pulled out of his embrace. 'I'll try harder, but I'll tell you this: if Howard ever sticks a bunch of red tulips in my face again, I'll not be held accountable for what I do with them!'

Dad laughed then, and though William didn't get the joke he was relieved it was all OK again.

A couple of weeks later, William was telling his dad about a teacher scolding a boy in his class. The boy had tutted, sending the teacher off into an even worse rage. When the boy was eventually allowed back to his desk, he sat down, and after a couple of seconds' silence, he tutted again.

'And?' William's dad said, eyes wide. 'Did she explode?'

William nodded.

'Like a red rag to a bull,' his dad said.

'What?'

'It means something that's sure to make someone angry. If you flash a red rag in front of a bull, it will charge at you.'

William nodded again. 'Like a red tulip to Mum.'

His dad started laughing, and that glorious thing happened; something ignited, and they kept going till they could barely breathe and their stomachs hurt.

20

By the time December arrives, moist and grey, and the walks to and from college are in the dark, William is enjoying himself. The putting on of his cassock and the graceful, weighty swing of the gown at his ankles makes him excited and eager to get to morning practice, or even better, evensong. With Martin at his side, talking, laughing and singing their way from school to college, scrunching down the gravel avenue towards the chapel, William's heart expands to make space for his new home. The classrooms, the austere dorm, and the dining hall heavy with its smells, are no longer strange to him and have no more nasty surprises, but it's in the chapel that he feels himself expanding. It's in here he is often so happy, so full up with joy, he has to wiggle his toes and fingers to stop himself laughing, or whooping or bouncing up and down.

'I know it's just a building, but it doesn't *feel* like just a building,' he tried to explain to Martin once.

'My dad doesn't care much about church, but he says that coming to hear us sing is like being hugged by God,' Martin offered. 'Is it like that?'

'Sort of, but the chapel feels like it*self*, not God. Bigger and older than us, but still letting us join in with a great game it's been playing for hundreds of years.'

Martin shook his head and laughed, but as usual, it made William feel better, not worse about what he'd said.

'Don't tell anyone else, but when I'm singing, it feels like the chapel is smiling at me.'

'That's Phillip, not the chapel! He smiles at your voice all the time, but he tries not to, he's not meant to have favourites.'

Missing the beginning of class every morning, William is spurred on by the constant need to catch up. It serves him well. The masters recognise he works hard and are impressed that, even though he seems joined at the hip to Mussey, he never gets into trouble. Classes are to be endured, prep a daily task to be completed. Fortunately, William finds he does have endurance, he is able to complete his prep, and he even has time to cajole his reluctant, restless friend to finish his.

■ ■ ■

With seasonal music oozing through his pores, he walks with Martin and two other choristers along the corridor towards the history room. It's three weeks before Christmas, on a Wednesday morning, almost at the end of William's first term. His fingers are a lilac colour from the cold and his nose is runny. William likes this particular classroom, which may be more cramped than others but is twice as warm. Martin holds the door open, bowing and gesturing extravagantly for them to go before him.

The cosy fug of bodies and the hum of radiator heat register first. He becomes aware that everyone is listening to music before he recognises what it is, but when he does, he comes to such an abrupt halt that Martin bumps into him.

Next to Mr Hawthorn's desk is an upright square of pale wood with a metal mesh circle at its centre. The music coming out of it is well known to William; the blunt simplicity of the tenors' plainsong about to bloom, the swooping harmonies and embellishments, the not quite human top C of the treble's solo. Martin nudges William and flicks his head in the direction of two empty desks. William doesn't move, held by silence like a basket holding the wonder of what's just happened and the expectation of what's about to come.

Allegri's 'Miserere'.

He was five, sitting on his father's lap, staring at the record player's leathery red and black casing, the stylus riding the grooves of the shining vinyl that rolled round and round and round.

'Why are you crying?' Evelyn laughed, reaching across to ruffle his hair. He slid from his dad's lap, knelt by the record player, so close he could smell the heat and the plastic, see the slight undulations as the record revolved, the wisp of dust gathering on the needle.

'Again. Put it on again, Mummy!'

When Evelyn told him that this beautiful, *beautiful* sound was made by a boy just a few years older than him, his world cracked open. If a boy like him could make a sound like that, what other magic was possible?

'That'll be you soon,' Martin mutters, as he pulls him by the sleeve to sit down.

'Mm,' William replies. He unzips his pencil case and starts to sharpen a lead so blunt it's almost flush with the wood, but he is too brisk and the new point snaps off, wedging itself between the blades of the sharpener. In the many hours they have spent together, William has told Martin all sorts of things. Martin is an exceptional listener, mainly, William realises, because he loves a story. So less than a term in, Martin knows William feels time spent with his uncle keeps his father from disappearing. He's seen his photo of Howard, bookended with the identical brothers. He knows that Evelyn is pained rather than comforted by Robert and Howard's presence and is determined that her son won't go into the family business, but *use his gift* and do something musical. He knows William feels as if he's flying when he sings, and that a place at the front of his skull buzzes when he hits the high notes. It feels as if he's told Martin most things, except, to his surprise, this; singing the solo for Allegri's 'Miserere' is what he's here for.

'You all know this piece of music, of course,' Mr Hawthorn says once it's over, walking back and forth before the blackboard, throwing and catching a small piece of chalk, 'but does anyone know the background to it?'

William's hand punches the air. Martin turns to him, surprised.

'Lavery, want to come up and tell everyone?'

William is on his feet before he's even finished saying, 'Yes, sir.'

'How did you hear the story, Lavery?'

'My dad. I used to listen to it every day when I was about five.' He looks at the floor, suddenly a bit embarrassed and a bit wobbly. 'He found out all about it for me.'

'Like all good stories,' Mr Hawthorn says, 'the truth is contested, and there are different versions. Let's see which one your father told you.' William glances at Martin who gives him a smile.

'In the old days, the "Miserere" was only sung in the Sistine Chapel in Rome. The Pope wouldn't let it be sung anywhere else. He wouldn't even let it be written down. So all the fancy bits – the *abbellimenti* – were passed down from one soloist to another. Anyone who tried to copy it or perform it somewhere else was thrown out of the Catholic Church.' He glances at Mr Hawthorn, wondering if he's telling the right version. He nods for William to continue. 'In those days, people used to travel around Europe for months and months to visit the big cities.'

'It was called the Grand Tour,' Mr Hawthorn interjects, 'very popular in the eighteenth century. That's actually why we're talking about this today. Carry on, Lavery.'

'People would go to Rome in Lent to hear the "Miserere" and Mozart went when he was fourteen. He went back to his hotel room and wrote it all down from memory. But to make sure he'd got it right, he went back again on Good Friday with the rolled-up music stuffed in his hat.

'Was he caught?' Martin shouts, forgetting to put his hand up. 'Was he chucked out?'

William looks again to Mr Hawthorn, in case he wants to deliver the punchline, but he smiles and nods at William.

'He was caught, but he wasn't chucked out. The Pope said well done and made him a knight!'

'Very good, Lavery,' says Mr Hawthorn, sitting down with a book. 'Have you seen the translation of the letter Mozart's father wrote to his wife from Rome?'

'No, sir.' William is excited.

'Sit down, well done. I'll take it from here.'

Mr Hawthorn rests the book on his lap and reads. '"You have often heard of the famous 'Miserere' in Rome, which is so greatly prized that the performers are forbidden on pain of excommunication to take away a single part of it, copy it or to give it to anyone. *But we have it already*. Wolfgang has written it down and we would have sent it to Salzburg in this letter, if it were not necessary for us to be there to perform it. But the manner of performance contributes more to its effect than the composition itself. Moreover, as it is one of the secrets of Rome, we do not wish to let it fall into other hands . . ."'

William finishes writing his paragraph about the Grand Tours of the eighteenth century. Martin's large head is resting on his hand. William nudges him with his foot.

'Wake up, I'm going to ask a question.'

Martin shuffles in his seat and starts to write slowly.

'Sir, I've finished. Can I see the letter?' William says.

Mr Hawthorn holds up the book for William to take. Then, as if he too had just been woken by William, he suddenly stands up.

'Six minutes left, gentlemen. I need to get your prep sheets from the office. Work quietly. Stay in your seats.'

The book is heavy and the pages are thick. William puts it flat on his desk. He reads the letter, printed in a font that looks like handwriting, and then rereads the bit that made the back of his shoulders tingle: *But the manner of performance contributes more to its effect than the composition itself.* He picks up his pencil and quickly starts to copy the slanted script into his rough book, with the feeling of urgency that overcomes him sometimes. He doesn't have long here. Choristers leave at fourteen, to make way for the purer, younger voices. Not having arrived until he was ten, William worries he won't be able to cram all he wants into this short time. The 'Miserere' is what he wants most.

He jumps as Martin's hand slaps down on his page.

'How did you do that?' The murmurs of the other boys grow louder as they relax into Mr Hawthorn's absence.

'What?' says William.

'The handwriting!'

'What about it?'

'It's identical! How did you do it?'

'I copied it.' He continues to write as he speaks. 'Mum taught me to write before I went to school, so I wrote like her. Then my teacher told me I had to write like him, so I did. It's easy.'

'Do mine.' Martin puts his own rough book over William's.

William copies out the last line of Martin's writing. Martin's smile is infectious. They grin at each other.

'You haven't a clue, have you?' Martin rests his hand on William's shoulder.

'What?'

'How useful this is.' He reaches across to William's rough book and turns to a clean page. 'Can you do your mum's without having anything to copy?'

'Of course.'

Martin puts one hand on the top of his head in excitement. 'Write this,' he whispers. 'Dear Mr Atkinson, please excuse William from all homework this term. He is worn out and on the verge of collapse. Yours sincerely, Mrs Lavery.'

William laughs.

'Or . . .' Martin looks up to the corner of the ceiling, his broad teeth resting on his lower lip. 'Dear Mr Atkinson, William was sick over Christmas. The doctor thinks he is allergic to fish, and says that he mustn't eat kippers.'

William briefly imagines the relief of not having to swallow the soft bones every Friday, before shaking his head. 'Imagine the trouble if I was found out.'

'You could do one from *my* parents.' Another wave of inspiration washes over Martin's face. 'Or anyone's!'

'Why would I do that?'

'You'd charge. Tuck rations.' He sits up straighter and twists to face William. 'We could be a team! I find the customers, you write the letters.' His eyes dart round the room. 'You'd have to do them before the Christmas holiday, then they can take them home and post them from there, so they'd have the right postmarks!'

'I'd have to write the envelopes as well.' William surprises himself by talking as though he is actually going to do it.

By the time Mr Hawthorn has given out prep questions, Martin has a list of boys to approach and William has a tangle of wire wool in his guts.

Mark Nettles is first, a tiny boy in the year above them. They are in the dorm, due at supper in ten minutes. Martin nods at Mark's pocket.

'Have you got everything? Sample writing? Note paper? Envelope?'

Mark nods back, his pointed face serious as he pulls out an envelope.

'One of my mum's letters is inside.' He talks to Martin but passes it to William.

William can feel the spring of the folded letter squeezed into the envelope. He pulls it out and smooths it on the bed. The writing is a neat, italic script, not unlike his teacher in class two.

'And I've written what I want you to say on the back of the envelope.' Mark points.

William turns it over.

Dear Mr Atkinson,

Mark keeps feeling faint during evensong on Wednesday after rugby. Our doctor thinks if he doesn't have to do Games he won't feel faint and will sing better.

Yours sincerely,

Mrs Nettles.

William kneels down next to the bed, leaning the fresh paper on the dorm bible. 'Tell me if you think I get anything wrong.'

'Don't worry, Mark, he won't.' Martin looks smug. William hopes he won't let them all down.

It doesn't take long and when it's done, the boy's face seems to lose its sharp edges and his eyes soften.

'Brilliant!' He stands holding the letter.

'Hang on, I've got to address the envelope so you can post it from home.'

'Impressive.' Mark hands it back.

'Get a move on, we've got to go and eat,' Martin says.

'Just think!' Mark laughs as they leave the dorm. 'No Games!'

'And only half your tuck allowance for the first half of next term, plus this week's.' Martin pats Mark on the back.

As they walk into the dining hall and Cook's face lifts ever so slightly when she sees him, William feels he's crossed a threshold.

During the last week of term, he writes three more letters: one to get Charles out of dips due to a weak chest; one for Anthony, asking for bigger portions at lunch because the doctor says he's too skinny; and finally for Martin (against William's advice), whose mother demands that the tuck shop starts stocking shoe lace liquorice.

William's first term ends in a sugar rush, as he and Martin chomp through Black Jacks, Fruit Salads and Bazooka bubble gum. Often, when he slides his hands into his pockets, they land in sticky sweet wrappers. Smiling, he sucks the goo from his fingers and runs to catch up with Martin, who is always striding a few paces ahead of him.

21

He wakes to 'Ding Dong Merrily on High'. Their flat is small enough to be filled with the noise coming from any one room and the smells of cooking from the kitchen. Today, it's bacon and the rich coffee made in the metal jug from Italy. Pulled from the back of the cupboard to make the black syrupy stuff he loves to smell, the jug is synonymous with special occasions. His bedroom door swings open, the music and aromas increase, and Evelyn dances in with a tray, wearing her nightie, a Father Christmas hat, and green tinsel round her neck.

'Happy Christmas to his Lordship.' She moves towards his bed, hips swinging one way and the tray in her arms the other.

'Happy Christmas, Mum.' He grins, sitting up and putting his pillow behind his back. She places the tray on his lap; a mug of cocoa with a swirl of evaporated milk on top and a plate of bacon, eggs and fried bread.

'I'll be right back,' she says, dancing out of the room. The music is turned up, and seconds later Evelyn returns with her own tray, identical to his, except with coffee instead of cocoa. She settles herself on the end of his bed and piles her fork with egg and bacon. William dips his fried bread in the deep yellow yolk. They both concentrate on the food, moving their heads to the music and smiling as they catch each other's eye.

William, a faster eater after a term as a boarder, puts his tray on the floor and then reaches under his bed for the parcel.

'You know, William,' Evelyn says, taking her last mouthful,

'whatever you've got me for Christmas will be a disappoint-ment. You shouldn't have bothered.'

William smiles, puts the parcel on the bed, lifts the tray gen-tly from her lap and sets it on the floor next to his.

'Yeah, yeah,' he says, 'I know, all you want for Christmas . . .'

'. . . is you!' she finishes, as she has done for as long as William can remember. 'But never more true than *this* year. Oh well, best get this palaver out of the way.' She pulls at the wrapping paper, feigning boredom. The paper rips to reveal the corner of a picture frame. The facade, also part of their ritual, is dropped as she quickly sweeps the paper aside and studies the photograph, scanning the sixteen ruff-necked boys in purple and white. He sees her eyes land on him, standing next to Martin, holding his music at just the right angle.

'Go on then.' He leans into her arm, nudging her with his elbow. 'Say it.'

Still fixed on the photo, she leans back against his body. 'I love it! I take back everything I said before – this is *much* better than you, any day.'

William's present is a bike, waiting for him in the communal shed next to the allotments. His old one is still there, ridicu-lously small. He goes for a ride round the park at the end of the street while Evelyn starts lunch. He can only just reach the ground, so he's a little nervous, but thinks by Easter he'll have grown into it.

For the first few days at home William had woken at six, when Matron would have marched through the dorms with her bell. There is a particular pleasure simply lying there not having to get up, gazing at his bedroom, at the spindly bookshelf, the yel-low and red spines of *The Boys' Book of Heroes*, *The Hardy*

106

Boys, *The Famous Five* and two bibles, one black and one red. William's eyes rest for longest on the cowboys and Indians rampaging across his curtains. He was just nine when the exciting new fabric had replaced the yellow calico he'd known since birth. A giant, hanging story book, with the rangy sheriff striding out of a hotel, and to the left, two Red Indians looking up a mountain, one with leather tassels running the whole length of his outstretched arm, and the other balancing a long spear on his shoulder. Above them, a friendly-looking cowboy with a gun stands next to a carriage with white, billowy sides. The final image is of three cowboys, galloping towards William with pistols.

He has not forgotten the excitement of these curtains. They signalled a turning point, when his mum stopped looking sad all the time. He was still woken every night by her sobbing, which was so awful he worried that she might choke and die. But at least in the mornings she'd smile and do things like buy him cowboy and Indian curtains.

'It's called Hiiiigh Noooon!' she said with a twangy drawl, pulling them across his window for the first time. They enjoyed westerns at the cinema, had already seen Gary Cooper in the film from which the images had come. The galloping cowboys on the curtains were probably heading down the mountain to kill the Indians, but it all looked friendly and jolly.

Lounging in bed, soaking in his familiar surroundings, has been pleasant. So has not standing over the bath for morning dips, or practising piano before breakfast. William often feels drowsy on sugar and so much warmth and comfort. He sloughed off the chorister boarder easily and settled back into his old self, eating as much as he wants, cuddling up on the sofa with Evelyn and a story book, even though he is too old. The knowledge of how happy he makes her, just by breathing and being close to her, drapes over his shoulders again like a warm, heavy cloak. There are moments, however, in their cosy flat when he feels a little trapped. When his mother's loving eyes on his face are too much. Too caring. Too intense. There are moments when he misses the bracing discipline of his life in Cambridge; the independence of only thinking about himself, the busyness of not having a spare minute to lounge around and wonder what to do next. Late in the dark afternoons, his overfed body sometimes aches for the brisk walk through the college grounds and into his beautiful chapel.

22

He must have fallen asleep. Fred Astaire and Ginger Rogers have disappeared. Something else is on now, but he can't work out what it is. Evelyn is in the kitchen. Without moving a muscle, he knows.

It's Boxing Day, and as usual, Uncle Robert and Howard are coming for tea, and as a result, Evelyn is in a bad mood. He can tell by the chink of cutlery on ceramic, the slosh of water in a mixing bowl, the shriek of a baking tray being pulled from the oven.

William is never hungry when they have posh tea because he will have been in the kitchen, *helping*. It's their joke. 'William, can you help me with the washing up?' Evelyn says, handing him a mixing bowl, or a whisk, or a spoon covered in something raw and sweet.

Sitting up on the sofa now, his bare feet touching the carpet, he feels guilty. If he'd wanted to, he could have been a real help this year, spreading the marge and fish paste, spearing the cheese and pineapple cubes with cocktail sticks, sprinkling the trifle with hundreds and thousands. But he didn't want to be in the kitchen, wary of what Boxing Day does to his mum. He's tired and irritable, and thinks how nice it would be if he could trust her to make Uncle Robert and Howard feel welcome. Instead of trying to jolly her along with jokes and helpfulness, William walks into the kitchen on the offensive.

'Mum?'

'Yes?' She doesn't turn from the sink where she's scrubbing burned bits off the baking tray.

William sits at the stool in the corner. 'Was there a memorial service for Dad?'

'A what?'

'A memorial service.'

'No.' She continues to scrub, her whole body vibrating.

'We sung for one at college to celebrate a professor's life.'

'Memorials aren't for the likes of us, William.'

'Pity.'

'Why?'

'You might have let me go to that.'

Evelyn turns, and her iron look confirms that there is no softness in his mother, nor will there be until Boxing Day is over and done with.

'When someone can tell me what there is to celebrate about losing your husband and having to raise a child single-handed, then we'll hold a memorial.' She turns back to the sink and swills out a cream carton. 'But don't hold your breath.'

'Well, don't take it out on Uncle Robert and Howard.'

'Well, don't you do that thing you do with the two of them.'

'What thing?'

'All of you. Together. I might just as well disappear.'

'We don't want you to.'

Evelyn is still for a moment, then starts back at the baking tray. William decides to leave her alone until they come.

In the lounge he looks at the old photograph on the bureau. Evelyn's holding baby him; his dad's arm hangs loosely around her shoulder. Howard and Robert stand a little to the left. Everyone's laughing, looking at Howard who has probably just said something funny, his hands splayed, eyebrows raised. From time to time, Evelyn puts the photo in a drawer, but he always finds it and puts it back out.

By the time his parents met, Robert, Howard and his father had been a tight unit for over ten years. Robert and Paul were sent to different secondary schools, a chance for each of them to be their own person. Neither had felt the need for that but they respected their parents. Paul met Howard on the first day and said he'd never needed to look any further for friendship. He invited Howard home one afternoon that week, introduced him to Robert, and from then on, outside school, the three of them were inseparable. The Three Musketeers, William's grandparents called them. William likes to imagine them as boys his age, swashbuckling around his grandfather's funeral parlour. He isn't clear exactly how Howard became part of the family business, or when he moved into the house. It had something to do with his parents getting married and buying the flat down the road.

They arrive with a cold waft of outside, woollen scarves folded over ties, V-neck jumpers and white shirts. Both men have big presents wrapped with ribbons, two for Evelyn and two for him. Under their little tree lies a solitary package for both of them, small, shallow, rectangular. William will not present them with the box of handkerchiefs this year. His mother can. Instead, he wraps his arms round Robert's waist, rests his face against the soft blue wool. Robert chuckles and taps out a rhythm with the palms of his hands on William's back.

'Happy Christmas, boy wonder.'

Howard ruffles his hair. 'Good to see you, William. You've got tall!'

'We shouldn't be surprised, but hasn't he just?' Robert holds William's face in his hands a brief moment, then turns to his mother.

'Happy Christmas, Evelyn. Good to have him back?'

'What do you think?' she replies snippily. 'Sit down and I'll finish in the kitchen. Sherry? Tea?'

'Sherry,' they reply together.

Howard sits on the settee, Uncle Robert in the armchair opposite. William places himself on the floor between them by the coffee table.

'Here you are, William.' Robert puts the two parcels before him.

'Thanks, Uncle Robert. Thanks, Howard.'

As William unwraps the 250-piece puzzle and an LP – the soundtrack to Leonard Bernstein's *West Side Story* – he chatters about his first term. He keeps a close eye on Uncle Robert; his thick brown hair, straight nose, the dimple in his chin, and – his favourite bit – the three sharp creases that fan out from the corner of each of his eyes when he smiles. Which is nearly all the time, as William relaxes quickly back into entertaining them. He's more outgoing and extrovert with Howard and Robert than with anyone else. It's a hangover from all the time he spent with them and his father, when he was always the centre of attention.

When Evelyn comes back in with glasses of sherry and nuts in a wooden bowl, the three of them are rocking, silent with laughter.

'What's funny?' she says with a bright smile, putting the tray on the table.

In a perfect Donald Duck voice, William says, 'I've been singing the "Te Deum".'

They collapse into laughter again.

Evelyn straightens the cloth and sits at the table. 'It always worries me you'll damage your voice doing that,' she says, and bites into a crab paste sandwich.

Later, Howard sits cross-legged with William at the coffee table and they start the jigsaw of the Cunard liner. Howard smells woody and crisp. They wonder if the piece in William's hand is the grey sky, or the metal of the boat. They give up and concentrate on the red funnels. Uncle Robert and Evelyn are talking at the table about nothing. He asks if she needs the window frames painting, because he wouldn't mind doing that. She says no, but thank you. After a while, he asks if they can play the LP they gave William.

William says, 'Yes please,' before Evelyn can say something unkind.

He and Howard carry on with the puzzle; Uncle Robert and Evelyn listen to the music with their eyes shut. Eventually they go into the kitchen and wash up.

Howard relaxes, swings puzzle pieces in the air in time to the music. Soon, every rummage in the box for a piece, every attempt to fit one into place, has become a giggled piece of choreography.

William wonders, suddenly, if Martin has sung 'Myfanwy' to his family yet. 'I've got a song to sing you all.'

Howard puts down a puzzle piece, smiling. 'That would be *marvellous*! What is it?'

'"Myfanwy" – I can do it in Welsh if you like.'

'I can't help it, William!' Evelyn sighs and flops onto the sofa two hours later. 'I miss your dad. Especially at Christmas. You can understand that, can't you?' She picks up the tea towel that lies next to her.

He shrugs, sitting back down at the jigsaw, running his fingers over the completed funnels. He steals a glance at her. She's twisting the tea towel round one hand. He looks back at the remaining pieces in the box and spots the fluffy bit of steam that connects the funnels. He and Howard were hunting for that for ages. He slots it into place.

'But I *like* being with him.' His eyes stay fixed on the box. 'It's the next best thing to being with Dad.' He forces himself to look at her.

'Not for me. It just makes me sad.'

'Well, I wish being sad didn't make you nasty! I wanted to sing a song for you all, but you looked so mean when you came back from washing up, I couldn't.'

She stares at him, the tea towel now draped over her red flecked skirt, then sits upright on the edge of the settee. 'Well, maybe next year I'll just stay in the kitchen and you can have a far better time without me.' She leans back, then sits up straight again. 'And I'll ask you not to call me nasty, William.'

'They miss him too, you know.'

She walks to the table and slaps the towel down. 'I wouldn't mind, if just once, Robert came on his own! Why do they *always* have to be together, when I haven't got anyone to be together with!' She marches out of the room and slams the door.

William moves his fingers again through the puzzle pieces, trying not to think about anything except the brown piece of luggage he needs.

Hours later, the completed jigsaw on the coffee table is the only evidence that Robert and Howard were there at all. There is something else, but it's hidden under William's pillow. He's sure Howard wouldn't have done what he did if he'd known William was watching through the window. As the two men walked down the path, there was no mistaking the anger on Howard's face. At the dustbin, he pulled the packet of hand-kerchiefs from under Robert's elbow, lifted the lid and dropped them in it. William saw the sudden swing of Robert's face to Howard's, but they were too far away for him to see their expressions. While Evelyn was in the bath, he sneaked down and retrieved the handkerchiefs. He didn't know why, but it felt important.

William is in bed now, dipping in and out of sleep, when Evelyn slowly pushes the door open and sits on his bed.

'I'm sorry, William,' she murmurs, 'I'll do better next year. I promise.'

William exaggerates his breathing, keeps his eyes closed. How can she feel lonely when she's got him? He'll probably forgive her in the morning but tonight he wants to stay angry. Wide awake now, he remembers another Christmas and because images of his father come so clear and strong, he lets it play out, even though he knows full well it will end with him feeling sorry for his mother.

There was a game his father and Robert played with him that filled him with a paroxysm of excitement and dread. The brothers would stand side by side in their undertaking suits, one in a rubber monkey mask. Whoever was masked would say in a sinister voice:

'Which is your uncle and which is your dad?
Choose the wrong one and the monkey goes mad.'

When they weren't working, it was easy to tell them apart. William's dad wore sloppy jumpers and cords. Robert was smarter; slacks, V-neck jumpers and a tie. At work, they wore name badges, and everyone had to trust they weren't messing around. They could well have been, after a childhood of making mischief with friends and teachers. Even their own short-sighted mother could only tell the difference when she was close up.

If William guessed right, he was hoisted onto the unmasked twin's shoulders and paraded round the room. Part of William wanted to get it wrong for the thrill of being chased round the room, pinned down and tickled mercilessly by the monkey. But he always tried to get it right, he wanted to be able to tell the difference. Eyebrows, nostrils, teeth, lips, ears, hairline, would all be studied by his young, eager eye. Nothing. He couldn't tell them apart.

It was the day business closed for Christmas when they made Evelyn play the game. William was six and the funeral home full of people; undertakers and local clergy. The office was cosy, with glasses on every surface, and crumbs from the mince pies his mother had brought through straight from the oven. William was rolling on the floor, being tickled by his dad in the monkey mask. Everyone seemed happy. There was red and green tinsel woven around the mirror on the wall and a fake Christmas tree in the entrance hall with coloured lights.

'Evelyn, you try!' said the vicar of St Chads, his apple cheeks scarlet after a glass or two of sherry.

'No, thanks!' Evelyn smiled back, lifting her glass to him.

'Come on, Mrs Lavery!' said one of the undertakers. It was clear from the murmurs and laughs that everyone wanted her to.

'All right then.' Evelyn rolled her eyes. William was nervous for her. He noticed Howard sit down in the corner. His father and uncle left the room and returned quickly, one in the mask. Evelyn's eyes flicked from one to the other. The unmasked face was deadpan, looking straight ahead.

Evelyn lifted her hands and rested her fingers in the indent

116

of her temples. 'If I could see *both* your faces, I'd be able to do it, no problem.' There was a hint of panic in her eyes. The room was quiet.

The twins stood, motionless. William slid his hand into his mother's.

'Howard, can you help?' asked an undertaker.

'No!' Evelyn snapped. 'I don't need it!' She looked for a second longer. 'I think Robert's got the mask on.' She tried to smile, tried to look as if she was enjoying it, but her set jaw, the buzz in the air around her, twisted William's stomach.

The masked brother jumped onto a nearby chair, making monkey noises and gestures, then dropped down and started to chase her.

'Paul, is it you?' she screamed as she ran around the office. 'Is it you?' The monkey closed in on her and picked her up.

'Is it you?' she screamed, hitting him in the chest. 'Tell me!'

'Yes,' said the masked face, gently putting her down. 'It's me.' William's dad took off the mask and laid it on the desk. People clapped and laughed as he folded Evelyn into a hug. Her face was so vividly red, William thought she looked ready to burst into flames.

When William passed Howard to get a chocolate from the big tin, Howard said softly, 'Want to know the difference?'

It seemed momentous that Howard could tell when his mother couldn't. William nodded.

'Robert has a *tiny* blue vein in his temple, right here.' Howard touched the dent in William's head. 'Tell your mum, but don't tell her I told you.'

Later, his mother sobbed on the settee, being cuddled by his dad. 'Evelyn, it's OK.'

'You humiliated me!'

'William,' his dad said, 'give your mother and me a moment, please.'

William ran to the kitchen, grabbed a biscuit from the jar shaped like a cat, then sat with his back to the closed door to listen.

'It was just a bit of fun.'

'I hate it when the three of you join forces against me. *Hate* it!'

'We weren't joining forces.' His voice was low and quiet; he was amused, not cross, William could tell from his cuddling voice.

'Howard can *tell*.' She wasn't using her cuddling voice. 'How do you think that makes me feel? Everyone laughing at me because I can't tell my own husband apart from his homosexual brother!'

William stopped chobbling in case they heard him in the deep silence that followed. He didn't know what that word meant, but he could feel the shock of her having said it from the quiet. He couldn't imagine his father's face. William licked a crumb from his bottom lip and felt it on his tongue. All he could hear was the soft whistling of breath through his nose.

'And you expect me to sit back and watch the three of you get your claws into William,' she started up again, 'until he thinks his only future's in this bloody place.'

'Claws?' His dad sounded baffled. 'That's how it feels?'

'There's a big world out there, I want him to feel he has choices.'

'Of course he will. Give me some credit, Evelyn.'

His mother exhaled loudly. 'Robert and Howard – they're always *there*. And if William goes into the business . . . I know it sounds pathetic, Paul, but sometimes, I think William loves them as much as he loves me and you.'

118

William had leapt up then, pulled the door open and charged in, climbing onto her lap and holding her face in both his hands. 'I love you most! I promise!'

'Well hello, Mr Elephant Ears.' His dad laughed. 'Evelyn, you know I love you most too, don't you?'

'How much?' she asked, softening.

He looked out of the window. 'Enough to throw the monkey mask away.'

She leant into him and the three of them were a lovely tangle of laps and arms and cheeks. 'I'd love that.' And even though William thought he'd miss the monkey game, he'd rather not see his mum so scared and lonely again.

'Mum,' he said after a moment of cuddling, 'Uncle Robert has a tiny blue vein, just there.' He reached up and touched her temple.

'Really?' Dad said. 'Well spotted, William.'

'Howard told you, didn't he?' his mum said.

William shook his head, remembering his promise to Howard.

'Yes, he did.' She patted his back. 'You don't have to lie.'

He looked up at her; she was still soft and cuddly, but there were tears in her eyes again.

■ ■ ■

Tired and sad at the memory, as he knew he would be, William pulls back his sheets and gets out of bed. He finds her watching television, with only the weak twinkle of the Christmas tree lights, and sits next to her on the settee.

'Hello, William.' She lifts her arm and he snuggles into her.

'Hello, Mum.'

119

She kisses the top of his head and they watch Billy Cotton and Vera Lynn's Boxing Day Party.

'I love you most, Mum,' he says at some point. She tightens her arm for a second around his shoulder and kisses the top of his head.

23

Even with the stocky cast iron radiators on full, the assembly hall is hard and heavy with cold. Mr Atkinson's shoulders seem rigid beneath his gown, and he isn't looking at any of them as they sing 'When a Knight Won His Spurs'.

Once they are seated and the headmaster starts to speak, William suddenly needs the toilet.

'It pains me to have to start the term with a disciplinary matter.' Mr Atkinson hasn't even said welcome back, or Happy New Year. Martin nods at William's bouncing left leg and frowns. William tries to sit still. 'But I have received what can only be described as ridiculous letters purporting to be from parents requesting idiotic schoolboy favours. I am not a fool and will not be treated as one by foolish boys who should know better. All those involved – you know who you are – will come to my office straight after assembly.'

Mark Nettles, sitting along the row from William, twitches his head to the right slightly, but doesn't look at him. He can't see the younger boys, Charles and Anthony, from where he is. A pulse beats in the ball of his sweaty right foot. He remembers Charles whimpering through the night in William's wet pyjamas back in September, and imagines how frightened he must be now. Martin's face is innocent and calm as ever, singing the hymns as if he means it, closing his eyes for prayers, listening to the notices. William struggles to stay on his seat. The dark green tweed of Mr Atkinson's trousers and the shine of his brogues, once admired by William, are now filled with menace.

'Those boys coming to see me, wait outside my room,' he says after the last hymn, gathering his papers from the podium, 'I'll be along shortly.'

'I'm going to be sick,' William says, as he and Martin walk along the corridor. Mark, Charles and Anthony are still in the body of boys funnelling through the hall door.

'They should have thought of better requests,' says Martin as they climb the broad stairs. 'It's their fault, not ours.'

'Shoe lace *liquorice*?' William says.

Martin puts his head to one side and purses his lips as they arrive at Mr Atkinson's office. 'Fair point.' It is beyond William how there can be even a ghost of a smile on Martin's face as he leans against the wall.

The others appear. Even though Mark is four years older than Charles and Anthony, he is barely taller than them.

'My dad's going to go mad if he hears about this.' Mark glances at the younger boys. 'We didn't write the letters! Why should we get punished for something we didn't do?'

'Yes!' says Anthony, in a bold voice that doesn't match his frightened eyes.

William's buttocks tighten, imagining the whacks he'll get as scribe of all four letters.

Mark jabs William's chest. 'You did it! You need to own up.'

'Rubbish!' says Martin. 'You'd have thanked us if it had worked.'

'But it *didn't*' – Mark's pinched face is getting redder – 'that's the point!'

Martin ignores him and turns to William. 'Go back to class, quick, before Mr Atkinson comes.' He nudges him away. 'You don't need to be here.'

'What?' says Mark, two deep furrows at the top of his delicate nose. 'He's the *only* one that needs to be here. He wrote the letters!'

'The letters were from *your* parents, asking for things *you* wanted.' Martin is calm and matter of fact. 'Go on, get lost, William, quick.'

'But I did it!' William says.

'No, you didn't.' Martin shakes his head. 'I did.' He turns to the others, his body still loose and easy. 'And if any of you say any different, I'll make your lives so miserable you'll wish you'd had a whacking from Atkinson every day for a week, instead of having me to deal with.'

Charles clamps his lips together, fighting tears.

'No,' William says, 'that's not fair.'

'Go!' Martin pushes him hard, so he stumbles backwards.

He looks at the others. They're resigned; they're not going to argue. Before he has time for any other thoughts, he walks away as quickly as he can, fizzing with shame, already regretting it, but knowing he isn't going to turn back.

24

FEBRUARY 1959

It's a high-wire act, this solo, like floating above a canyon. Getting up there isn't the problem; William can get to an F, never mind a C. The problem is holding the G in perfect pitch, rock steady, without cracking or fading while all the parts below are changing. Allegri's 'Miserere'. It still thrills him how his breath, his voice, can fill the chapel, soaring up to its high ceiling, piercing the silence, or slicing through other voices. And when he's a soloist, there's the thrill of knowing the others' voices are there to frame and magnify his own. It's magic. Pure magic.

He thinks he's done a good job; buoyed by the lingering sense that *he* was soaring, not just his voice.

Phillip is looking into the distance, as if William's voice is visibly hanging there. William doesn't take his eyes off him.

'Not bad,' Phillip says eventually, still considering what he's just heard. 'Remember, it's not reaching the high notes, it's keeping control of what's either side.' Finally, he looks, lightly, briefly at William. 'You mustn't swoop up, and then of course,' he says, as casually as if he's talking about how to butter a piece of bread, 'it's too easy to smudge the quaver ornament on the way down.' He smiles a little. 'But we'll get there. No doubt about that. Right, let's move on . . .'

'It's like Narnia,' says Martin, as they approach the frosted copper beech. A wren sits on the grass to the left of the path cocking its head at them as they pass, fearless of the noisy procession of boys.

'Imagine Matron on a sleigh. Our very own White Witch.'
As usual, it pleases William that Martin's laugh makes the boys
ahead turn round to see what they're missing.

This is William's second term of his second year as chorister.
He is almost as tall as Martin now, though much slighter. The
rolling grind and crunch of the gravel through the soles of his
shoes still satisfies him, and the tall plane trees on either side
of the path still salute him as they did when he first arrived. If
anything, he feels it all the more keenly now, aware that it can't
go on forever. Although he came late as a chorister at ten, it is
forgotten now. The younger boys who started last September
only know William as a soloist, and best friends with the other
main soloist, Martin.

'Your mum'll be cock-a-hoop,' Martin says. The grass looks
like starched sea anemones, and the trees are bony and dark
against the vivid sky. Small clouds of breath bloom from sixteen
mouths.

It's passed now, but even the most fidgety novice choristers
felt it. Sometimes, something happens to this gang of boys, who
fart and burp and pick their noses, when they *know* that what
they produce is bigger and better than they are. Afterwards, stepping in puddles, telling jokes, it fades. But they never forget it.

'You punched that C in the mouth.' Martin leaps over the
silver slash of water on the path.

The robust breeze plays with Martin's dense hair, buffets
William's face and whips round his ankles. But singing Lent
music has put a breath of spring in the air for him.

'Thanks.' He grins. 'I just wish it went on for longer.'

Martin laughs. 'Than twelve minutes?'

'Mum says she could have it on all day and then get into bed
and fall asleep listening to it.'

'She won't sleep between now and Ash Wednesday when she finds out.'

William laughs. 'Once I'd been accepted here she cried every time she looked at me for about a week.'

'She's like a fairy godmother,' Martin says as they reach school.

'Why?' William sits down in the vestibule to change his footwear.

Martin stamps his foot into his shoe. 'She's beautiful, she's strong. She'd do *any*thing to make you happy.'

'So would your mum, wouldn't she?'

'It's different. You're the only one. It's all about *you*. There are so many of us, it's never all about me.'

Martin has been soppy over William's mum since he saw her running down King's Parade with William on her back. Late from an afternoon's exeat, William had said he couldn't eat a Chelsea bun *and* hurry, so Evelyn told him to get on her back and eat the bun, while she hurried for both of them. Martin had seen it from across the road, where he was with his own mother. What he'd liked was not so much her running along with an eleven-year-old on her back, but that she could do both those things *and* laugh.

'She can be annoying too, you know,' William says, walking down the corridor to history. 'I know for a fact she won't want Uncle Robert and Howard to come to hear the "Miserere".' When Martin took a big solo last term, his parents, grandfather, two brothers and twin sisters had all come. Seeing so many of them there just for him had made William sad.

'Surely she'll want them to come for this?'

'She'll say something like, "Life is hard enough without having to sit on a pew with Robert and Howard on display." What

126

does she even mean? I *hate* it, Martin, hate it.' William notices that Martin's pale cheeks have gone a little pinker.

'If your dad was still alive,' Martin asks, 'would Robert and Howard come to hear you?'

'It depends who won the argument. Mum would have wanted Robert to come on his own and Dad would have said that wasn't fair.'

'Are you going to tell her you want them both to come?' Martin leans into the classroom door.

'Yes, in my next letter.' William pulls at his tie as he and Martin enter. He's much too hot and he has the feeling there's something about to explode in his head.

'She's just trying to protect you,' Martin says as they walk to the two empty desks at the back.

William finds the statement so odd and bewildering, he doesn't reply.

The dry dollop of mashed potato thuds onto his plate. Usually he's ravenous by morning break, let alone lunchtime, but he doesn't feel hungry today.

'Thank you.' William smiles at Cook, whose eyes soften when she sees him. He doesn't slip in early any more in the mornings like he did in his first year to watch her make breakfast, her corseted torso bumping occasionally against his, but he always makes sure to be friendly.

'William, want to join me?' Nigel Wynne, a slender, graceful boy, is head chorister now. 'Where's Martin?' Nigel looks round the dining hall.

'Head's office.'

'What for this time?'

'Back-chatting.'

Nigel smiles. 'Do tell.'

'He was messing around in history this morning. Hawthorn told him playing the clown isn't funny. Martin said, "With respect, it *is* funny, sir, that's the point of clowns."'

Since William let the others take the blame for the letters he wrote last year, he has refused to take part in any of Martin's shenanigans; stealing sunglasses in Woolworths, smuggling a college duck into Matron's bedroom, or dropping a bottle of cochineal into the porridge. Martin always seems to find someone else to get into trouble with and never puts William under any pressure. William's aware of an understanding amongst the boarders, that he is somehow under Martin's protection. The stories of the wee-soaked pyjamas and the forged letters are part of school folklore. William sometimes feels a bit cut off from the other boys because of it, as if he can never quite get on with anyone else on his own terms. He is grateful for Nigel inviting him to sit with him.

'Well, if he gets a whack, we'll all be treated to a close-up of his bruised backside tonight.' Nigel laughs.

'And every night this week, to watch it change colour.'

'Sometimes I think he likes it.' Nigel's smile drops to a frown. 'Are you OK? You look a bit odd.'

'I think I've got a temperature,' William says, touching his damp forehead.

'You can't be ill,' Nigel says, 'not until after Ash Wednesday.'

In the song room the following day, William takes off his gown, which is now above his ankles and has long stopped whispering over the ground, soaking up mud and puddle water. He's glad to sit down after the walk from school and hasn't even got the energy to laugh at Martin's impression of the organ scholar's squint. He wishes he had a bit more oomph. When

Phillip arrives and asks them to warm up with some scales, William takes a breath and a loud volley of coughs bursts from his mouth.

For two days he fights it, won't admit he's ill, can't *bear* the thought that he might not be able to sing the 'Miserere', but then Phillip sends him to Matron halfway through practice and he almost passes out on the way.

■ ■ ■

It's flu. Full-blown, vicious, drawn-out flu. William is in sickbay for ten days. The fever, the aching arms and legs, and the raw red of his blocked nose mean he doesn't think of much at all to begin with. He feels hard, dried up inside and most of all, angry. Ash Wednesday comes and goes. Matron tells him that Nigel took the solo as she bustles around his bed, filling his glass with lemon barley water, replacing his bundled handkerchiefs with two ironed ones on his bedside table. William stares at the ceiling and pinches his left thigh between two fingernails until it hurts more than thinking about Nigel singing his solo. He continues to do that for the rest of the day and by evening has to switch to his right leg.

After a few days, Martin is allowed to visit him for fifteen minutes in the afternoon. The sickbay is south-facing and filled with intense spring sunshine. William's head throbs and his limbs *still* feel filled with concrete.

'Bad luck, but it'll be yours next year,' says Martin, landing heavily on the end of William's bed.

'You don't know that,' William replies, 'my voice could break, or one of the younger ones might get it. Charles is good enough.'

'Rubbish. You're the best.'

129

Lying in sickbay, he's been dry-eyed and brittle, but Martin's solid presence on the bed, his friendship, is making him tearful.

'How was Nigel?'

'All right, I suppose.' Martin looks him in the eye. 'Nothing special.'

William doesn't believe him, but appreciates the loyalty.

'At least this way,' Martin says, 'we've got time to work out how to make sure your uncle and Howard can come next year.'

William stares at the blue stitching on the bed blanket. Two days ago, he heard Matron telling the nurse that a master had got the sack.

'I'd heard things about him.' Nurse's low voice carried much better than she must have thought it did. 'He spends the summer holidays in Italy, with a *man*.'

'Then he had to go,' Matron said. 'Even a *hint* of degeneracy around the boys is too much.'

The trouble with being in sickbay is that William has nothing to do but *think*. So when he isn't feeling almost physically sick with disappointment and jealousy, he is thinking about Robert and Howard being degenerates. William does and doesn't want to talk about this now. He leans forward to check that Matron is still in her little office at the end of the room. She's on the phone.

'Martin?'

'Yeah?'

'Uncle Robert and Howard . . . do you think . . . they're . . .' He tries, but just can't say it. 'You know.'

Martin puts his head to one side then nods. 'Probably.'

'So, when you said Mum was protecting me, you meant from them?'

Martin scrunches his face, as if from a stab of pain. 'Some

130

people think they shouldn't be left alone with children, but I'm sure my parents don't think that.' He looks at the floor for a while, then back up at William. 'I bet your uncle would never hurt you.'

He hears Matron saying goodbye, the heavy clunk of the receiver into its cradle. 'You should probably go now,' William says, embarrassed that Martin seems to know more about his family than he does, although also relieved to know that Mr and Mrs Mussey would be kind-hearted towards his uncle. 'I still feel ropey.'

William doesn't mind having a few more days lying in bed, not having to talk to anyone.

25

JANUARY 1961

Martin's eldest brother, Richard, is waiting for them at Pulborough station, leaning against a blue Ford Anglia, cigarette balanced on his bottom lip. In his final year at Oxford, Richard is a thinner, taller version of Martin.

'Hello, Squirt.' He slaps Martin on the back, and then holds his hand out. 'Hello, William, I'm Richard. Climb in the back, I'll put your case in the boot.'

'Where's Mum?' Martin says, sitting next to his brother.

'Cooking supper with Flo. All hands on deck.'

William has been invited to spend some of the Christmas holiday with Martin's family every year of their friendship, but William has never been able to imagine asking Evelyn, so he never has. But this is William's last year as a chorister, his last year with Martin as his companion, whose stories for the past three years of his boisterous, bohemian family have entranced and entertained William. Evelyn agreed, when he kept his promise to himself and asked her in the first five minutes of their exeat visit in December. She was disappointed; her smile was too quick and sharp, and she'd flicked away her cake crumbs with a force that was meant for something else. Nevertheless, he decided to take her at her word.

The highlight of the first bleak day back in Cambridge after Christmas has always been sitting at supper listening to Martin tell him about the Mussey Boxing Day Play. Who fell out with who, which soft furnishings were purloined for costume and sets, whether they remained in place for the duration, which boys played girls and which girls played boys – gender reversal was evidently mandatory. It sounded such indulgent fun, putting aside a whole day to write, cast, rehearse, make the set and costumes, and then of course perform it. The older the Mussey children get, the more elaborate they have become and the later the performance time. Last year, they didn't take to the stage until 11.30 because Richard insisted mid-afternoon that he rewrote the script in rhyming verse.

Excited and nervous, with his suitcase packed for the new term, which will begin in three days' time, William at thirteen had never travelled on the train alone before, so it was agreed that Martin would meet him at Paddington and they would travel from there to Storrington together.

'What are we eating?' Martin asks his brother.

'Chicken.'

'One of ours?'

'Two, actually. You're honoured, William,' says Richard, turning his head, 'a two-chicken supper!' He puts the car in gear and swings out of the station. 'Talking of food, has Martin introduced you to the Fitzbillies Chelsea bun?'

'Of course I have! We're allowed out on a Saturday afternoon now,' Martin answers.

'Martin buys two,' William says, keen to join in, 'and finishes them before I've even got mine out of the box.' He's rewarded by Richard's hearty laugh.

'How many solos last term, Squirt?'

It's a routine question, William can tell. Martin has his head to one side, thinking. 'At least seven but to be honest, I've lost count.'

'Git,' mutters Richard.

Martin twists round, grinning to William. 'I've already beaten his solo score.'

'What about you, William?' Richard asks, throwing his cigarette butt out of the window and leaning his elbow on the ledge. 'I hear you're pretty good.'

The answer is thirteen – five more than Martin. 'Not sure,' William says, 'around ten?'

'I'd say more,' Martin says, 'he's bloody good. He's bound to get the "Miserere" this term.'

It's Flo who first greets them when they walk through the broad, glass-panelled door into the vast, peopled kitchen. With thick glasses that magnify her eyes slightly, she holds Martin's face in her hands and kisses both his cheeks noisily. She looks old, William guesses in her seventies, with grey curly hair close to her head.

'You must be William.' She grips his hand.

'Welcome, William,' a female voice calls from across the room. It takes him a second to locate Mrs Mussey, who's walking to the table with a serving dish, smiling at him. Just short of six foot, Mrs Mussey is the tallest mother William has ever met.

'Hello, William!' He's hit by the unison volley of voices.

'Hello.' For a moment, William feels completely overwhelmed and doesn't dare meet anyone's eye.

Everyone's on the move, carrying things to the table, pulling things out of cupboards, filling a water jug; adults and teenagers in a melee of movement and noise in a kitchen bigger than the floor plan of his entire flat. Mr Mussey's hand on his back exerts enough pressure to push him towards the table, a huge, cross-hatched thing that sits in the curve of the generous bay window. Martin has already slid onto the ledge of the bay which is padded with long cushions, indicating for William to join him.

Like iron filings, the bodies in the room converge and sit, and all the hustle and bustle becomes an energy focused on the serving bowls. Sitting opposite him on high-backed pine chairs are Imogen and Isobel, Martin's terrifyingly pretty twin sisters, and Richard. Mr and Mrs Mussey sit at either end and it must be the third brother, Edward, sitting on the other side of Martin.

'Roast Henrietta and Mabel tonight. God rest their souls,' Mr Mussey booms, red hair flopping over his brow as he sets to Henrietta or Mabel with a carving knife, with all the latent energy and enthusiasm William has always enjoyed in Martin.

'Flo, are you sure you don't want any meat?' Mrs Mussey says over her shoulder.

William wonders where Flo is going to sit, but she has a coat on and is standing with her back to them, laying a piece of foil over a plate.

'I'm fine with this, thank you.' Flo smiles from the back door, the plate balanced in one hand. 'Goodnight.'

'Goodnight, Flo,' the family shout back, some turning, some carrying on with what they're doing.

'She goes off meat when we eat something she's known since it hatched,' Richard tells William, as Flo closes the door with a waft of cold air. 'The softest cook in Sussex.'

William assumed Flo was one of the many aunts or godmothers or family friends Martin has talked about. He didn't know *families* had cooks. Martin has never mentioned a cook!

Richard and Martin reach across the table and prod their forks into the meat as soon as it flops away from the carcass onto the serving plate, the crispy crinkled skin separating from the flesh as it falls. At home, Evelyn brings his plate to the table, already served. Does he reach out and help himself? Does he wait? Martin saves him by dropping the second two slices he takes onto William's plate, and proceeds to take two servings of everything, one for William, then one for himself; roast potatoes, mashed potatoes, cauliflower cheese, peas, carrots and gravy – the sort of meal William would have expected at Christmas or a special Sunday lunch.

'What a sweet boy you are,' says Mr Mussey to Martin, rubbing his head. 'Do you see that, darling? He's actually thinking of someone else.'

'Just as well.' Mrs Mussey piles carrots onto her plate. 'If you don't dig in quick here, William dear, this lot will strip the table bare before you've located your cutlery.'

She has silver-streaked blonde hair that hangs down beyond her shoulders, scruffy and slightly matted, as if it could be home to an exotic bird. She sticks out her bottom lip to blow strands of it away from her face. Her flesh looks firm under her floating floral dress, no mound at her middle. When she leaps up from her seat and strides across the kitchen to get the pepper, he notices her calves flexing and thinks he wouldn't be surprised were she to hurdle the table.

A few mouthfuls in, William dares to look at Isobel and Imogen. They have inherited their mother's blonde hair, except theirs is sleek and straight. Their limbs are long and golden and William struggles not to stare; partly because they are stunning and he doesn't get to look at girls very often, but also because, apart from his father and uncle, they are the first set of identical twins he's been able to have a good look at. He won't be able to tell them apart away from the table, where Imogen is opposite Martin and Isobel is opposite him, but as Richard and Martin insult each other, Isobel often meets his eye and smiles easily at him, whereas Imogen seems to avoid it – which is what he'd do if he was being stared at by a stranger. Isobel seems keener to follow the conversation and chip in, whereas Imogen goes for long periods concentrating on her food, occasionally pushing her silky curtain of hair over her shoulder. William also notices how the sisters glance at each other at the same time, raise their eyebrows in exactly the same way, and his favourite bit is when Imogen reaches over and pulls Isobel's hair out of the way before it trails in the gravy. Isobel carries on as if she'd done it herself. He finds that very satisfying.

He glances at Mr Mussey, who's watching him with a light smile on his face. William feels himself blush and concentrates on Edward, who is wishing that chickens had four legs. He's conscious he should join in the conversation; he hasn't said a word yet. They'll think he's an idiot or rude. He promises himself at the next silence, he'll ask a question. Twice he has taken a breath, but then someone else bursts in and it's rare that only one person is talking.

Eventually, there's a significant pause and he says, much too loud and fast, 'How was the Boxing Day Play?'

After all the over-talking, interrupting, laughing, there's a united snapping of attention. Everyone's looking at him and it's completely silent. He's said something wrong.

'Didn't Martin tell you?' Imogen eventually says.

He glances at Martin who is grinning with food-filled cheeks.

'I wanted to surprise him,' Martin says.

'We postponed it,' says Richard, reaching for more chicken. 'Till tomorrow, so you could be in it.'

Wrapped up in coats and scarves, William and Martin are sitting in adjacent apple trees with their legs dangling over the unkempt grass. The darkness is softened by light from the kitchen. Surrounded by an old brick wall with eight apple trees, two cherry trees and a pear tree, the garden is like something out of a picture book.

'I'm worried I won't be any good – in the play.' William rubs his finger along the fissured tree bark. He adjusts his position to ease the pressure of his waistband, which has been digging into his middle since the second helping of apple pie.

'That doesn't matter,' Martin says, emitting a cloud of breath. 'Aren't you pleased?'

'Yes,' William says, 'and petrified.'

Martin laughs. 'There won't be any cousins, so it won't be quite such a big deal.'

'Oh!'

'They came on Boxing Day. They're back in London now.'

William doesn't mention his surprise at Flo, or how pretty his sisters are; he doesn't want to discuss any of it, he just wants to enjoy it. And anyway, he is so touched that this big, sophisticated family would rearrange things just for him, he would probably cry if he opened his mouth.

Evelyn wouldn't like the sprawling clothes on the landing, or the old newspapers scattered across the sitting room, or the splats of toothpaste on the bathroom mirror, but William loves the idea that style and elegance don't depend on cleanliness.

'Your house is splendid,' he says, taking off his trousers, his legs goose-bumping instantly. William wonders that no one has drawn the curtains, but without neighbours to overlook them, he can see why they wouldn't bother. The room contains four single beds, but still, there are broad swathes of space in between them.

'Thanks.' Martin strips off his vest and drops it on the floor.

'Our flat is *tiny* compared to this,' William says, glancing at his skinny body in the wardrobe mirror across the room.

'I bet it's cosy. It's freezing here unless we have a heatwave.' Martin's voice is distorted from within his pyjama top. 'And I bet your mum keeps everything tidy.'

Martin won't hear a word against Evelyn; *So elegant, lipstick that makes her mouth look like slices of fruit, butter biscuit baker.* But tonight William finds himself drawn to the Amazonian mother figure of Mrs Mussey, with her broad-brush approach to housework and mothering.

'It's strange, isn't it?' says William, settled into the trough of the bowed mattress, under sheets that though musty are smooth and heavy. 'Before Cambridge we had completely different lives. Then for four years we'll have done almost exactly the same thing every day, and then for the rest of our lives we'll do completely different things again.'

'Do you think you'll do music or funerals?'

William told Martin long ago that his father and Robert clearly wanted him to go into the family business, while Evelyn wanted him to have a life in music. After his dad had died, Evelyn had been very keen for William to join a reputable choir and couldn't have been happier when the choirmaster thought it was worth his while trying for Cambridge, even though he was nearly ten.

'If I'm good enough, music, I think.'

'You're good enough,' Martin says.

'What about you?'

'I don't like to think about it.' Martin climbs into bed and pulls the miniature chain hanging from his bedside lamp. There's a soft ping as the brightness folds away. 'I can't imagine life without you.'

In the darkness, smiling at the warmth of Martin's friendship,

William rolls onto his side and decides not to waste his time here worrying about how cold it may feel once it's gone.

'By the way,' Martin says a few minutes later, once William's mind has started a lazy drift from thought to thought, 'Mum says if you keep staring at the twins like that every mealtime, I'm to pour cold water over you.'

'I wasn't staring at them like *that*!' William is wide awake. 'It's because they're twins. Promise me you'll tell her.'

'*You* tell her,' Martin says, rolling over to face the little sprigs of cherries, blueberries and apples that sit in neat diagonal rows across the wallpaper, and have bloomed back into visibility now William's eyes are used to the dark.

If he begs, Martin will only tease him more, so he waits. Just as he starts to think he's waited too long and Martin's asleep, a soft voice says, 'I'll tell her before breakfast. Don't worry.'

26

When Isobel and Imogen saunter into breakfast in plaid skirts and Aran sweaters, hair sleep-rumpled and gorgeous, William realises that overnight his interest in them as twins has been superseded by his appreciation of how very, very beautiful they are.

The girls sit down opposite him, lazy and languid, with their smooth, gently freckled skin that looks sprinkled with brown sugar, their green eyes and dark eyelashes, their lips, like Martin's, full and cushioned. Just as he starts to imagine what it might be like to kiss them, Mrs Mussey places a bowl of something hot in the middle of the table and he forces his eyes down to the food before him.

'Would you like some, William?' Mrs Mussey asks, holding her hair back in a ponytail in one hand, her other poised with a spoon over the bowl. To William's surprise it contains rice – not something he's ever had for breakfast.

'Yes, please. What is it?'

'Kedgeree,' says Edward, plunging his own fork into the bowl, receiving a rap on the knuckle from Mrs Mussey's spoon. 'Have you not had it before? I can't imagine life without kedgeree.'

'Doesn't say much for your imagination, Edward,' says Imogen, buttering her toast. Martin laughs, and Isobel, William notices, is smiling.

'It's haddock, rice and boiled eggs, William,' Mrs Mussey says, putting a helping onto his plate.

'Thanks – my mum doesn't like fish,' he says, hoping to

imply they would otherwise have eaten it regularly, along with cornflakes and sliced white toast with Robertson's marmalade.

'Richard,' says Mrs Mussey as she gets up from the table, skimming her hand over his hair, 'can you try and get on stage by eight at the latest tonight? We've got about ten people coming, including Mrs Wickers who slept through it all last year. And your grandfather will be driving home afterwards, so it's not fair to keep him too late.'

William thought how wonderful it would be if his mother, Uncle Robert and Howard could be in the audience to see how he was part of this cultured family.

Richard is intent on scraping the serving bowl of the last of the kedgeree. Mrs Mussey steps back towards the table.

'Did you hear me, Richard? Answer when I speak to you.'

'Yep, that's fine,' Richard answers. William hopes they are on stage by eight, because if not, he knows he'll feel anxious.

After breakfast, the young people migrate to the sitting room around the polished oval table, swept clean of the *National Geographic*, *Punch* and *New Statesman*. Richard summarises for William's benefit that they write the play before elevenses, for which Flo is, as they speak, baking biscuits. After elevenses and before lunch they allocate roles and do a run-through. After lunch they divide into two teams – one for costume and one for set. After tea break it's dress rehearsal. William calculates they will have said their lines only twice before the performance.

'Do we keep our scripts in case we forget our lines, or will there be a prompt?'

Everyone laughs.

'No. No prompts. No script, really,' Martin says, 'you remember or you make it up. It's all part of the fun!'

'And at least one of the boys usually shows off their arse or todger at some point,' Isobel says.

He looks at Martin – he's never mentioned this, William is sure of it. 'OK.' He tries to look relaxed.

'Let's crack on, shall we?' Richard lights a cigarette then balances an A4 pad on his knee. He looks round at everyone with a smile. 'Scenario?' he says, pencil poised.

'Operating theatre,' shouts Edward.

Richard nods and writes it down. 'Setting?'

'Rome, 1945,' says Imogen.

'Why not?' says Richard, writing it down. 'We can have fun with the accent.'

'1945?' says Edward.

'The year we were born,' offers Isobel.

'Theme?' Richard doesn't look up from his pad.

'Unrequited love!' shouts Martin, eyes wide, colour high in his freckled cheeks.

'We had that last year,' says Imogen, on the verge of boredom again.

'Not last year,' says Edward, 'it was definitely revenge last year – Imogen got cross at Richard even though he was only acting.'

'You were alarmingly hateful, Richard,' Imogen says.

'Unrequited love it is then.' Richard glances at his watch. 'Title?'

'*Open Heart Surgery*,' shouts Martin in another explosion of enthusiasm.

'Or *Love under the Knife*?' suggests Edward.

'What about *Wounded Heart*?' dares William.

'Marvellous, William,' says Richard, '*Wounded Heart* it is.'

As everyone claps, William gets the feeling that they've all been waiting for him to say something, simply so they can all agree with it.

By 11 a.m., when Flo enters the sitting room preceded by the smell of baking, the play is written and William has radically revised his understanding of what it means to write a play. He's a female nurse in love with the handsome doctor (Richard) who in turn is in love with another nurse (Imogen), who is in love with the patient being operated upon (Edward). Martin is a patient in love with William's character. The only consolation of being cast as a woman is that William won't be called upon to show his arse or his todger.

The day passes in a frenzy of improvisation, dressing up, good-humoured arguments, and the filching of furniture and household items. The operating table is an old door from the barn balanced on dining room chairs. A selection of flannels from a selection of bathrooms are surgical masks. Operating instruments are gathered from the cutlery drawer, and the patient's heart is a piece of liver out of the fridge, donated by a reluctant but forbearing Flo.

In spite of being able to remain fully clothed, on balance William still regrets being the only one to switch gender. As a male character, he most certainly would have had some opportunity to be amorous towards one of the twins, and perhaps even better, have one of them be amorous towards him. Instead he is left having to feed Edward spaghetti and have his bottom pinched by Martin. At the eleventh hour, during the dress rehearsal, Richard decides that for the close of the play, everyone delivers a kiss on the lips to the person they love. William would have preferred to have left it at the bottom-pinching, but now he has to take Richard's face in both hands and smack a hearty kiss on the lips. And he has to endure the same treatment from Martin.

At least the idea makes Isobel laugh, and at least they only have to do it once. In rehearsal they are allowed to air-kiss, with the proviso that when it comes to it, there'll be no holding back.

By late afternoon, William's overcome with a longing to go to his room for a while and be on his own. They're all wonderful, but so noisy and lively and demanding. His face hurts from all the expressions he's had to make in the many conversations he's had, and he still hasn't got used to just how many of them there are. How Martin must have missed them when he first came to Cambridge. How quiet and lonely the dorms must have seemed compared to this mayhem.

Over supper, they aren't allowed to talk about the play so as not to spoil it for the audience, who are outnumbered by the cast. But something must have leaked, because Flo serves lasagne, which William discovers is an Italian dish. He isn't sure about the slippery sheets of pasta and he's starting to get very nervous.

27

Imogen is an astonishing few inches from his face, concentrating, tongue poking out of the side of her mouth.

'Blue suits you, William.' She waves something in front of his face but it's a blur. 'Now, mascara. Whatever you do, don't blink. Trust me and keep your eyes *open*.'

'OK,' he says, palms tingling to rest on her hips that are there, right in front of him. But as she puts the brush on his lashes, both eyes slam shut.

'You nincompoop.' Imogen laughs. 'Look!' She holds a mirror to his face.

The black smear runs from under his eye all the way to his nose, but it's the blue arcs of his eyelids that alarm him.

'What are you doing to me?'

'Making you look like a woman, what do you think I'm doing?' She's enjoying his consternation and he decides to milk it.

'My mum'd have a fit,' he says, but instantly regrets it. He doesn't want Imogen to think his family prudish, so adds, 'Though Uncle Robert and Howard would *love* it,' and then regrets that too.

'Who's Howard?'

William feels the rise of a flush to his face. 'Part of the family business.'

'And a good friend of your uncle's?' She smiles in a way that makes him even more uncomfortable.

'Yes,' he says.

Imogen's wiping under his eyes with cotton wool drenched in something chemical and cold. 'You know that sort of thing doesn't bother us, don't you?'

'Of course,' he says, as casually as he can.

'Did Martin tell you Dad's firm worked on the Lady Chatterley trial last year?' William remembers how one of the boys rented his dog-eared copy out for a daily rate. Martin boasted that if it wasn't for his father, the book would still be banned and he didn't need to pay to read it, thank you very much, they had a copy at home. 'His motto,' Imogen continues, mercifully ignoring William's high colour, 'is anything goes, as long as it goes with kindness.'

'For a kind woman, Mum's not always kind to them,' he says, disarmed by the sentiment.

'Look up,' she says, coming at him again with the mascara wand, 'and don't blink.' She's leaning into his face again. 'Would she rather Howard wasn't part of the family business?'

'Perhaps,' he says, finding it easier to talk to the ceiling than her creamy face. 'She'd also prefer that Robert didn't remind her so much of my dad.' He glances back at her, so close he can see the downy hairs above her top lip. 'They were identical twins too.'

'Yeah, Martin told me.'

'And,' he continues, pleased to know Martin talks about him to his family, 'it could be she thinks the two of them will lure me into the family business.'

'Would you want that?' She is still focusing on his eyes with fierce concentration.

'I want to do something with my voice. So does she.'

'I don't know why I'm bothering with this mascara, your eyelashes are incredibly thick.' Imogen stands back for a moment and takes a stubby-looking pencil out of her make-up bag. 'Martin adores your mum. He says she's stylish and beautiful and *worships* you.' She rummages in the bag and finds a sharpener for the eye pencil. 'It must have been horrid for her, after your dad died.'

'Yep,' he says, stunned at what an intimate conversation he finds himself in, 'really horrid.'

Imogen starts colouring in his eyebrows. 'But you know, it's OK to be critical of someone you love.' She rubs with her thumb, blending the colour. 'It doesn't mean you love them less, or that *everything* about them's wrong. Open your mouth.' William feels the velvety lipstick glide on. 'You soon learn that with a rabble of siblings like mine. See as much of Robert as you want, I say, but show your mum you love her too and aren't about to turn into a debauched undertaker.' She's tickling his cheeks now with a large, whispery brush. 'Unless that's what you want.' She laughs.

'It's not,' he says as quickly as he can, still sounding nonchalant.

She laughs again, collecting brushes and zipping them up in the bulging make-up bag, then holds his chin in one hand and surveys him. 'You make a gorgeous girl, though it's more to do with those cheekbones and big blue eyes than anything I've done.'

William curses his fair skin as he feels the blood rushing to the surface again, but their talk leaves him feeling grown-up, as if he's just gone through a rite of passage; discussing not only the difficult bits of his family, but his own sexuality – with Imogen Mussey!

■ ■ ■

An hour later, William is playing Sophia, with whom Martin's character, Giovanni, is in love. William hasn't mastered the finer plot points of the play, beyond who he's supposed to love and who loves him. The rest of it involves him being greeted with, 'Ciao bella!' by just about everyone, and having to repeat it sounding as female as possible, which isn't too hard, as he has a fine contralto voice to call upon. As the curtain, taken from the boys' bedroom, is yanked up by Edward, William judges it prudent to throw all he's got into his 'Ciao bellas', so from the outset and unrehearsed, he lowers one hip, resting his hand lightly on it, bends his other knee a little and pats his bubbly blonde wig.

Mrs Mussey is tickled right away and, as her throaty chuckle gets louder, she sets off not only the rest of the small audience, but the cast too. By the second act, when the liver/heart is removed from Edward's character, as soon as anyone delivers the line, 'Ciao bella!' in William's direction, the audience starts laughing in anticipation and the cast is reduced to giggles.

Intoxicated, William stretches out his performance, waiting hand on hip, bent knee, for the mirth to build; then, with a powerful falsetto and an overblown accent, he replies, 'Ciao *bella*.'

By the final scene, audience and cast are swimming in a sea of endorphins. William has been camping it up for an hour, hidden behind the make-up, wig and ridiculous voice. When it comes to the final falling-domino scene of kisses, he's able to participate wholeheartedly in the giving and receiving of a hearty smacker in the evidently insatiable hunger for yet more laughter. The whole thing is so exciting and fun and warm, and smells of make-up and cotton sheets, with lights making the stage so bright and sparkly, that he feels he has crossed over into an altogether more exciting and vibrant life than he had

149

imagined possible for himself. He is touched beyond measure when the cast has taken its bows and everyone drops hands to applaud him, the unexpected star of the show.

He inhales the smell of hot milk and chocolate as they form a line near the range, where Flo ladles out cocoa from the large pan. When Imogen puts an arm round his shoulder, he worries that the sudden erection must be visible through his frock.

'William!' she says. 'You certainly connected with your inner diva.'

'He did, didn't he?' laughs a delighted Martin.

'It's that beautiful voice he's got in there.' Flo taps his chest.

'Martin tells me you'll be doing the "Miserere" this year,' Mr Mussey says. 'Mind if we come to hear you?'

'I might not,' he says, face burning, 'but if I do, of course. That would be great.'

'You wouldn't sing for us now, would you, boys?' says Mrs Mussey, seated at the kitchen table with her father. 'Before Grandad goes home?'

Martin looks expectantly at William, who nods back.

'What shall we do?' says Martin.

'"Myfanwy"?' William says.

Martin pulls a face. 'Bit of a downer? And they heard it three years ago.'

'But it's about unrequited love,' says William.

'Oh, let's have that, Martin!' Mrs Mussey looks from one to the other. 'We could do with a bit of calming down.'

'We can do it in Welsh or English,' William offers, becoming gradually conscious of the make-up and dress he's wearing.

'Welsh!' a few voices shout. This lot seem predisposed to favour the more challenging option. William was astonished to discover earlier that the Musseys think it's cheating to look at the picture on the box when you do a jigsaw.

'But you have to tell us what it means first,' says Imogen, looking solely at William.

'Let's go back into the sitting room.' Mrs Mussey gives an arm to help her father up. 'We can all sit down and you can give us a translation before you sing.'

William and Martin stand where they performed the play, while every chair is landed on by the adults and every space on the floor occupied by the young Musseys.

Martin nods at William. 'You tell them about the song.'

William suddenly feels raw, standing there in drag, about to tell them something so beautiful and tender. As if he's about to peel off a layer of skin.

'It's about a boy who loves a girl called Myfanwy. They've promised to be together, but he knows she doesn't love him any more, so although he's heartbroken, he releases her from the promises she made to him.' William is much more aware now than he was during the play of the faces watching him. 'Because more than anything, he wants her to be happy. In the last verse, he asks her to hold his hand one last time, but only to say good-bye.'

'Oh, dear God! I'm welling up already,' says Mrs Mussey, pulling a hanky out from her sleeve and dropping it on her lap in cheerful readiness.

'Sounds marvellous, boys, off you go,' says Martin's dad, who sounds weary and might just want to go to bed.

With their vocal cords already warm and elastic, they start, with what Martin would call a juicy, plum pie sound. In spite of all the excitement and adrenaline of the evening, William relaxes his eyes so he can focus on the sound, not anyone's face.

151

They're done and there it is – that heavy beat of silence – the mute thump of emotion before the startled burst of applause. Martin's grandfather stands and claps with his hands above his head. Imogen and Isobel both whistle with their fingers in their mouths, clapping each other's spare hands. Mrs Wickers is crying. He and Martin bow and bow again, so drawn out is the clapping. William allows himself to look at everyone's faces, meet their eyes, but it's not until he notices that Mr and Mrs Mussey are holding hands that he realises he is holding Martin's, with no idea how they came to be like this. He gently pulls it free.

William finally drops onto the soft mattress shortly after midnight for his last night before returning to school. Martin only just walloped down on his seconds ago, but his breathing already seems to be deepening.

'Martin?'

'Mmm?'

'I've had a great time.'

'Mmm.'

'Thanks for inviting me.'

'You're welcome – *Bella*.'

William is asleep within seconds.

He can't breathe. The huge, sinewy mermaid is writhing on top of him. He struggles to free himself from her strong, wet tail which is coiling round his waist. Her mouth is all over his, salty, sea-swilled. He gasps and recoils and doesn't understand why he should have an erection when he is so revolted by the fish woman on top of him.

Wait. He *really* can't breathe. The mermaid has vanished. He

152

is awake, but his mouth is still covered; a body weighs down on his. In a panic, he shoves it away, is finally able to breathe in, ready to shout out, but a big fleshy hand stifles it.

'Shhh, it's only me.' Martin's whisper is quieter than breath. His face eclipses the room.

'What are you doing?' William's heart is flinging itself against the cage of his ribs.

'I thought you wanted it.' William feels Martin's erection against his stomach. He pushes him away again, twisting his face from Martin's.

'Well, I *don't*.' His throat strains with the force of such whispering. 'Get off!'

Martin looks at William, a crease at the top of his nose, then pulls away suddenly, drops back against the pillow. William glances at him. His eyes are silvery from the moonlight glancing in through the naked window.

'Bloody hell, Martin,' William whispers. 'I didn't know.'

'I didn't either. I just wanted to kiss you.'

'I'm sorry.' William talks to the ceiling. 'I don't.'

Martin returns to his own bed, his pyjamas bright in the moonlight.

28

Evelyn's burgundy tweed dress is tight at her small waist. A cardigan the same colour is draped round her shoulders. Ash Wednesday is two weeks away, and as Martin had predicted, the 'Miserere' is William's. In his pocket, folded up with his exeat, is a letter from Uncle Robert. He doesn't know when he's going to get it out, but he knows at some point he'll have to.

Last night, having refolded the crumpled letter and put it in his trouser pocket ready for the next day, William calculated that he and his mother must have had twelve lunches at the Copper Kettle over the last three and a half years. There are other cafes, but they have always sat and gazed out on King's Parade, at the lace-like stonework, the glassless windows and slender pillars tipped with crosses. Evelyn, always luminous at seeing him, has brought funny stories and baked treats in a box. She's always dug for details of his chorister life; lessons, Martin's misdemeanours, what nice things Phillip has said during choir practice. There have been times, of course, when hiccoughs of irritation interrupted their chatter, but on the whole, they've enjoyed their lunches and he's looked forward to seeing her.

'So, how's that scallywag Martin?' Evelyn pulls the cardigan round her shoulders before resting her forearms on the table and leaning towards him. 'Any tales to tell?'

The pebble of pain plummets his body again. It's been a month since he stayed at the Musseys'. He and Martin still sit together in choir and still sleep in adjacent beds. Outwardly everything is the same. But really, everything is different. Martin can't look him in the face. Bold, badly behaved, unabashed Martin can't meet his eye. William has tried to talk about it, wants to say it's OK, he's sorry he's not, but it's OK. Martin, though, has become skilled at avoidance and it's rare they talk about much at all.

'Not really.' William shrugs. 'He's calmed down a bit this term.'

'I bet that's a relief to his parents. So' – Evelyn nudges his knee under the table – 'how are you feeling about your big day?'

Over his mother's shoulder, William sees the approaching waitress. 'Fine, but can we talk about Uncle Rob—'

She closes her eyes and holds both palms towards him. 'Before we get into that, I've got some *big* news.' Her eyes open wide, and her sudden smile and taut, petite body tell him that whatever it is, it's going to affect him too. William is suddenly nervous.

The waitress stands at the table, notebook poised. 'Ham, egg and chips twice, please,' Evelyn tells her, 'and two glasses of water.'

She watches her walk away then breathes in sharply. 'I've been thinking. You'll be leaving here in four months. We need to find you a good school and make sure you keep your music going.'

A wriggle of excitement moves in him. He's been trying not to think about what's next. Most of his friends, including Martin, will head off to other boarding schools, with reputable music departments and, more often than not, older siblings already there. He's assumed he'll be going to the local school back in Sutton where his old primary friends will have been for the last three years. It worries him that going back, he'll become ordinary again.

'Thanks.' He smiles at the waitress who delivers their water.

'I've think I've found somewhere we could actually afford a whole house. With a garden! But most importantly, the local school has an outstanding reputation for music *and* it's a part of the world where young men, and older ones actually, are expected to sing. There are *three* different choirs within a ten-mile radius!'

'What do you mean, part of the world? Where is it?'

She clasps her hands together. 'Swansea!' Her eyebrows lift. 'South Wales.'

William stares back. It's only now he notices her hands are trembling.

'It's by the sea! We could even get a house with sea views! A new start, just the two of us.'

He can't help but catch a breath of her excitement. Living by the sea. Singing. A house with a garden. He smiles again. 'When would we go?'

'This summer, ready for you to start school in September, and I'll look for a job!'

'Wow.' He sits back in his chair.

'And you'll never guess what?'

'What?'

'When I leave you today, I'm driving to Wales for two weeks to check it out. Then, I'll come straight from there to hear you sing the "Miserere"!' She leans back for the first time. 'I've got a good feeling about this, William. A really good feeling.'

'Where will you stay?'

'In a B&B – I'm thinking of it as a little holiday. Then if I like it, you and I will go to look at houses and visit the school as soon as term ends.'

The prospect is certainly a lot more exciting than spending

the summer in Sutton Coldfield. 'Have you told Uncle Robert?'

She shakes her head. 'Not yet, no need.'

Their food arrives; he stares at his plate for a moment. 'They'll miss us.'

'They'll miss *you*, William, let's be honest, but I'm sure they'll manage.'

He reaches into his pocket, hoping her good mood will make this easier. 'I wanted to talk to you about Ash Wednesday. You told me in your last letter Robert couldn't come because of his back.'

'Yep.' A slash of poppy red has bloomed on each of her cheeks. She concentrates on her plate.

Embarrassed and sad for her, he says, 'You told him not to come.'

She swallows and her mouth shrinks. 'What are you talking about?'

'I wrote to him, about how excited I was.' William puts the letter on the table. 'And he sent me this.'

Evelyn stares at the small brown envelope with four lines of Robert's neat, italic script and wipes her mouth with the napkin, leaving a smudge of lipstick on it.

'*When* did you write to him?'

'I write to him every week.'

Evelyn smooths the napkin across her lap. 'You've never mentioned that.'

'I knew you wouldn't like it.'

'Nonsense!' She tries a little laugh.

'It's not,' William says, trying to keep his voice gentle, 'you know it's not.'

They both eat for a few moments, then William picks up the envelope, pulling the blue paper from it. '"Of course,"' he reads

157

slowly, '"I wouldn't miss hearing you sing the 'Miserere' for the world, but your mother thinks the pressure of having her, me *and* Howard would be too much for you. I thought of coming on my own, but I'm afraid I'd be too sad to leave Howard out, so I'm sorry, William, we won't be there for this one. I hope you understand, I must respect your mother's wishes."' William drops the letter on the table.

'Robert's been economical with the truth,' she says softly.

'How?'

She lays her cutlery down, though her plate is half full, and puts her hands in her lap. 'Turning up at the flat late at night, crying and carrying on about Howard having a right to hear you sing, isn't *respecting my wishes.*'

'He did that?' The chips in his mouth are too big and dry.

'I was worried the neighbours might call the police!' Her face creases in irritation. 'Oh, for goodness' sake, William, why are *you* getting teary?'

'You made him cry!' William wipes his eyes with the back of his hand. 'How could you? He must have been *so* upset.'

'So was I!' Evelyn frowns. 'And now to find out the two of you have been going behind my back writing letters.'

'It wasn't like that. We just knew you wouldn't like it.'

Evelyn leans forward, her body nudging her abandoned plate. 'What else don't I know about?'

He just looks at her.

'What else?' she repeats firmly.

'In my first term, I was homesick and didn't want you to worry. Robert sent me Dad's old blanket.' Evelyn's mouth is a straight line, her eyes hard and bright. 'He comes to evensong once a term. He drives all the way, then drives back straight afterwards. And when he gets home, he writes to me about the music.' William's eating as he speaks. Evelyn's cutlery still lies either side of her plate. 'But he's never said anything unkind about you. Ever.'

Evelyn looks down momentarily. 'I've been honest about how hard it is to even look at Robert sometimes, but this isn't about that. I'm worried about you getting dragged into the family business.' She frowns again. 'You've got talents. It would be a waste.' She pauses and shakes her head. 'A *complete* waste.'

'What about Dad,' he says quietly, 'do you think *he* wasted his life? Were you ashamed of *him*?'

'Never!' She looks almost afraid. 'But William, you're *special*. You've got a gift. Please don't throw it away.'

'Relax,' he says, dipping a chip into the scarlet pool of ketchup, 'I want to stay in music. Uncle Robert won't change that. But if we move to Wales, I'll always want to stay in touch with them and you can't stop me.'

She sighs. 'Of course.' She finally lifts her cutlery.

'But Mum?'

'Yes?'

'Be honest, that's not the only reason you don't want Howard to come and sit in the pew with you and Robert, is it?'

'I'd rather it just be me, but I know I wouldn't get away with that. I just don't want to have to share it with them and that's the truth.'

'Is it? Really?' He's surprised he feels more sad than angry. The memory of her failing the monkey mask test that Christmas, and how gentle his dad was with her afterwards, when she'd spat out the word 'homosexual' as if it was poison. 'Are you sure it's not because you're ashamed of them?'

'Does Howard come too?' Evelyn's suddenly crisp and alert. 'On these evensong visits?'

159

'Yes.'

Evelyn scrunches up her face.

William leans forward and takes her hands. 'Mum, please, I *want* them both to hear me sing. I promise, they won't turn me into an undertaker, or a homosexual!'

'William!'

'Mum! I live in a boarding school, do you think I don't know about this stuff?'

'OK! I admit it. If they both come, first of all, I won't get a look in, you know what it's like. And second, yes, I'll be embarrassed. So shoot me!' She takes a deep breath and sits back. '*Please*, William, let me have this one day, without all the *stuff* I have to deal with when I'm with them. I just want to enjoy it. And not think about anything but being the proudest mum on the planet.'

There's no point arguing, nowhere for them to go with this. 'OK, Mum, but it's not what I want. At all.'

She's radiant in her relief. 'Let's order pudding, and then I'll hit the road to Swansea! New life, here we come!'

He orders jam roly-poly and makes small talk, but he can't stop images of a distraught Uncle Robert pleading with his mother late at night.

29

The days are getting longer, but at 7 p.m. that evening, it's already pitch black. William and Martin are sitting on the vestibule bench, back from evensong, leaning down, changing shoes, almost cheek to cheek.

'Good time with your mum?' Martin says quietly, busy with his shoe laces.

'Yes and no,' William replies, also focusing on his feet. This is the first conversation Martin has initiated all term. 'She told Robert he couldn't bring Howard on Ash Wednesday because it'd be too stressful for me having them all there, but she told me it was because his back couldn't take the journey and the pews.' They remain on the bench as the others start to head upstairs. 'So I called her out on it.'

'And?' Martin sits up and looks straight ahead, but William feels his concentration.

'She apologised, but still doesn't want them both there. She always feels left out. Plus she's embarrassed.' He realises what he's just said and feels a rush of blood to his face. 'Sorry!' Martin turns to look at him.

William is relieved just to be looked at again by his friend. 'Martin, I'm so sorry . . . at your house . . .'

'Shhhh!' Martin puts his hands over his ears and shuts his eyes. 'I don't want to talk about it.'

'OK.' William lightly touches his arm. 'I won't.' After a moment's silence, William decides to carry on as if that last bit hadn't happened. 'I told her it was OK, but it's not. I'll always wish that they could have been there and however much they want to, they'll never go against Mum's wishes.'

'No, she'd have to invite them herself,' Martin says simply. 'Come on' – he stands up – 'we should go.'

The idea lands and pierces like an arrow. 'You're a genius!' William says, running to catch Martin up on the staircase. 'I write to them pretending I'm her. She apologises and says she wants them both to come!' They stand outside the dorm, across the threshold from pre-supper mayhem.

Martin's scowling. 'Last time we tried this trick it didn't go too well.'

'We were stupid ten-year-olds,' William says. 'I'm leaving here soon. This solo is what it's all been about for me. I've got a tiny family. I want them there!' He pauses. 'So would Dad.'

'And what then? Your mum gives them a big hug as we process in?'

'I don't care. I just want them to hear me sing. Whatever happens after can take care of itself. Anyway, it'll be rammed. They might not even see each other until it's over.'

'But don't they live in the same street? Your plan only works if they don't see each other between now and next Wednesday.'

'They won't! Mum's going to Swansea for two weeks – I think we're moving there in the summer, by the way – she's coming straight from there.'

Martin studies William's face. 'What about the postmark?'

The solution comes easily: 'I'll send a postcard from here – I've got one in my locker – I'll say she's just said goodbye to me on our last exeat and knows I would want them both there, so she wrote the card while she was still in Cambridge.'

'It's risky.'

'Since when have you not liked risky?'

Martin smiles a little, shrugs his shoulders. 'Fair comment.'

Over supper, Martin eats his way through the steak and kidney pie, evidently with nothing more to say. William knows that Evelyn would be furious to see Howard in the chapel with Robert, and they would be mortified to be there against her wishes. The letter, when he sends it, will be a ticking time bomb. But he knows something else too, and it feels bigger and stronger than all the other things; the 'Miserere' is not just any piece of music. And if his mother, his uncle and Howard are there to hear it, to hear him sing it, somehow, eventually, it will be all right. Plus, it's such a relief to be speaking to Martin again, it coalesces in William's heart as the right thing to do, the answer to everything.

Quiet and pensive over supper, Martin becomes riotous once the bedtime routine begins. William wonders if it's out of relief, that they are maybe inching back to their old way of being.

Eleven boys, including William, are in bed, while Martin stands on his, surveying the room. He claps his hands, looks at the wall clock.

'Four minutes. Someone? Anyone?'

Martin throws off his pyjamas, wobbling a little on the mattress as he balances on one leg, then the other. Excitement jitters from bed to bed. Martin beats his chest, his gaze sweeping the room for a taker. When William first saw Martin do this, more than three years ago, his body was hairless. Now there is a soft red cloud around his swinging penis and under his arms.

'Come on! Someone!'

More than once, Martin has leapt from bed to bed on his own, unable to draw anyone else in, but sometimes, like tonight, he won't stop until someone joins him. Most have accepted the challenge, but not William, unable to imagine being bold and reckless without any pants on. And there is always the real possibility of being caught. The last time, Martin was given five whacks, and since it was by no means the first time, an appointment with the school psychiatrist.

'OK,' says William, climbing out of bed, discarding his pyjamas and jumping up alongside Martin. And he thinks no matter how embarrassing this is going to be, it will have been worth it for the smile on Martin's face right now.

'Get a move on!' someone says. 'Only three minutes left!'

'You go clockwise, I'll go anti,' says Martin, gesticulating the directions, turning William round, their bare rumps nudging against each other.

William feels the scrutiny of the dorm, but the rush of adrenaline is an unexpected surprise. He's ready for this. Martin lifts a three-fingered hand. 'Three.' He flips one finger down. 'Two.' Then another: 'One!'

At first William's alarmed by the skid of the bed he lands on – his hands wheel and he thinks he's going to fall backwards, but he recovers and propels himself from one bed to the next, light and fast. He hears the scrape and slide of each bed as Martin thumps down on them. His willy waving above the laughing faces, William is high on the thrill of thrilling others.

They slam into each other and fall onto Martin's bed, chests pumping with laughter. Martin's breath pours into William's ears. The softness of Martin's thigh presses into his. William is not aroused, but not repelled either. He's got his friend back.

When silence fills the room like a thunder clap, William turns his head, although there's no need to, because he already knows Matron is standing in the doorway.

30

William stands before the desk, breathing the thick scent of dust and polish, not knowing what to do with his hands.

'It pains me to see you here under these circumstances, Lavery.' The daffodils glow on the window ledge behind Mr Atkinson's head, also burnished by the sun's glare.

'You're a fine chorister. Mr Lewis says perhaps the best he's ever had. But we can*not* allow a boy who misbehaves in such a way the honour of the most prestigious of solos. You understand that, don't you?'

'No!' His face burns as he steps closer to the desk. 'I'll do anything, sir.' His voice sounds ridiculous, high-pitched. '*Please*, sir!'

'You should have thought about the consequences before you joined in with Mussey's perverted pranks.'

William's head buzzes. He'll be gone in June, and for the rest of his life, all he'll remember is that he never got to sing the 'Miserere'. Flu first time, and now Martin, with his stupid games. A wall of tears is building behind his eyes, and he wonders, what if he gave in to them? What if, for the first time in four years, he let his body have its say? What if he dropped to the threadbare rug, sobbing at Mr Atkinson's feet?

Mr Atkinson stands up suddenly and pulls open the desk drawer. 'The best you can do now, Lavery, is take your punishment like a man.'

It's only then that William realises how very much he doesn't want to be beaten. The sun has inched to the left and no longer illuminates the flowers, but instead the piece of birch that Mr

Atkinson has slid smoothly from the drawer. So light and thin, it surely can't hurt that much? Tucked into his underpants are two handkerchiefs, one for each buttock, which Martin pinched from the laundry cupboard.

'Make sure you visibly flinch after the first one,' he said, putting the handkerchiefs under William's pillow after lunch, 'or he'll hit you harder the second time.'

'You said you never flinch.'

'I don't, but I go in there so often, I've got to keep my self-respect somehow. It's a one-off for you.'

Now he's actually standing there, William wishes he'd asked Martin, who is waiting his turn outside the study, to tell him exactly what was going to happen.

Mr Atkinson stands next to William, and his heart takes off like a trapped bird. What now? Does he bend down? Does he wait to be told to bend down? How far does he bend? All the way? Halfway? Why the *hell* didn't he ask Martin?

'Bend over.'

'Please let me sing, sir!' William can't help himself.

'*Down!*'

He hasn't anticipated how intolerable this moment would be: face to the floor, backside offered up. He probably didn't need to bend this far; he's touching his toes. The silence is absurd and humiliating.

When it comes, the crack of pain is far worse than he imagined. His body jolts upwards. He bites his mouth and tastes blood. Upside down, he can see Mr Atkinson's pressed black trousers, and when the crease shifts quickly to the left, William braces. The cane hits exactly the same spot, as does the next and the next, leaving his flesh twitching.

Mr Atkinson walks back to his side of the desk, puts the cane

166

in the drawer and sits. William stands ramrod-straight, fists clenched. Their eyes meet and Mr Atkinson's gaze drops down to the rug so quickly that, for the briefest of seconds, William is sure it's shame he sees on his headmaster's face.

Martin straightens from his slouch against the wall, but William doesn't acknowledge him. Rushing to the toilets, he hears Mr Atkinson.

'You again.'

Standing against the cubicle wall, taking care that his roaring flesh doesn't touch anything, William swipes at his tears and wishes he were bigger than this, that he could laugh it off, parade his wounds like Martin, as if they're trophies. But it hurts too much and he is too angry. It's the first time in his life he's been hit. The lack of emotion affronted him the most. If he had to be assaulted, a bit of passion, an overflowing of anger would have at least made more sense of it. And as if that wasn't punishment enough, he's lost the solo and didn't even see it coming. He hates Mr Atkinson.

Sooner than he expected, William hears heavy footsteps that stop outside the cubicle.

'Over and done with now.' Martin's soft voice echoes a little in the empty toilets.

William doesn't want to need Martin at this moment, but at the sound of his voice, he does. It's not a good idea for William to let him into the cubicle, lean on his chest and sob. But that's what happens.

'How many?' Martin says, when William can speak.

'Four. You?'

'Six. Listen, get the handkerchiefs out of your trousers. I'll put them back before we forget.'

167

William reaches down the back of his trousers and pulls, but he grabs the waistband of his underpants by mistake. He cries out at the bite of pain.

'I wish I wasn't so pathetic!'

'You're not. You're the best boy in this whole place, and in two weeks' time, it won't hurt any more, and you're going to sing the solo of your life.'

'No, I'm not.'

'You're kidding!'

Crying again, William shakes his head and suddenly, it's Martin he hates. His stupid, selfish bed hop has lost William everything.

'This is *your fault*. It's *all your fault!*'

He still can't get at the handkerchiefs, so he turns away from Martin to face the cubicle door and yanks his flies down. 'Bloody hell, Martin!' he says, again unsuccessfully trying to grab the fabric down his underpants. 'You never said it would hurt this much!'

'I'm sorry. I'd forgotten what a shock it is the first time.' From behind, Martin gently pulls William's waistband back. 'Let me do it.' He reaches inside William's trousers. 'Hold your breath a moment. It won't hurt forever, I promise.'

In the brief second before the door flies open, William knows there's someone outside, but there is no time to stop crying. Daylight floods the cubicle, and Charles and Anthony stand gaping at William's twisted face, his open flies, Martin's hand down his trousers.

'Get off him!' Charles shouts at Martin, and both boys start to pull William out of the cubicle.

'I'm fine.' William shakes them off. 'Get lost!'

'Anthony, go and tell a master!' shouts Charles. Anthony looks at William and Martin as if needing their permission.

'Don't!' says William, zipping up his flies. 'I'm OK.'

'He was hurting you!' Charles is breathless. 'We heard!'

'If this gets back to the masters' – William's voice is surprisingly commanding – 'I'll make life hell for you. Understand?'

The boys look uncomfortable, glancing from Martin to William.

'Tell them, William,' Martin says quietly, 'tell them I wasn't hurting you.'

William sees it flit between the two boys; the thrill of thinking they've interrupted a forbidden act. He knows full well how quickly it will spread. How easy for all of them to believe that this is what their friendship has really been about these four years. William can see exactly how the next few months will go: the giggling, the knowing looks, the sudden quiet when they enter a room.

No, he decides, he simply won't take it. It was Martin, not him, who caused all this. Quickly buttoning his waistband, he turns to Martin. 'I've told them not to tell a master, isn't that enough?'

A tap drips. Martin's eyes fill, the first time William has ever seen that happen.

'William,' Martin says, '*tell* them.'

Charles and Anthony look at William, waiting. *They're loving it*, he thinks, taking a step out of the cubicle. They separate to let him through.

'Just stay away from me, OK?' William says over his shoulder to Martin and strides out into the corridor, stuffing both handkerchiefs in his pockets.

A week later, William is called back into Mr Atkinson's study. Phillip has persuaded him that never has a boy wanted a solo so much, and never has a boy with a voice quite like William's graced these chapel walls. So Mr Atkinson tells William that though it is highly unusual to reverse a disciplinary measure, he will sing the 'Miserere' on Ash Wednesday after all.

This headmaster will have plenty of time to reflect on that decision, and on how things might have played out differently for William if he hadn't given in to the pleadings of his passionate choirmaster.

Part III

FAMILY BUSINESS

31

SEPTEMBER 1965

'Can't I take yours, Uncle Robert?'

They're in the hallway, about to leave for the station. Howard is putting William's suitcase in the car boot. The large case contains seven pairs of new Y-fronts, two pairs of pyjamas, two shirts and two T-shirts, a pullover, two pairs of slacks and a blazer. Eighteen-year-old William is wearing his new suit. Also in the case are the clothes he will need for training in the embalming room: a pair of white surgeon's boots, a plastic gown, a plastic apron, two pairs of strong rubber gloves, one pair of plastic arm sleeves and a face mask.

Uncle Robert frowns at the book William is holding. 'It's so tatty!'

'That's why I like it.'

Together they survey the worn grey book in William's hands, *Embalming – Theoretical and Practical* by Edwin Frank Scudamore FBIE.

'You'd rather that scruffy old tome than the new edition I got you with the nice gold lettering?'

'Yes.' William smiles, tightening his grip on it. 'It was Dad's.'

Robert smiles. 'Of course you can have it. As long as I get to keep the new one.'

Ten minutes later, the three of them stand on the station platform. The oak trees are on the turn, yellow flashes amongst the green. A breeze washes over William's face as he hugs Howard. He feels self-conscious in his black suit and tie and posh overcoat, but trusts his uncle's judgement that it will show respect to the family he's staying with. The Finches are another third-generation undertaking family. They live in Stepney, a half-hour walk from the Thames College of Embalming where William will be studying for a year.

A cotton wool cloud dabs the sun out, and as William turns to Robert, he suddenly feels scared.

'Remind you of anything?' Uncle Robert asks.

'A bit,' William says, used to Robert's ability to tune in to his feelings, and already trying to resist the memories of the first time he left home.

'Remember, you can come home at the weekends at the drop of a hat. No blummin' exeats needed.'

'I know, but I'll try and get on with life in London. Christmas will be here before we know it.'

'You know your bed's always here for you.' Robert puts his hand on William's arm.

'I'll work hard and I'll make you proud.'

'I'm already proud.' Robert looks at Howard, who stands, tranquil as ever, a gentle smile on his face. 'We're already proud.'

The train pulls in and William hugs Robert, and though he's never done it before, he kisses him on the cheek. Then he hugs Howard again, who squeezes back tightly. He picks up his suitcase and briefcase and climbs aboard.

'Don't wait to wave, I'll get sad,' he says, suddenly wanting to be on his own.

'Good idea,' Howard says, 'or we'll all be bawling our eyes out.' He chuckles, and softly turns Robert round. The diamond ring on his little finger winks at the sun before he folds his hands behind his back and the two men walk away from the train. William sees them turn slightly towards each other – Howard is saying something – and then, in perfect unison,

174

without turning, they each lift both their hands and wave.

As he sits next to the window on the tired upholstery, with a spring nudging him in the backside, William is unexpectedly overwhelmed with a sense of his mother. Not the mother who moved to Swansea without him and now manages the biggest music shop in Wales, but the mother who took him to Cambridge, who knelt on the gravel in her stockings to tell him how proud she was, trying so hard not to cry. He stares out of the window, not bothering to wipe his face until he feels drips on his hand.

The harvested fields snap across his vision like rolling sand dunes. Alone in the carriage, he glances at his watch just as the train plunges through a tunnel and he has to wait for the flash of returning daylight to see the time. Still well over an hour before he arrives in London, with the challenge of the Underground.

He hasn't told his mother he's off to London to start his formal training. Uncle Robert might have told her, he supposes. He knows they write to each other now; the frostiness started to thaw a year or so ago. He knows that makes Robert happy but he has never felt comfortable with it himself. The last four years, since leaving Cambridge so abruptly, only make sense if he keeps holding his mother accountable for what happened. As another train suddenly rips by in the opposite direction, William sits back and closes his eyes. It's no good; rocked by the train, with late summer gold flashing across the countryside, he can't withstand the memory of saying goodbye to her all those years ago, and the feeling it brings of being totally loved by her, the centre of her universe.

He's lived with Robert and Howard since that nightmare Ash Wednesday, when he refused to even finish his final year.

175

Evelyn had arrived straight from Swansea to hear William sing, fizzing with excitement and intent. In two short weeks, she'd found a house, a job, a school with Eisteddfod ambition keen to welcome a Cambridge chorister. She would move there as soon as possible to get settled during William's final term and he'd join her there for the summer. Walking into the college chapel, that was her glittering plan. A short hour later, everything had come crashing down.

When none of them – Phillip, Mr Atkinson, his mother or Robert – had even put a dent in William's resolve to leave Cambridge immediately, the only option was for him to stay temporarily with his uncle while Evelyn got settled in Swansea. That he ended up staying four years, through his O and A levels, was a surprise to everyone.

For the first few weeks with Robert and Howard, William put all his effort into forgetting the last four years had even happened. He schooled himself to block any memories as soon as they appeared. He wouldn't listen to choral or church music, he wouldn't sing, and he wouldn't allow himself a moment's hesitation before dropping Martin's unopened letters in the bin.

What he swore he would never forget, however, was that all this was his mother's fault.

William leans down now, to click open the lock of his new briefcase and grip the broad spine of Scudamore's opus, hoping that the weight of it, the dusty smell, the small text and detailed drawings, can work their magic. Six months ago, once he was accepted on the course, William started to read his father's textbook and found it an unexpected treasure, light relief when he wasn't studying for A levels. He'd known about veins and arteries, but a *retromandibular* vein? A *superior mesenteric* artery? He was mesmerised, laughing out loud when he found out there were *two* circulatory systems in the human body: the pulmonary circulation loop and the systemic circulation loop. In the past weeks, he has romped through the dense text and meticulous illustrations, finding he can easily retain the most outlandish names, from the lateral circumflex femoral vein to the dorsalis pedis artery. Following the surge of fluids through the cardiovascular system, William couldn't understand why people don't talk about it more often.

It takes a while, but eventually Scudamore transports him from his past, with its lingering presence of Evelyn, and into his future as an embalmer. The pull of the decelerating train an hour later drags him from the complex world of hypochlorite disinfectants. After replacing the book and locking the briefcase, he slides his arms through the silky tunnels of his coat sleeves, picks up his bags and steps off the train.

32

'William Lavery. Is that Lavery and Sons, Sutton Coldfield?'

'Yes, sir.'

William and three others are being shown the workrooms in the basement mortuary. He expected desks, but there are none. The small group stands between the two fireclay embalming tables. Lying on one is a cadaver, covered with white paper. Arthur Mason, Director of the Thames College of Embalming, tall, congenial yet authoritative, is greeting each of them individually.

'I knew your father, William.' Arthur stands with his hands behind his back, his head slightly inclined and dipped – the undertaker's quiet air of compassion undergirded by expertise. William nods. Undertaking is a family business; it would be unusual – embarrassing even – if your family was not known. But it pleases him again, that choosing this work, this way of life, he has aligned himself to his father. Most of the time, this is a comforting thought. Only occasionally does he wonder if his father might have preferred him to have made choices that aligned him to his mother instead.

'Is your uncle well?'

'Yes, thank you, sir.'

'Good.' Arthur turns to the stocky, ruddy-faced man to William's left, older than William, but possibly still in his twenties. 'And you must be Roger Turner. How's Mr Turner?'

'Not too bad, sir,' Roger replies, a friendly, easy smile on his face, 'though I think he's ready to ease off. That's why I'm here.'

William expected to be the youngest. He knows that small undertakers often only have one qualified embalmer and it's quite usual for the son to work for many years in the business before qualifying in this particular aspect. William pushed to start young, because he knew that his interest lay in the morgue, not the funeral parlour. To be left alone to work with the dead, not sit with the pain of the bereaved like Howard does, talking them through the endless decisions they are generally totally unprepared to make; coffin size, coffin finish, flowers, orders of service, music. He knew from his early days in the morgue with Robert that doing something so personal and important, but not having anyone watching you, not even the person you're looking after, suited him perfectly.

What William notices first about Simon Drake, the third man, is how his eyelashes flash white in contrast to his dark suit. William has never seen anyone quite so pale, as if his skin has never seen the sun. The Drake family business is in Worcester. Arthur, it turns out, trained with Simon's father.

The fourth and final man is the nearest in age to William, but since they gathered here half an hour ago, William has been keeping his distance.

'And you, young man, must be Ray Price?' Arthur says.

It's no surprise that Arthur doesn't know Ray's grandfather, or father. William feels some pity for the young man, who probably doesn't even realise how out of place he looks, how everything about his appearance confirms his ignorance of the undertaking world. Embarrassed on his behalf and only vaguely aware of what clannish prejudices are moving within him, William has deliberately stood on the opposite side of the table to Ray.

'Yes, sir,' the young man says abruptly. He is small and wiry,

179

with haywire black hair. His suit is rumpled and his white cuffs are grubby.

'And you're going to be working for Lightfoot's in Leeds?'

'Yes, sir, if I qualify.' His strong northern accent surprises William.

William has noticed, and is sure everyone else will have too, that Ray's fingernails are dirty and ragged. How long before he realises this won't do, before he makes adjustments? Decorum, cleanliness, tidiness, are all parts of the whole that communicate respect. And although right now they are in a basement morgue, not a mourner in sight, you never forget who you are serving.

'Well, Ray, you couldn't be in a better place if that's your goal.' Arthur's voice takes on a more formal tone, hands clasped at his stomach. 'Thames is the largest embalming company in the country and the best known training institution. Many local funeral parlours can't afford in-house embalmers, so by providing top-quality services at reduced rates, we get a steady supply of cadavers on which you can learn your trade.

'In here' – he gestures at the room – 'you will watch demonstrations, but more importantly and more commonly, you will stand alongside your tutor, either myself or Norman, my deputy, and watch us work, gradually practising aspects of the procedure yourselves. Occasionally, you will go out to homes or hospitals to accompany embalmers, but the bulk of your work will be in here.' He pauses and looks in turn at each of them, enjoying, William thinks, the assumed gravity of the moment. 'And if you work hard and pay attention, what you learn here over the next twelve months will turn you into some of the best embalmers in Europe.'

Ray's eyes dart all over the room. For William, Simon and Roger, nothing in here is new; the embalming tables, the trolleys with buckets and drainage trays, the cadaver. They will all have had access to mortuaries and chapels of rest from an early age. In fact, William will have been a relative latecomer at fourteen.

Arthur walks towards the door, beckoning them to follow. In the far corner of the adjacent, smaller room are two stacks of six stretchers, and embedded in the wall, cool storage chambers.

'These are actually an ex-air raid precaution.' Arthur lays his hand on the basic-looking steel frames, each with five wooden slats, painted white, running lengthways. On each corner is a metal bracket which enables them to be stacked. 'Simple, but they do the job. Bodies are stored here, and taken through to the demonstration room next door.'

William wishes he felt kinder, more generous towards Ray, but being near him raises unease in himself, an unease that takes him back further than his first weeks with Robert, when he stood next to his first cadaver with his uncle's hand on his shoulder. What bothers him today, glancing every now and then at Ray, is the knowledge that he, eight years ago, and almost dizzy with the unfamiliarity of it all, was just as much of an oddball himself. And who knows what those four years in Cambridge would have been like had he not been rescued so early and so completely by Martin and his friendship, which both cocooned him and propelled him out into chorister life. He's not unaware how perverse it is, that rather than wanting to offer the same kind of rescue to Ray, to go out of his way to ease his passage into a new world, William resents Ray for the mirror he presents him with. Well-practised, William swats the image of Martin from his mind.

'You'll learn your trade here. Observing good practice and practising yourselves are the heart of what we do. Nevertheless, there's no avoiding the theoretical knowledge you need. At the end of each day, you'll be given a written question from your tutor, and that evening, you'll answer it to the best of your ability, using Scudamore. When your tutor has time, you'll go through your answers together.

'So' – Arthur claps his large hands – 'let's get to work.'

As they follow Arthur back to the demonstration room, William glances at Ray's feet, anticipating correctly that his shoes are scuffed and worn.

The subdued, dreamy light from the single opaque window high up on the wall snaps into something hard and bright as Arthur turns on a lamp next to the table. Once they are all gathered, with notebooks balanced on clipboards, he slides the paper sheet from the body.

33

'It's slave labour.'

Ray and William are waiting to order drinks while Roger and Simon save the table at their first lunchbreak.

'Rubbish.' William bristles every time this man opens his mouth and shows his ignorance. 'We've got to practise on real bodies. We can't just play around and then throw them away, so it's better we help with a real embalming. What's the other option?'

'*They* pay *us*, Einstein.'

'But they're training us! Everyone pays to be trained, don't they?'

'No.'

William thinks Ray is making up for not knowing anything in class by being such a know-it-all now.

'Apprentices get paid,' says Ray. 'Not much, but something.'

William hasn't thought of that – he doesn't really know much about how things work in the wider world. The barman is taking his time to wipe down the counter at the other end of the room, chatting to regulars. He wishes he'd hurry up and take their order so they can get back to Roger and Simon. He doesn't want them to think he and Ray are a pair just because they're young.

'I was offered a car mechanic's apprenticeship back home,' says Ray, 'and they'd have paid me.'

'Maybe you should have taken it.'

Ray pulls his mouth down and hunches his shoulders. 'Car

mechanics are ten-a-penny there – and badly paid. The funeral home said there'd be a job waiting for me if I qualified here and they'd cover my rent while I trained.' He shrugs again. 'Didn't seem a bad idea – a year in London, with a job at the end.'

'It's so *still*.' William mimics Ray's response when Arthur pulled back the sheet from the cadaver.

'Well, son,' Arthur said, a smile playing at his lips, 'we'd all need to worry if it wasn't.'

Ray looked quickly at their laughing faces. 'I'll get used to it.' He nodded. 'Don't you worry.'

'Ha bloody ha.' Ray's face remains deadpan now, as he raises his hand to catch the barman's attention, who finally starts to amble towards them. 'You seriously think I'm the weird one, don't you? You think, because that was the first dead body I've seen, I'm somehow second rate!'

'What can I get you, gents?' The barman rests both meaty hands on the counter. His sideburns curve around his cheeks like lamb chops.

'Three pints of bitter and a lager shandy for the lady, please,' says Ray, with the ease of a man who's ordered many drinks from many bars.

William promises himself he'll never order a shandy again in Ray's company. 'I don't think you're second rate, I just don't get the impression that you want to be an embalmer,' William says, as the barman moves to the pumps.

Ray laughs. Wholeheartedly. It's the first time William's seen his face rearrange itself and he notices what even, white teeth he has.

'And again,' says Ray, enjoying himself now, 'you *seriously* think I'm the weird one because as a kid, I didn't dream of stuffing dead bodies for a living?'

'It's not weird if it's what your grandfather and father did.' William knows he's not being fair. He hadn't spent his childhood knowing this is what he'd do. It was only after the life he'd expected had vanished that he realised how well he was suited to the quiet, hidden work of an embalmer. Nevertheless, his irritation makes him add, 'And we don't *stuff* bodies. We look after them.'

He reaches out and takes the tray from the barman, leaving his change on the counter.

■ ■ ■

William's first time alone with a dead body was with Kenneth, the old man who lived down the road.

It was late September. Evelyn was in Swansea, and because she'd been gazumped on the house she was buying for them, he'd had to start school in Sutton until October half-term. He'd taken to doing his homework in the office adjoining the morgue rather than in the kitchen. Robert was looking after Kenneth, who'd died that week.

'Can I watch?' he said, appearing at Robert's side.

Robert's hands were suddenly still. 'If you like. I've nearly finished, we're onto the H.'

'What's that?'

'It's a mnemonic, Pack Her Cotton Dress Clean Today Please. We use it for the final bits and bobs, once the body's embalmed. H stands for hair, C for cosmetise, and D for dress.' He turned to William. 'Sure you're all right with this?'

'I'm sure.'

'Right then.' He reached for the leather cosmetics bag behind him. 'Let's get this hair sorted.'

'Robert?' Howard called from the office. 'Can you come here a sec? I've had someone on the phone wants to book a double funeral for next week. There's a few logistics I need to check with you.'

The embalming was complete, so Kenneth looked much more himself than he would have done an hour ago; pinkish, not waxy yellow, plumped lips almost smiling, and convex eyelids due to the little caps over the eyeballs. When Kenneth was ill, William had twice delivered a casserole for him. He hadn't stayed long, but served the food on a plate and helped him up from the armchair to the table. At fourteen, William had towered above Kenneth, and as he helped him from armchair to dining chair, he noticed what a very neat dome Kenneth's head was, and wondered why he didn't grow his comb-over long enough to reach all the way across. From his vantage point above Kenneth, William could see his wiry eyebrows, like feelers.

Uncle Robert and Howard were deep in conversation, and without thinking, William leaned across to the cosmetics bag and took the black comb. He swept the fine hair carefully across Kenneth's mottled scalp, then trimmed back the longest eyebrows with the tiny silver scissors.

Robert came back in just as William had removed a solitary whisker from Kenneth's left nostril.

'William!' Robert said. 'What have you *done*?'

'Sorry.' William put the tweezers down.

Robert shook his head quickly, smiling. 'I wasn't admonishing you. He looks marvellous!'

'Really?' William looked back at Kenneth.

'Really!' Robert stood close. 'You've tidied those eyebrows up without butchering them. And the hair! It's perfect. He looks his very best self.' Robert looked up from Kenneth and frowned at William. 'He didn't bother you?'

'No.' William smiled. 'He was very polite and kept his eyes closed the whole time.' They both laughed. 'I liked getting on with it. No one watching.'

Robert patted William's back. 'You'll be ready for an audience again one day,' he says softly.

'No, I won't.'

'That's how you feel now, it's still raw. I'm just saying, don't rule singing out. Never say never.'

'Never.' William dropped the tweezers in the cosmetics bag and it was right then that the idea landed. 'I want to be an embalmer like you and Dad.'

Robert let out a gentle laugh. 'You're fourteen! I'd rather see you out making friends than hanging around in here with me and Howard.'

'I don't want friends. I'm no good at it.'

Some of the boys at Bishop Vesey's Grammar had been at the same primary school as William. Thankfully, none had shown the slightest interest in what had happened to him while he was away. He'd tried to fit in these last couple of weeks. He'd even sat with a few of them in the cinema car park on Saturday night, eating fish and chips and drinking cider. The trouble was, not one of them could ever be anything like the friend Martin was. And if he could throw that away, what business did he have making new ones?

The discipline of his chorister days meant he was a good student without looking as if he was trying. He was friendly and polite, but made no attempt to get to know anyone, joined no clubs, and if he was invited out after school, he declined with a smile and a no thank you.

Robert sighed. 'If your schoolwork doesn't suffer, you're welcome in here any time, my boy – though your poor mother'd be appalled.'

'It's none of her business.'

'Come on now, she's your *mother*.'

William sighed. 'Why don't you hate her?'

Robert turned to face William. 'Because I know grief, William. Your father has been dead six years, and I still think of him every day. I need to do that with a clear conscience and a lightness of spirit. Your father *loved* your mother. If I hold on to bad feelings towards her, I couldn't ever think of him without guilt. And I couldn't bear that. So, when enough time has passed, I'll hold out my hand to her and I'll keep doing so. No matter if she refuses it, slaps it, or bites it off for that matter. She was the light of your father's life. And anyway, you'll be off to live with her soon.'

William looked back at Kenneth, and gently smoothed his hair again.

34

William doesn't feel immediately at home at the Finches'; how could he? But he does feel welcome. Mr Finch, with furry little hoods of grey eyebrows, is formal yet warm. Mrs Finch is tiny, and wears slippers with a strap of light, feathery fluff, and high heels. When he first arrived, he was moved at how they took his hand in both of theirs. More than a handshake. Their daughter, Gloria, a trainee nurse, was eating out on his first night. After shepherd's pie and peas, he excused himself to go and do his homework.

Now in his room, with its two single beds and striped wallpaper, he looks at his envelope, pristine, full of promise. *Name the branches of the carotid arteries and trace the arteries and veins a particle of fluid from the big toe to the left ear would use.* Roger and Simon opened their envelopes that afternoon but William slipped his into his briefcase for later.

After being with strangers all day, he takes comfort in lifting the familiar Scudamore from the shelf, flicking through it to find the right chapter, smiling at the musty breath of it and how it feels like a bit of his uncle's and dad's souls right there before him. He reads it thoroughly, then composes his answer, first in rough, then neatly. Two hours pass in which he has happily disappeared from himself. The knock at the door is gentle, but it still makes him jump.

'Cocoa in ten mins if you want it.' The voice is bold. London. Female. Must be Gloria.

'Thank you,' he says, listening to the footsteps going downstairs.

Is he meant to follow her? Will she bring it up? If she does, should he ask her in? If he goes downstairs, should he bring it back to his room, or should he sit down there with them? He sits at his desk, checking his watch every few seconds.

At four minutes and counting, he is delivered. 'Come on down,' calls the voice, 'it's ready.'

She's waiting in the galley kitchen doorway, with a tray holding two cups and a plate of biscuits. 'Take this to Mum and Dad, and then we can have ours in here. They're watching *Armchair Theatre*, and no one's allowed to speak, or Dad loses track.'

William takes the tray from the attractive young woman he thinks is roughly the same age as him, catching his thumb between her fingers as she hands it over. The silvery TV light reflects off Mr and Mrs Finch's spectacles. He gently puts the tray on the small table in between their two seats and leaves with neither acknowledging his presence.

'Thank you, William,' Mr Finch shouts, making him jump in the doorway.

'Yes, thank yoooou,' sings Mrs Finch.

'My pleasure,' shouts back William. 'What's so funny?' he says to Gloria.

'You're very polite.' She smiles, wiping a circle of cocoa from the work surface with a sponge.

'Costs nothing, but earns you a lot,' he said, surprised at how readily his mother's words trip off his tongue.

Gloria's green eyes shine as she laughs again. She pushes herself up onto the counter and William is struck by how athletic and light on her feet she is. She is a good four inches shorter than him. He also notices her padded curves; how nice it would be to rest his hands on that gentle bulge of her hips through her pretty dress. 'That's yours there.' She nods at a green cup and saucer. 'And help yourself to biscuits out the tin. I'm Gloria.'

'Nice to meet you, Gloria,' he says. The cocoa is strong, with small, petrol-y bubbles on top. 'Thank you for this.'

'My pleasure,' she says. 'What was in your envelope tonight?'

She's obviously used to Thames College students in her house, so he responds in kind.

'I've been naming the branches of the carotid arteries and tracing the arteries and veins a particle of fluid from the big toe to the left ear would use.'

'You look as though you've been enjoying yourself.'

'I have.' He laughs at himself. She joins in; her giggle is rich and textured.

'Gloria! Close the door,' shouts Mrs Finch, 'your father's already in a muddle.'

'Sorry,' Gloria shouts, jumping down from the counter and crossing the kitchen.

'You don't have to stop talking,' Mrs Finch shouts, 'just keep it down.'

'Why are *they* kissing?' Mr Finch says. Gloria keeps her hand on the door; head inclined and a warning finger held to her lips, she winks at William. 'I thought she was married to the lawyer,' Mr Finch says.

'She is!' Mrs Finch replies. 'That's the point, he's her bit on the side. Keep up, you daft bat.'

Having gently closed the door, the two of them laugh as quietly as they can. Some cocoa slips down William's windpipe and Gloria has to pat his back as he splutters over the sink.

That night, lying in bed, remembering, William smiles. He likes how Gloria makes him feel. Even coughing over the sink with cocoa stinging his nostrils, he was enjoying himself. And still now, he can feel the sensation of her hand on his back.

191

It's Friday and it feels very natural sitting opposite Gloria on the counter at 9.30 in the evening, with Mr and Mrs Finch watching TV in the next room. As the week has progressed he's found out that Gloria is one year older than him, has an older sister who's married with two children, living in East London. Last night William asked if her father had ever put pressure on her to join the business.

She looked at him as if he'd said something stupid. 'Think about it. Have you ever met a female embalmer? Have you ever seen a sign outside a funeral home that says, Blah Blah Blah and Daughters?'

He shook his head. 'You're right, I haven't.'

'I'm not complaining. It got me off the hook – I'd rather save lives than pickle bodies. Mind,' she added, 'you'll not find better people than in the funeral business. And if I ever have a daughter, and she wants to follow in her grandfather's footsteps, I won't have a problem with it.'

Then they'd talked about Egyptians pulling brains out through the nostrils, but he found his mind kept jumping back to the thought of Gloria with a baby daughter.

'You've painted your nails,' William notices now. 'Nice colour.'

'Thanks!' she says, smiling at her splayed fingers. 'I always do them if I've got two days off in a row.'

'I used to paint nails for my uncle in the morgue.' He'd never offer this to a normal girl, but he's confident she'll understand. The risk pays off.

'I did too!' She grins. 'For Dad. I loved it! Especially how when you hook their hands over the edge of the coffin they don't budge an inch.' She laughs. 'I used to think it meant they

192

really wanted it doing, the way their hand just stayed put. I was only thirteen.'

'I was fourteen,' he says, and they laugh again. 'Actually, that's still my favourite bit; the cosmetology.' Encouraged by her warm delight in anything he says, he confesses, 'I love it all: hair, make-up, nails.'

'Maybe you should be a beautician.'

'No.' He laughs. 'It's after we've gone through all the other stuff, I like being able to say it's all over now, we're just going to make you lovely for your family.'

Gloria stretches her leg out to gently kick his shin. 'You're a talker, then. Dad natters his way through an embalming.'

'So does my uncle,' William says. 'He tells them about the weather. I tend to stick to explaining what I'm doing.'

She tilts her head and a thick curtain of auburn hair falls across half her face. 'What, everything?'

'I sing during those bits.'

Her laughter is kind and William couldn't feel more pleased with himself as he goes up to bed an hour later.

■ ■ ■

As early autumn had taken hold in Sutton Coldfield, William discovered that he found the presence of the dead calming, and the sight of his uncle quietly, skilfully looking after them equally so. He had five more weeks until half-term and his move to Swansea, but he found the more time he spent in the morgue, the more he liked it. There was a relief in looking at a corpse; nothing more could hurt them. Nothing more could be done or said. He'd yet to see a dead body that didn't look peaceful.

He was relieved to find he didn't mind the visceral nature of

193

it either, wasn't at all squeamish when the sharp trocar pierced a heart, or stomach or lungs, to drain off the fluid. He didn't have to look away when the needle went through the roof of a mouth and into the nostril to keep the jaw from hanging open.

He couldn't help but register the intrusive and, yes, even though done by his gentle uncle, the violent nature of some of it. So once the P for packing (which, he was shocked to discover, meant shoving wodges of cotton into *every* orifice) was done, and they got to the H and C, he felt a sense of relief. It had quickly become very natural, standing next to Robert, to say, 'All done now, Stanley,' or June, or Terrence, 'all finished.'

Doing this quiet, intimate work in the peaceful morgue, and with no audience, was enormously appealing. The simplicity and privacy of it won him over. No performance, no audience, no humiliation. As the distance between him and his chorister days increased from days and weeks to months, his future as an embalmer acted as an anchor for his present and some kind of hope for his future.

He let the routine of his days carry him. From one lesson to another, to lunch, usually on his own if he got his way, though sometimes he put up with someone's small talk. Then straight home, his bag heavy with textbooks, to a warm, quiet welcome from Robert and Howard, who carried on around him, delivering tea and biscuits and taking a quick glance at the work he was doing. Sometimes, looking up from his books, William imagined Evelyn at work in a very different environment; moving lightly amongst polished pianos, hulking double basses and cellos, glinting trumpets and flutes. In those early days, when she still thought he was going to join her there, she wrote to him about it; ordering obscure sheet music for customers, recommending local teachers to parents, stock-taking. Yesterday a man had come in to buy a kazoo and asked her to recommend a good teacher, and the piano tuner's young guide dog had cocked its leg on a drum kit. It impressed him really, her persistence in trying to entertain him, but it was now ingrained in him to brace himself against her, hold her responsible, never forget. So no, he didn't write back to her, even though sometimes he felt a twitch of humour, the urge to respond, to continue with a piece of nonsense she had started. But he always managed to resist. While his mother knew from practical, matter-of-fact letters from Robert that he was healthy, going to bed on time and doing his homework, she had absolutely no idea that William had been helping in the mortuary and was often entrusted to take sole charge of the H and the C of Pack Her Cotton Dress Clean Today Please. She had no idea of the growing resolve that he wasn't going to Swansea at half-term. But then neither did Robert and Howard.

35

'William!'

As William folds his morgue clothes ready to place in his locker, his heart plunges at the sound of Ray's voice. It's Monday, week two. After a full day of working alongside Arthur, he's looking forward to getting back to the Finches'. He wonders what the question in the envelope will be and whether Gloria will be wearing her checked slippers tonight, or if she'll be barefoot, with those small toes that wriggle about in their stocking covers as she sits on the counter swinging her legs. He hopes the envelope he's just slipped into his briefcase will give him something to talk about with her. She enjoys anatomy as much as he does.

'What?' he says, without looking up from folding his plastic gown.

'Can I come to your digs tonight so we can work together on the theory?'

'That might be awkward.' William finally looks Ray in the eye, but continues folding. 'I live with a family and I don't know what the deal is with visitors.'

'No worries' – he remains upbeat – 'you could come to mine. I've got beers.'

William glances at his watch. 5.05. Dinner at 7.00. If he goes to Ray's, helps him as quickly as he can, he could be back for tea, and the rest of the evening wouldn't be disrupted. If Ray comes to the Finches', he might never get rid of him.

'I can come for an hour now, but that's it. They're expecting me for tea.'

Ray's smile is genuine, a rare showing of his even teeth. 'Thanks, William. I could do with a hand.'

It's the truth. Twice this week William's heard Ray's tutor say they'll need to spend more time together on his assignments.

'I live just round the corner.' Ray stuffs his gown into his bag in a big ball.

'If you fold it, it won't look such a mess when you put it back on.' He's sick of looking at Ray across the embalming table in his gown that's so rumpled it doesn't even hang straight.

'I'll do it later.' He grins, patting William on the back. 'Let's get this bloody homework out of the way.'

'It's not much, but it's home – isn't that what they say?'

Ray holds the door for William, who is out of breath from the three-flight climb. It took them twenty-five minutes to walk 'just round the corner', so it's already 5.30. The soles of his shoes stick to the lino that curls up in the doorway. Ray flings his bag across the room onto the unmade bed. In the corner is a tiny sink. Against the wall to their right, a camping stove sits on a table, surrounded by dirty plates and dishes. There's a clothes rail with one jacket on a hanger, but trousers and shirts are draped over the rail. A yellowing net curtain hangs from a wire halfway down the window.

Ray takes off his tie as he kneels next to the iron bedstead that reminds William of boarding school, with its skinny mattress. Ray pulls two bottles from under it, drops them on the blanket, and gets a bottle opener from a basket on the small Formica table. He pops the lids off and passes one to William before he can say no. He's not a fan of beer, and he doesn't want the Finches to smell it on him when he returns.

'Take a seat.' Ray gestures to the rickety wooden chair next to the table as he sits on the bed and lights a cigarette. Straightening one leg, he pulls a brown envelope from his pocket, bent now into the curve of his thigh. With the cigarette hanging from his bottom lip, he pulls out the question, drops the envelope on the floor, and reads, squinting his eyes against the smoke.

'I hate this.'

'What?' says William, noticing it is now 5.45.

'Doing this. I thought that's what I was paying for. They want to get us up to speed as fast as they can to do their dirty work, but we have to learn the difficult stuff on our own.'

'If you think embalming's dirty work' – William takes a swig of beer – 'I'm not sure you're going to last.'

Ray drops the paper on the bed next to him and sits forward, towards William.

'Now I've got you to help me, I can't fail.'

'Let's get on with it. I haven't got long.' William regrets how mean-spirited he feels when he's with Ray.

'Jammy bastard.' Ray drags on his cigarette. 'A family to go home to, hot meals. Bet your room's better than this, eh?'

'What's your question?' William nods at the paper discarded on the bed.

Ray reads it out. It's the same one William had on his first day.

'Where's your Scudamore?'

Ray waves his hand under the bed till it bumps against the book. He pulls it out and bats away the dust on it.

William takes it from him, leafs through it and lays it open on the right page. 'OK,' he says, 'I visualise the arteries like branches of a tree.'

Ray looks from the book to smile at William.

'What?' William says.

'It comes so naturally to you.'

'I've watched my uncle, so it makes sense, and anyway, I had this question last week.'

Ray stubs out his cigarette on a saucer next to his bed. 'I know you think I'm useless. I probably am, but it gets on my nerves how smug you all are.'

'Just write down this bit. I've got to go.'

Ray starts copying out the paragraph William has highlighted. 'Drink your beer then.' He points at the bottle on the floor. William knocks it back in five gulps.

Ray's handwriting is thankfully fast and neat. It's 6.50. They'll be sitting down to eat in ten minutes and he thinks it will take him at least half an hour to get there.

'What's the problem?' says Ray. 'So you'll miss tea. How old are you, ten? Stay here and we can have another beer, get fish and chips.'

'Laugh at me all you like, but I *want* to sit down for a meal with a nice family and, if you must know, their daughter.'

Ray's sly smile and knowing look make William regret what he's just given away.

'Now *that* I understand!' He finishes his beer. 'Bugger off then, I've got this now.'

'Thanks,' says William, feeling sheepish, getting up and putting on his jacket. 'Make sure you include all of the arteries and veins that are relevant; you lose points for every one you miss.' Ray doesn't move to open the door or say goodbye. He just watches William with a smile that makes him uncomfortable.

'Bye then,' William says as he backs out of the door. Ray merely raises the empty beer bottle.

He runs full pelt back to the college and then to the Finches', not trusting himself to navigate the route from Ray's. It takes thirty-five minutes and by the time he bursts into their dining room, he's out of breath, sweating and a little light-headed. Mr Finch is serving apple pie. All three of them turn in surprise. His sausage, mash and peas are on his plate, with a hint of white where the fat has congealed on the gravy.

'I'm so sorry!' he says, chest heaving. 'I was helping someone with their homework.' Unable to speak, he breathes heavily. 'He lives further away than I thought.' He unbuttons his coat. 'I came as fast as I could.'

'Well, you're here now,' Mrs Finch says, 'eat up. It'll be cold but I'd rather it not go to waste.'

'Of course not.' William dashes into the hall to hang his coat up. He pulls his sweater close to his face. It reeks of smoke. He takes it off and leaves it over his coat.

Mrs Finch inhales noisily as he sits next to her. 'If it wasn't too early, I'd think you'd been doing your homework in the pub, William.'

'No!' he exclaims. 'I was at Ray's.' Before he can do anything about it, a burp rips from his mouth. He looks at his hosts earnestly, feeling his face flush. 'Mrs Finch, Mr Finch, please don't think I'd ever take your hospitality for granted. Ray's not from an undertaking family and he's struggling with the work. He asked me to help him, and I thought I ought to. He offered me a beer.'

He finally steals a glance at Gloria. Her lips are clamped together, her eyes sparkling.

'Apology accepted, William,' says Mr Finch, 'but be here on time for meals in the future, unless you've told us otherwise in advance.'

Mrs Finch pats his hand. 'It sounds as if you were trying to do the right thing.'

'What's this chap's name again?' Mr Finch says, before blowing on his apple pie.

'Ray Price,' William says, lifting a fork of cold sausage and potato to his mouth. 'I'm not sure he's going to make it,' he says as another burp explodes from his mouth.

It's too much for Gloria; her full-throated laugh fills the room.

'Sorry,' William says again. Gloria flings her head back. Her abandon is irresistible and soon they are all laughing.

36

William wonders if he will always be reminded of uncooked chicken at this moment; the slack, loose skin, the absence of urgent blood that you expect when flesh is sliced open. It's their first post mortem case. A fifty-nine-year-old man.

Three weeks into their training, they've watched several embalmings, helped suture, and raised veins and arteries. A post mortem case is a completely different matter. The body has already been opened by medics examining the internal organs to determine the cause of death. Their rough and ready suturing has to be undone, the sternum reopened, the organs taken out again. Once the body and the organs have been treated, the sternum is put back and the skin stitched together – this time neatly. It takes hours.

Arthur has a different suturing style to Uncle Robert – he holds the needle at a different angle and his movement is less fluid – but the result is the same; a perpendicular ridge down the torso. As he stitches, Arthur's tall frame hunches in concentration over the body. The careful needlework will never be seen by the family – it will sit beneath the gown, or suit, or whatever clothes have been chosen – but still, Arthur takes his time. It matters. Somebody loved this man and even if there's no one left to mourn him, he's still a person, and embalmers have to believe that people matter. If they didn't, why would they do their job every day?

Two and a half hours after he started, Arthur ties off the suture.

'Ray?' he says, breathing out heavily and finally looking up. 'What's the mnemonic we use for remembering completion procedures?'

Oh no. When Ray's put on the spot, he never knows the wretched answer, however simple and obvious. This one could be particularly painful, because he might try and guess it. At least he's cut his fingernails and knows now to keep them clean. William imagines him at the sink in his bedsit, scrubbing at his hands. His hair is still matted and haywire.

Ray stares at the window for a moment, then lifts his eyebrows. 'Fold her frock and put it in the drawer?'

Arthur's jawbone twitches but his face remains expressionless. 'And what do you think that stands for, Ray?'

Ray catches William's eye and winks. William shakes his head slightly and looks back at the body.

'Can't remember, sir,' Ray says, with that terrible cheerfulness.

'William?' Arthur says.

'Pack Her Cotton Dress Clean Today Please,' he says quietly.

'Correct.' Arthur turns his body towards Ray. 'Say it.'

'Pack Her Cotton Dress Clean Today Please,' Ray speaks loudly and clearly. William knows that this cocksure manner is only to save face and that when he goes back to his bedsit it's another story, but he wonders if he should tell Ray how annoying it is.

'And William, please tell your colleague here what it stands for.'

'*Pack* is pack orifices. *Her* is set hair – or shave as appropriate. *Cotton* is cosmetise, if necessary. *Dress* is dress as directed by family. *Clean* is clean all mortuary equipment. *Today* is tidy up and check stocks. *Please* is attend to personal cleanliness.'

'Thank you, William.' Arthur clasps his hands. 'I'd like you to take charge of these proceedings with Ray as your helper, and please give a running commentary on what you're doing and why.'

'Yes, sir.'

'Good. And Ray?'

'Yes, sir.'

'Humour is important – embalmers need it to keep sane. But I'm telling you now, you will *not* use humour to cover your ignorance. I will *never* find it amusing that you have failed to learn even the most rudimentary of things. Things have got to change. Do you understand?'

While William agrees with Arthur, he sorely wishes he'd say these things to Ray in private. Roger and Simon, working with Norman at the next table, can hear every word, and each public humiliation stokes Ray's resentment, which William will then have to endure at the pub. Outside, a car with a hole in its exhaust splutters, darkening the window high up on the white wall. Ray meets Arthur's stare.

'I understand, sir.'

'Good,' replies Arthur. 'Off you go, William, and ask Ray to assist as and when you need him to.'

William moves closer to the table. Neither Ray nor Arthur has any idea just how familiar he is with Pack Her Cotton Dress Clean Today Please, nor what a salvation it was when he found himself back in Sutton Coldfield. In fact, in his mid-teens he used to worry sometimes about how much he loved the H and the C.

. . .

If mourners commented on how their loved ones looked so peaceful, so *themselves,* Robert didn't tell them it was the work of his fifteen-year-old nephew, but he always passed on the compliment.

'That's down to you. I may do a decent job, but they can't see those bits. What means most to them is the part you played.' And he'd touch William's shoulder, or rest his hand briefly on his head, even though by now, William was taller than him.

Sometimes, as he finished up on the H and started on the C and found he instinctively knew what colour eyeshadow to put on, how much or how little blusher, what nail varnish, William wondered if he was a poofter after all – that's what they were called at his new school. Sometimes he wished he was. He could be like his uncle and Howard. He could get Martin back – he need never have lost him.

But it was girls he liked. When the bus stopped at Sutton Coldfield Grammar School for Girls and they streamed on, it was their faces, legs, and the imagined shape of their breasts under their uniforms that William thought about. Sometimes, when he couldn't summon the will not to, he'd think of Imogen Mussey and those intense few days at their home. He always regretted that indulgence though, because it inevitably led to Martin. It seemed every good thought in his head had to lead to something bad. The thrill of the bed hop to the humiliation of a beating. The kindness of Martin to the cowardice of William's betrayal of him. The beauty of the 'Miserere' to the shock of his mother's spite.

Stop it. Forget it. All of it.

. . .

'So, first is Pack,' William states now, looking briefly at Arthur and Ray before pincering a sizeable chunk of cotton wool with large metal tongs. 'For pack the orifices.' Lifting the man's thin legs and bending them back towards his stomach, as if he's a giant baby, William inserts the wad up his backside.

37

'I've got a proposition for you, William.'

They're walking to the pub at lunchtime, beneath a late November sky of vivid uninterrupted blue. Their breath hangs briefly in little clouds as they walk along the narrow pavement, hands deep in pockets, elbows bumping. There are as many leaves on the ground now as on the trees. Those still on the branches wave in the wind, their outlines defined without over-lapping foliage. William feels an urge to reach up and pluck the lower ones off, to bring them to their inevitable end more quickly.

'What's that, then?' he says without enthusiasm.

'I'll pay you in beer to be my private tutor.' Ray smiles. 'I need to qualify, William,' he says, more seriously. 'You can help me, you're bloody brilliant.' He looks ahead for a few paces then back at William. 'What do you think?'

'Pity I don't like beer,' William replies. Ray went some way to redeem himself that morning by being an attentive helper throughout the completion process. He made no quips, asked questions, and congratulated William at the end in Arthur's hearing.

'No problem,' Ray bats back. 'There's plenty of water, hot or cold, your choice.' They laugh, slowing down as they arrive at the pub. 'So, what do you think?' Ray pushes the door and holds it open for William as the stale smoke blends with the fresh air.

'We can give it a go' – William rests his hands on the bar – 'but after two weeks, either of us can decide to stop. And I don't care what you say, I won't miss my evening meal, so it'll have to be straight after class and it can't be for longer than an hour.'

'Couldn't we do it later on?' Ray looks happy. 'After you've eaten?'

'No. That's when I do my homework.' *And talk to Gloria in the kitchen*, he thinks.

'Deal!' Ray's face is transformed, and William thinks not for the first time that if Ray took any trouble with his appearance, he could be handsome. Ray reaches into his pocket as the barman nods his head at them.

'A pint of bitter, and for you, William? This one's on me.'

'Half a pint of cider, please,' William says to the barman, who nods again and walks away to the pumps.

'How about, in return,' Ray says, 'I give you a bit of advice, man to man. My guess is you're not the most experienced when it comes to the ladies, and I've got the feeling you're soft on this Gloria.'

William shrugs, looks down at the bar and bends back a corner of a beermat.

'Pretty, is she?'

'Very.' William can't help grinning.

Their drinks arrive and Ray pours a pile of change into the barman's hand, who counts it then gives him some back. They head towards what has become their spot in the corner by the window. William takes his first gulp of cider. It flows down his throat easily.

'Have you made a move?' Ray says.

'I'm not sure what that means, but we talk a lot,' William says. 'She makes me cocoa every night.'

'Steady on, that kind of behaviour could land you in a lot of trouble!'

208

'Take the mickey all you want!' William can't help but laugh. 'I like talking to her and I like drinking cocoa.'

'If you do want to step things up, and you need any advice, I'm your man. Let's just say I've packed an orifice or two in my time.'

William winces, can't help it.

Ray's confidence visibly falters. 'I know you think I'm a loser, but you could at least try and hide it.'

'I don't think that,' he half lies, feeling guilty, 'sorry.'

Ray softens at the apology. 'Who'd have guessed there were boys in this world who spent Saturday mornings putting make-up on stiffs?' Ray warms to his theme. 'Not me, that's for sure.'

'Not *every* Saturday.' William laughs. 'And not until I was fourteen.'

'Why fourteen?' Ray frowns. 'Is that the age of initiation?'

'It's when I moved in with my uncle.'

'Why?'

'It's complicated.'

'I might not know where a carotid artery flows from and to, but I'm sure I can follow your living arrangements.'

William is relieved to see the time on his watch. He gulps down the rest of his drink and picks up his coat. 'Right, I'm off.'

Ray looks at the clock on the wall. 'We've got ten minutes yet.'

'I haven't. I'm going out with Arthur.'

'Where?'

'Home visit, council bigwig. His wife wants him embalmed at home.'

'I see,' Ray says, his face closed down, smile gone. 'Golden Boy to the rescue.'

Arthur has never invited Ray to a home embalming, and

209

this is the third time William has been asked. But the flicker of sympathy William feels is extinguished by a sudden and strong feeling of superiority.

'Talking of advice, I've got some for you.'

'What's that then?' Ray stands and puts his coat on.

'Get a haircut. Even if your marks improve, you won't get asked on any home visits looking like that.'

William's afternoon goes well. Arthur praises his work and professional, solicitous manner with the councillor's widow. But the whole thing is sullied for him because of the fiery colour that rose on Ray's face before he had time to laugh it away.

• • •

If his mother had come to get him sooner, before the summer holidays, William would have gone. But after the gazumping, the new house wouldn't be ready until the end of October, and the unexpected promotion she got when her boss had a heart attack meant she was incredibly busy, so it was agreed he'd see the half-term out in Sutton. Before Ash Wednesday, the thought of moving to Wales had some appeal, but after he'd gone cold turkey on choral music and promised himself never to sing in public again, the last thing he wanted was Evelyn pushing him to join a male voice choir. And anyway, by then, William was certain about his future. He kept telling Uncle Robert and Howard he wanted to stay with them, but neither seemed to hear him.

And then, half-term arrived and one day there she was, all perky and bright getting out of her new Ford Anglia, which, William noticed with irritation from his window, matched her burgundy lipstick and shoes.

210

Robert, Howard and Evelyn were standing in the hall, the first time they had been together since the dreadful evening of the 'Miserere'. Still in his room, he put the suitcase that Robert thought had been packed for two days back on top of his wardrobe, breathed in deeply and walked downstairs.

'Here you are!' Evelyn watched him descend, beaming. She registered his empty hands and her smile hardened. 'Everything's ready for our big adventure.' She tried to take his hand but he pulled it out of her reach.

'I don't want an adventure.'

Evelyn didn't miss a beat. 'You'll meet people your own age. *All* the young men down there sing in choirs.'

'I don't want to sing. I want to be an embalmer. Here.'

'How can you possibly know that?' Her smile was getting weaker, her tone sharper.

'Because I've been doing it. Every day.' From the corner of his eye, he saw Robert and Howard look at each other.

'For goodness' sake, Robert.' Her head swung to him. 'A fourteen-year-old boy spending his time in a funeral home? What were you thinking?'

'It was my idea,' William interjected. 'I'm good at it, aren't I, Uncle Robert?'

Robert looked, helpless, from William to Evelyn.

Frustration swept afresh across her face as she turned on the two men. 'Will you ever accept that William is *my* son, not yours!' Robert and Howard met her furious gaze with their own, but said nothing. 'It's such a *waste!*' She turned back to William, thumping the side of her thighs, making her bag slide down her arm. 'You've got a gift. I won't let you throw it away.'

'If anyone threw it away, it was you.'

At that, Evelyn's body stiffened. All her agitation and

frustration seemed to concentrate on her stillness. She studied William's face as if Howard and Robert weren't there any more. 'Are you going to hold that moment against me until the day I die?' she asked softly.

William shrugged, worrying that if he spoke, he'd lose his resolve.

'You know, William, I think I miss you as much as I miss your father. I don't know where he's gone, but the boy I raised has disappeared.'

He really thought he might be about to cry, and for some reason, at that moment, he knew this must be avoided at all costs. He turned his back on all of them, climbed the stairs, closed the door to his room, and sat on the bed.

'Evelyn, this was *not* my doing.' Robert's voice eventually broke the hostile silence. 'I've never encouraged him and I've never countenanced him staying here beyond this week. This . . . this determination has come from him alone.'

'You say that' – William recognised his mother's tone; shaky but steely all at once – 'but ever since he was born, you've wanted to get your hands on him. I've seen the way you look at him, like he's yours!'

'Really, Evelyn?' said Howard, with an edge of anger in his voice. 'Still this? You know, the tragedy is that Paul adored you. You never had anything to be jealous of.'

'I did!' she batted back. 'I was jealous of how you came swanning into this family with enough love for *everyone* when I only seemed to have enough for Paul and William. You made me look as if I never had enough love.' There was a pause, then: 'What are you grimacing at, Robert?'

'Do you want William to hear this?' Robert replied.

'Of course I don't!' She raised her voice. 'But what I want and

212

what I get rarely match up, Robert. I *want* my son to come and live with me, but evidently he doesn't.'

'So what are we going to do?' Robert said. 'Frogmarch him to the car?'

During the next silence, William found himself worrying that they hadn't even offered her a cup of tea. It was three hours from Wales to here. She must have been thirsty, and hungry. William tasted salt in the corner of his mouth. He wiped his face.

Then her feet were running up the stairs and his door opened so fast, he jumped. Her eyes were hectic, but she stood in the doorway composed, and when she spoke, it was slow and calm.

'I can't force you to come with me, and I can't force you to forgive me, so I'm going. I love you, and there'll always be a home for you with me, but I'm not going to write any more letters for you to ignore, or call you on the phone for you to refuse to speak to me. When you're ready, I'll be there.'

William waited a minute, then followed her down the stairs.

'I'll be in touch about sending you money,' she said to Robert as she walked out of the front door. Robert stared at the ground, flexing his jaw.

'Don't you want a cup of tea?' William couldn't help but shout from halfway up the stairs, gripping the banister.

She turned, and for a brief moment, they actually saw each other. Breaking the connection, she shook her head. 'Not to worry, I'll get something on the road.'

So they stood on the driveway and watched her get in the car. She didn't even look at him before she drove away.

He watched her car reduce to the size of a postage stamp, a small but powerful pressure point of pain in his sternum.

38

It has taken him twenty-five minutes to walk from the station to the avenue on which the Finches live. His hair is freshly trimmed and he wears his new winter coat, half price in the Boxing Day sale at Rackhams. Howard, his shopping companion since he was thirteen, thought this one particularly dashing. His fifth Christmas without seeing his mother. He's ready for the new term. Ready to see Gloria.

The cool air shoots into his lungs like peppermint. The branches of the plane trees lining the street are thick black fingers reaching for the blue sky. His leather shoes hit the pavement with a crisp *clap-clop* as he lets his suitcase swing loosely. The metal clasps on either side of the handle squeak briefly with each of his steps. His left hand is deep in the silk lining of his pocket, clasped tightly round the key to the Finches'. He's missed Gloria over Christmas and has decided to be more forthright about his feelings. He takes no notice of the semi-detached Georgian houses, the few traces of dirty snow on the pavement. The avenue is simply a broad funnel of excitement, down which he's happily tumbling towards her.

At the doorstep, he imagines for a moment that this is his house and that inside, his wife is waiting for him.

'Hello! I'm back. Anyone in?' The hallway is warm. It's not the feel of an empty house.

'In the kitchen, William. Happy New Year.'

Even lovelier than he remembered, that full, textured voice, the slight Cockney inflection. Smiling, he puts his suitcase on the bottom stair and hangs his coat over the blue ball next to the yellow one, on which Gloria's russet coat hangs as usual. No other coats.

'Happy New Year to you too!' he replies. 'Kettle on?'

'For you? Always.'

He smooths his hair and walks down the busy brown carpet towards the stippled glass of the kitchen door. Pushing it open, he thinks of his resolve to be bolder.

'Hello, favourite Finch.'

'Better not tell my parents that!' she bats back, grinning too as he stands in the doorway.

There's rock and roll coming from the transistor radio and there's a plate of mince pies on the counter. It's warm and cosy and Gloria is smiling her most lovely smile at him. But his has disappeared and he's not even looking at her, or the pair of scissors in her one hand and the comb in the other. He's looking at the man sitting on the chair that's normally in the dining room, with a white towel round his neck, smattered with black semi-circles of cut, wet hair.

'Ray! What are you doing here?'

Remaining very still as Gloria takes the scissors to his head, laying her free hand on the bare nape of his neck, Ray replies, 'What does it look like? I'm getting a haircut.'

Sitting on the counter, almost enjoying the scorch of hot tea down his throat, William watches Gloria carefully wipe the hairs from Ray's neck.

'There you go. Smart as the best of them, Ray. No one can have a go at you now.' She looks over at William. 'You should give them what for, William.'

Fury bubbles in his chest, but he keeps his face blank. 'Who?'

215

'Those miserable buggers on your course who told Ray to get a haircut.'

'Maybe they were trying to help,' he replies, looking at Ray. 'Everyone wants you to do well, you know that, Ray.'

'Well, I think it's rude,' says Gloria, taking the broom from the cupboard and making decisive sweeps across the lino, gathering Ray's hair into a silky wet pile at her lovely feet.

William slides down from the counter and takes the dustpan and brush from the cupboard under the sink. He kneels before Gloria, sweeps up the hair and tips it in the bin. Ray jerks upright. 'Oh, I was going to send a lock to my mum!' He winks at William.

'Help yourself.' William gestures at the bin.

'Anyway, William,' Gloria says, bright and breezy, 'how was your Christmas?'

'Good, thanks.' He hops back up on the counter, determined to look at home. 'I helped in the mortuary a lot.'

Ray laughs, and William could kiss Gloria when she says, 'Good for you, I bet your uncle loved having you back.'

'What about you, Ray?' William puts the pad of his finger on some toast crumbs left on the worktop; one, two, three of them. 'How was Leeds?'

'Didn't go.' Ray shakes the towel in the sink, fiddling with his collar, and then sits back down. 'There was snow forecast and I didn't want to get stranded.'

'And would you believe,' Gloria says, hands on curved hips, 'his landlady went away for two days and left him without any heating or hot water! At Christmas!'

Ray looks from Gloria to William and back to Gloria, mouth turned down, his eyebrows slightly raised.

'Awful,' William says, not believing a word, and then, because he can't stand it any longer, 'So how did you—'

The front door opens and Mrs Finch is in full flow coming towards the kitchen. 'They may be half price, but do we *want* psychedelic curtains in the lounge . . . William!' He jumps down from the counter; she approaches with open arms. 'Welcome back!'

'Happy New Year, Mrs Finch,' he says as she squeezes him round the waist. Mr Finch stands behind, in William's sightline. 'Happy New Year, Mr Finch.'

The kitchen is full of them now. Ray is the only one sitting, in the chair that shouldn't be there.

'My! Don't you look smart, Ray!' Mrs Finch rests her hands on Ray's shoulders. 'I told you Gloria would sort you out.'

William is confused. Mr Finch claps his hands and says, 'So, William, we did it. Are you pleased?'

'Pardon?'

'Took you up on your suggestion.'

'What suggestion?'

'What other suggestions have you made?' Mr Finch laughs. 'Offering the spare bed in your room to your friend.'

On 27th December, Ray had hand-delivered a letter to Mr and Mrs Finch introducing himself, a friend of William's (more like a brother really – after all William had done to help him). He described his impoverished digs, his struggle not coming from an undertaking background, his desire to qualify. How William was going to help him and had mentioned there was a spare bed in his room, and didn't think they'd mind another lodger. He knew this was presumptuous, but after spending such a miserable Christmas, he thought he'd got nothing to lose. The worst that could happen was that they'd say no – which he'd quite understand.

217

All this William picked up from the torturous meal they've just eaten. He was the only one who'd come off badly if he contested everything. So William nodded and smiled and laughed at Ray's jokes, who, transformed by his haircut, has well-tended nails and clothes less rumpled and grubby. William felt himself grow smaller with every joke Ray uttered and every burst of laughter from Gloria's mouth. It was not in him to compete, so he sat there growing quieter and smaller and meaner.

'You don't seem very pleased to see me,' Ray says, once they're in what used to be William's room, alone for the first time.

'What did you expect?' he stage whispers, not wanting the Finches to hear. 'Why didn't you ask me first?'

'I didn't think you'd mind. I thought we were friends.'

'What if I don't *want* to share a room – with a friend or anyone? You should have asked me, Ray!'

'And you'd have said no.' He drops the pretence. 'And I couldn't stand being in that place any more. And, though it's obviously not mutual, I like you, William.'

Ray snores. William lies on his side, feeling dark and coiled up inside. Ray is underhand and opportunistic. But once examined, his own feelings aren't pleasant either. It is true he doesn't want to share a room, but he hasn't said all the other things that are true; that he finds Ray crude, his ignorance embarrassing, that he is threatened by him and jealous of the laughter he so easily drew from Gloria.

That night he dreams he's back in Cambridge. He and Martin are waiting in the bathroom for Matron to give them the dips.

'Martin, you've got boobs!' William says, and Martin laughs, cupping his puppy flesh in his hands and pouting his lips. When he wakes, William is left with the light feeling their friendship gave him. What he wouldn't give to have Martin lying in the other bed now.

39

The thick, yellow quality of the light tells him it's later than it should be. Ray's bed is empty, unmade as usual. William sits up, snatching his travel clock from the lace doily on his bedside table. Ten o'clock. Saturday. He puts it back and flops down again. Even though there's no college today, he'd normally be out of the house by now.

When he had the room to himself, he'd do a couple of hours' study first thing, then wander down Bethnal Green Road, looking but not buying from the market stalls, get a paper and sit in the small cafe on the corner and have a go at the crossword. But with Ray in residence, he doesn't like to study in his room. He feels awkward about how much time he's happy to spend with his tatty old Scudamore, how calming and reassuring he finds it to understand more and more about the internal workings of the human body. He'd never tell Ray how privileged he feels to walk around knowing what there is under people's skin, a whole miraculous universe of efficiency and movement. As if he's been entrusted with the secret of everyone's insides. It pleases him, as he looks at someone in the street, that he'd know which is their external and which their internal carotid artery, that he could name every single bone in their skull. Yesterday, Arthur asked him if he'd ever considered medicine. He was pleased at the implication, but was sure he'd found his vocation. He'd like to share the thrill of this knowledge with someone, but he won't with Ray. He feels himself closing down.

He's polite with him as they sit squashed at their little table, which wobbles and creaks as they lean on it to write. William often finishes the half-hour tutoring with a headache. He has to flex his jaw and breathe in and out afterwards. Sometimes, he catches wafts of Gloria's perfume on Ray's clothes, and it's all he can do not to tip him off his chair.

With William's help, Ray's written work has improved, and his physical presentation no longer causes offence. His dark hair is parted and combed, his nails clean and filed. But still he shows little aptitude for the work, which William finds infuriating. Sometimes, when it's just the two of them carrying out a procedure, he simply intervenes, taking the instruments from Ray's clumsy hands and doing it himself. Ray rarely complains, but yesterday, when William snatched the aneurysm hook off him, he muttered, 'I know I'm useless, but why should *you* be so angry about it?'

William did not reply as he easily separated the neck tissue to find the vein that had eluded Ray.

The truth is, William thinks he'll never stop resenting Ray for lying his way into the Finches' home. He feels personally robbed, with the theft continuing day by day. He no longer ends the evening with a cup of cocoa and a chat with Gloria. She asks him, but she asks Ray too. As if he doesn't spend enough time with Ray as it is.

During the week, William's escape is Scudamore, but he quickly realised he needed something else for the weekend; to get him out of the house, out of himself. A poster for a Millais exhibition at the Tate Gallery got him there for the first time. One visit was all it took.

Big, beautiful and free; the Tate, the National Portrait Gallery and the V&A invite him in, to sit, to wonder, for as long as he wants. Paintings quickly become old friends to revisit, and no matter how long he spends strolling through the galleries, there is always something new to win his heart.

By ten o'clock on a Saturday, he'd usually be on a bus and on his way. But this morning, stepping onto the landing, the air feels still and cold, as if he's the only one in. He washes, dresses, then runs lightly down the stairs, feeling the relief of solitude. He pulls some bread from the waxed paper bag, lights the grill and lays the slice under the popping flame, turning it just at the right time. There's a new jar of the lime marmalade Mrs Finch sometimes buys because she knows he likes it.

He drops two spoons of tea into the dark earthy pot. He flicks on the radio and pulls the toast out; perfectly brown and crisp each side. His bare feet are warm and comfortable. Tony Bennett is singing 'I Left My Heart in San Francisco' and the margarine is melting nicely on his toast. He sips the tea and wipes the crumbs from the counter before taking a bite of the bread. Leaning against the worktop, he hums, then sings softly, blending his voice with Tony's, so used to not singing it feels transgressive. He sings louder, and it's good to feel the vibration in his chest and throat.

He turns the radio up and takes his plate to go into the dining room.

Gloria stands in the hall in her coat, cheeks red from outside, delight all over her lovely face. 'My God, William!'

'Sorry!' he says. 'I didn't hear you come in! I wouldn't have made such a racket if I'd known I wasn't on my own.'

'Racket?' she says quietly. 'It was bloody beautiful!'

He smiles at the floor. She comes closer and touches his hand, seeking eye contact by dipping her face below his.

'Talk about hiding your light under a bleeding bushel.' She

puts her bag on the floor, unbuttons her coat and swirls it off her shoulders, talking all the way down the hall to the coat hooks. 'Why on earth aren't you in a choir or something?'

He holds his half-eaten piece of toast which is now limp, over-soaked with marmalade. 'I was once,' he says. Gloria reappears and sits herself on the counter. 'I was a chorister for four years, in Cambridge.' He quickly drops his toast in the bin and rinses his plate under the running tap. 'Tea?' he says, pointing at the teapot.

Gloria swings her legs, her hands on the edge of the worktop. 'Thought you'd never ask.' She's grinning, looks as if she wants this, to be talking to him, like old times. 'Why haven't you ever told me?'

He reaches over her head to the cupboard and takes out a delicate cup. He pours the tea, holding the strainer above its rim, feeling the steam over his face. Eventually he shrugs his shoulders.

'It's never come up. Like it never came up that you cut hair.' He sees her surprise, as if he's slapped her with no warning.

'I'll cut your hair anytime you want, William.' She's defensive. 'I just thought you'd got that covered.'

The silence is too deep, too charged for either of them to pretend that they haven't entered strange and difficult territory, that everything is normal. The click and push of the front door is followed by a cool swill at William's ankles. There's a movement in the hallway, a darkening of the light.

'I'll respect that you don't want to talk about it,' Gloria says, 'but whatever it is, you can always talk to me.'

'What about?' Ray leans casually against the doorframe.

'Not for your ears, mister.' Gloria's voice is suddenly, dramatically bright and light, and though William knows she's doing

223

this to protect him, he's annoyed that Ray has put an end to their conversation.

'I'll mind my own business then,' Ray says, unperturbed by the brush-off. 'So' – he grins and rubs his hands together – 'still on for the dance tonight?'

William remembers a dance being mentioned, but he can't dance, or compete with Ray's constant charm offensive, so he said no.

'You bet,' Gloria says, picking up the bag she left on the floor. 'You coming, William?'

'No, not tonight.' He turns his back on them to rinse his cup under the tap.

'Pity,' she says, 'got myself a new pair of shoes specially.'

40

It's nearly two weeks since that unfinished conversation, two weeks since Gloria and Ray went dancing. It's been raining all day, and there's a bare tree branch that taps on the dark bedroom window with each gust of wind. Ray's at the cinema with a cousin who's in London for two days and Gloria's downstairs watching telly with her parents. William is at peace. If Gloria and Ray are out together, he can't settle. He tries to lose himself in his studies and sometimes it works, but when the front door finally opens and they're home, he realises that the gentle click and grind of the key in the lock is what he's been waiting for. Then he has to contend with Ray coming to bed, but at least when he's in their room, he's not with Gloria.

The branch scratches the window again at the same time as a gentle knock at his door. For a moment, he's confused.

'Hello?'

The door opens slowly, shushing across the carpet. 'All right if I come in?'

'Of course.' He tries to look casual, though Gloria has never come into his room before.

She leans on the door she's quietly closed behind her. The red cable-knit jumper is bulky, leading him to imagine the hidden contours of her upper body.

'Everything all right?' Gloria, normally so at ease with herself, is subdued, awkward.

'Yes, thanks.'

'I miss our chats.'

'Me too.' He makes a long job of putting his pens and ruler in the jam jar on the desk, concentrating on his hands. 'They're really piling the work on.'

'You could take half an hour's break, couldn't you?' She gathers her glossy hair in one hand and coils it round her fingers. 'Just a quick chat over cocoa, William, I'm not asking for the whole evening.'

'I'm sure Ray would be happy to oblige.' The barb is out before he can stop it.

'Yes, William' – there's a sting in her voice now too, and she's no longer leaning against the door – 'but I was talking about you, not Ray. And in any case' – her face is all frustration now – 'why can't the three of us be in a room together!'

'He moans if I keep the light on to study, so I have to get it done before he goes to bed.' He hates how he sounds, hates the crinkle at the top of Gloria's nose, drawing her dark eyebrows together, but he can't stop. 'And frankly, I'm with him all day. Why would I want to stand around in the kitchen with him in the evening as well?'

'Because I'm there too?' Her voice hardens to match his; her arms fold quickly across her chest. William's shocked at how angry she suddenly is. 'I came to tell you two things.' Her voice is loud enough to make William worry that Mr and Mrs Finch will hear. 'First, I miss talking to you, but you clearly have your reasons for staying away. Second, Ray has asked me to go out with him.' She's glaring at him. His eyes keep dropping to the carpet but he forces them back up to her face. 'Proper, like,' she says, 'and I just wanted to see if you had anything to say about that.'

What to say? He stares at her now. *What to say?* They consider each other in a stony, hard silence and a coldness cascades through his insides, as if Matron is under his skin giving him the dips. But, miraculously, his shoulders rise, as if of their own accord, in a casual shrug.

'I thought you already were. Do what you like, Gloria.'

Apart from a slight shift in her jaw, Gloria remains motionless, her green eyes boring into him. When she speaks at last, her voice is entirely different; soft and quiet, and not quite hers.

'Well, at least we both know where we stand.' She opens the door. 'Goodnight, William.' The click of the latch behind her is unhurried and deliberate. He stares at his dressing gown that hangs on the door peg, drab and limp.

Spring is ruined. The white and green of snowdrops, daffodils luminous with sunshine and proud scarlet tulips become one with the sharp discomfort of watching Ray and Gloria.

At dinner, Ray is shameless, his hand at Gloria's back, creeping under her jumper or up her skirt a little, as their knees touch beneath the teak table. Lying in the same room as him each night, wondering what he and Gloria have got up to, sets William's insides against themselves. He's pretty damn sure what his roommate is thinking about as he tosses and turns for the first half-hour after he gets into bed. And when William is woken by the rapid creaking of bedsprings, he's disgusted. The keenest torment, however, comes from within. It's himself he loathes. She asked him, *asked* him if he minded her going out with Ray. If he knew what had stopped him telling her the truth, he might find some peace, some way of coming to terms with it.

By the time the Finches' garden is a frenzy of rhododendrons, poppies and delphiniums in the crisp May sunlight, William and his cohort are three quarters of the way through their training. Nights are long and mild. William continues to excel and Ray continues to scrape by, but the jokes at his own expense and his generosity at the bar each lunchtime have won Simon and Roger over and Ray is accepted as part of the group.

Over dinner, Gloria scolds Ray and tells him he needs to buck his ideas up. Ray says he's sure that once he gets a job in a good undertakers, he'll fly. When he says things like that, Mr Finch remains silent, and Mrs Finch says things like, 'Well, let's see.'

With four months left at college, William glances at the *Room to Let* ads held by the criss-cross elastic on the newsagent's noticeboard. He always thinks he'll come back and look when he's not with Ray, but he hasn't yet.

41

William arrives home in time for Mrs Finch's Sunday roast and knows immediately that something is wrong. They're already seated, which is not unusual; William routinely arrives home just in time to slide into his place at the table. Meticulous in helping clear away and wash up, he's polite and helpful, but gives nothing of himself away. If he's ever on his own with Mr and Mrs Finch, he relaxes a little, but he's still on his guard for fear he'll tell them their daughter deserves better than Ray Price.

At the Tate all morning, William has been looking at the Pointillists. Last week he found if he stood in front of Millais' *Ophelia*, half an hour could feel like five minutes. Forgetting everything except the thick gloopy elegance of a Van Gogh, or today, the miraculous precision of a Seurat, gives him respite. Galleries and museums were not part of his early childhood, but the chapel at Cambridge taught him that genuine works of art have the stamina to captivate the same pair of eyes again and again.

Entering the dining room today, the silent animosity feels as colid as the table. None of them looks up. Mrs Finch's face doesn't break open with a smile; no, 'There you are, William.' She's piling mashed potato onto her husband's plate, with a loud clatter of metal spoon on china. Mr Finch's eyes are on the table-mat in front of him, hands resting either side of it. Most disturbing is Gloria's left hand, misshapen by the pressure of Ray's grip.

'Hello,' William feels compelled to say.

'William,' says Mr Finch, barely moving his face.

'Hello, William,' says Gloria quietly.

'Everything OK?' he asks, looking briefly at each of them.

'You've caught us at an awkward moment,' says Mrs Finch.

'Should I leave?' he says. 'I can eat out.'

'Stay where you are.' Gloria is stern.

'Would you just cut the wretched chicken, Reg!' Mrs Finch snaps.

Mr Finch leans across and starts slicing. William is hungry and, as the white meat tips and falls away from the carcass, he's tempted to reach out and grab a piece of crispy skin.

Mr Finch glances at William, his upper body juddering with the rapid carving. 'I'm afraid we've just had bad news, William.'

Gloria drops her head. Ray squeezes her hand again. She pulls it out of his grip and places it in her lap.

'I'm not sure I like you describing it as *bad* news,' Ray says, and William sees Gloria close her eyes for a second.

Mrs Finch, who has been half standing, half sitting, dishing up and handing out the plates, drops to her seat and rests her head in one hand, hiding her eyes.

'I'm pregnant, William,' Gloria says. 'Up the junction, up the duff, whatever you want to call it.'

Mrs Finch starts crying quietly.

'Oh!' William feels hot.

'So, we're getting married!' says Ray, a rictus grin on his face. 'In fact, we'd like you to be our best man, wouldn't we, Gloria?'

'Oh!' he repeats.

Mr Finch looks at his wife, transfers the bowl of roast potatoes from her placemat to his and unceremoniously drops them onto everyone's plates.

William realises he can't stay a second longer. 'I think it's best if I leave you all to it.' He's standing now. 'Thank you, Mrs

Finch, it looks lovely, I just . . .' Words won't work for him, and it's all he can do not to run down the hallway to the door.

'Bloody hell, William,' says Ray that night in their room, 'what the hell was all that about at lunch?'

'Shut up,' William says, turning to face the wall. 'Shut the bloody hell up.'

'I don't see why *you're* in a state. It's me who's got to get hitched all of a sudden, me who's going to have to work for her bloody father, when I was hoping to live a little.'

Before he knows it, William is out of bed. 'And it's *me* who loves her!'

Ray stares up at him from the edge of the bed where he sits in his vest and pyjama bottoms. 'You saying I don't?'

'You wouldn't catch me complaining if I was in your position.'

'But there's the difference, William. You're not in my position, because you *let* me take her from under your nose, and didn't do a damn thing to stop me.' He shakes his head. 'I thought at least you'd put up a fight' – he laughs – 'and the stupid thing, William, is that you wouldn't have had to fight very hard. You know, when I asked her out, she said she needed to clear something up, and I thought, damn, she's going to ask you – give you a last chance to declare your love, or something daft. But I'm guessing she can't have, because I can't believe even you would have been that stupid.'

William steps towards Ray, his chest like a bellows, feeling the only conclusion for the forces at work in his body is a thump on Ray's nose.

'Oh, sweet Jesus,' says Ray softly, looking intently back at William. 'She did, didn't she?'

231

William can't speak.

'You idiot.'

William clears his throat to try and stop the weird fluttering sensation.

'You bloody idiot.' Ray climbs under his sheets.

William sits on his bed, hating himself far more than he hates Ray. What if he'd told her that yes, he *did* mind her going out with Ray? He minded with every muscle, every bone, every drop of blood in his body, that he knew he could make her happy – he *knew* he could. But not now Ray's baby is nestled inside her warm body.

'All that matters,' he says, exhausted, 'is that you look after Gloria.'

'I know, I know,' Ray says quietly, 'I'm not a complete bastard.'

William gets back into bed. 'Don't ask me to be your best man.'

'Oh, come on, I haven't got any other friends in London.'

'Ask Roger, or Simon.'

Gloria and Ray are to be married in three weeks, on 23rd July, in the local registry office. The hope is Gloria won't be showing too much. William can tell already. It seems he knows her body too well; the curve of her stomach, the fullness of her breasts. It's torture.

Six days after William walked away from his roast dinner, he and Gloria are the only ones at home. This rarely happens. Mrs Finch is at her sister's, Ray's on an evening home visit with Mr Finch. Now it's a given that Ray will work for him, Mr Finch is taking an interest in his training. Assignment finished, William slips down to the kitchen for a cup of tea. After the scream of the kettle has died down, and the fridge door has clunked open and shut, and his teaspoon has been swilled under the tap and dried, William has no more excuses to ignore the sound coming from the sitting room.

Gloria's sobbing connects with some deep anxiety he doesn't understand. She must know he's in the kitchen, that he can hear her crying. He fights the strong feeling he has that he mustn't intrude, quickly makes a second cup of tea and takes them into the sitting room.

'Cuppa?' He holds it out to her, waits for her to thrust her tissue up her sleeve.

'Ta,' she says, sniffing a few times. She doesn't look at him as he sits next to her.

'You OK?' he says after a few moments.

'It's going to be awful.'

'What is?' *Her life,* he thinks, *her marriage?*

'The wedding. There'll be hardly anyone there.' She's about to cry again. William's arm lifts to rest across her shoulders, but he lowers it. 'Ray said his family are Catholic and would only disapprove, Mum's too ashamed to invite her family, so it'll just be my sister's lot and Dad's brother and his family – who I can't stand.'

She looks at him for the first time. 'Oh, William! This isn't the sort of wedding I thought I was going to have!'

'It's not the sort you deserve,' he mutters.

'And you won't be best man!' She frowns. 'It'd make a bad day bearable to have you there, being kind and calm.' It melts him to hear her say that. 'Too good for us, are you, now I'm pregnant?'

'No. No!' He's appalled that's what she thinks. 'That's not why.'

233

'Why then?'

Is she daring him? How can he? He's not just sitting next to Gloria, but her and Ray's unborn child.

'Of course I'll be best man,' he says softly, 'I'll be the kindest, calmest best man to set foot in the Stepney registry office.'

She leans her head, heavy, on his shoulder. 'Thanks, William.' He doesn't dare move until she sits back up.

Later in his room, he remembers the nights he spent listening to his mother's sobbing after his father died. He feels leaden with the same sadness and impotence.

The sun is burning away the glisten of last night's rain on the pavement, and a soft layer of mist surrounds Ray and William as they walk to college, for most of the way in silence.

'I've told her I'll be best man,' William says eventually over a fierce chirruping in the swaying hedge. Ray's shoes graze the pavement as he stops suddenly.

'Thank God for that. Pity you couldn't have said that a week ago and saved Gloria all that upset.'

'She said none of your family are coming.' William walks on.

'Shotgun weddings aren't their style.'

'But eventually they'll want to see their grandchild, won't they?'

They've reached the college's grey edifice. Ray looks at his watch then leans against the wall. William does the same. 'Their *grandchild*, is the fruit of our sin. Don't worry, I'm not depriving our child of anything.'

'That's tough.'

'They're the least of my worries. I've just got to get married, pass my exams, and be a father. That's enough for now.'

Following Ray up the steps, William thinks, not for the first time, if he was going to spend the rest of his life with Gloria, and her luscious body was the home for his baby, he'd happily run over hot coals to college every morning and still have a smile on his face.

42

He's with her when it happens.

'Come on you, let's have a last cocoa together, for old times' sake,' she says when he meets her in the kitchen. 'You'll be gone in a couple of days!' She puts her head on one side and beams her warmth at him. 'What do you say?'

William has found a room just round the corner from college. His landlady is ancient but pleasant. It'll only be for two months and then he'll be back in Sutton with Uncle Robert and Howard. He's got used to the ache in his heart, and to make life as easy as possible for Gloria he's acted cheerful and normal, and they are almost back to how they were before Ray turned up. Mr and Mrs Finch are in the sitting room watching *Armchair Theatre*, just as they were on his first night back in September. Ray is upstairs.

'All right.' He smiles and sits himself on the counter next to the kettle. It's worth the effort to hide his feelings to draw that smile from her. She turns and bends down to lift the milk bottle from the fridge. William's heart kicks and he feels the jump of blood rush straight to his face. A huge crimson flower is blossoming across the back of Gloria's skirt.

'Gloria!' he shouts instinctively. 'You're bleeding!'

The milk bottle clatters into the sink and Gloria twists round to look. 'Oh God!' She looks at him, her face creased and helpless.

Mrs Finch is there already, taking Gloria by both arms. 'Let's get you to the loo. Reg! Get the car ready, we're going to the hospital.'

They all go, except William. Ray carried Gloria back down the stairs without his shirt on, so William took off his and gave it to Mrs Finch for him.

The sudden silence thunders through the hallway after Mrs Finch snaps the door shut behind them, even though he was there ready to do it for her. He turns and sees the heavy, gummy drops of blood on every stair tread. He goes to the sink and puts cold water in the bowl, takes a knife from the cutlery drawer and a Tupperware box from the cupboard. He gets the worst of it off with the knife. The smell doesn't bother him – he's used to far worse. He gets his own nail brush and, with salt and cold water, scrubs at each crimson spot. Concentrating on what he's doing, he can manage. *Just get this beige carpet clean before they come home.* That's all. He knows nothing about miscarriages, but hopes because they got to the hospital quickly, she'll be all right.

Staring intently at successive small patches of carpet, he doesn't notice the failing of the light until he's reached the top. He flicks the bulbous switch and doesn't see any red or rose blush on the stair carpet. He gathers the damp toilet paper he's used to soak up the water and turns towards the bathroom to flush them away, glad he's saved them from this, at least. But there's more blood on the landing and he chides himself for not anticipating that. Finally, after more scraping, dousing, scrubbing and blotting, it's done. With tight shoulders and aching head, he wishes that someone could at least have called him from the hospital to say what's happening. Hands full of soggy, stained loo roll, William pushes open the door to the small toilet.

A sharp cry punches out of his mouth. In spite of his ignorance, he's pretty sure the gaudy mess in the toilet bowl means

237

Gloria and Ray are no longer expecting a baby. He stares at the scarlet muddle for a few moments, then, with goose bumps on his bare arms, William grips the Bakelite handle and pulls the chain.

43

'Isn't she beautiful?' William says.

Gloria still has her arm hooked through his, even though the walk is over.

'Mmm,' Gloria says, tilting her head at *Ophelia*, at the upturned hands and the half-open mouth.

'I don't think I've ever seen anything so lovely,' William says, smiling from the painting to Gloria and back to the painting again. 'Look at that tree trunk! I could reach out and stroke it – and those flowers on the water – and how real her hands look!'

'Mmm.'

'You don't sound impressed.'

'I am, it's just a pity she's dead!'

'I'm used to that, aren't I?'

She takes her arm from his and slaps his shoulder. 'You nutter,' she says, and starts to giggle. An older couple come to stand next to them. They turn from the painting to Gloria as she continues to laugh, and a small *tut-tut* can be heard as they focus on the canvas. Gloria looks at William and opens her eyes wide. Now she really can't stop.

William doesn't care about the couple. He doesn't care about the security staff noticing them. He wants to run to the nearest phone box so he can tell Mr and Mrs Finch, *I've made her laugh – she's laughing!*

'What are you up to this morning, William?' Mrs Finch politely asked when William joined them for breakfast that day.

'I'm off to the Tate.' He glanced at the piece of paper in

Gloria's hand, and the sight of the familiar slanted handwriting flung a pulse against his throat. 'Everything all right?'

She exhaled then nodded. 'At least now I've heard from him I can get on with forgetting him.'

'Sooner the better,' Mrs Finch said quietly.

Gloria flicked her wrist to open the folded letter and scanned it. '. . . "best that I cleared off. I don't think you or anyone else would want me sticking around . . ."' Her voice was harsh. Mr Finch dipped his head and studied his toast. 'He's right, isn't he?' Gloria swept them all with her bold gaze.

William caught Mrs Finch glancing at him. Mr Finch didn't look up. She ripped the letter in two, laid the pieces next to her plate, and took a gulp of tea.

'So, William, the Tate. You love it there, don't you?' Her skin was still pale, and she hadn't curled her hair, so it looked longer and thinner than normal, and her head smaller. All William has wanted to do since her return from hospital is hold her. Sometimes the feeling is so strong he has to fold his arms. He imagines nothing in return. He just wants to wrap her up and make her feel safe.

'I do,' he replied, 'I love the building as much as the paintings. And you can get a pot of tea and a cake for two shillings round the corner – a bit pricey, but worth it.' He was talking too much, but didn't want to lose her interest. Encouraged by the faint amusement on her face, he asked, 'Want to come with me? It's only a short walk from the bus stop.'

'Why not?' she said, glancing at her mum and then out at the garden, at the warm July morning. 'It's a nice day, isn't it? About time I got out.'

Mr Finch put his hand on his daughter's back and gently rubbed it. 'Good idea.' He rummaged in his pocket and put a pound note on the table. 'Tea and cakes are on me.'

Mrs Finch smiled and winked at William.

'Tea?' says William now, taking Gloria's elbow and leading her away from *Ophelia*.

'I've never been to an art gallery before,' Gloria says, her heels clicking on the wooden floor.

'Neither had I,' he says. 'There was a lot of art at Cambridge, but it was literally part of the furniture, so I didn't take much notice.' They turn left into the next room, past portraits of serious-looking men, and the light-catching gold of an enormous frame surrounding a dark, foreboding landscape.

'Why did you start coming?' Gloria cranes her neck before and behind William to take in what's on his side of the room.

'To begin with, it was a free-time filler that made me feel I was making the most of London, getting to see its treasures.'

'And now?' She turns her head to him.

'It's hard to explain.' He points left as they leave the gallery. 'I don't know much about art, but when I come out, I feel better, bigger on the inside. Look, here we are. You find a seat, I'll get the tea and stop talking rubbish.'

She stops in the cafe doorway. 'You're not talking rubbish. You say lovely things.'

He queues for the tea and teacakes, watching the butter dissolving into the teacake as the woman takes his money. As he walks towards Gloria sitting with her back to him, he plans to talk about the tutting lady; he wants to laugh with her again. He has to concentrate on the tray because the metal milk jug has been overfilled, but Gloria turns to look at him and his mouth goes dry. Laying the tray carefully onto the melamine table, he leans across and pats her arm. Her sobs are barely audible, but it must be clear to everyone in the cafe that she's crying.

'Sorry,' she says, touching the corners of her eyes with the pad of her finger. William notices the two women on the adjacent table have only crumbs left on their plates and he hopes they leave soon. He sits down.

'I'll be all right, won't I, William?'

'Of course you will,' he says, leaning towards her, 'it only happened three weeks ago.'

'I know I was barely pregnant,' she says, her breath catching, 'I wasn't even showing.'

'You were,' he says. She's staring at him and he thinks he'd probably do best to keep quiet, but she looks so eager, he carries on. 'Everything about you was different.'

Gloria watches him for a moment, then blows her nose on a paper napkin. 'It's the guilt.' She's matter of fact now. 'When I knew I was pregnant, I cried all morning.' She leans towards him, so their heads are almost touching. 'What if the baby knew I didn't want it?' she whispers. 'What if that's why I lost it.'

He takes both her hands; she pulls one away to wipe the drips from her chin but slides it back. William's elbow is nudged by the departing woman next to him, trying to tuck her chair back under the table.

'That *can't* be right.'

'I *did* feel like a mother,' she says, 'and that mattered more than all the other stuff – the shame, the rubbish wedding.'

'You'd have been *great*.' The words hang heavy and final. 'And you *will* be great,' he adds.

She looks at the table. 'What if that was my only chance? I'm used goods now, aren't I?'

'Don't ever call yourself that! And anyway, no one even knew you were pregnant. I did, but that's different.'

'Why?' She's waiting for him. Again.

242

A waitress has appeared next to them. 'We're closing in ten minutes.'

'Thank you,' says William, glancing at the pretty young woman. For a brief moment he imagines his heart being free to flirt with her, to start something new and fresh, without all the hurdles that lie between him and Gloria, without all these failures and missed opportunities weighing him down. The waitress clears their table and walks away, her flat shoes squelching on the floor. It's a fantasy. His heart isn't free, so why bother imagining it is?

'Maybe I won't be able to get pregnant again. Or maybe I will, but I'll keep having miscarriages.'

'I'm no expert,' he says, feeling woefully inadequate, 'but I'm pretty sure lots of women have miscarriages and then have healthy babies.' He stands and slides his jacket on, then pulls her coat off the chair and drapes it over her shoulders. 'I think you should try and be positive, for your own sake.'

'Easier said than done.' Gloria gets up.

'Another quick wander in the gallery before we go home?' William stands up. 'If we go in the opposite direction, we can do a loop and have one last look at *Ophelia* before we go.'

'Is that what you normally do?' There's a slight smile on her face.

'Yes.' He smiles back.

Even though he's on edge, he feels a lifting, a lightening at the delicate colours and textures of the Millais, the seeming miracle of transparent, colourless water rendered so perfectly. By paint! It's a relief to be standing there without the need to speak. Eventually, Gloria says quietly but clearly, 'I never loved him.'

Grateful that she's looking at the painting and not him,

grateful that he can reply to the painting and not Gloria, he asks, 'Why did you go out with him?'

'He was funny. Charming. We had a laugh.' She pauses and turns to him, but he keeps his gaze on the painting. 'And he *asked*.'

After a few minutes without either of them moving, she says quietly, 'I'm not sorry Ray's buggered off. But I am sorry I've lost my baby.'

And that's enough. He feels softened, yet bold enough to put his arm through hers. 'Uncle Robert said on the phone last night that they're booking tickets for the Ladies' Dinner Dance in Nottingham. It's the annual posh do for the Midlands Chapter of embalmers, don't know why they call it that.' He's talking faster and faster, suddenly desperate that she comes. 'It's on 22nd October, the day after I graduate. Want to come? It'll be something to look forward to.'

'Yes.' She puts her head on one side and smiles. 'Why not?'

44

NOVEMBER 1970, SUTTON COLDFIELD

The pile of tiny coffins reaches to the ceiling. He has to stand on a chair. His slurry-coated hands slip on the wood; he can't get enough purchase to pull it down. On tiptoe, he manages to hook one finger over the coffin's edge. His ankles wobble as he pulls it towards him. As the white casket tilts downwards, it knocks him back and a child's body flops out onto his chest. He hits the ground and the crushed skull nestles under his chin, the dried, bloodied hair scritch-scratching his throat. A woman kneels down, looks at the body draped over him, and starts to scream. He sits up.

The screaming continues; he feels the hot rush in and out of his lungs, Gloria's hand on his back.

'All right,' Gloria whispers, sitting up too with her arm across his back, her head on his shoulder. 'Shhh. I'm here.' It's him doing the screaming.

'Sorry.' He feels the sweat on his forehead.

She lies down and pulls him next to her, lays his head to her chest. 'Try to sleep.' Gloria's breathing starts to deepen and he tries to enjoy the gentle rise and fall of her. But of course, he won't go back to sleep. He hates that so many of her nights are disturbed like this – have been since the very beginning of their marriage.

He's only twenty-three and already married three years. He still marvels at being loved by her. The joy of it can make him want to shout out loud. On his own, in the mortuary, he'll find himself smiling at the very thought of her, at something funny she said at breakfast, or a kindness shown to him, or Robert, or

Howard. But on nights like tonight, it's guilt he feels, and before he can stop himself, his mind takes him back to the cold, dank phone box in the cheerless dusk after the Aberfan funerals. He said goodbye to her, resolved to forgo his own happiness for the sake of hers. He often tries to resist the memory, to walk himself out of that phone box and the conversation they're about to have. But it's so powerful it usually holds him hostage, like tonight, until it's run its course.

'Are you finished?' she'd said.

'Yes.' And there was indeed a sense of being finished, his clouded breath suspended above the heavy mouthpiece.

'Just so I'm clear' – Gloria spoke a little louder now, as if talking herself back into being – 'you're saying that because of what happened to those poor children, you don't want any of your own?'

'You weren't there, Gloria. The pain's too *big*. I couldn't bear it, I just couldn't.'

He heard her breathing, imagined her flowery fresh fragrance. She felt very close, as if he could have put his finger on the cross-hatch of the receiver and been able to feel her bold, soft lips.

'William' – her assured voice was back – 'I love you too. If you don't know that by now, you're a world class idiot.' He couldn't help but smile. 'I have a suggestion. Is that allowed?'

'It won't change anything.'

'Couldn't we, after all that's happened, just enjoy being in love? Not having to pretend we're not? Don't you think we deserve a bit of happiness? We're young. We can worry about children later.'

'No!' He trampled the bubble of joy in his throat. 'You can't marry me thinking I'll change – I won't. And you want children.'

246

'No, William!' She sounded angry. 'It's you I want, *you*!'

And in the silence that followed, with the cold of the concrete floor seeping through his soles, he dared to believe she was right and let himself fall into her gorgeous, naive love. They were married six months later.

■ ■ ■

As Gloria rifles through the basket of varnishes the morning after the nightmare, the familiar chunk and rumble of small glass bottles draws a smile from William.

'This one all right? She holds up a pearlised pink.

'Yep. Give it your best, she was a beautician. It's the first thing her daughter will look at.'

'What's her name again?'

'Barbara.'

'Come on then, Barb.' Gloria takes the left hand in hers. 'Let's get you gorgeous.'

Saturday mornings are William's favourite. With Robert and Howard playing golf, he and Gloria have the house to themselves. They take time over a cooked breakfast. Gloria tells stories from the hospital where she's now a psychiatric nurse, often putting a funny spin on things that couldn't have been much fun at the time. Their best times have always been chatting in a kitchen, with hot drinks and comforting food.

Occasionally, after breakfast, he'll have a weekend embalming to do. He's let off washing up then and, once Gloria's finished in the kitchen, she comes through to help with the cosmetology.

'I wonder what'll happen to her business.' Gloria gives Barbara's hand a rub before she starts filing the nails.

'Her daughter ran it with her.' William sprays the mortuary

247

table with disinfectant. 'They both lived above the shop. I suppose she'll just carry on.'

'Same set-up as us.' Gloria blows the dust from the filed nails and hooks the fingers over the side of the coffin.

William leans against the wall and watches her. She hasn't put her own make-up on yet, and her face is pleasantly pale and stark. *My wife*, he thinks.

'Do you mind us still living here?' he asks.

She picks up the nail varnish and looks at him. 'One day, I'd like a place of our own, of course I would, but each month without us paying rent, we've got a bit more in savings. There's no hurry, Robert and Howard are sweethearts.' There's a gentle *tick-tick-tick* as Gloria shakes the bottle. She laughs. 'Do you remember just after we were married, and I asked Howard how he'd fallen in love with Robert?'

'And he went the same colour as the tomato ketchup.'

Gloria laughs again, the gurgly, lush laugh that William wants to record he loves it so much. 'And Robert leapt up and started washing up, even though we hadn't finished eating.'

As a child, long before he understood their relationship, William knew, without any displays of physical affection, that Robert and Howard belonged to each other. When Howard put on one of his funny voices – Donald Duck, Popeye, Bugs Bunny – William saw the change in Robert's eyes, a visible softening. He and Gloria laughed in private that Howard still owned a house a few streets away, still had his mail delivered there, still spent a couple of nights there each week. But it sometimes makes William sad that they feel the need to keep so much of their lives hidden.

'Stick the radio on, William,' Gloria says.

He finishes wiping down the table, throws the paper towels

in the bin, walks to the radio on the window ledge. It's the Jackson 5, 'I'll Be There', and Gloria immediately joins in. William waits a moment, then harmonises. The mortuary is the only place he'll sing. Unlike him, Gloria can move her head to the music without it affecting the careful strokes of nail varnish. The DJ's banter washes over them for few minutes.

'We're invited to a christening,' Gloria says, 'Paula at work. I'd like to go to this one.'

'You sure?' He turns, holding the disinfectant to his chest.

'I like Paula.' Gloria is bent over, her face near the nails, but now she sits up straight, holding the brush over the bottle. 'And it's what people our age do, celebrate when friends have a baby.'

William kneels to put the container away in the cupboard. His back to her, he tries to slacken his jaw. Gloria doesn't miss a thing; she knows every physical manifestation of his inner world. She screws the top on the bottle, returns it to the basket, walks over to him and bends down to kiss his forehead.

'I'm going to this one, and if you'd rather not, fine. But don't try and stop me.' She ruffles his hair. 'I'll see you when you're done.' Her slippers slap her feet as she leaves. William remains crouched before the cupboard, the slow, heavy mingle of guilt and frustration in his gut.

She persuaded him that his aversion to parenthood shouldn't stop them getting married, but he's never been able to put his anxiety aside. Two months before their wedding, Gloria told him if he offered her a get-out clause one more time, she'd stand in the street and scream. He believed her, so he stopped.

William stands up now and walks to the coffin, unhooks Barbara's manicured hands. He breathes in the cool chemical whiff of the varnish.

'It's for her sake we shouldn't go, Barbara,' he says, 'not mine.'

45

Oddly, they've never actually argued about not having children. In the run-up to their wedding, it was a bust-up about Evelyn that he wasn't sure they'd recover from. Gloria had made it clear early on she wanted the full lowdown on his small, complicated family. It was hard, telling her the little he remembered about his father's shockingly quick death from cancer, about the close relationship that had existed between him, Uncle Robert and Howard, about his mother's insecurity, and him, slap bang in the middle of it all. Gloria was the only person in the world he'd told about his chorister days, about Martin and the horror of Ash Wednesday. She hadn't said a thing when he'd told her, just opened her arms and held him for a long time. He'd been so grateful for that; the feeling that no matter what, she was on his side.

But it was different a few weeks later, when he said it would be too awkward, too painful to have his mother at their wedding. He actually put into words that his mother was the villain in all this. She had cut short his time in Cambridge. She had broken up the family. She had left him to go to Swansea. It was all her fault.

Gloria looked horrified. He'll never forget the way she looked at him when he said that.

'You said she asked you to go with her to Swansea.'

'But she didn't *have* to go. She could have stayed in Sutton.' He got flustered and suddenly very angry. 'If you love me, Gloria' – his voice was quivering – 'you won't raise this again and you'll never ask me to forgive her.'

'I can't promise you that,' she said, as quiet and angry as him, 'but I pray to God that one day, you'll grow up and face this like a man.'

He stormed out of the house and didn't come back until late that night. But she was waiting for him, as if seconds, not hours had passed. She said if he wanted to marry her, then his mother wouldn't just be welcome at the wedding, she'd sit at the top table.

So that's what happened. Having put his own conditions on their marriage, he knew she had him over a barrel. Evelyn sat next to him at the wedding, but they barely spoke. He noticed how she smiled and talked with Robert and Howard, as if continuing conversations they'd been having without him knowing. Gloria held herself back, he could tell, for his sake. And that was the last he'd seen of his mother.

• • •

Monday morning and a full day ahead, with three bodies to look after. He does most of the embalming now. Uncle Robert and Howard handle front of house and admin, leaving him in the solitude he relishes; alone but not alone. After a big investment last year, the mortuary, though relatively small, is one of the most modern in Britain; rotatable porcelain embalming table, porcelain sluice, high-level extractor fan and a twin gravity stand. Everything has a place in the deep, high cupboards lining the walls. The three of them budgeted and researched it together, but it was William who took the lead, who knew what he wanted. The two older men were happy that for at least some of the time, William seemed at peace.

This morning, he checks the paperwork; the death has been

registered, it's a cremation, and both doctors have signed the forms. He wheels the table to the centre of the room and removes the sheet.

'Morning, Margery.' He touches her yellow waxy hand then reaches behind him to flick the radio on. The acoustics in the mortuary are dreadful really, like a cavernous bathroom, but he's grown to love it. It's Dana and 'All Kinds of Everything'; the simple tune has a kind of purity appropriate for this old lady with no wedding ring.

As he works, he hopes Margery will replace the bright flashes of the child's broken head nestling under his chin. 'Build Me Up Buttercup' now. The procedure comes so naturally to William that sometimes when he's finished, he can't remember carrying out parts of it at all, but his equipment and the state of the body tell him he has. He packs her orifices now, singing loudly, then gently lifts her into her coffin. He dresses her, cuts, files and cleans her nails, combs her hair, trims her eyebrows.

He has done a good job. But today is not a good day. The body has tormented him. Too big, too old, too clean, too whole. On a day like today, he'd prefer a post mortem job; a body already cut, disrupted and crudely stitched back up by the pathologist. And, God forgive him, on a bad day, he thinks that to find a child on the table might provide some sort of exorcism for the children of his dreams.

Later, he'll be aware of the look that flits between Howard and Robert over lunch, when he's *like this*. And he'll hear, when Gloria gets home in the evening, Robert and her talking quietly. He doesn't blame them. He sends Margery's body fluids down the sluice, wishing he could do the same with the contents of his fixated memory.

252

46

MARCH 1972

On Saturday 18th March, the morning of his twenty-fifth birthday, William is woken by Gloria kissing him loudly on alternate cheeks, twenty-five times, holding his face in her hands as she has every year since they've been married. He emerges from sleep smiling.

Having been sung to at breakfast by Uncle Robert, Howard and Gloria, and opened their gifts, it's now only the two of them. She's just sat on his lap in the kitchen and asked him if they can go to Cambridge for the day.

'I don't want to.' He snuggles into her soft body. 'It's my birthday, and you want me to be happy on my birthday, don't you?' He was hoping they could go back to bed.

Gloria reaches for her teacup on the kitchen table that's messy with birthday cards, wrapping paper, aftershave from Robert and Howard, a wallet from her. She takes a sip, puts the cup down and rakes her fingers through his hair. 'I think it would be good for you.'

'Enough.' William gently pushes her from his lap, stands, picks up his own cup and leans against the sink, immediately feeling damp seeping into his back. This is the third consecutive weekend she's suggested they take a train and go to evensong. 'Why make me remember things I want to forget?'

Gloria sits back down on William's vacated chair. 'Sometimes, I think all you *do* is try *not* to remember. It must be exhausting.' She picks up the unopened card they both know is from Evelyn and then gently rests it against the teapot. Later, she'll put it on the mantelpiece next to her own; one of the small, determined stands she takes to acknowledge his mother.

Looking across at him now, her face softens. 'I wouldn't ask to go to Aberfan, but evensong? In Cambridge? It's *beautiful*. What if you went, and actually enjoyed it?'

The teacup he's holding is suddenly so light and fragile, and his hand so tense, the only thing to do is hurl it at the wall.

William hates *World of Sport*, but Gloria leaves him alone when it's on, so with the broken teacup swept up and dropped in the bin, he's now in the lounge staring at Brian Moore talking about football teams he has no interest in.

Night sweats, bad dreams and waking flashbacks have been in their marriage from day one, a short six months after Aberfan, but Gloria seemed to take them in her stride, just as she seemed to take his determination to remain childless in her stride. It's getting on for six years since Aberfan. Six years! He'd hoped as time went on, his brain would calm down, that the electric-snap bursts of battered limbs, broken bones and most of all, parents' stricken faces, would start to fade. If anything, they're getting worse.

He has wondered about the other two Birmingham embalmers who went to Aberfan. Do they suffer like him? He knows Gloria would approve were he to get in touch with them. It's not the embalmers' way, he always concludes. At times it's a tough job, but William has always felt it's expected to bear those times quietly, with dignity.

William can't shake off the feeling, since Gloria made the move to psychiatric nursing, that she wants to cure him. He was pleased that unlike many of her friends, she never considered giving up work just because she was getting married. But when she talks about using his energy in the wrong way, and not facing things, he feels viewed through the lens of that Dr Kavannagh. Gloria says that other psychiatrists dismiss his talking therapy as hippy mumbo jumbo – so why she thinks everything he says comes from the mouth of God, he doesn't know.

Every time she suggests they go to Cambridge, so he can *face* things, he worries that what she really wants is for him to sort himself out enough to change his mind about children. Determined as he has been, he knows that this elephant in the room of their relationship will never go away. Even when she's too old to bear children, their absence will sadden her and judge him. It will never be settled. Ever.

He turns off the TV and quietly leaves the house to walk the ten minutes to the station, catching the earthy smell of imminent spring.

'Gloria?' he shouts up the stairs on his return.

'Yeah?' she calls from their room, and he recognises, with a beat of affection, how there's always hope in her voice, always the anticipation he's going to say something to please her.

He starts up the stairs, but she's coming down and they meet halfway. 'I've done something good.' He grins.

'What's that then?' She puts her hands on her hips, nonchalant, teasing, looking down from the higher stair.

He holds up the little oblongs. 'Train tickets to Cambridge. Today.'

Her slow, broad smile could warm the whole house. Her arms wrap round his neck and she pulls his head into her chest.

'And,' he says into the softness of her, 'I've booked us into a bed and breakfast, close to the station.'

Her arms tighten and she lets out a noise, untamed, that makes him laugh.

255

'I've wanted to do this for so long.' She lifts his head to look him in the eye. 'Thank you, William.'

'You're welcome,' he says, picking her up into a fireman's lift and starting up the stairs. 'We've got two hours.' Her slipper slides off and bumps down to the hallway.

47

'Thank God I brought the brolly.' Gloria looks through the mercury rain streaming diagonally across the window as the train slows into Cambridge.

'It never seemed to stop raining in winter.' William rests his hand on her knee. 'Our cloaks got so heavy, it made my shoulders ache.'

Gloria tilts her head and smiles. 'Poor little William.'

He squeezes her knee, making her yelp. They step onto the platform laughing, holding hands, and William lets himself hope they'll have a good time.

They drop their bags at the B&B first. It was a long shot, but he asked directory enquiries for the number of the guesthouse on Tenison Road that Mr and Mrs Mussey stayed in, always preferring to make a weekend of it even though they could only see Martin for two hours on the Sunday. As Gloria sits and bounces on the bed, running her fingers over the lilac candlewick cover, William wonders if the Musseys ever slept in this room, on this mattress. He tries not to think of Martin

It's cold for March. The little heater in the corner of the room clatters into life and they eat their sandwiches sitting on the bed. Afterwards, he puts his arm round her and rests his chin on her head, breathes in the smell of her hair. 'Plenty of time before evensong,' he says, pulling her down to lie next to him.

'Not enough for what you want.' She laughs, and they lie holding each other for a few minutes. When she sits up, pulls a comb from her bag and tugs it through her mane of hair, William watches, hands behind his head, smiling. She quickly puts her soap bag next to the sink, and the box of sandwiches she made for tonight on the mantelpiece.

'Come on then. Let's visit your old haunts.' She glances at the travel clock she's set up on the spindly bedside table. 'How long till evensong?'

'Ages.'

It has stopped raining. The sun silvers the tarmac, pavement and trees as they walk. Avoiding puddles, they turn right onto Station Road, passing huge houses with generous driveways and oak trees. Instead of turning right onto Hills Road towards town, William scoops up Gloria's hand.

'We've got time for a wander round the Botanic Gardens.'

'Did you go there a lot?' Gloria follows him across the road.

'Quite a lot,' he says.

He wishes he hadn't lied, because as they walk the gravel pathways round the gardens, pausing at the fountain, the giant redwoods, the lake, Gloria won't stop imagining a ten-year-old William. The truth is, he never once came here, but a lot of the boys did with their parents. He's brought her here now simply because he has no memories of it. Even so, the sound of their feet scrunching on the gravel and the fiery orange of the path threatens to pull him back where he doesn't want to go.

By the time they leave through the Bateman Street gates and start walking along Trumpington Street, he feels light-headed and slightly sick. The open gutter, a mini canal on either side of the road, intrigues Gloria, and she jumps back and forth over it a few times, then settles next to him and takes his hand.

There must be *some* new buildings in town – different shops and cafes – but his Cambridge was small; Trumpington Street, the sitting lions of Fitzwilliam Museum, King's Parade, Trinity Street, the Backs.

'That's the cake shop famous for Chelsea buns.' He has to make this the trip that Gloria is hoping for. 'Want one?'

She grins up at Fitzbillies. The sun is weak and watery, but still, the italic script glows golden on the wooden storefront. 'Go on then, we can save them for later.'

William leans into the door. The feel of it against his shoulder is the same, the ding of the bell is the same, and the sweet, yeasty smell is the same.

Two Chelsea buns, please, he says, infected by Martin's excitement at the syrupy thud into the crisp, white box. *Make that three,* Martin says at the last minute.

'Martin always got two,' he tells Gloria as they leave, 'and the first one was gone by the time we'd crossed this road.'

Gloria nearly steps into the open gutter. 'Whoops!' She grabs his arm. 'I nearly went in!'

'You wouldn't be the first,' he says, instantly regretting it, because now, here's Evelyn, twisting her ankle and landing with one knee in the water. She's looking up at him first in pain, then with a laugh, to stop him worrying.

To his dismay, he realises the pavement he and Gloria stand on is fragile as eggshells. At any moment, a memory could crack open the surface and he'll be swallowed whole.

'We often saw students fall into it on their bikes.' He attempts a laugh.

'I'm not surprised.' She squeezes his hand.

William falls silent, and as Trumpington Street becomes King's Parade, and – *Oh God!* – the Copper Kettle, Gloria's presence is less comforting, less real, as another woman returns

259

with her fragrance, the bright beam of her attention on him and butter biscuits in a Tupperware box.

'What? What is it?' Gloria turns at the twitch and wince of his face.

'Nothing.' He speeds up to try and shake it off.

'I understand,' she says evenly. 'This is where everything went belly up. I understand.'

He remains silent, noticing the Senate House, with its chalky glow. Looking down at the pavement, his feet move relentlessly forward and he concentrates on Gloria's hand tight round his.

'I just want to enjoy the singing. And be proud of you.'

For a brief second he imagines that; listening, with Gloria knowing this was him once. But as the pavement gives way to the cobbled forecourt, with the uneven brown, red and grey stones beneath his soles, he stops dead.

'I can't, Gloria.' He stares at the ground. 'I can't go in.'

'Course you can,' she says lightly, tugging him towards the entrance.

'No!' He didn't mean to shout. A couple on their way in glance at them. 'You go,' he says under his breath, 'I'll meet you in forty-five minutes.'

She puts her face close to his so he has to look at her. 'We've come all this way. Please. For me.'

He shakes his head. 'I can't.'

He marches twice around the perimeter of Jesus Green, then follows the avenue of London plane trees towards the river. He stops to watch a swan carve a velvety V in the water before walking under the bridge. Gradually he becomes aware of the repeated *thwock* of a tennis ball and two students on the courts to his right. The surface shines from recent rain. He watches the old tennis ball fly, ragged, between the students. If only he could do things others seem to do effortlessly; think about his past, knock it around like that beaten-up tennis ball, as if his memories could be prodded and poked without bursting open and destroying him.

He sits on a bench next to the tennis court and wonders how he'll make this up to Gloria. Maybe forget the sandwiches back at their bed and breakfast and go out for a meal? William checks his watch, stands up and heads back to the college.

From a distance, he can see the forecourt dotted with people, and even from here, he can spot Gloria's orange coat. She might be talking to someone, but he's too far away to tell. Getting nearer, he's puzzled by the group of men standing there. He speeds up, unsure of what mood he'll find Gloria in and wondering whether between them they've got the energy to salvage what's left of their time, to pretend that he's all right.

48

He wasn't mistaken; the men are down and outs, hanging around Gloria. Her voice carries on the spring breeze. Her bold, London voice. She's talking to a tall man, not scruffy like the others, with his back to William. He's close enough now to smell the acrid, pungent odour of the tramps. Gloria spots him; he's relieved to see she smiles.

'He brings me all the way to Cambridge for evensong and at the last minute he buggers off' – he knows this is for his benefit – 'does a bleedin' runner.'

'Abandonment withstanding,' a cultured voice booms from the broad body that stands between him and Gloria, 'did you enjoy it?'

'It was beautiful,' she says, glancing over the man's shoulder at William. 'I don't need my dopey husband to tell me that.' A gust of wind folds Gloria's hair across her face. She laughs and pulls it back.

She's looking at William, but he's no longer thinking about telling her how sorry he is in that moment of eye contact. He's no longer wondering about the men in dirty coats and tattered shoes. He reaches up and rests his hands on the broad shoulders, on the soft tweed. He feels his face split by a smile as the figure turns.

The man is startled. He looks back at Gloria before turning again to William, and then his wide, creased brow smooths. He laughs and his long arms reach out.

'William!'

Engulfed in a tight hug, William laughs too. 'Martin.'

William and Gloria sit at a table tucked in a corner of the crowded Eagle pub.

'I can't believe it!' Gloria sips her shandy, her eyes bright and excited, as if she's just met her own long-lost friend. She's put her bag on the spare seat and William has put Martin's requested pint of bitter on the table. She leans into him. 'I was all set to give you the silent treatment, but your faces when you saw each other!' She takes another sip, puts her glass down, and covers his hand with hers.

He shrugs. 'When I first realised it was him, it was just . . .' He pauses. 'Just *joy*! But now I can't stop thinking about what I did to him.' *Tell them, William.* Those tear-filled eyes.

'It didn't look as if that was *his* first memory, did it?'

'I suppose not.'

'How long did he say he'd be?'

'He just said he'd meet us here once he'd said goodbye to those men. He can't have thought he'd be long, or he wouldn't have asked us to get his drink.' He takes another gulp of whisky. 'Did you notice them in the chapel?'

'I was right in front of them,' Gloria says, nodding, 'but I could hear this posh voice talking to them, so I knew they were being looked after. I breathed through my mouth so I couldn't smell them and it was fine.'

'They wouldn't have been allowed in my day,' says William. 'Oh! Here he is!'

Martin threads his way through the bodies, navigating the narrow spaces as if he could do it with his eyes closed.

'William Lavery!' Martin sits and slaps both hands on the dark table. 'How absolutely bloody marvellous to see you.' He turns his beam from William to Gloria. 'And you too, Mrs

Lavery. Absolutely bloody *marvellous.*' He gulps the beer, then wipes his mouth on the back of his hand with expansive, exaggerated movements so familiar to William, he feels an ache. 'What brings you to Cambridge?'

'Gloria's always wanted to come and see where I misspent my youth.'

'And now I get to meet the person he misspent it with!' Gloria says.

The couple on the next table turn their heads at Martin's laugh – that *laugh*! 'Your beloved,' Martin says to Gloria, his voice deep and rich, 'was the finest chorister ever to have graced the college chapel.'

'Bit of an exaggeration,' William objects, but feels that warm wash of Martin's generosity.

'It's not, Gloria, ask Phillip Lewis. He'd back me up.'

'Do you still see him?' William straightens. 'Do you *live* here?'

'Yes and yes.' Martin nods, sitting back, his stomach pushing against the checked shirt. 'After university – I failed, by the way – I went to Ivory Coast with VSO for three years. Every teacher and tutor I ever had told me how selfish and lazy I was, so I decided to prove them wrong. Loved the people, loved the climate, could have stayed there, to be honest, but Mum got ill, and I came back to help look after her for the last six months.'

William tries to imagine robust Mrs Mussey on her deathbed. 'I'm sorry.'

Martin dips his head. 'It was three years ago now. Dad shed this mortal coil too, a year later. Wasn't any point for him without her.'

William is ashamed and sad. In another life, he would have been at their funerals.

'Anyway,' Martin continues, his broad face etched with fine lines, freckles still dotting his nose and cheeks, 'I came into a fair bit of dosh and went slightly berserk in true prodigal fashion. Did too much of everything that wasn't good for me, not enough of what was. Lived in San Francisco for a while, and London. Then I had a particularly painful break-up, and when I sorted myself out, had a think about what I was going to do with the rest of my life.'

'And you came back here?' Gloria's East London accent always turns up a notch when she's concentrating.

'Only for a sort of holiday at first, to reconnect with my musical roots. Music was one of the things I'd decided was good for me. On my first night, after a drink here, I was walking back to my bed and breakfast and came across two drunks sitting on the kerb singing. I sat down and joined in.' William laughs at how easily he can picture this. 'They were surprisingly good, so I taught them a few harmonies. It was a hoot. Then I taught them "Bird on the Wire".'

'What?' William asks.

'Leonard Cohen?'

William and Gloria shake their heads.

'Where have you been?'

'Sutton Coldfield,' they say together, making Martin laugh again.

'You should check him out,' he continues. 'The man's a genius, check that *song* out. It's what gave me the idea, and the name.'

'What idea?' Gloria asks, like a child on a story mat. 'What name?'

'The Midnight Choir. We meet every week in a church hall on Hills Road and once a term I bring them here. I have to tip

Phillip off, to have a word with the porter so we don't get turned away.'

'That's fantastic,' William says. 'How many of them?'

'On a good night' – Martin looks to the ceiling, counting – 'fifteen.'

'Is that your job?' asks Gloria.

'If only. I work in the Rare Books reading room in St John's library. Can you believe it? I have to whisper all day. Me!'

'What do you sing?' Gloria leans her elbows on the table opposite Martin.

'Pop songs, golden oldies, and hymns. They *love* a good hymn.'

'I'm glad you're still singing,' William says.

'Don't tell me you're not?' Martin frowns from William to Gloria.

There's a beat of silence. 'Oh, he sings every day.' Gloria leans closer towards Martin and whispers, 'But only to dead people. Similar repertoire to you; pop songs, old people songs – but no hymns.'

William sees the twinkle in Martin's eyes, getting the measure of her, warming to her humour. Martin turns from Gloria and puts his head on one side to look at William.

'But you're not in a choir?'

William shakes his head. 'My performing days are over. Unless, as Gloria says, the audience is dead.'

'So you joined the family business after all?'

William nods.

'Don't go all modest, William,' says Gloria.

He grimaces.

Gloria looks vexed, turning to Martin. 'He's the best embalmer in the country.'

'Don't be ridiculous.' William nudges her.

'With Uncle Robert?' Martin smiles.

'Yep.'

'How is he?'

'Good, thanks. Gets tired, but no real health problems.'

'And Howard?'

'Yep, still going strong.'

'We live with them.' Gloria leans under the table and, after a brief rummage in her bag, brings out the Fitzbillies box. 'Fancy one of these?'

'If you weren't married, I'd propose immediately.' Martin reaches into the box and bites off half a bun in one easy movement. 'So, William,' he says with sugar-speckled lips, 'how's the lovely Evelyn?'

Gloria looks at William, but he can tell she's not going to speak for him.

'Fine. As far as I know. We don't speak. She lives in Swansea.'

Martin leans back suddenly, 'But you were so close!'

'You know what happened.' William feels a stir of irritation. 'You were there.'

'But families do that; have dramas, hurt each other, fall out, make up.' Martin looks perplexed. 'It never occurred to me you wouldn't have sorted it out. You *adored* each other.'

'You could tell that, could you?' Gloria asks, intensely focused all of a sudden. 'Just from seeing them together?'

'I'd say. I was jealous as anything! I'm one of five and I could tell, seeing them walking along King's Parade, or coming out of the Copper Kettle, they *loved* being together.'

'Well, not any more.' William has to close this down.

'Apologies for venturing into difficult territory.' Martin turns his palms outwards briefly, and there's a moment's silence. 'Is that why you didn't go to evensong today?'

William nods. They all look at the table for a moment, then Martin sits upright. 'Oh!' he says, with renewed verve. 'I thought of you last term. We sang "Myfanwy". They loved it. Remember that? We sang it to my family?'

'Of course.' William continues to stare at the dark whorls on the oak table.

'The thing about that song' – this time Gloria does rescue him – 'it's got difficult memories for William.' A large group have left the bar, and suddenly it's a lot emptier and quieter. 'Do you remember that disaster six years ago? In Aberfan, when all those children got killed by the collapsed coal tip?'

'Course I do,' Martin replies, 'buried alive by the National Coal Board. I'll never forget it.'

'Well' – Gloria clears her throat – 'he went, as a volunteer, right after he qualified, and he sang "Myfanwy" to some of the little kiddies, when he was, you know, looking after them. And now it does funny things to him.'

William makes himself look at his old friend. 'I'm a head case. Lots of things do funny things to me, including choral music and in particular, you won't be surprised to hear, the "Miserere". I'm estranged from my mother, I haven't spoken to you, my best friend, since I left here, and I won't have children. Some days I'm fine, others not. I get palpitations, tunnel vision and flashbacks; awake or asleep, they get me any which way.'

Martin is still, hands in his lap. William feels a palpable sense of calm coming from him and remembers it was always like this; energy and mischief, but always this calm, intense listening.

'Well, bless your gentle soul,' Martin murmurs, as the door opens and a loud crowd of male students amble in. They sit in silence for a moment.

'What about you, Martin?' Gloria says. 'Have you got someone special? It can't be easy working with those blokes.'

'Not at the moment,' he says with a gentle smile.

'Well, that's a crying shame' – Gloria stands suddenly – 'cos I think you're lovely!' She looks around. 'Where's the loo?' Martin points behind her. 'I'll get another round on my way back. Same again?' They both nod and watch her walk away.

'How are your brothers?' William asks. 'And the twins?'

'Yep, all good.' Martin finishes his beer. 'Richard's a banker in Kemsing, Edward's a headmaster at a boarding school near Brighton, and the twins live in Worthing. All married with sprogs. Seven nieces, three nephews.'

William stares at his glass, then looks up. 'Martin, I'm sorry I didn't reply to your letters.'

Martin shrugs. 'Forget it. I'm sure I waffled on terribly.'

'I didn't even read them.' He holds Martin's eye. 'Couldn't bear to.'

'Fair enough.' Martin winces briefly.

'It wasn't. I couldn't read your letters because I felt so guilty.' William glances quickly at Martin, then looks down again. 'I missed you *so* much.'

'If you'd bloody well read my letters, you'd know that was mutual.' Martin's beefy hand slaps down briefly on William's.

William shakes his head. 'You're better off without me.' Suddenly, William is worried he's going to cry. He doesn't want Gloria to come back and find him in bits. She was finally having a good time.

Martin shunts forward in his chair. 'William, I choose to spend my time with men who've lost everything. They're not exactly straightforward, but they're far more interesting for it. They're *real*.'

269

William notices Gloria at the bar chatting to the barman, who's laughing at something she's said.

'OK.' William looks back at Martin. 'Consider us found.'

Gloria returns with a tray. 'Everything all right?' she says.

'Thank you, Gloria.' Martin lifts the drinks to the table, passing William's to him. 'Wouldn't have had you down as a whisky drinker.'

'What would you have had me down as?'

Martin considers. 'I seem to remember you having a penchant for ginger beer, but then you were only ten.' Martin and Gloria laugh, filling the pub and William's heart.

'Come on then, Martin.' Gloria rubs her hands. 'Spill the beans, tell me about my beloved when he was a choirboy.'

'Well, Gloria' – Martin drops his voice – 'how long have you got?'

'That man loves you.' It's after nine and they're desperate for their sandwiches waiting on the mantelpiece. A cyclist rolls through a deep puddle next to them and water fans off the tyres. Gloria tuts and bends down to snap the wet nylon away from her leg.

'I know.' They turn into the short pathway to their bed and breakfast. He pushes the key and wiggles it in the lock to find the connection. 'I love him too.'

'Good.' She pats him on the back as she follows him up the narrow stairs. 'Because in this life, we need all the people who love us that we can get, don't you think?'

'I do,' he says.

'Promise me you'll stay in touch. Visit him again? Maybe invite him to us?'

'Promise.'

49

TWO YEARS LATER

William has been sitting in the corner of Ruth's lounge for over an hour while Gloria talks to her friends. He doesn't like this room; the glass cabinet with wedding and baby photos depresses him and the bland rubbish playing on the stereo is like nails down a blackboard. Ruth is Gloria's closest nursing friend, and the last, except them, to start a family. Right now, he doesn't like her very much either and he positively hates christening parties.

A few months ago, he came back early from work and found Gloria on the kitchen floor, a tight knot of grief, knees gripped to her chest. He caught the misery on her face in the brief second before she could get it under control, readjust herself for him. She tried to grab the balled letter next to her, but he dipped down and got to it first. It was from her sister.

'I'll get over it,' she said, wiping her face with both palms. 'Just seems a bit greedy. She's already got three. Not sure I can get excited about a fourth.'

He sat on the floor and put his arm round her, kissed her warm head. She leaned into him, her body relaxing, and it amazed him how she could let him be her comfort, when it was him inflicting the hurt.

Gloria has no idea that every now and then he lets himself imagine a pregnancy; the heat of her joy, a baby arriving – always a girl – the soft flesh of small fingers closing round his. Neither does she know about the images that burst into his mind with all the vivid horror of his flashbacks. Images of terrible attacks on their baby's fragile body. The unbearable anguish of embalming his own child. Because how could he ever let anyone else do it? All this he keeps to himself.

On his most recent visit to Cambridge, he hoped to talk about it with Martin, thinking that his presence has an almost magical quality. But once he arrived, he felt the folding in of himself and let Martin's lively company be enough for both of them. He must have stayed with him more than ten times in the last two years. Sometimes with Gloria, sometimes on his own. It's best when she comes, and Martin cooks an elaborate meal, with wine and loud music, and flowers on the table, but mostly he comes on his own, wanting to give her a break.

Gloria is walking towards him now, carrying the baby in its ludicrous satin gown, followed by Ruth, who smiles at him and says, 'Want a cuddle, Uncle William?'

He shakes his head. 'No, thank you.'

Ruth mock frowns, looks to Gloria.

'Come on, William.' Gloria smiles, but there's warning in her voice. 'He's a poppet.' She holds the baby towards him, determined.

It won't take much, he thinks, *just reach out, take the child, and that delicious smile will sweep her face.*

'Come on then, little chap.' He stands, trying to sound confident. His hands close around the baby's sides, and he feels the tiny case of ribs under the slip and slide of the satin. The two women grin at him. He settles the baby into the crook of his arm.

'Look how relaxed he is!' Gloria says.

'Sit down with him' – Ruth looks eager – 'he might drop off.'

Carefully, William settles back into the seat, feels the weight of the miniature body relax in his arms, watches the eyelids, slower and heavier with each blink. Everyone else is standing

272

and he's aware of other guests smiling down at him. He concentrates on the baby, the adults now on the periphery of his vision.

A golden flicker at the edge of his left eye is the only warning, seconds before his body jolts at the certainty that the baby is dead. He struggles to stand, holding it with both hands. He shouts and the baby wakes. But how? It's dead, and all these people, all these parents are waiting for him. He must do it quickly, before it starts to decompose! He tries to run through the crowd. There's a cry of anguish. The baby is being pulled from his arms by an angry man. The father wants the body, but William mustn't give it to him! He tightens his grip on the screaming baby. He must get to work!

'William! William! Let go of the baby!'

Gloria. Her arms round him. Someone's sobbing. Where's the baby? The line of parents stare at him.

'All right now?' she asks, searching his face.

The film of sweat cools on his forehead. The cul-de-sac is full of parked cars. They lean on their bonnet in silence. The fresh air helps bring him back to himself, his surroundings. Her hand on his shoulder is gentle and so is her voice, but he senses she's angry.

'Get in the other side. I'll drive, but not yet,' Gloria says, soft but firm, slipping her hand in his jacket pocket for the keys. 'I've got things to say and you need to *hear*.'

Once in the car, he stares through the windscreen, exhausted. A gust of wind whistles through the air vent.

'They must hate me.'

'No.'

'Course they do. At least now they'll know I'm right about not wanting children.'

273

She twists urgently in her seat towards him. Her eyes are fierce and full of intent. They stare at each other for a moment, him braced against what's to come. Then her breath heaves in and out and she turns back to look out of the windscreen. 'I have *never* told *anyone* why we haven't got children' – she speaks quietly now – 'but you know what really pisses me off? Not that you don't want children, or wake up screaming. Do you think I could love anyone as much as I love you – who wouldn't be touched by the horror of what you saw?'

'What then?' he asks, just wanting to get home and sleep.

'That you don't *have* to put up with this. It's one thing in our home, our bedroom, but William, you scared me today. You could have hurt the baby.' Her voice wobbles. 'I just *know* there's help out there.'

'I won't let it happen again. Clearly, I'm not safe with children.'

'Yeah, you tell yourself that.'

The unfamiliar tone of sarcasm gets his attention. 'What do you mean?'

'You're scared of getting help, because of what else it will uncover. This isn't just about Aberfan.'

'Here we go.'

Gloria shakes her head, laughs an unpleasant laugh. He unwinds the window.

'What drives me crazy,' she says, 'is that you can't bear anything to be more than one story. You've blighted our marriage because you say you couldn't bear to suffer like those *poor* parents of Aberfan. Well, you know what? You're a bloody hypocrite.'

He didn't expect an attack. She's normally so gentle after an episode. A cat strolls onto the pavement and flops down into a plank of sunshine. Physically depleted, all he can do is stare at it.

'You've been inflicting pain every day for years. On your own *mother*.' She shakes her head. 'You can choose not to be a father, but you can't choose to stop being a son and she can't ever stop being a mother.' A couple are leaving the christening. They glance at the car, then, heads down and hands loosely clasped, they walk quickly towards their Morris Minor. 'You think you're this wounded, bleeding heart, but really, you're a tyrant who hurts everyone who gets close to you.' She waits. 'Well?' Her voice is sharp. 'Have you got anything to say?'

'You're right,' he replies eventually, eyes still on the cat licking its striped flank. 'I'm a tyrant who hurts everyone close to me.'

'So,' she says. He hears her swallow and catches the slight uplift of her chin. 'What are you going to do about it?'

'Simple,' he says, finally turning to look at Gloria's troubled, beloved face.

Part IV

MIDNIGHT CHOIR

50

For all he knows, he sleepwalked to the station. William has no memory of boarding the Birmingham to Cambridge later that day. He registers dashes of fields, fresh growth on the trees. The sun on his left burns through the glass and makes the dusty seat smell toasted. He didn't bring sunglasses, it's only March. The corner of a shirt is poking out of his suitcase. He doubts he can carry it to Martin's without the handle breaking, but has no cash for a taxi.

The walk to Jesus Lane tires him out, the sun a malign bore at his temples. He knocks the door and leans his head on the blue paint as he waits for Martin to come down the stairs.

He stands upright at the clink and rattle of the chain on the inside. 'Hello? Can I help you?'

William registers blond curls on broad shoulders. The black and white stripe of the rugby shirt hurts his eyes.

'Is Martin in?'

The face considers him, then turns and shouts up the stairs, 'Martin! It's for you!'

William thinks of introducing himself, but can't summon the energy.

'You should leave him in peace, you know,' the man says quietly, leaning in, 'he does have a life.'

William can only nod as he hears Martin thundering down towards them.

'William! Have I forgotten something? I haven't looked in my diary for days.'

'No,' he says, trying to raise a smile, 'I'm not meant to be here.'

Martin puts his hand on his shoulder and guides him in. 'Steve, this is my oldest friend, William.'

Steve smiles awkwardly. 'Sorry, William, I thought you . . . you must think I'm a complete arsehole.'

'Not at all,' William says, putting out his hand to shake Steve's but misjudging it and jabbing him in the stomach.

Steve turns to Martin. 'Sorry, I thought he was . . .'

Martin scrunches his face. 'You do look dreadful, William. Come on in.' He gestures up the staircase. 'Steve, put the kettle on, would you?'

'Sure.' Steve bounds up the stairs like a big cat.

'I'll get this,' is all Martin says about the suitcase. 'Up you go.' William feels the steady pressure of Martin's flat palm all the way up the stairs.

The sitting room's bay window is full of the fresh magnolia leaves. The patterns of their shadows flicker and dance over the wooden floor. On the table are two willow pattern plates with half-eaten bacon sandwiches, a bottle of brown sauce, two mugs.

Steve appears from the little kitchen off the sitting room. 'Tea or coffee?'

'Coffee, thanks. Black.' He thumps down onto the sofa and leans forward, his head in his hands. He feels the shift and sway as Martin sits gently next to him.

'Do we have a problem?'

William's throat constricts at the *we*. 'We do,' he says, grateful for how Martin never lets him feel alone.

Steve puts the coffee onto the little ebony table carved into the shape of an elephant. 'I've got things to do, I'll see you later.'

'Thanks, Steve,' he says.

After a few light bounds down the stairs, the door opens, closes, and then silence.

'Who's he?' William asks. 'I hope I didn't interrupt.'

Martin shrugs. 'Just a friend, don't worry about it.' He shifts in his seat to face William. 'What is it? What's happened?'

A weight pushes on his chest. He breathes in, sips the strong filter coffee and puts it back on the table. He stares at the pot plant's two-toned leaves, vivid against the ebony wood.

'William?'

His eyes wash warm. 'I've left her.'

'You can stay for a while, on two conditions.'

Martin has come into his bedroom to open the curtains. William covers his eyes as light slices his pillow. He's obviously slept all night, but as he remembers where he is and why, William feels bone-tired.

'Thanks. What are they?'

'You help me with the choir.' Martin pulls the sash window down an inch and leans against it, arms folded.

'I'm sorry, Martin.' He shakes his head. 'Anything else, just not that.'

'I could do with the help and there isn't anything else.' He has a hint of a smile on his face.

William can't help but smile back. 'I don't have much choice then, do I?'

Martin steps towards the bed and pats William's leg. 'Marvellous! OK. I'm off to work. Today's task is to type up the words for the new songs we're working on this week. Scores are on the table, next to the typewriter. Then go to the reprographics department at college – one good thing about working in the library – say I sent you, and get twenty copies.'

281

'Can I do it tomorrow?'

'I've got other things for you to do tomorrow.'

William closes his eyes again.

'Problem?'

With his eyes still closed, he says, 'I'd hoped I could just rest for a while.'

'I came back to Cambridge in a similar state, but at least I had the gumption to know what I needed. *Nourishment*.'

William opens his eyes to see Martin moving back towards the window.

'OK, I'll try.'

'Can't ask more than that, can I?' Martin pulls the window down a few more inches. A wave of air cools the room as he walks to the door. 'Oh!' He leans his head back in. 'The second condition.'

'Yep?'

'When I come back tonight, you tell me what's going on. You clearly weren't up to talking yesterday, but if you're staying, I deserve an explanation.' He disappears before William can answer.

'Martin?' William calls out.

'Yes?' he replies from the landing.

'Is Steve living here?'

'No.' The door opens and Martin's head reappears. 'And that's a third condition. No judgements.'

'Of course not,' he says, disappointed that Martin would think he even needed to ask.

Once the door slams, the sudden and complete silence feels almost hostile. William pulls the duvet over his head, but knows within seconds he won't be able to sleep again. He flicks it back and stares at the quarter-paned sash window. *What's happening at home now? What's Gloria doing? What conversations is she having with Robert and Howard?*

To remind himself why he's doing this, he imagines Gloria with a family that has nothing to do with him. His stomach pitches him out of bed and he makes it to the bathroom just in time to hurl last night's chicken pie across the cracked sink.

51

It's dark by the time William finishes telling Martin. The windows and curtains of the sitting room are still open. The budding horse chestnuts on Jesus Green glow a coppery gold under the street lamps.

Martin tilts the teapot over his mug for a last brown dribble, drains it in one gulp and stands. 'Did you get the lyrics copied?'

William nods to the piano against the wall. 'Over there, in the folder.'

'Good. We need three more ring binders, can you get them from Smith's tomorrow?' He reaches in his back pocket and puts two pound notes on the table. 'I'll go straight to rehearsal from work, so you need to sort yourself out with food and meet me there.' He closes the window, draws the curtains, takes their mugs to the kitchen, and then walks back through the living room. 'Goodnight, William.'

'Is that it?'

Martin pauses near the door and looks at William, his eyes unusually fierce. 'Yes, that's it,' he says eventually and leaves.

William doesn't move. The creak of Martin's footsteps on the floorboards stops after only a few minutes. He wants Gloria, pictures her waiting for him in bed, her cotton nightie soft and pretty against her skin, brushed auburn hair dark on the white pillow. He closes his eyes. What would peace even feel like? he wonders. Can he remember ever feeling it?

Yes. And there he is, back in his mother's kitchen after a nap, watching her take biscuits out of the oven.

· · ·

'Good evening, gentlemen.' Martin's eyes dart from one man to another; comfortable, authoritative. One copy of the lyrics that William had copied for him yesterday sits neatly on his broad lap. 'I hope the week has been kind to you.' The chairs are in a circle. He and Martin set out fifteen; four are empty. The men smile or nod; one waves a raggedy arm. 'This is William, an old friend from my chorister days. He's going to help us for a few weeks.'

William nods with a quick smile, looking at no one in particular. He's very uncomfortable, in part because of the company, but also because he's worked so hard during his adolescent and adult life to ignore the past he shares with Martin. To be so casually introduced in this way seems somehow brazen, like a violation.

'So.' Martin lays the music under his chair. 'Let's warm up with some laa-ing, shall we?' He checks the square clock on the wall. 'Jenny should be here any minute, but we can manage this bit without her. Everyone up.' Martin stands and there's a rumble and shriek of chair legs.

The narrow windows that run around the top of the church hall are slightly ajar, but still, the smell of the men is bitter and musty. William decides not to try and identify the individual odours. They all seem to be wearing coats, though some of their clothes are so tattered and layered, it's hard to identify what the items originally were. Martin, as usual, is in baggy cords and an open-necked shirt.

'Remember, breathe from here,' Martin says, his paw of a hand over his stomach. Some men adjust their posture, some don't. He sings them their note, bottom D.

This is the first time William has heard Martin's adult singing voice. They all knew, as choristers, that however exquisite their voices, there was no guarantee they'd be anything special later on, but Phillip always said their discipline and training would stand them in good stead to make the best of what they were landed with. William's not at all surprised, though, that Martin is a lush, resonant bass.

He leads them up and down their scales and arpeggios. William is impressed. The overall sound is pleasing, albeit a bit gritty. He does his old trick of differentiating the voices, and this makes him notice individual faces, dissolves his sense that they are one, messy whole. He notices the delicate bone structure of the tenor opposite, his wire-wool hair roughly brushed and parted. He sees the wide-open mouth of the man to his left, with a front tooth missing.

'William, can you give the files out, please?' Martin points to a lopsided table in the corner and the pile of A4 ring binders, with 'Midnight Choir' written on the spines. They slither and slide in his arms as he walks round the circle. The men take the folders in both hands, two feet flat on the ground, sit up straight.

'Number three then, to finish the warm-up. William, you're going to have to play piano. Do you mind? I don't know what's happened to Jenny.'

He hasn't touched a piano since he left Cambridge. Walking across the hall, he wishes that Martin had warned him he might be called on to play, but then the door opens and a woman William guesses to be in her forties runs in.

'Sorry, Martin, I had a puncture.' She hurries over to the piano, taking off her coat as she goes. 'Had to go back and get my husband's and I can't cycle very fast on his. Hello, gentle-men.' The woman waves quickly to the group and a 'Hello,

Jenny' comes back. They like her, William thinks.

'Not to worry,' Martin says, 'we're just going to finish the warm-up with "Danny Boy". This is William, Jenny, an old friend who's helping out for a bit.'

'Hello, William.' She smiles, laying her coat on the top of the piano and opening the lid.

Martin gives her a minute to find the music, then raises his hand and nods at her. She plays a few bars of the introduction, her back and head swaying. It's striking how the men are holding their books. Straight-backed, heads up. Martin has been channelling Phillip.

It's patchy of course, but there's also a richness to it William didn't expect. They're really singing. And somewhere in there are one or two good voices.

On William's left is a gangly, skinny man, impossible to age, but his long hair and wispy beard are mostly grey. He's on edge, eyes flicking to William often, but never resting long enough for William to smile at him. He's not on the right page and isn't singing, but William is wary of helping him. He's wary of all of them. But by the second verse, he can't stand it any longer. He leans across, flicks forward two pages and points briefly at the words they are singing now.

'But come ye back when summer's in the meadow,
Or when the valley's hushed and white with snow.'

The man nods, looks briefly at him, but still doesn't sing, and after a few seconds starts turning the pages again.

'David can't read,' the man on William's right says. William is embarrassed at his faux pas and barely acknowledges the comment. 'He's deaf,' the man adds.

'Oh,' William mouths back, nodding. He sings along quietly; he doesn't want to be heard.

'Right. Let's get serious about this, shall we?' Martin's eyes are bright; he looks even taller and broader than normal. He eyeballs the men, one by one, and extends his hand. 'Come on. Mean it.' His hand closes to a fist. '*Mean* it.' He looks briefly at the lyrics, rests the tips of his fingers over his heart, then seeks out each man's gaze again. '"And I shall hear – I *shall* hear, though soft you tread above me."' His lively eyes sweep the room. '"And all my grave will *warmer, sweeter* be." Come on. Gentlemen, make me believe it! "For you will bend and tell me that you love me."' He pauses again, then adds softly, '"And I shall sleep in peace until you come to me."'

Really, Martin? William thinks. Can any of these men here know they're loved? *Really?* Can any of them sleep in peace? But the men are watching Martin. They're captivated.

'Let's do it again, from "And I shall hear", and remember, don't leave me in any doubt' – he glances to the piano – 'thank you, Jenny.'

They sing it again and from the first syllable, the difference is astonishing. A wave of energy floods the room, powerful and tender.

'Yes!' Martin beams, his torso bending and weaving with the music, and William is aware of certain muscles in his face. It's been a long time since he has smiled like this. And for the final chorus, he lets himself sing like he hasn't sung for even longer.

'That's more like it!' says Martin, triumphant, looking at William and nodding briefly.

'Bloody hell,' says the man next to him, looking at William. They're all looking at him, they're all smiling, except David, who's looking up at one of the windows.

Martin chuckles. 'It's a thing of beauty, isn't it, gentlemen, that voice? Enjoy it while you can.' He's still grinning as he dips his head and rifles through the folder. 'Right! Number six next. "What a Wonderful World". Ready?' He looks up and waits for the men to find their music, then nods at Jenny. 'Here. We. Go!'

'Some of us had good jobs,' says the man who told him David was deaf, as most of them cluster in the corner over tea and biscuits. 'See that bloke with the blue hat?' William looks and nods. 'Cambridge graduate. Solicitor. And that one there, in the wellies? Teacher.'

'What about you? Sorry, I don't know your name.'

'Colin.' He eats two bourbon biscuits, barely chewing them, and some brown crumbs lodge in the fringe of moustache that hangs over his pale narrow lips.

'Accountant.' William notices that amongst the layers of anorak, cardigan, shirt, deep inside there is a badly knotted burgundy tie. 'Never thought I'd end up with the likes of him.' He nods to David who's making wide gestures and guttural sounds at Jenny. She's nodding and smiling back at him, and before he can stop himself, William thinks how good Gloria would be, here with these men.

'Hello, William,' Jenny says, her shoes clip-clopping over the parquet floor to him. 'Thanks for coming along.' There's a smudge of pink lipstick on her tooth.

He shrugs, thinks better of telling her he has no choice. 'I'm happy to help.'

'They're a good bunch,' she says, surveying round the room, 'and Martin is *wonderful* with them. I can't tell you what a good job he does.'

'If nothing else, it's great hearing him sing after all these years – he's a bit deeper these days.'

Jenny smiles at him, and he wipes his front tooth. 'Thank you.' She laughs and wipes hers.

William feels Martin's hand close round his arm. 'I'm going to ask you to sing with me after the break to show how the tenor part works for "Sweet Caroline", all right?'

'I've never sung it in my life.'

'You could do it with your eyes closed.'

William glances at Jenny and Colin, and raises his eyebrows. 'All right.'

After rehearsal, after singing to them, with them, William finds it easier to talk to the men; as if they've exhaled together and can breathe more easily. He knows a handful of names: David who's deaf and looks like Catweazle, Phil with the missing tooth, Andrew who's softly spoken but belts out the songs so hard his voice cracks. And Colin, the biscuit-eating accountant. They're given sandwiches before they leave, cut into quarters, filled with fish paste, tinned salmon and egg, which disappear into mouths, pockets, and even under one woolly hat. David comes back from the door to shake William's hand, which he finds unexpectedly touching.

'Do you ever think it might be painful for them? Singing about love and how wonderful the world is?' William leans on the wall while Martin locks up.

'What did you feel? In the room?' Martin drops the keys into his coat pocket and they start walking. 'Did you feel they were in pain when they were singing?'

'No,' he has to admit, 'but I felt awkward singing it with them.'

'Just because they've lost everything, doesn't mean they've stopped being human. I'm guessing most of them have probably been in love. Most of them have probably thought at some point, the world was a good place. The way I see it, singing about it keeps them in touch with who they were, are, could be. I don't know, William, but when they really connect with the song, with the lyrics and music, it feels like it's doing good, not harm. I'm damned if I'm going to look for songs that aren't about love and life and loss and pain and joy. This is being human.' He briefly raises both arms into the air. 'I treat them like humans.'

William reaches across and pats Martin's back.

'Anyway, never mind them, did *you* enjoy it?' Martin says, twisting his body briefly towards William as they turn right to cross Parker's Piece.

'Yes.' William smiles. 'Actually, I really did.'

'What did you enjoy most?'

'Just singing.' He's still grinning.

'Nothing like it, is there?' Martin talks to the pavement.

'Seems not.' He laughs, and Martin puts his arm round his shoulders and pulls him briefly towards him. 'You're great with them, Martin, really great.'

'Doing what you love brings out the best in you.'

'So, David doesn't sing, but comes every week?'

'Never misses. We sang in a service last Christmas and he stood there in the second row giving the congregation the evil eye, didn't open his mouth once.' Martin laughs.

As they walk the diagonal path, cyclists shoot by. William finds himself keeping to the very edge of the path, while Martin wanders to and fro.

'I had a chat with Colin.' William wants Martin to know he made an effort.

'You got him on a good day. His wife left him when he wouldn't get help for the booze. She hooked up with some high flyer and last year moved their two kids to London. It kills him. Big house, private schools. He's not allowed to even see them.'

'Ouch,' says William.

'Some days, he looks ready to kill.'

'The room must be full of stories like that.'

'Yep, but for an hour and a half, they can leave that at the door and have a good sing. They might have lost everything, but no one can take their voices.'

'Who's Jenny?'

'Member of the church. She organises the rota for people to provide the refreshments and sandwiches. Quiet saints, the lot of them.'

Once they reach the cast iron lamppost in the middle of the common, William turns to Martin. 'You're disgusted with me for leaving Gloria, aren't you?'

'Not disgusted.' Martin looks straight ahead. 'It just seems such an unnecessary mess, William. You're surrounded by people who love you. Surrounded.'

'It's not easy being loved by people you keep hurting.'

'For fuck's sake.' Martin speeds up, head down, then stops dead momentarily. A cyclist swears, swerving to miss them. 'Do you think anyone deserves being loved, *really* deserves it?' He shakes his head and starts walking again. 'You're not special, William. You're like all of us. Sometimes we're the best we can be, sometimes the worst. It's called being human.' They head left towards Drummer Street. 'I don't know how to help you sort yourself out, but I know how you looked this evening. Alive. And surely, the point of being on this earth is to *live*. If

292

singing brings you back to life, warms your heart, stirs your blood' – he comes to another halt and faces William, putting a hand on each of his arms – 'don't you think it's your duty to bloody well *sing*? As if your life depends on it?' He lets go and walks on, his brogues a steady beat on the pavement. 'It's all I've got, William.'

William rushes to catch up and get into time with Martin's long stride. They continue in silence. After a few moments, he counts four footsteps, inhales.

> *'Myfanwy, may your life entirely be*
> *Beneath the midday sun's bright glow,*
> *And may a blushing rose of health*
> *Dance on your cheek a hundred years.'*

Martin's voice slides in instantly, easily, alongside his. Two more students pass on their bikes; they slow down, smiling as they go, one bike lurching towards the other.

> *'I forget all your words of promise*
> *You made to someone, my pretty girl*
> *So give me your hand, my sweet Myfanwy,*
> *For no more but to say "farewell".'*

They come to a standstill outside the Methodist church and bellow the last note into the Cambridge sky, arms aloft, hand in hand.

Martin opens the front door to his flat and William follows him in, talking to his back. 'I can't make Gloria happy. She deserves to be happy.'

Martin walks up the stairs. 'OK, William.' He shakes his

head. 'If that's what you want to tell yourself.'

And there it is again; the cocktail of fear and anger he felt in the car with Gloria. A bloody hypocrite, she called him. He reaches the top of the stairs, the familiar darkness rising in him, the same overwhelming dread.

'Tea?' Martin calls from the kitchen, but William goes straight to his room.

52

The thick, white-tipped buds of the magnolia in the back garden are so hefty they look in need of hinges to open. The shared back garden is scattered with purple crocuses, which already he and Martin have inadvertently trampled on. Some recover and stand themselves up again; some stay prone on the lawn, their squash of purple and yellow insides exposed.

After three weeks, William has a routine. He gets up once Martin's left for work and sits at the table overlooking Jesus Lane, at cyclists hurtling to nine o'clock lectures, and Midsummer Common filling out for early spring. The first whiff of freshness and soil still takes him back to Gloria dating Ray in London, but there's something else now too; relief, for the Midnighters. The clocks have gone forward so it's light when they leave choir. On nights when he has felt the chill in the air as he undresses for bed and goose bumps sweep his bare legs, he thinks of Colin, and David and Andrew. He wonders how cold they are, where they're sleeping, if they're hungry. The night air is still cool, but its bite much softer.

Watching life flow past, and with a second cup of coffee, William sometimes calls Uncle Robert. William promised to keep in touch and it's the least he can do. Howard has found a locum to help two days a week. Gloria went back to Stepney at first and then last week she went on holiday. Where, or who with, he doesn't ask, but he's relieved.

Once he's done errands in town – printing lyrics, sourcing music, liaising with the church to organise a piano tuner – he returns to the flat and pulls out one of Martin's LPs. Sometimes he simply listens, eyes closed, concentrating, and wonders how he's survived without this beauty all these years. It amazes him that classical music, so important to him for so long, has never been a part of his marriage. In the evenings, he goes to concerts that Martin can get them into for free.

For the last two weeks at Midnight Choir, he's worked with the small group of tenors for half an hour, leaving the basses to Martin. Initially, he was so nervous, he didn't notice much beyond his own shaking hands and bland comments, but last week was different. For twenty minutes they lost themselves to each other, and the sound they made when they came back as a group and sang to the basses was so much better, William could have punched the air.

'Martin's a hard act to follow, but you taught us well,' Colin said, and William felt a rush of pride and gratitude.

'Thanks, Colin. You've got a lovely voice there.'

'*I've* got a lovely voice?' Colin laughed softly. 'You're our very own Pavarotti.'

William twiddled with the button on his cuff. 'Do you like opera?'

'Used to,' he said. 'I saw him live once in Covent Garden.' The remembered pleasure reached his eyes, so that William noticed for the first time what an unusually deep green they were.

This morning, he forces the old sash window down a few inches, and studies the lemon centres of the milky magnolia flowers. Leaving the window open, he gathers up his and Martin's bowls, rinses them off under the tap, then sits down at the table.

The phone's shrill ring makes him jump.

'Cambridge 57912?'

'William! How are you?'

'Uncle Robert, hello. I'm OK, what about you?'

'Missing you. Keeping our heads above water.'

'How's the locum?'

William hears his uncle inhale before he speaks. 'I've let him go; he wasn't much help I'm afraid. Gloria's father has been coming from London for two days a week, but can't do it much longer. If it comes to it, we'll just have to give some business to Bunts.'

'I'm so sorry.' Robert's time is usually spent working out how to take business off Bunts, not give it to them. Robert doesn't respond. 'I'll be back soon. How's Gloria?'

'Still away. Comes back in two days. But heartbroken, William. Heartbroken.'

He's empty, can't think of anything to say.

'Just stay in touch, all right?'

'I've promised.'

'You'd better. Anyway, the reason I'm calling is to let you know I've just forwarded something to you in the post from your mother, and I'm not asking, I'm telling. You must open this one, William. And if you need to talk about it, I'm on the end of the line. Any time, night or day.'

His mouth has gone dry. Is she ill? He's spent years ignoring his mother and justifying his behaviour to himself, but he's always known at some point, he'll have to square up to it all.

'Suppose there's no point me asking you what it is?' He attempts a lightness of tone.

'It's her news, not mine.'

53

'So,' says Martin to the group, scraping his hand through his thick hair. 'There's a spring festival at my old college next week, which means we get another chance to hear the "Miserere". Hands up who wants to come?'

Every hand goes up. Fifteen here tonight. Colin leans towards William smiling, and grasps his cuff to lift his hand up. William snatches it away so quickly Colin flinches.

Martin hasn't warned him about this. He feels tricked. 'I'm not going.'

'Why not?' asks Colin. Everyone's listening. 'It's free.'

'I know. I just don't fancy it.' William looks round and sees Jenny's watchful gaze on him.

'So, seventeen of us then,' Martin says without so much as a glance his way. 'Marvellous. And cocoa afterwards at the Copper Kettle.'

A few of them cheer.

'Are you really not going to come?' Martin sits with a cup of tea on the settee later that night.

William shakes his head, still embarrassed at his reaction to Colin.

Martin puts his arm across the back of the sofa and looks at William for a moment. 'We've never talked about it, have we? Your "Miserere".'

'No,' William says from the other end of the long settee, 'and I'm grateful that you haven't tried.'

Martin frowns. 'But you *loved* that piece of music. Why deprive yourself because of one unfortunate incident over half your life ago?'

William stares at Martin, teeth sinking into the soft sides of his mouth.

'The music is still the music, it's bigger than one choirboy's cock-up. It's bigger *and* better than that' – he takes a drink of tea – 'and so should you be.'

'Back off, Martin.' William's on his feet, a mug in his hand that needs to be flung against something. 'You think you know everything about me, but you don't know how it *feels. That's* what I can't cope with. How it feels!'

Martin stands too, less than a foot away from him, and gently takes the mug from his hand.

'Well, ponder this, Mr *Damaged*,' he says softly, 'you don't know how I felt when I kissed you. Trust me, you have *no* idea. Or when you let the other boys think I'd molested you. If I'd let those things be more important than the people involved, I wouldn't have talked to you when I saw you outside college with Gloria, and I certainly wouldn't have let you come and live with me.'

It's true, of course. Every word Martin says is true. What if he'd chosen differently? What if all that had happened could have made him a bigger person? If each disaster had been a crossroads at which he could have taken a better path? It's too painful to dwell on.

'I'm not coming.' William puts his hands in his pockets. 'I've sung with you, I've listened to music I swore I'd never listen to again, but I'm not going back to that chapel to hear that piece of music.'

'The men will be disappointed,' Martin calls after him as he leaves the room.

'I'm sure they'll get over it,' William calls back. 'Goodnight.'

He gets changed, washes briefly in the bathroom, then walks over to the small mantelpiece over the blocked-up fireplace and picks up the small rectangle of thick white card with wavy gold edging.

Evelyn and Frank invite you to their wedding
All Saints' Church, Mumbles
Saturday 4th May at 2 p.m.
And afterwards at the Langland Court Hotel.
(Apologies for short notice, we decided life's too
short to waste any chance of happiness)

At the bottom, in the familiar italic script he was so skilled at forging, she has written, *Time to move on? It would mean the world to me if you came.*

■ ■ ■

The severed arm is warm and wet in his hands.

'Take this outside,' Jimmy says. 'Hold it up and ask the parents whose child it belongs to.'

'I can't!' he says.

Jimmy is shoving from behind. 'Yes, you can!'

He's struggling to turn and run back inside. Jimmy pushes him again and he stumbles out into the crowd of mothers. They're mauling him, trying to get the arm. His chest heaves in and out; a terrible screaming starts. Strong hands are clasped round both his arms.

'William! Wake up. You're dreaming.'

He's sitting up in bed, breathing heavily with the familiar blend of distress and relief. Martin's next to him in T-shirt and underpants. He wonders briefly where he is and why Gloria isn't there. He tries to quieten the panting, relax his tense arms, open his fists.

'I didn't know if I should touch you or not.' Martin looks shaken.

William flops back onto his pillow. 'Was I yelling?'

'I'll say.' Martin smiles weakly. 'I've kind of been waiting for it to happen, but you still scared the life out of me.'

'You've been waiting for it to happen?'

Martin picks up the blanket that has fallen off the end of the bed and starts folding it. 'Gloria told me once about the screaming, that's all.'

Martin sits back on the bed in his underwear, hair tousled, T-shirt rucked up his back, and it suddenly feels like boarding school. William laughs suddenly. 'I'm not easy, am I?'

Martin smiles. 'You know I've always preferred interesting.'

William's eyes blur and he doesn't fight it. 'I've made such a mess of everything.'

'For the gentlest, most kind-hearted person I know, you are extraordinarily good at making a pig's ear of things.'

A warm tear trickles into his ear. 'You're a good friend, Martin.'

'I can see the music bringing you back to yourself. You shut it out as if it was the thing that hurt you, when all along, it's been the thing that can save you.' He puts a hand firmly on William's leg. 'Listen to it, sing it, teach it, breathe it, in and out, every day. You'll get there.'

'Mum's getting married,' he blurts out, pointing to his mantelpiece. 'She wants me to go.'

Martin goes over and peers at the invitation. 'Wow.' He straightens and turns back to William. 'That's big.' He sits back on the bed. 'Will you?'

William shrugs. 'I'm so bloody confused.'

'Where are you going?' William asks as Martin stands up. He doesn't want to be on his own yet.

'It's three in the morning,' Martin says, walking out, 'where do you *think* I'm going?' His head appears back round the door. 'To make us cocoa, of course.'

54

Colin isn't at choir. This concerns William more than he would have expected. There's a fragility to all the Midnighters, but there's something about Colin that particularly moves William. His way of holding his music so carefully in his hands. How he takes off his filthy donkey jacket and places it on the back of his chair, just so. William feels the chasm between what Colin has become and what he used to be; it settles in his chest and doesn't go away until he's walking home with Martin. He's come to enjoy his sessions with the tenors. He doesn't even mind that David always chooses to join them and spends the whole time staring at him.

During tea breaks, Colin's told William that his ex-wife and two children live in London with her new husband, with his high-paid job in the City – though not as highly paid as Colin's was five years ago, before he drank himself into oblivion with guilt over a miserable one-night stand. He has no visiting rights. He hasn't seen his children for over a year. He wonders how his son is getting on at secondary school. He wonders if they call this man Dad. He wonders what his wife says to them about him.

Tonight, William takes the tenors to work on 'Can't Help Falling in Love'. It's not easy, because Gloria loves this song and they're missing Colin, who always gets it first time. William is singing louder than normal to help drag them along. He wishes, as he's singing, that he'd just once sung it to Gloria, *really* sung it. She'd have loved it. He could have hammed it up, but meant it as well. Ready to quash the thought, as he's quashed a hundred thousand thoughts of her before, William decides to let it be, to let the music bring her to him. *Let me feel the love and the sadness*, he decides. And as he stands, beating time with his right hand, singing at almost full throttle, David steps out from the little huddle, his raised palm towards William. Everyone keeps singing as David approaches him. Inches away from him now, David's whiskery face intent, blue eyes questioning, curious, he lays his palm on William's chest. The pressure is warm and firm, and William feels the vibration from his singing against David's splayed hand. The two of them maintain eye contact as David grins. Still with his hand on William, he twists round to look at the others. No one stops singing, but they all smile at the smiling David. When they've finished, he walks back to the group, snatching his hand into the air, as if he's just touched something hot. A small round of applause breaks out, and although William isn't quite sure what it's for, he joins in.

Later, as they're eating and loading up with sandwiches, William stands on a chair and asks if anyone knows where Colin is. No one does.

'What do you do when one of them goes missing?' William asks on the way home. Parker's Piece is soggy after a short shock of a shower and the surprised earth smells strongly of the new season.

'I run a choir, not a hostel.'

'Aren't you ever tempted to do more?'

'I give them a place to be human once a week. That's my contribution.'

The next day, William makes sandwiches and a flask of sweet tea and spends five hours wandering round Cambridge: the benches on Midsummer Common, Parker's Piece, Jesus Green; the porticos of Eaden Lilley and Joshua Taylor. He sees other Midnighters, but not Colin. He does the same the following day, repeatedly circuiting the city centre in case the moment he'd turned a corner Colin had arrived.

'It's a pity if Colin misses the "Miserere",' Martin says the next morning, putting on his anorak. 'He absolutely loves it. I'm going straight from work, and then we're having cocoa after at the Copper Kettle so I'll be late back. I'm not going to ask if you'll come, but I bloody well wish you would.'

'Have a good day.'

He hears Martin run down the stairs and the door opening. Instead of the door slamming shut, Martin's steps come back along the hallway.

'William?' he calls up.

'Yes?'

'Have you looked in the Botanic Gardens?'

William almost runs there, frustrated for not thinking of it himself. After walking the pathways and a quick stride through the hothouses, William sits by the fountain for an hour and a half, the packed lunch on the bench beside him. As well as sandwiches, there are now two Jaffa cakes, an apple and a Club biscuit – as if Colin is a child or an animal he can lure with treats. His body tightens with anxiety as he imagines Colin in a gutter, Colin collapsed, drunk, or injured. In every imagining of him, William sees, buried under his layers, that burgundy tie round his neck.

He thinks of David at their last choir practice and it's as if he can still feel the hand on his chest. *It's no good*, he thinks. *I can't cope with this. I'm made from different stuff to Martin. I can't bear the pain.* Standing up, he imagines telling Martin he won't be coming to choir any more, and asking if it's still a condition of him staying in his flat. Maybe it's time to go home, anyway. He likes to think Gloria's had a few weeks to accept they're finished, that perhaps she is ready to start thinking about a different future.

Instead of crossing Parker's Piece, he turns right down Mill Road, an area he never visited as a chorister. Martin calls it the guts of Cambridge, which William thinks might suit him better right now than the historic centre. A tattered tweed coat and a pair of shoes with flapping soles catch his eye. The vagrant is walking down a gravel path he's never noticed before. At a distance, he follows him into a graveyard full of wonky headstones covered in lichen, leaning into the earth at extreme angles. Tired, he sits on a bench against a wall.

'William?'

Colin looks different. Like himself, but turned up a few notches; cheekbones sharper, hair wilder. He slumps down on the bench.

'I've been looking for you for days. Where've you been?'

'London.'

'How long for?'

'As long as it took me to beg my train fare back.'

'Here.' William hands him the bag.

Colin looks at him, holding the bag tentatively. 'For me?'

William nods.

He opens it and puts a sandwich straight in his mouth. He reeks of booze. William has never been conscious of it on Colin. Some of the men drink heavily before choir, but William wonders now if Colin deliberately arrives sober.

'Did you see your children?' William asks, after letting him eat for a few moments.

'My daughter. From a distance. Opposite the school gates.'
Colin is talking to the gravel path. 'She looked happy. Laughing
with her friends.'

'You didn't speak to her?'

He shakes his head. 'It was enough to watch her for a few
minutes.' He stretches out a leg so he can reach into his trouser
pocket. He unfolds a small piece of worn paper and hands it to
William. It's a family photograph; recognisably Colin, with his
wife and two children who look about five and seven. He points
at the girl. 'That's Katy. She's taller now and her hair's shorter.'

'Is that their address?' William points to the reverse side of
the photo.

Colin nods.

'You said you didn't know where they lived.'

'I could never show my face, so I may as well not know.'
Colin's head drops. William's afraid he's going to cry. 'When
she took them to London, my wife said if I got myself straight,
I could see them.'

'Martin told me you couldn't.'

'I can't if I'm on the booze. And I can't come off it, so it's the
same thing. And anyway, I don't want them to see me like this.'

'Tea?' William holds up the flask.

Colin nods but looks in the bag. 'Club biscuits. Haven't
seen these since they were in my kids' lunchboxes.' His body
straightens all of a sudden. 'What's the time?'

William checks his watch. 'Ten past five.'

Colin stands up, lurches to one side and then falls back onto
the seat. 'It's today, isn't it? The "Miserere". Come with me.'

'No, thanks.'

'Suit yourself.' Colin starts to walk in the wrong direction,
dropping the photo. 'Thanks for the food.'

'You've dropped your picture.'

'I know.'

'Don't you want it?'

He shakes his head. William watches from the bench as twice, Colin stumbles, but when he actually falls and knocks his shoulder on a gravestone, William bends down to pick up the photo, runs over to him, lifts his arm and puts it over his shoulder.

It takes them half an hour to get to the college. With his forehead dripping, his right arm stiff from supporting Colin, and his armpits sticky and damp, William breaks his promise to himself, and for the first time in thirteen years, walks through the college gates towards the chapel.

55

The doors are as high as he remembers. Their scale is grand whether you're four foot or six foot. Still majestic and lofty, yet still (and this surprises him), *still* it feels as if he's being welcomed. Trusting Colin to support himself now, William enters the narthex and a waft of ancient air leaves a grainy taste on his throat.

'Come on, William, you're in for a treat,' says Colin as they cross the threshold.

And here it all is; the rich ceiling, the glint of gold on the floor, and the deep colours, as window after window fills the chapel with refracted light.

Colin spots the others and sets off in a stumbling half-trot. The men shuffle up to make room on the pew. Jenny is here, excited and alert, pointing out something in the order of service to one of the men, a scarlet scarf over her jacket. William sits on the end with Colin to his right, but from further down the row, Martin stands up and waves his hands for everyone to move along so he can sit next to William at the end of the pew.

'You've come.' Martin pats him briefly on the leg.

'By accident,' he mutters.

He picks up the order of service: Rachmaninoff, Purcell, Weelkes. Old friends.

The pews are filling; raincoats, tweed jackets and anoraks like in his day, but now, bright wool scarves trail the floor, an afghan coat, a rainbow cardigan with toggles. There's a flash of purple and white to his left, and here they come. He feels a surge of adrenaline, as if it's him about to sing. Tiny and slight, tall and rangy, plump and spotty, in cassocks too long and too short, the boys process past, their light surplices billowing and white.

He glances down the line of Midnighters; they breathe heavily, sit awkwardly, crusty boots undone, dirty laces trailing. Maybe they're his protection, his ballast against the past; broken men, sung to by little boys, certainly no angels themselves. Ordinary yet extraordinary, all of them. A rush of wonder flows through him. Maybe Martin was right, his family debris is insignificant compared to this grandeur, this depth. Ridiculous, he knows, but the feeling that this chapel loves him is strong as ever. Here's Phillip! Still thin, more stooped, head tilting to one side with that sense of purpose, a job to be done. The choristers peel away, flowing into the stalls on either side of the aisle.

It's then that William discovers there are no barriers to time travel here. Because nothing has changed; the candle holders, the lights, the kneelers, the ironwork at the end of each pew. As the boys take their places and arrange their music, William can't stop the descent to a place deep within. He's in dual time now, alongside the grown Martin and his shuffling, smelly Midnighters, but equally, alongside his thirteen-year-old self, about to sing Allegri's 'Miserere'.

'The sacrifices of God are a broken spirit.' The dean's words are as familiar to William as his own name. 'A broken and a contrite heart, O God, Thou wilt not despise. Let us humbly confess our sins to Almighty God.'

There's nothing to be done. Time and place have buckled, and William is caught in the very moment from which he has been running for thirteen years.

56

Lined up in the narthex, the choristers feel the bulge of expectation in the air. Usually on high days, William imagines the
chapel's excitement at having so many extra bodies. Today, there's
no space in him for that kind of fancy. He is simply terrified.

He looks left at Martin, who stares straight ahead. Since the
caning two weeks ago and what happened afterwards in the toilets, he and Martin haven't spoken, haven't looked each other in
the eye. Yesterday, in the changing rooms after rugby, someone
shouted, 'Don't stand with your back to Mussey!' and William
simply carried on buttoning his shirt.

The organ starts, loud and riotous, and William could scream
at it all. Here he is, on the day he's dreamed of since he was five,
and yet he's never felt as wretched and anxious. At the threshold of the chapel, Martin dips his head close to William, so swift
and sudden it makes him jump.

'Did you send the letter to your uncle?'

'Yes,' William replies. 'I should have listened to you.'

Martin raises his eyebrows and exhales, cheeks like ping-
pong balls. 'What did you say?'

'Not much – "Just leaving Cambridge for Swansea. Back in
two weeks for William's big day. Please come. Both of you. I'm
sorry."'

Martin says nothing.

Too late now; his mother, Uncle Robert and Howard are in
there. Perhaps they've already spoken, worked out what he's
done. The possibility that Evelyn could be anything but furious

311

to see them is now so completely ludicrous, he hates himself.

He won't try and spot them. He breathes in sharply, and resolves that for the next hour, he's a chorister and principal soloist. That might be enough. If not, well, he'll worry about being a son and nephew afterwards.

A hard slice of daylight widens to their right. Sixteen boys turn to see William's mother dashing in. She notices William immediately.

'Sorry!' she mouths, two or three yards away, hand on her panting chest. 'There was an accident.'

The clerk appears, black cloak swinging with the speed of his approach.

'You'll have to wait until after the choir have processed.' His hand is at her elbow, guiding her away from the boys.

'Of course. Sorry.' She points at William. 'I'm his mother.'

Martin is staring at Evelyn and William hears him swallow. As they start to process, William fixes on the colour-flecked glow of the windows behind the altar and lets the faces of the congregation, turning so eagerly to watch them, remain a claustrophobic blur.

Setting his music down, his decision to ignore everything except Phillip and the music is obliterated, because here's Evelyn, tiptoeing in on shiny high heels. With the pews ranged at the sides, facing the aisle, no one can sneak in unseen. William doesn't recognise a single thing his mother is wearing; coat, bag, scarf, shoes. All new. She stops before a pew on which the people aren't too squashed and waits for them to create a space for her. To her left, William is shocked to see Mr and Mrs Mussey. When he stayed at Christmas, they said they'd like to come if he got the solo, but he assumed Martin would have told them not to.

312

It's not until Evelyn's removed the silky yellow scarf and accepted an order of service from the man to her right that William realises, with a hot rush of blood to his face, that Uncle Robert and Howard are sitting directly behind her.

'The sacrifices of God are a broken spirit: a broken and a contrite heart,' the dean begins, 'O God, Thou wilt not despise.'

Robert and Howard are smiling uneasily. What *has* he done? Evelyn glances at the order of service, but her body is turned towards the choir. Towards William.

'Let us humbly confess our sins to Almighty God.'

'We have erred, and strayed from Thy ways like lost sheep. We have followed too much the devices and desires of our own hearts.' On a usual Wednesday evensong, the dean's words are answered with a smattering of subdued responses. Today the swollen congregation booms back at him. 'We have offended against Thy holy laws. We have left undone those things which we ought to have done; and we have done those things which we ought not to have done; and there is no health in us.'

If only he could undo the things he ought not to have done recently. As the congregation thunders its way through the Lord's Prayer, Uncle Robert and Howard still look uncomfortable. His mother remains focused on William, with what Martin would call her slices-of-fruit smile.

With not so much as a glance at Phillip, William sings the responses he has sung hundreds of times.

'*O Lord, open Thou our lips.*
And our mouth shall shew forth Thy praise.
O God, make speed to save us.
O Lord, make haste to help us.
Glory be to the Father, and to the Son, and to the Holy Ghost;

As it was in the beginning, is now, and ever shall be:
world without end. Amen.
Praise ye the Lord.'

The congregation sits and there's a settling, a concentration of focus onto the choristers. The main event. In the silence, William opens his music, and for the first time in four years, approaches a solo without his eyes locked onto Phillip's.

A nudge from Martin and a split second late, he joins in.

'*Miserere mei, Deus . . .*' Trebles, tenors and basses blend, like the easy flow of water over pebbles in a stream. *Have mercy on me, O God.*

Uncle Robert is looking at William now.

William pulls his attention back to Phillip and notices how tight his choirmaster's face is and how intense his gaze on him. He stays for two bars.

'*Secundum magnam,*' they sing in unison.

Now the tenors lead – '*misericordiam*' – now basses, now trebles, whose rising voices hint at their imminent, startling ascent.

But William can't help himself. Evelyn, Robert and Howard are all watching him intently. He sings with the trebles and basses as they weave together, silken and soft into the gently stretched close of the line, '*Tuuuu-aaaam.*' *According to your great kindness.*

Back to Phillip, whose eyes are fierce now, demanding his attention, but they're in the first deep basket of silence and after that, the basses have another whole line before they even get to him.

Evelyn still has no idea. She gives him a gentle nod.

'*Et secundum multitudinem miserationum tuarum.*' The plainsong blossoms, powerful and mellow, filling the chapel.

According to the multitude of Your mercies.

What's Howard doing, rummaging at his feet? Uncle Robert is reaching forward to his mother; he wants her to know they're there, before he sings.

'Dele iniquitatem meam,' the basses finish – *Do away mine offences.*

Uncle Robert's hand is on her shoulder. The first solo is coming for him. Phillip will be leaning forward, his inclined head ready to nod his invitation. But look! Evelyn jumps and spins round. Robert gives a muted wave and – oh! – a flash of blood in Howard's hand. Tulips! He's giving her red tulips! Only the back of her head is visible to him.

The music gathers.

With swift efficiency, Evelyn knocks the flowers from Howard's hand and slaps his face. Robert's body jumps in surprise and the tulips fly upwards, towards the startled saints above. Single scarlet petals take wing, following their own trajectories for a second before drifting down, to land on a shoulder, a head, a forearm. The bouquet lands with less grace on Mr Mussey's lap.

William's throat locks. He can't breathe. Now! *'Amplius lava me ab iniquitate mea.'* Sky diving without a parachute. The chapel fills with the otherworldly, almost inhuman sound. Pure. Perfect. Top B.

Wash me thoroughly from my wickedness.

The clerk swoops down on Evelyn like a raven and holds her elbow. He's taking her away. She looks over her shoulder at him she leaves.

Here it comes. *'Et a peccato meo munda me.'*

Top C.

And cleanse me from my sin.

315

Drop down to the B. Rock-steady as the tenors weave and curl around it.

Howard has a red stripe on his cheek. His mother has been removed from the chapel. His uncle's eyes are tiny silver saucers.

He can't stand this. He can't look any more. Yet now, the simple act of switching his gaze back to Phillip is like a jump from one planet to another. But he must stop this torture, return to the safe place of his choirmaster's face. And it's only then, when he sees that Phillip's concentration is not on him at all, but on his friend beside him, that it hits him. With an icy tingle running from head to toe, William realises he hasn't sung a single note. It was Martin all along.

There are four solos left. He won't waste a second more on his despicable mother. He's back and he's ready and it's all he has left. William breathes, straightens, focuses entirely on Phillip. With two bars to go, he follows each note on the score, his eyes switching from music to Phillip. Music, Phillip. Nothing. Else. Phillip. Music.

But Phillip doesn't lean towards him. Doesn't even look at him. As if William has ceased to exist, it's Martin Phillip invites. And the next time, and the time after that, and the time after that, even though William's concentration doesn't waver for a second.

Once it's over, all twelve minutes of it, Phillip finally looks at him. And in that moment, William feels not just the disgrace of his choirmaster's disappointment, but everyone's; the other choristers, his family and every member of the bloated congregation.

Abruptly, it's intolerable for him to remain a second longer. He's not even aware of making a decision. His body takes over,

316

scrambling out of the choir stalls, treading on feet as he goes, running down the aisle. As he passes Uncle Robert and Howard, his foot lands and slips on a thick green tulip stem. His arms wheel back for a second, but he manages not to fall and runs on, breath loud and coarse, feet slapping the tiles.

In the vestibule, he sees his mother, still held at the elbow by the clerk. He keeps running, out into the flat light of cool spring, through the quad, past the Porters' Lodge, onto the street.

Eventually he squats and leans against the low wall, gripping his head.

'William!'

It's her, running towards him. And not far behind are Uncle Robert and Howard. He stands, knees shaking. And now, here they all are, together on the pavement.

'Happy now?' Evelyn's eyes narrow at Robert. She tries to take William's hand but he pulls it away. 'I told you it would put too much pressure on him.'

'You *asked* us to come, Evelyn!' Howard snaps, his cheek still red.

'I asked you *not* to come.' Her jaw's so tight it's a wonder she can speak.

William sees Howard's desperate glance at Uncle Robert, then at him. In that second of connection, William sees that his uncle realises who wrote the letter.

'You hit Howard.' William turns on his mother. 'You *hit* him.'

For a moment she looks appalled. 'He attacked *me* – with those bloody flowers!'

William sees the bewilderment on Howard's face. 'She's always hated the flowers, Howard, she used to throw them away.' He's punishing her. 'Didn't you, Mum?'

'I just wanted you to leave the three of us alone!' Now she's crying. 'All I wanted was to be a normal family, not bloody Lavery and Sons! I didn't want flowers – I wanted my family!' With a clenched cry of frustration she pushes Robert in the chest. 'Why couldn't you have died instead of him!'

'Evelyn!' Howards shouts. 'For God's sake.'

A calm comes over William. He turns slightly away from Robert and Howard so he's facing his mother. He's never felt so angry and so powerful.

'If someone had to die,' he says softly, 'I wish it had been you.'

Evelyn stops crying and stares at him.

'William,' Robert says, his voice low, 'enough.'

'*You* ruined today and I'll never forgive you.' He carries on as if his uncle hadn't spoken. He glances at the chapel over his mother's shoulder. A gust of wind moves his hair. 'Take me home.'

The air around them bristles with the shock of what's happened, with what's just been said. Evelyn stands looking at him, blinking. After what seems a long time, she inhales suddenly. 'You can't just *leave*.'

'I already have.'

'But I'm going back to Swansea tonight. I've got an interview tomorrow. I've got to sort out a house, school for September. As soon as term's over, I'll come and get you.'

William sees the shock on Robert's face. He knows nothing of Evelyn's plans.

'You've only got a few months left,' she says, 'it'll be fine.'

'I am not going back.'

Evelyn looks stupefied. 'Well, you can't come with me yet, I'm in digs, there's no room.'

'Then I'll stay with Uncle Robert.' The two men stare at the

318

ground. 'I can, can't I?' he asks them.

'Of course you'd be welcome,' Robert says, clearly unable to look at anyone, 'but it's up to your mother.'

William thinks she's going to cry again, but then she gathers herself, assembles one last bit of strength.

'Very well,' she says, staring at William, 'just until I've got everything ready.'

William notices three gowned men striding through the gates onto the forecourt; the clerk, Phillip and Mr Atkinson. Once they see William, they all come to a halt. And behind them, in the entrance, three more figures appear: Martin and his parents.

57

'That'll do me,' Colin says softly once the choir has processed out. 'That was heaven, that was.' His Scottish accent, often barely discernible is pronounced. 'Who wouldn't want to come and hear that? Tell me, William, cos I can't understand how anyone in their right mind could not want to hear *that*.'

'It's a long story.' William stands, light-headed, desperate to get out.

'All right?' says Martin on William's other side, and for a moment, William is completely disorientated at the sight of him.

'Let's go to the Copper Kettle, Colin,' he says, ignoring Martin. 'I need some fresh air, they can meet us there.'

Walking through the quad and out into the spring-fresh air, Colin still reeks of alcohol, though he seems to have sobered up and matches William's fast pace.

'Incredible really,' Colin says, as they pass the stately Senate House, over the cobbles and onto King's Parade. 'They're just kids, but I swear they pull heaven down when they sing like that.' William looks up from the pavement at Colin. He doesn't normally talk like this. Their eyes meet. 'Yep, that'll do me, thank you very much.'

A Ford Capri roars down the parade towards them. They stand and watch the car, polka-dotted with rust, shoot by with a gravelly roar. It screeches to a halt at Great St Mary's.

'Daft bugger's going to have to go back exactly the same way he came,' Colin says.

'I'll buy you dinner, Colin, what do you fancy?' William is ready to walk on, but Colin doesn't move.

'Thanks for making me a packed lunch.' Colin pulls William into a clumsy hug. The skin of his neck is soft and acrid. 'And for singing with me. You're a good man.' He lets go and looks back at the car as it jerks through a three-point turn. Abruptly, he starts walking. William has to run to catch him up.

'What's the hurry?'

The sound of the car accelerating, snorting and hiccoughing through the gears irritates William. He deliberately doesn't look round, but as the roar intensifies, he can't help but glance to his left as the car approaches.

'Bye, William,' Colin says softly, stepping into the road.

The impact knocks his body onto the long blue bonnet, across the windscreen and off onto the other side of the road, before William even cries out.

The blue light pulsates across King's Parade. A vivid ribbon spools from Colin's mouth and over his left cheek. His grip on William's hand is firm, though his open eyes are unseeing. Jenny kneels on the other side of Colin, stroking his head and talking to him. Then they stand and watch as the ambulance men manoeuvre him onto a stretcher. The other Midnighters clump together on the pavement with Martin.

Once the stretcher has been secured in the ambulance, the driver beckons William away from the open door, out of Colin's earshot.

'Has he got family?' he mutters. 'They need to come to the hospital. As soon as possible.'

'OK.' William nods, reaching into his pocket for the photo Colin dropped in the cemetery. 'I'll get someone to call them, but can I come with him in the ambulance?'

'All right. Get a move on though.'

William runs over to Martin. 'Can you call his wife?' He puts the grubby photo in Martin's hand, face down so the writing is visible. 'Tell her to get to Addenbrooke's. Quickly.'

'OK.' Martin glances round. 'Damn, where's the nearest phone box?'

'No. Go home to do it. I need you to bring some things to the hospital. You might want to write them down.'

'No problem.' Martin produces a tiny black diary from his jacket pocket and pulls out the pencil from the spine. 'What do you need?'

'Two towels, scissors – the sharpest you've got – a flannel, a bar of soap, razor, shaving cream, toothbrush, nail clippers, a flask of hot water, mouthwash and a newspaper.'

Martin nods, still scribbling as William climbs into the ambulance.

58

'Colin,' William whispers in his ear, 'I'm going to tidy you up. Your family are coming.' In a private room in Addenbrooke's hospital, there's no longer any grip to Colin's fingers and his breathing is shallow. 'The doctors think I'm bonkers, but who cares?'

Martin holds Colin's hand while William kneels in the corner with the bulging plastic bag and takes out the newspaper, laying it flat on the floor.

Martin glances from Colin to the photo they've propped up on the bedside cabinet. 'You've got your work cut out.'

'Watch me.' William rolls one of the towels and angles it under Colin's head. He hacks off the outer three inches of hair, dropping it onto the newspaper. Dipping his fingers in warm flask water, he teases through what remains, breaking the lugs. Looking every now and then at the photo, he combs it, parts it, and cuts again.

'How long have I got?' He asks without looking up.

'They left London about half an hour ago, so I'd say less than an hour.'

'What did you say to her?'

'That Colin had been in an accident and wasn't going to make it. That I knew the three of them were always on his mind, and if they wanted to say goodbye they should come now.'

William's hands are still. 'What did she say?'

'Once she'd ascertained who the hell I was, she asked what state he was in and would it upset the children.'

'And?'

'I told her not to worry about that.'

'Well done.' William gets on with the final touches to the hair. While William tips hot water onto a flannel, Martin leans in towards Colin and starts to sing 'Myfanwy'. William wipes Colin's face, rubbing at the corners of his eyes and the encrusted edges of his lips. The skin feels thin and tired against the pull of the flannel. Shaving cream expands like a living thing on his palm. William is soothed by Martin's voice, the resistance of the stubble to the razor, and the clear path of fresh skin that appears with each stroke.

William trims the eyebrows, then shapes them with his dampened thumbs until they lie sleek and thick, with a touch of grey. Martin's back at the first verse, but William has no idea how many times he's sung it. With the remaining water, he washes Colin's hands, dragging his nails through the bar of soap, then scooping out the gunge with a nail file. He cuts the fingernails down to a slim arch of white. Once the hands are dry, he files each nail. Finally, he dowses the toothbrush in mouthwash and carefully slides it into Colin's mouth.

Colin looks ten years younger, thinner, smaller. William smooths the left eyebrow again with his thumb and then sits next to the bed opposite Martin.

'Sing the last verse with me,' Martin says, nodding towards Colin's other hand, which William scoops up.

'He was in London,' William says after a few moments of silence. 'He watched his daughter come out of school.'

Martin exhales. 'Poor thing. At least he got back for the "Miserere".'

The room smells of soap, shaving cream and antiseptic. It's dark outside. William stares at Colin's neat crescent thumbnail.

'If I'd had my wits about me, I could have grabbed him. Saved him.'

Martin shakes his head. 'Try not to waste any time on that, William. You did more for Colin than anyone.' He smiles gently.

The second hand on the wall clock clunks its way through another minute.

'We'll miss him, won't we?' William swallows. 'All of us, I mean, the whole choir.'

'Yep.' Martin nods. We'll have to sing something special next week. To remember him.'

Neither of them speak for a while. Colin snatches at breath, making them jump, but then seems to settle, his mouth hanging a little open.

'How was it then?' Martin's voice is barely a whisper. 'Being back there.'

'Horrendous,' William answers, 'it was the first time I actually *let* myself remember the whole thing. God! It was awful.'

'I've always wanted to tell you,' Martin says, 'I was hoping Phillip would let you back in after you missed the first one. It's bothered me that you might have thought I stole it from you.'

'I *never* thought that. Imagine if you hadn't! What would have happened then?'

'We'll never know.'

'I've been so ashamed, Martin, for so long. The most spectacular ballo up in the history of the choir.'

Colin gulps for air again. They watch him for a few moments until he's quiet once more.

'It's not how I remember you,' Martin says. 'And I bet you anything it's not how Phillip remembers you. If you were the worst, you were the best too. Stunning. Absolutely stunning. However' – Martin sits up a little straighter and looks William full in the face, a hint of mischief in his eyes, a twitch at the corner of his mouth – 'there's no denying, it was the most delicious moment of high drama, you ripping down the aisle like a bat out of hell.' He smirks. 'You should have seen Phillip's face! He didn't move a muscle, just stared after you!' Martin lets out a giggle. 'I thought I was going to have to conduct the choir, as well as sing the solos.'

Martin puts his head back and laughs. William recognises this moment for what it is, sees the chance, and decides to take it. After thirteen years of wrestling it down, William allows the whole messy bundle of suppressed memory to surface. And like a miracle, laughter bubbles up with it.

'You're forgetting my skid on the tulip halfway down the aisle,' he says through the laughter.

Martin's face lights up and his body ripples with mirth. 'Oh yes! *Much* more decorous than a banana skin!'

Soon, both of them are fighting for breath, holding their stomachs. Martin's face in laughter is timeless and William feels thirteen again; the same boy, but this time, free.

The shriek of trolley wheels in the corridor brings them back to themselves, their bodies relaxed, their faces aching.

'God, that feels good!' William says eventually. 'I never thought, in a million years, I'd be able to laugh about that.' He inhales deeply. 'I feel cleaned out.'

Martin nods. 'Best medicine and all that.'

'Thank you, Martin,' William says.

'You know me, always up for a good laugh.'

'Not for that.'

'Oh.'

William watches Colin. 'For everything. Saving the "Miserere". Being pleased to see me outside the college with Gloria. Letting me stay.' On the periphery of his vision, he can see Martin's face looking at him. He finally looks back. 'I don't deserve you.'

Martin smiles and shakes his head slowly. 'I've told you before, no one deserves anyone.'

'Thank you.'

Martin nods at Colin. 'You've performed a minor miracle here today, my friend. He can't tell you himself, but it's a fact that he'd be extremely grateful for this.'

A surge of hope pushes on William's lungs. He's not sure for what, but it propels him to the foot of the bed. 'Let's make sure the sheets are tucked in at the bottom – if his wife sees the state of his toenails, we're rumbled.'

Once they've both attempted a hospital corner, Martin rubs his hands together. 'Right! I'm going to find us both a disgusting cup of tea.'

William rolls the newspaper up and drops it in the bag, putting everything else on top of it. He places it in the corner then sits and waits, looking at Colin; his jawline, the gully of flesh between his nose and mouth, his pale pink lips. He decides when he gets back to Martin's, he's going to put the 'Miserere' on. Loud.

His back is to the door and, although they arrive in silence, he knows they are there. She's slender, in high heels and a bright green coat, flanked by a teenage boy with shoulder-length wavy hair, and a younger girl, holding her mum's hand with both of hers.

'Hello.' The chair scrapes loudly as he stands. 'I'm William.'

'Are you the man who rang Mum?' says the girl who has Colin's chin and nose. They remain in the doorway.

'No, but I sing in a choir with your dad.'

'We didn't know Colin sang in a choir,' the woman says, and

then, as if by saying his name she's suddenly aware of him in the bed, she walks forward and the children follow.

'What happened?' the woman asks quietly. 'They said it was a road accident?'

'He was hit by a car.'

'Was he drunk?' the girl says.

Her brother flinches. 'Katy!'

The wife's red nails splay across her mouth and a tear sits on her eyelash. William notices a chunk of diamond, swivelled to one side of the skinny pole of her ring finger.

'You said he'd look different, Mum,' says the girl. The boy takes a step nearer the bed.

'I thought he would, darling.' She looks up briefly at William.

'Can he hear us?' The boy's deep voice has that unstable quality, as if at any moment it could veer off into a squeak.

'I think so,' William says, 'he squeezed my hand when I told him you were coming.'

The girl runs round to stand next to William and takes Colin's hand. 'Hello, Daddy,' she stage whispers.

The wife takes the other hand.

'I'll leave you to it.' William backs away from the bed.

'No!' the wife says quickly, nodding at the seat in the corner. 'Please stay. I didn't know he had friends here.'

William sits.

'He's not squeezing my hand, Mummy.'

'He's very weak, love.'

William hadn't planned to say anything, but finds himself speaking to the boy. 'I know he was wondering how you were getting on in your new school – Daniel, is it?'

Surprise and pain sweep the boy's face. He moves closer to his mother. 'Can I, Mum?' He holds Colin's hand, so all William

328

can see of it are the fresh white crescent nails. 'School's fine, but I still miss you.'

Five minutes later Colin stops breathing, but not before three people have said goodbye and placed a kiss on his fresh forehead.

Part V

ABERFAN

59

Martin pours them both a coffee. The morning sun whitens the curls of steam rising from the cups. They haven't been to bed yet.

'Where is it?' William stands with his head on one side, flicking through Martin's records.

'Depends which version you want.'

'Don't care.' He turns to Martin. 'You choose.'

Martin takes two strides to stand next to William. He pulls one out almost immediately and flashes its cover briefly at William; it's a recording from King's College.

'Sit,' he says, walking to the record player.

He does as he's told and closes his eyes. He hears the slither of the paper sleeve, the bump and crackle of the needle. Feels the give of the settee as Martin settles next to him.

'All right?' Martin asks twelve minutes later.

William opens his eyes and nods slowly. 'Still here.'

'Didn't spontaneously combust.' Martin smiles, then a hint of a frown creases his forehead. 'Did you imagine you were in the chapel?'

'Further back.'

Martin nods. 'You listened to it with your mum.'

'And Dad.' He smiles. 'On his lap, actually.'

'Butter biscuits in close proximity?'

William laughs, and the tear tips down his face. 'Almost certainly.' He takes a sip of coffee and they sit in silence for a while.

'Martin, do you think Colin held on? I mean, waited, till they'd come to say goodbye?'

Martin tilts his head. 'Possibly. You did tell him they were coming, didn't you?'

William sniffs and twists to face Martin. 'Can I borrow your car for the day?'

'Of course. What for?'

'To go and see Mum.'

'In that case, I'll give you the keys, but only once you've had a couple of hours' sleep.'

William looks at his watch; it's just after six. 'You're right.' He stands up. 'If I go to bed now I could leave at ten.'

Martin pulls him into a short, fierce hug. 'Well done, whatever happens,' he says, close to his ear, 'well done!'

• • •

By the time he drives into Mumbles, it's early afternoon and a smooth, shining expanse of sand stretches towards the glittering water. During the hours in the car, William has resisted practising what he's going to say. Several times though, he's found himself smiling at the thought of his mother's pleasure, and a sense of relief keeps stealing over him. Pulling the steering wheel right to climb the steep incline of Plunch Lane for the second time in his life, William feels the tacky pull of sweat under his arms.

The immaculate front lawn and window boxes spilling over with pink petunias, profuse yet tidy, are very Evelyn. The door to the house is stippled glass, with three strips of yellow wood emerging from the bottom left-hand corner, like inverted rays of sunshine. When he came here after the Aberfan funerals, he didn't even manage to get out of the car. This isn't an option now, so as soon as he's turned the engine off, he climbs out and strides down the path. By the time he's reached the door, his heart is thumping in his throat.

The simple two-tone bell is loud, but somehow, William can tell it's echoing through an empty house. There's no flicker of movement through the bobbled glass. She's out. Nevertheless, he presses the bell again. And again.

'She's not here.' A very Welsh voice comes from his left. The woman next door has stepped out onto her front garden. She's tall and skinny, with bulky pink strips of sequins on her slippers that twinkle in the sun.

'Do you know when she'll be back?'

The woman shakes her head, turns her mouth downwards. 'Not until late. She's gone to Sutton Coldfield.'

Something flickers in his belly; panic, some sense of betrayal. 'That's a long way,' he says, in an effort not to ask a direct question; after all, they're complete strangers.

The woman smiles, almost conspiratorially. 'She's gone to pick up her daughter-in-law.'

For a brief, insane moment, William wonders who that could be. He stares at the sequins across the woman's feet, notices her varnished toenails through the beige mesh of her tights.

'She's going to help Evelyn get ready for her wedding.' The woman's face tightens in concentration on William. 'Can I tell her who called?'

'No.' William is already back at his car, opening the door. 'Thank you. It doesn't matter.'

60

A flock of daffodils stand proud and golden in the late afternoon sun on the patch of grass at the turning into their street. From this distance, the Lavery and Sons sign looks small and understated. It's taken him three and a half hours to drive from Swansea to Birmingham. He called Martin from a service station and asked if he could keep the car for a few days; he was going home. Now, finally and unexpectedly parked beneath the Lavery and Sons sign, all he feels is tired.

The forecourt is empty and the relief is immense. He'd wondered if he was going to find Robert and Howard entertaining Evelyn and Gloria, and where on earth he'd fit into that. After staring at the illuminated tulips under the window, he gets out and lets himself in. The grandfather clock in the hallway stands sentinel, tick-tocking over the unassuming order of Howard and Robert's carefully lived life. He hangs his anorak on the hook furthest to the right, as he used to. The adjacent one, Gloria's, is empty. He stands for a moment, listening to the silence of the house, then heads through the adjoining door at the end of the hall to the funeral home.

The mortuary is clean, orderly and silent. All as it should be. He places his hands on the table. If there was a body waiting, he wouldn't hesitate; that would calm him, let him disappear for a while. Instead, he checks on supplies in the cupboards, turns the taps on and off, fiddles with the instruments. Eventually, he walks back through to the house.

Walking into his bedroom is the hardest. The orange poppy

duvet and matching curtains, the oak dressing table, the leather armchair, just as they always were. He scans the bare surfaces; the antimacassar stretches out on the dressing table, not rumpled and rucked without any perfume bottles or tissues. No hand cream, bracelets, safety pins or lipstick. No nurse's silver fob watch. He opens her wardrobe and a few wire coat hangers rock gently. It's worked. He left her so she could leave him. And now, he sees, she has.

He must have fallen asleep, but wakes to the sound of car doors closing. There's a click and then a swish of carpet downstairs.

'Robert? Howard?' He moves quickly to the top of the landing, not wanting to scare them.

The men stand, faces upturned; identical expressions of surprise, swept away by broad smiles. As William comes down the stairs towards them, Robert's arms lift, like a child to a parent.

They embrace while Howard stands with one hand on Robert's back and one on William's shoulder.

'Why didn't you tell us you were coming?' Robert stands back and grins at William.

'I didn't know I was,' William answers.

'I'll put the kettle on,' says Howard, squeezing William's elbow.

'*Please!*' William realises he hasn't eaten or drunk anything since this morning.

'Toast and Marmite?' Howard claps his hands together.

'Yes!'

'Just to keep you going,' he says, disappearing into the kitchen. 'We've got toad in the hole in a couple of hours.'

William and Robert go to the sitting room, hearing the rumbling kettle, the chink of a teaspoon, the opening of the fridge, through the open serving hatch.

'How long are you staying?' Robert says. 'How long have you been here? Is that your car in the driveway?'

'Robert!' Howard laughs from the kitchen. 'Too many *questions*, give him a chance.'

He sits on the sofa. Robert, on the armchair opposite, stares at him, smiling but intense and enquiring. Howard comes in with three mugs of tea and a packet of gypsy creams.

'Start on these while the bread's toasting.'

'Thanks.' Howard's flouting of the savoury before sweet rule has always struck William as quietly, delightfully anarchic.

'So, what's going on?' Robert slides to the edge of the seat, towards William. 'Are you all right?'

'Sort of.' He shrugs. 'I went to see Mum this morning.'

'In Swansea?' Robert is shocked. 'From Cambridge?'

He nods.

'Why?'

William takes a gulp of tea, holds his mug in both hands. He glances from Robert to Howard and sees the same intensity of gaze upon him. 'It's gone on long enough, hasn't it? We don't have forever.'

Robert quickly wipes his cheek with the back of his hand.

'But she wasn't there,' he says, 'she was here, wasn't she? Picking up Gloria.'

'How do you know?' Robert's cheeks are pink.

'Her neighbour told me.'

'And you drove straight back here?' Howard passes him the plate of biscuits. William takes one.

'Didn't know what else to do.'

'You missed them by less than an hour,' Robert says softly.

'We're just back from taking them to Spaghetti Junction,'

338

Howard says. 'Your mum was worried she'd get on the wrong way and end up in Ipswich.'

'Were you going to tell me?'

'What, that she's been here?' Robert gestures with open hands at the room.

'That she and Gloria have somehow become best friends.'

Robert looks to Howard first, then to William. He exhales, shakes his head. 'Glory be, William, none of us knew what to do for the best. But you should have talked to her,' he says, with a pleading in his face.

'I couldn't! She'd have persuaded me to stay! Just like she persuaded me to marry her in the first place!'

'She was in such a mess' – Robert frowns – 'and she kept saying she wanted to see your mother.'

'Why would *that* matter so much?' William asks. Again, he sees the helpless glance between the two men.

'William.' Howard sounds matter of fact. 'These things are between you and Gloria, not us. You need to speak to her.'

'I've told you, I *can't*. Gloria getting to know Mum isn't going to help anyone.'

'You're not in a position to judge that, William. Not until you've spoken to Gloria.'

'Are you going to the wedding?' Howard picks his mug up and takes a sip.

'I wanted a proper conversation with her. I won't be able to do that at the wedding. Don't you think it will be odd, just being there but not being able to talk?'

'Maybe,' says Howard, 'but this whole situation is odd, always has been. It'd be one hell of an olive branch, don't you think, being there, with a big beautiful smile on your face, as she comes down the aisle?'

'If Gloria wasn't going to be there it would be a lot easier,' William says.

'How about you do this for your mother,' Robert says, 'and then deal with Gloria afterwards.'

'Easily said.' William can't help but smile at the hopeful looks on their faces. 'But OK. I'll try.'

'Hallelujah!' says Robert. 'Will you go back to Cambridge in the meantime?'

'I've got to get Martin's car back to him.' He smiles at them. 'But I'm home now. You can leave the mortuary to me, I'll take care of everything.'

61

William gently lifts the seventy-three-year-old man into his coffin. The embalming has taken him two hours. He quickly puts him in the tweedy suit and checked tie his family has provided. The sun casts the golden glow that appears in the room mid-morning. He's nearly finished; the man's sparse hair only needs a quick comb. It feels good to be back in here, doing what he does well.

After two quick knocks, Howard comes in. 'Martin on the phone for you.'

William puts the comb on the man's chest and goes through to the office. 'Martin?'

'How are you doing?'

'OK. Just finished my first embalming. Still trying to get to grips with Mum's wedding.'

'Are you going to go?'

'Yes. Howard pointed out it would be the mother of all olive branches.'

Martin chuckles, then after a pause asks, 'How do you feel about seeing Gloria?'

'Terrified.'

Another pause, and he hears Martin inhale suddenly. 'She rang me, from your mum's. She says that if you're going, it might be good – for everyone – if I came too.'

William sees Howard looking up from his desk. 'Easier? How?'

'They think you'd have me, if you needed someone. And so

would Gloria, I suppose.' He lets out a weak laugh. 'Think of me as ballast.'

William wants to be indignant at the two women making arrangements for him, but all he can think is how good it would be to have Martin there. 'I could drive down after work in your car next Friday, stay the night and then we could leave first thing.'

'It'd make more sense for me to come by train to Birmingham and then drive with you from there. Saves you going to and fro.'

'You sure?'

'Absolutely.'

'Thank you. Robert and Howard want to get there in time for a pub lunch. They hate being hungry at weddings.'

'The prospect is getting better by the minute.'

Apart from sleeping, embalming, and eating comfort food served by Howard and Robert, the only other things William does in the next week are buy a grey suit, so there'll be no mistaking it for his undertaking uniform, and arrange for an audition for the City of Birmingham Symphony Orchestra Chorus. Boys in his sixth form played in the CBSO youth orchestra, but Robert recently told him about their brand new amateur choir, all set to perform challenging works to the highest international standard. William applied before he let himself think about it too much and has been invited to an audition in a week's time.

Very quickly, it's Friday, with the wedding tomorrow. Howard is cooking beef bourguignon. The kitchen is relaxed, full of the smell of itself. William is laying the table, and Robert is getting a head start on the washing up with the saucepans.

'Quick drink before we eat?' says Howard. 'Beer? Gin and tonic?'

They sit at the table; him at the end, Howard and Robert on either side.

'Ready for tomorrow?' Robert asks.

'Not sure.' William flips the caps from the three beers and slides a bottle in front of them both. 'Have you, even for a moment, felt sad for Dad?' he asks Robert. 'That she's marrying someone else?'

'I'm sad at how short his time with your mum was, but if anyone knows that this is what he'd want for her, then it's us.'

Howard lets out a mixture of a sigh and a gentle laugh, and nods. Are they referring to something he should know about?

'William,' Howard says, apparently reading his confusion, 'you do remember, don't you? What he said to us just before he died?'

'No,' he says, 'I wasn't there. You were, but me and Mum got there too late.'

'You don't remember at all?' Robert seems incredulous.

'I remember you both leaving us on our own with him, but he was already dead. And Mum was so upset we'd missed it. She was talking to him, and I was embarrassed for her, because I knew he'd already gone.'

He's suddenly at the edge of a precipice, a feeling that something's coming to push him from behind. A pulse is thumping in the ball of his right foot.

'That's not what happened, William,' Robert says.

Howard gently puts his beer down on the table.

'Your mum had been at the hospital all day,' says Robert. 'We'd been looking after you. She called us early evening and said we needed to come. When we got there, she was in quite a state. She hadn't eaten, hadn't even had a cup of tea or been to the loo. We said she should take a few minutes.'

'She didn't want to,' Howard said, 'but she went anyway.'

A smell: antiseptic, something sickly sweet. A cloudy glass on the bedside table. Wanting to leave with his mum, but wanting to stay. The door to the memory flies open and it's all there before him.

His dad has lost so much weight, his hip bones make miniature mountain peaks under the sheets. His face is all juts and dips. No longer Robert's identical twin.

Robert lays his hand on Dad's arm. Howard's firm hands are on William's shoulders, pushing him gently towards the bed.

'If you don't say goodbye now, you might wish you did later.'

His dad's eyes open. His neck twists to face him. A bony hand lifts slowly and rests briefly, clumsily on his head, before sliding off. How light and weak it feels! This hand that tickled and lifted, cuddled and played.

'Where's Mum?' The voice is as weak and clumsy as the hand.

'Having a wee and getting a cup of tea.' It all sounds so silly and he wishes he hasn't said it.

'She'll be back in a flash, Paul,' says Robert gently.

His dad's finger points at each of them. 'The Three Musketeers.'

'What'll we do without you?' Robert strokes his dad's arm, his voice all over the place. Howard remains behind William but his hands tighten on his shoulders.

His dad's lips are cracked and his pale tongue keeps trying to lick them. Robert takes a tissue and dowses it in water, then dabs it on his lips. Paul lies still as his brother tends to him, then raises his hand again. He's going to speak.

'Keep them close, Robert. Please keep them close.' His throat rolls and bobs in his scrawny neck. 'And if she finds someone else.' His arms lift from the bed and he puts both thumbs up.

Then, with no warning, no fuss, but instantly and completely, he's gone. Doesn't even close his eyes. The shock shoots down to William's feet and up to his head.

'No!' Evelyn's at the door. She approaches the bed. 'No!'

Robert and Howard stand back, Robert silently sobbing. Howard takes his hand. It's the first time William has ever seen them touch each other.

'It was seconds ago, Evelyn. It was peaceful,' Howard whispers. Robert's head hangs as if his neck has no strength. His tears are dropping onto the lino and William thinks he can't *bear* this. He wants to run away, he wants to go with his dad.

'Evelyn,' Howard says, 'we'll give you some time on your own with him. Shall we take William?'

'No! Please don't take him.' The desperation of the 'please' punctures William's heart.

As Robert and Howard exit the door, Robert's shoulders heave up and he lets out a deep, deep sob.

William is terrified. How long can something hurt this much? He's shaking, watching Evelyn lie on the bed, tuck her head under his dad's chin. 'Paul,' she sobs, 'you didn't wait for me.'

Inches from her crying face, the eyes that haven't got his dad in them any more sit like cold marbles in deep sockets.

Robert is still crying in the corridor. The bed is shaking with his mum's weeping. And his dad's body without him in it revolts him. And he just can't *stand* this! He's rooted to the spot. Imploding. Exploding.

They leave the hospital an hour later. She puts her arm tightly around his shoulders as they walk, and pulls him to her side.

'It's you and me now, William. You and me.'

He remembers his dad's raspy voice – 'Keep them close, Robert' – and his eight-year-old heart knows that somehow, his world is always going to be out of kilter from now on.

62

'Is the plan still to meet for lunch?' Martin says, glancing over at William in the passenger seat.

They're half an hour out of Swansea. They've listened to music, they've sung and they've laughed. They haven't talked about anything that matters.

'Yes, there's a pub not far from Mum's.'

'I'm going to duck out, if you don't mind.'

'You? Give up the chance of food? What's going on?'

'I'm going to meet Gloria.' He winces. 'She's scared.'

'Fair enough,' he replies, realising that now they are close, so is he, that he could do with Martin's company. But mostly, the thought of Gloria being scared to see him squeezes his heart. 'Where are you meeting her?'

'Midday, somewhere on the seafront.'

'I assumed she'd be with Mum.'

Martin shakes his head. 'Apparently it'll just be her maid of honour at the house.'

The electric pop of the idea straightens William's spine. 'In that case, I'll duck out of lunch too. You can drop me off at Mum's.'

Martin raises his eyebrows. 'Are you sure?'

'I'm sure.'

'She'll be busy, and how will you get to the church?'

'It's the local one, it can't be that far.' With a kick of adrenaline he adds, 'If it goes well, I might even get a lift!'

'Can I help you?' The woman at the door is about Evelyn's age, and for a second, William searches her face for signs of his mother, but then realises of course it's not her. 'We're a bit pre-occupied at the moment,' she says, already poised to close the door with a polite smile.

'I've come to see Evelyn.'

Both hands fly to her mouth and she takes a step back. 'Dear Lord, it's William, isn't it?'

He nods.

'Hang on.' She pushes the door carefully until the catch clicks gently shut. Her figure darts to the left. William studies the concrete slabs under his feet. Then a change in the light makes him look up and his lungs inflate suddenly. Even through the opaque glass, her movement, the angle of her arms at her side, the tilt of her head, is as familiar as an old ache.

The door opens. Huge curlers, quilted dressing gown buttoned to the neck, red slippers. Full make-up. Different. The same. She stands with her hand on the door, still and silent.

'Well,' she says, a ghost of a smile lifting one side of her mouth, 'if it isn't his Lordship.' She talks softly. 'It's good to see you, William.'

She leans towards him, one arm held out, and he thinks for a moment she's going to shake his hand. But she's reaching to his face. She touches it gently, briefly, then puts her hand in a pocket.

'Let me look at you for a minute. William James, twenty-six years old.'

'Hello, Mum.'

'Hello, William.' She steps back and gestures into the hallway. 'Are you coming in?'

She leads him into a spacious sitting room, awash with light

348

from the large bay window made up of small rectangular panes, some with distorting balls of glass.

'Have a seat.' She points to a generous plush sofa. Once he's sat down, she sits opposite on a matching armchair with wide arms. The woman who answered the door comes in. Her cheeks are scarlet and she holds her hand to her chest.

'Evelyn, the car will be here in an hour and we've not done your hair or nails yet.'

'I won't stay long,' William says, 'I just wanted to see you before you got married.'

Evelyn looks at her friend. Is it panic or excitement he sees in the flash of her eyes?

'We'll be fine, Norma. If you do my hair and nails now, you can get ready while William and I have a few minutes.'

Norma nods. 'Just pretend I'm not here.' She picks up a comb then quickly puts it down again. 'Tea?'

'I'll make it,' says William, 'you start her hair.'

'Grand!' Evelyn's smile is radiant, and he was right, she *is* excited. 'The kitchen's on the right, you'll be able to find everything.'

When he comes back in with a tray, the last of the curlers is coming out and Norma starts combing his mother's hair. Evelyn has a permanent half-smile on her face, but her hands are tapping in her lap.

'You look well, Mum.'

'And it would be a sad thing, if I didn't have a spring in my step on the day I'm getting married, don't you think?'

'What's he like?' William busies himself, putting mugs of tea within reach of both women.

'He's a wonder, William.'

'Good.' He's suddenly at a loss for words.

349

'So,' she says, pleasant, open, but with a poise that strikes him as a kind of defence, 'what's your news?'

He feels sorry for Norma, who gently nudges Evelyn's head down so she can get to work, looking at his mother's hair with forensic concentration, as if to reassure him that nothing else going on here is of the slightest interest to her.

'CBSO are starting a new choir. I'm auditioning next week.'

Evelyn looks up suddenly. No surprise, he thinks, that someone would want to marry her with that radiant face. They may as well be in the Copper Kettle talking about his latest solo. He wishes he was as composed as her. He can't sit still, inches forward to the edge of the sofa, notices the large bricks of the chimney that dominate the room, his own wedding photo on the mantelpiece.

Norma shakes the hairspray and fills their half of the room with it. She looks at the clock. 'Half an hour, Evelyn. I *wish* I could leave you two alone, this is killing me, but both of us need to get changed and I haven't done your nails yet.'

'I'll do her nails,' William says. Both women look at him with such identical surprise, he can't help but laugh. 'I do it all the time in the mortuary.'

Norma's hand goes back to her chest. Evelyn glances up at her. 'Welcome to the world of Lavery and Sons, Norma.'

'I'm pretty damn good at nails actually, Norma.' William smiles. 'How about you both get changed, then I'll do your nails, Mum.'

Evelyn gives a sharp nod and stands up quickly. 'Game on, Norma!' She puts her hands on her friend's shoulders and pushes her from the room. 'Let's get a shuffle on!'

He follows them out with the tray and goes into the kitchen. From behind a closed bedroom door, he hears the soft slap of hands and the thud of what he takes to be jumping feet. Grinning, he washes and dries the mugs before going back into the lounge.

He goes straight to the alcove to the left of the chimney, where he noticed the skinny spines of Evelyn's records standing fresh and pristine, even though she will have listened to all of them many times. Of course, they're meticulously alphabetised, so it takes him less than ten seconds to find what he's looking for. He lays it on the turntable ready, then sits back down and waits. As soon as he hears a door open, he jumps up, puts the record on and returns to the settee. The sound quality is even better than Martin's.

Miserere mei, Deus: secundum magnam misericordiam tuam.
Have mercy on me, O God: according to Your great kindness.
Et secundum multitudinem miserationum tuarum,
dele iniquitatem meam.
According to the multitude of Your mercies, do away
mine offences.

The door swings open to reveal a younger-looking, elegant Evelyn, in a fitted cream dress with an orange rose pinned to it. There's a bottle of nail varnish in her hand and her mouth is open ready to say something, but when she hears the music she stops.

'Sit down, Mum.' William holds his hand out to her. She gives him the bottle of varnish. It *tick-tick-ticks* as he shakes it.

Amplius lava me ab iniquitate mea: et a peccato
meo munda me.
Wash me thoroughly from my wickedness: and cleanse
me from my sin.

Quoniam iniquitatem meam ego cognosco: et peccatum
meum contra me est semper.
For I know my faults: and my sin is ever before me.

She sits next to him and their eyes meet briefly before he gently takes her left hand in his. Carefully, he draws the brush, plump and glistening with orange varnish, down the length of the nail. The sound is so good, the choristers may as well be in the room with them.

Tibi soli peccavi, et malum coram te feci: ut justificeris in
sermonibus tuis, et vincas cum judicaris.
Against You only have I sinned, and done this evil in Your
sight: that You might be justified in Your saying,
and clear when You are judged.

He lays her hand down in her lap and she offers him the other. He feels the tremor in it, the warmth of the blood in her body.

Asperges me hyssopo, et mundabor: lavabis me,
et super nivem dealbabor.
Purge me with hyssop, and I shall be clean: wash me,
and I shall be whiter than snow.
Auditui meo dabis gaudium et laetitiam: et exsultabunt
ossa humiliata.
Let me hear of joy and gladness: that the bones which
You have broken may rejoice.
Averte faciem tuam a peccatis meis: et omnes i
niquitates meas dele.
Turn Your face from my sins: and blot out all my misdeeds.

Second coat. He has so much he wants to say, but right now, her warm, soft hand is in his, and he is making her beautiful for her wedding and they are listening to Allegri's 'Miserere'.

Cor mundum crea in me, Deus: et spiritum rectum innova
in visceribus meis.
Create a clean heart, O God: and renew a right spirit
within me.
Ne proiicias me a facie tua: et spiritum sunctum tuum
ne auferas a me.
Do not cast me away from Your presence: and do not take
Your holy spirit from me.
Redde mihi laetitiam salutaris tui: et spiritu principali
confirma me.
O give me the comfort of Your help again: and 'stablish
me with Your free spirit.

Once it's over, he looks up to meet her eyes, which are fixed on him.

'I'm so sorry for how I treated you, Mum.' He's worried he might cry.

She smiles gently and puts her hand on his. 'I tore you in two with the way I treated Robert and Howard.' She withdraws her hand and sits back. 'You know, there's a madness that comes with grief. For a good few years after your father died, I had a layer of skin missing.' She rubs a hand slowly the length of her arm. 'I was raw. The sight of your uncle was like having salt rubbed onto that rawness.' She scrunches her face. 'I was so jealous they still had each other. I've apologised to them, but I'm glad I can apologise to you now. I hated how close you were to them, when really that was a wonderful thing.'

'I'm glad you're getting married. Dad would be too, I'm sure of it.'

'Thank you, William. I'll never forget him.'

'I know.' They sit in easy silence for a few moments. 'I didn't think you'd actually go to Swansea without me.' He didn't plan to say this, and worries he sounds churlish.

She nods. 'I didn't think you wouldn't come! For the first six months I changed the bed in the spare room every week, so it would be fresh if you turned up.' She shakes her head. 'What a terrible mess we can make of our lives. There should be angel police to stop us at these dangerous moments, but there don't seem to be. So all we're left with, my precious son, is whether we can forgive, be forgiven, and keep trying our best.'

'We'd best go for it then, hadn't we?'

'Let's.' Breathing in sharply, she splays her hands and surveys her nails, the exact colour of the rose pinned to her dress. 'Nice job, William. Who'd have thought it?' She lays them neatly on her lap. 'You know, I only pretended to drop out of your life, I've kept a very close track on you. I know more than you think.'

'What do you know?'

'You muddled along at sixth form, excelled at your embalming training. You did a brave and difficult job at Aberfan and you're left with the scars of it. You married a wonderful woman, insisting you'd never be a father, and you walked out on her because you thought she'd be better off without you.'

'I know you meant well spending time with Gloria . . .'

The door whooshes open and there's Norma, transformed in a sky-blue silk dress, full make-up and hair in a chignon. 'Five minutes, Evelyn.'

'Well, look at you!' Evelyn raises her eyebrows and smiles at her friend.

354

Norma makes a quick curtsy, then her face creases in distress. 'Dear Lord, *all* I want is for you to have time on your own, but the car's about to pull up!' She looks at William. 'You'll come with us, won't you? In the car, I mean?'

'I'd be honoured – and late if I didn't; I'm on foot.'

Evelyn stands. 'Right then, Norma!' The business is back in her voice as she waves her fingers in the air to dry them. 'Where's that daft little purse you insist I have to use as a hand-bag?'

'Here.' Norma steps into the hall and comes back to slide a small silky bag on a chain over Evelyn's hand.

'Well, how about this for a wedding present, eh Norma?'

'Thank heavens for waterproof mascara,' says Norma, grinning.

'And quick-drying nail varnish,' Evelyn adds.

There's a gentle tap at the door.

'It's the driver,' Norma says. 'Nice job on the nails, William!' She darts out to the vintage cream Rolls-Royce and stoops at the window to talk to the driver. 'You two sit in the back,' she calls, straightening up and running round to the other side to get into the front passenger seat.

Once they pull away, Norma starts chatting loudly to the driver.

'So,' Evelyn says, as the car descends the lane's steep incline, 'you do know this wonderful wife of yours is going to be there?' Now they're minutes from the church, William feels a thrill at the thought, but tries to ignore it. 'I know what you're *trying* to do, but you owe her one more conversation.' Evelyn suddenly looks out of the window and William sees they've arrived. 'I have to say, William, much as I love you, your timing could have been better. We're there already!'

355

'Well' – Norma twists round to face them – 'one way of having a *bit* more time to yourselves would be if William walked you down the aisle.' She looks, triumphant, at Evelyn, then William. 'What do you say to that, then?'

He can see the leap of joy in her face as Evelyn turns to him.

63

The church porch smells of dusty paper and cold stone. Norma has taken her seat at the front after making sure there's a space for William.

'What music are we walking in to?'

'Vivaldi. *Four Seasons*.'

'Nice, which one?'

'Winter, violin concerto in F minor.'

'Classy!'

'What would you expect?'

'Mum?' He looks straight ahead.

'Yes, son.'

'I love you the most. Always have.'

There's a puff of breath, then she squeezes his elbow. Evelyn slides her arm from William's and stands directly in front of him. 'I need you to tell me one more thing, William.' Her gaze on him is steady and serious and it makes his stomach pitch.

'What?'

'Do I have lipstick on my teeth?'

'No.' He laughs. 'You're all clear.'

Once the music starts, there's a rustle of bodies as people stand, and although it's a small church, he's shocked to see that every single seat is taken.

'Blimey!' he says.

'Plenty of time for you to get to know this crowd,' she says, as if reading his mind. 'Your lot are on the front row, left-hand side.'

And there they are; Martin, a head and shoulders above everyone else, having a good look round. Next to him Howard and Robert, and next to them, nearest the aisle, chestnut hair, straight-backed: Gloria.

Racing pulse, walloping heart, wet palms.

'I'll have my mind on other things for the rest of today,' Evelyn mutters through a smile, nodding at people as they start their solemn, in-time-to-the-music walk. 'You concentrate on Gloria.'

He feels suddenly helpless, terrified at the approach. Unknown, smiling faces like a field of exotic flowers. Howard twists round and catches William's eye, then nudges Robert who also turns and then whispers to Gloria. William braces himself, but she doesn't turn.

The man waiting for Evelyn is tall, with thick grey hair and a slight tilt to his body. As he turns, William can see his left leg is at a strange angle.

'There he is!' Evelyn whispers, as if surprised to see him.

'He must hate me,' William whispers back, conscious of the smiling vicar they are heading for.

'Nonsense,' Evelyn says, 'he's not that kind of man.'

They've arrived. Frank nods at William lightly and smiles. Then his eyes land on Evelyn and William is left in no doubt that this man is in love with his mother. Not until she has slid her arm from William's and reached out to take Frank's hand does she let out a sob; a short, wild cry. Frank puts his hand on her back, and she breathes in and straightens. She looks across at William and winks.

Without her, he feels horribly unanchored, exposed. Quickly, he slips into the space next to Gloria. They both look straight ahead as everyone sits.

358

'Welcome, all of you, to this joyous event,' says the vicar, opening his arms, 'the wedding of our beloved friends, Frank and Evelyn.'

So close to Gloria after all these weeks, he breathes in her perfume, the fresh shampooed smell of her hair, and his stomach flips. William doesn't need to turn towards her to see the difference. Doesn't need to look. He simply knows. Gloria is pregnant.

'This wasn't deliberate. I promise.' Gloria puts her hands on her rounded stomach.

The graveyard is littered with confetti. Frank's family have been summoned for the photos, and Gloria has accepted William's invitation for a quick walk. Later, he will describe the service as an out of body experience. Standing next to her during the hymns, he was stabbed by unexpected moments of joy so intense and physical he had to channel the surges of energy into his singing. The first time, verse two of 'Praise, My Soul, the King of Heaven', he made the vicar physically jump. Martin joined in so it wasn't just him who drew attention. He didn't understand how this thing he'd never wanted could make him so happy. Maybe it was simply being next to her again.

'I believe you,' he says now, hands in his pockets to fight the impulse to hug her, put his fingers through her gorgeous hair and touch her changed form.

'Well, good. I'm glad that's straight.' She still won't look at him properly. 'And I'm pleased you and Evelyn have talked,' she says after a pause, 'at long, bloody last.'

He nods. 'Yes, at long bloody last.' Their feet crunch on the gravel pathway for a few steps.

'I wasn't going to let her be cheated out of being a grand-mother as well as a mother.'

'You did the right thing. You've always been better than me at that.'

'You big *pillock*, William.'

He expects a smile to slide across her face, but there isn't one. She's angry. Of course she is. Wives aren't like mothers. They can stop loving.

'How are you?' He gestures at her stomach and, even though she's unhappy with him, there's an involuntary flutter of ela-tion in his own belly.

She shrugs. 'I'm dealing with it.'

Pink and white scraps of confetti skitter across a gravestone in front of them. A burst of laughter comes from the church. They'll need to go back soon. He wants to hold Gloria's hand, which hangs, elegant, by her side, still with her wedding ring on, he notices. His mother and Frank are walking towards the car.

A fresh breeze rolls confetti across the gravel and over Gloria's cream shoes. She kicks her foot to shake it off. In front of the church, Evelyn is climbing into the lovely old car as Frank holds the door, with a smile splitting his face. The door clunks shut and the car drives away past a crowd of waving people.

On impulse, William reaches out for Gloria's hand, but she shakes her head. A gust of wind cools his face. There are more clouds than blue sky now. Looking across at Gloria's stately, heavy form, he suddenly knows exactly what he needs to do next. And he so wants her to be with him when he does it.

'Gloria?' He stops walking and is grateful that she stops too, and for the first time, looks him in the eye.

'What?'

'I'm going to Aberfan. Will you come with me?'

'That's what you've got to say to me, is it?' Her eyes are ferocious; he notices how tightly she's gripping the handles of her bag. 'Only I'd *wondered* whether you might ask me how I've managed since you've been gone thinking I'm going to be a single mother. I thought maybe you might ask me about that, William!'

'I'm sorry,' he says, blinking against the instant burn of tears.

Gloria stands steady, glaring at him. 'I was going to tell you I was pregnant. I was trying to work out the best way to do it. Then there was that awful bloody christening. And then you just . . . just left! How could you do that to me, William?'

The cool breeze strengthens. His hands are cold; he wants to take hold of Gloria's. 'I wanted you to be free of me.'

Gloria shakes her head, lets out a sorry laugh.

'Please come with me to Aberfan.'

'When?' A strand of hair is blown diagonally across her face, but she does nothing to move it.

He shrugs, glances round at the departing cars. 'Tomorrow?'

Her green eyes seem to give up some of the animosity, searching his face for something. 'All right.'

He lets go of the breath he didn't realise he was holding. 'Thank you, Gloria.'

'I'll need the loo a lot,' she says, not returning the smile.

'Of course.'

She turns her back on him and heads for the church. 'Now leave me be for a bit,' she says over her shoulder, 'I can't take too much of you at once.'

'OK,' he says, watching the familiar swing of her hips, the purposeful heel-toe of her walk, conscious he's watching so much more than Gloria; part of himself, part of them. 'Thank you,' he shouts.

She raises her arm as she walks away and he can't tell if it's in dismissal or acceptance.

64

Once she's eaten the sandwiches William made for them in Evelyn's kitchen this morning, Gloria sleeps all the way from Swansea to Merthyr Tydfil. When she wakes, she still doesn't speak, turns herself away from him to look out of her window. It's disconcerting. From the moment William met Gloria, she has talked. His adult life has been narrated by her. Driving through the valley villages – Cilfynydd, Troedyrhiw – she would normally have laughed, attempting to read them out loud. So many times, he wants to start a conversation with her, but feels he has no right until she has said what she needs to say to him. In spite of all this, unbidden arrows of joy keep piercing him as he steals glances at her.

'You've probably got a lot to get off your chest,' he finally says, as they drive through Pentrebach, two miles from Aberfan. 'I understand, so feel free.'

Gloria continues to gaze out of the passenger window, across the valley, yellowed by the afternoon sunshine. 'Let's do this first.'

In William's mind, Aberfan knows only the night-time; with the roof of Pantglas school forever crumpled, poking at weird angles out of the landslide like a broken umbrella. Aberfan's streets are forever dark and tacky underfoot.

To arrive in broad daylight, with green trees vivid against a blue sky, disturbs him, as has passing the new school on the edge of the village, with children all over the playground.

Where the coal waste bulldozed through stands a community centre, behind which he parks Martin's car. While Gloria goes to find a toilet, William walks a few paces to stare at an electric-blue climbing frame and roundabout, at some swings with cheerful red frames.

He hears Gloria approaching from behind. She stands by his side.

'This is where the school was,' he says. A small dog waits for its elderly owner to catch up, then sniffs at the roundabout.

How human imagination and will could contrive to transform the Aberfan he knew to what it is now utterly confounds him. He finds he doesn't want to stare at a playground, a community centre. He's come to see heroic men crawling over the carnage, with blackened skin, haunted eyes and shovels in perpetual, desperate motion. He's come to feel the slurry underfoot, hear the lorries groaning in and out of the village.

'I'm going to look at the memorial garden.' Gloria walks on past the playground. She pushes the iron gate inscribed with the words, *This is the site of the Pantglas School*. William follows and they stroll amongst the neat rectangles of manicured lawn with small trees and plants bordering tidy, clear paths. 'It's the footprint of the school.' Gloria points at the patches on their left and right. He wonders how much more she knows. How much time she's spent finding out about this place that has such a hold on him.

He nods, momentarily transfixed by the marigold orbs in the borders between the path and the lawns. The calm order of the place offends him. For all she thinks she might know, Gloria has no idea. No visitors will have *any* idea of what happened here. He turns his back to the mountain and looks across at Moy Road. The old houses to the right look so normal, so intact, their windows edged with brick surrounds, like gappy white teeth. Who'd know that he peered through those windows and saw black piles of filth, with branches, bricks, toys, parts of broken piano sticking out of them? He remembers a stiletto shoe poking out from a black mound halfway up a staircase, white and bone-like.

The air smells of grass. A magpie lands on top of a small cherry tree. To the left, sloping down and away from them, are two rows of modern houses. This was where the original houses were completely destroyed. Is one of them Betty's? Is she still alive? William looks to the right, the route from the school to the mortuary.

'I want to go to the chapel. You don't have to come.' He's starting to wish he was alone. He has nothing to say about this Aberfan to Gloria.

'I'll come.' Gloria puts her hands in her pockets.

They walk along Moy Road for a few yards, then left down a short, steep side street that leads to the chapel. William doesn't remember the gullies that run between the houses, grass poking up through the tarmac and washing hanging across them. He doesn't remember anything beyond the chapel and the school, but this metal handrail that runs down the path he does, because he saw a woman hold on to it when her knees buckled.

Halfway down the incline he stops dead.

'What?' Gloria says. 'What's the matter?'

'It's gone.'

'What's gone?'

He rubs his temple to stop the buzzing and walks to the bottom of the path. He stares at the dark building with its modern brick tower that only now, he notices, has the shape of a cross embedded into the stone.

'This isn't it!' He looks left and right to see if he's got the wrong place.

'They must have knocked it down and rebuilt,' Gloria says softly. 'You can understand why.'

Something moves across William's scalp, like a twang of elastic. 'Why? We didn't do anything *wrong* in there!' He hears how high and broken his voice sounds. 'They shouldn't have knocked it down!'

He steps closer to the bleak building and touches the metal railing. It all seems so empty and still without the mothers, headscarves tied under their chins, winter coats held across their chests, without the coal-dusted miners, exhausted and determined, the Salvation Army with their tea, Kit Kats, and the kindness of whisky and cigarettes.

It's all so *ordinary*.

An explosion behind them makes them both jump. They turn to see an old Ford Cortina race down the narrow street, the driver's window wound down.

'This is where they had to wait,' William says turning back, rubbing his hand along the railing. 'The parents.'

'Where you had to hold up the little boy's shirt?'

He feels the slide of warmth and the pressure around the side of his palm as Gloria slips her hand into his.

'But it wasn't like this.'

'That's good, isn't it?' Gloria speaks quietly, not taking her eyes from the chapel. 'You wouldn't want it to stay the same forever, for all the people who have to go on living here? Would you?'

He shakes his head and frowns. 'But if none of it's here . . . if it's only in my head . . .' Something is falling within himself. He sounds mad. He doesn't want Gloria to think he's mad. He exhales; a bark of breath. 'It's an adjustment.'

'Of course it is.' Her grip tightens. 'But you can do it. Just like with your mum.'

'What do you mean?'

She continues to look at the chapel. 'You've realised people change; in fact, they couldn't stay the same, even if they wanted to.'

He looks ahead too, holding her hand. He's holding her hand. Maybe he'll be all right.

'I think I'll visit the graves,' he says, 'but it's a bit of a climb. Do you want to sit in the car, or on that bench in the playground?'

'No, I'll come.' She looks at him. 'I'll just have to take it slow.'

They walk back up the side street and turn left, away from the memorial garden and community centre and then right onto the lane that leads to the mountainside cemetery. The oldest graves sit at the bottom, skewed and sunken; grey, green and white with lichen and moss. But higher up the mountain, white semi-circles loop their way across the slope in two long rows; giant Polo mints, bright against the sky. William wants to run to them, but it would look odd and Gloria is by his side, so he slows his step and stares ahead.

'Bloody hell, don't they like their hills?' Hands on hips, Gloria breathes heavily for a few seconds before starting again.

Eventually they stand on a level path before the graves. Graves, William reflects for the first time, that have been here for seven years now. Although he's close enough to touch them, he has the strange feeling that he's moving further away. The years feel fluid, as if they are draining through him. The emptiness he felt staring at the new chapel starts to inflate, to fill with a lightness that lets him breathe.

Beneath each loop of a headstone are individual memorials; angel's wings, hearts, open bibles, scripture verses, poems, photographs in gilded frames. He walks slowly, reading everything.

> *If all the world was ours to give*
> *We would give it yes and more*
> *To see the one we loved so much*
> *Come smiling through the door.*

Halfway along the first row, Gloria sits on a bench behind him and blows her nose. William wants to find the grave of the girl with the perfect hand, but he can't remember her name. There's a photograph of a smiling boy, hair neatly parted, new second teeth too big and spread out in his mouth. The broken bodies of these children he never knew alive have sat under the surface of his memory for so long, it's as if they're part of him. Yet this is not the memory of the parents, or the community. It's his. His and Jimmy's and Harry's and the other embalmers'. It's what binds them together, and what separates them from the rest of the world.

William glances over his shoulder as a woman in a blue coat sits next to Gloria. He turns back to the graves.

'Hello,' says Gloria, 'am I on your seat? I can move.'

'That's all right, plenty of room for three.' The woman chuckles. There is a pause, then: 'Where are you from?'

'Near Birmingham, but we've been at a wedding in Swansea. You live here, do you?'

'Yes, love. My whole life.'

'Well,' says Gloria, bold and kind, 'my sympathy for the dreadful losses you've had to endure.'

'Thank you.'

William walks along the row.

A precious flower, lent not given
To bud on earth and bloom in heaven.

'Why have you come?' The woman's voice is gentle. 'I hope you don't mind me asking, I just always wonder what brings people here.'

Gloria clears her throat. 'It's not morbid curiosity, I promise you. My husband's an embalmer. He came to help when it happened.' William doesn't turn round, but a heat rises in him to hear Gloria call him her husband. 'He wanted to pay his respects.'

'I remember them,' the woman says, 'a *terrible* job. A terrible kindness they did for us. Something none of us wanted to think about.' William stares at the photograph of the smiling boy.

Gloria drops her voice, but he can still hear. 'He came back for the funerals, but this is the first time since.'

'He came to the funerals? That's more than I did. I didn't go to my own child's funeral. Imagine that!'

'I can't imagine any of it,' Gloria says.

'The guilt of it would have eaten me up if it wasn't for something that happened. My own little miracle that kept me going. Still does.'

'What was it? Do you mind me asking?'

William walks on a little but stays within earshot. He stares at the inscriptions, listening to the soft rhythm of the woman's voice.

'There's a lane me and my little girl used to like, alongside here. She'd zoom along on her scooter with my shopping bag hanging off the handles, full of things she'd collected. Bits of

369

fern, wildflowers, blackberries, anything she could pick and drop in the bag.

'On the day of the funerals, I told my husband to go for both of us, and I went up there. I could see everyone, but they couldn't see me. I sat against this almighty big rock that she used to draw on with her chalks. I wondered if any of it would still be there, but we'd had so much rain it had washed away. It was like I had a God's-eye view. I watched people putting their flowers on the huge cross. They'd come from all over the world, those flowers. Everyone looked so small. And I thought – how can we bear this? How can we possibly bear this pain? I wished we'd *all* died that morning. All of us together. That would have been better, I thought.'

William is desperate to turn round but he can't.

'And then this *racket* came from nowhere, above my head. It was a bloody helicopter, full of photographers! Well, that nearly polished me off. It was *my* girl who'd died, *my* heart that was breaking. What did the rest of the world want to be doing with us? And then it started, this beautiful, *beautiful* voice from behind me. Singing "Myfanwy", a song that means a *lot* to us in the valleys.'

'Yes' – Gloria's voice is low – 'I know it.'

'I didn't dare move. Whoever it was thought they were alone. So I just leant against that rock, watched the dirt thrown on the grave of my precious girl and let this – angel, whoever he was – be my voice. I let him sing that lovely, sad song, from me to my little girl. And now, if I'm on my own here, I sing it to her myself.'

At last William turns. Had he looked after her daughter, held up a piece of her clothing? Was she one of the mothers who sank to her knees at the sight of it? Was she the girl with the perfect hand? And today, this woman sits next to Gloria, in a cheerful spring coat with apricot-pink lips. *Humans beings are extraordinary*, he thinks.

'And I went back down that hill,' she continues, glancing at William, 'and I didn't feel any better, but somehow I had hope, that in time, I'd be able to bear it.'

Gloria looks at William. She won't cry, but he knows she wants to.

'William, come and say hello to this lady.'

He walks towards her, his hand held out.

'Hello' – her grip is firm – 'welcome back.'

'Thank you,' he says, connecting with her intense gaze. 'Can I ask you something?'

'If you like.' She nods, a slight smile lifting her mouth.

'When I was here, a woman turned up at the chapel and helped us get the children ready to be identified. Betty. Her house had been knocked down. Do you know her?'

'Course I know Betty.' The woman smiles. 'Everyone knows everyone here. They rebuilt her house. You'll have seen them on the way in. Very swanky, they are. All mod cons.'

'Do you think she'd mind if we visited her?'

The woman stands and smooths her coat. 'I'll walk you down, shall I?'

65

The doorbell is shrill and tinny. There's a movement, the blur becomes a neat figure, and the door opens.

'Look, Betty!' The woman presents them as if they're quarry she's hunted down. 'I've brought you some visitors.'

Betty looks at Gloria first, registers the pregnancy. 'Who's this?' She smiles. Her hair is grey, her floral dress is not smothered by a man's jumper, and she's wearing slippers not wellies. Her face has more lines and is fuller. But to William, she is exactly as she was.

'Betty.' He moves towards her. 'I'm William Lavery. I was a volunteer embalmer.'

Betty's hands lift to hold her face as she breathes in. 'Oh my word! Would I ever forget you?' She moves over the step to hug him, wrapping her arms tight round his waist, her face unashamedly pressed against his chest. He feels her small hands gripping his back.

'And this is . . . ?' she asks, letting go of him, smiling at Gloria.

'My wife, Gloria.'

She puts her hand softly on Gloria's cheek. 'Tea?' Her eyes are tiny blue lakes.

'I could *murder* one,' Gloria says, her smile creeping across her face, 'after I've used your loo, if that's all right?'

Betty stands back a minute and holds both of Gloria's arms. 'You look exhausted. How about we bring the tea up for you in my spare bedroom and you have a lie-down?'

Gloria smiles her gratitude.

Betty puts her hand on Gloria's back and points inside. 'Top of the stairs, left for the loo, first right for the bedroom. Sheets are clean.'

Gloria hugs her. 'I love you already, Betty.'

Betty laughs, and together she and William watch Gloria walk into the house. Each stair gently creaks as she climbs them.

'Come in the kitchen while I make a pot of tea.'

William follows. 'So, this is your new house?'

'Not so new now.' Betty smiles and reaches for mugs, kettle, tea, barely having to move. 'How come you met Mary?'

William leans against the worktop in the galley kitchen. 'Gloria got talking to her at the graveyard.' Betty nudges him to the left to get into the fridge. 'She told us on the day of the funeral how she went up the mountain, and heard someone singing "Myfanwy".'

'We all know that story. Her angel.'

William says nothing. Betty stops pouring the milk. 'Oh Lord, was it you?'

'I came back to pay my respects but I didn't want to intrude, so I went up behind the cemetery and when that wretched helicopter appeared' – he shrugs – 'it just came out of me.'

She shakes her head. 'We were all hit hard, but some buckled more visibly.' She stirs the tea and then puts the lid on the pot and concentrates on him. 'Mary was one of those. But she's had two more children since. Boy and a girl. Lovely, they are. So you see, you didn't just help all those parents say goodbye to their little ones, you helped Mary live with herself.' She pours a mug and hands it to him. 'You take this up to her.'

Awkward at crossing the threshold, William can tell, even with Gloria's back to him, that she's fast asleep. He puts the tea down on the wicker bedside table, in case she wakes thirsty, and walks light-footed out of the room and back down the stairs. Betty is sitting in the lounge, a square room with a sofa and two armchairs arranged in a triangle around a glass coffee table.

'She's flat out.'

'Bless her. When's the baby due?'

It hits William that it hasn't occurred to him to ask. 'I don't know.'

'What?' Her face is half frown, half smile.

'Long story.' He sits on the sofa opposite Betty. 'I didn't know until yesterday she was pregnant. I left her two months ago.'

She studies him, as if waiting for an alternative version that makes sense. 'You're telling me,' she says eventually, 'this is the first time you've seen each other for weeks and weeks? And you've come *here*?'

A clock chimes hurriedly somewhere in the house. A cat runs in and jumps onto Betty's lap. She lays her hand on its back and it lies down.

'I thought if I could make my peace with Aberfan, I might be able to make peace with myself.' He nods his head at the stairs. 'And her.'

'So, whatever troubles you've been having' – she leans back in the chair, crosses her legs – 'are mixed up with what happened here?'

'Yes,' he says, wondering from the look on her face and the comfort of her presence why on earth he didn't think to come and speak to her sooner. 'I've had dreams, from the day I left here, and flashbacks when I'm wide awake. On the day of the funerals, I decided I couldn't even *think* about having children. It was *unbearable*. I told Gloria, right from the start. I tried to break it off, but she wouldn't have it.' The teapot and mugs sit on the table between them, and a plate of biscuits with a paper

374

doily, but they remain untouched. There's a building pressure in him, to tell her what he's kept locked up so tightly. She's perfectly still, watching him, and it takes him right back to the moment she stood opposite him in the chapel vestry, waiting for him to pull back the blanket from the first child. 'What I've never told anyone . . .' He pauses, needing to swallow. 'Is that if I even think about having a child, spend a few seconds imagining what it would be like, I get these images in my head of its damaged body on a morgue table and me having to embalm it. Because if I had a child and they died, I couldn't possibly let anyone else do it, could I?' His eyes fill and when he manages to look at Betty, he sees that so have hers. 'I left her because I thought it was the kindest thing I could do. Let her have a life with someone else. But I didn't know she was pregnant. I would never have left if I'd known.'

A heavy creak at the top of the stairs gets both of their attention. They look from the staircase back at each other. The long moment of silence is like a held breath, then Gloria's footsteps move quickly across the landing, a door closes, the chain flushes, more footsteps, then silence.

'Right.' Betty stands after a few moments' quiet, and the cat tumbles onto the floor, looking around confused. She sits next to William on the sofa and holds both his hands. 'God knows we've suffered in Aberfan and it's been *hell*ish. Long, hard and hellish. But we're still here.' Betty's intent gaze holds him like a hug. 'And we've managed to laugh as well as cry, and there are new children and the school is full and there are reasons for living. Lots of them. What you did here, that *terrible* job, made unbearable moments bearable. And in my experience, that's what happens. When we go through impossible things, someone, or something, will help us, if we let them. And in our darkest days, William, you helped us. Now, at some point, God forbid, you might need help. And I believe you'll get it.' She frowns a little. 'And it seems to me that if Mary could find the courage to risk all that agony all over again, you can take that risk too.'

William soaks in Betty's words, her presence, her goodwill. He feels no need to say anything.

'You do love Gloria, don't you?' Betty asks.

'Oh, yes,' he answers, and the resolve with which he says it releases something, something he's held tight, like a clenched muscle.

Betty pulls a tissue from her sleeve and drops it in his lap.

'Now,' Betty says, 'this is all very private, but I seem to be slap bang in the middle of it, so I'll say my piece and then I'll be done. All right?'

'All right,' he says softly.

'It seems to me, that out of all this pain you've put people through, including yourself, a very good thing can come' – she glances up the stairs – 'for all three of you. The end of this chapter and the start of the next is that you become a father, knowing *far* better than those who've never seen the suffering you have, just how precious this child is, *even* before it's arrived! And that, William, seems a bit of a gift, don't you think?'

He nods.

'So.' Betty's hands rub together, sending a gentle rasp into the room. 'I'm off out for a couple of hours. I won't be back till teatime. I'll get fish and chips and you can stay the night if you like.'

She lifts the tray and takes it to the kitchen. 'This'll be cold, but help yourself to anything.' She comes back into the living room, unhooks her coat from the peg and slides it on in one swift, easy movement. She gives him a wave and closes the door behind her.

He sits, until the *click-clack* of Betty's rapid footsteps has faded. He takes off his shoes, puts them by the front door and then climbs the stairs. He's sure Gloria overheard him talking to Betty, so she might be waiting for him, but there's a stillness to the house that makes him think she's fallen back to sleep. If so, he won't wake her. He'll lie down beside her, next to the living flesh and bloodness of her miracle body, and when she opens her eyes, he'll make her another cup of tea and sit down on the bed with her. He'll ask her forgiveness, he'll make sure she knows how much he loves her, and then he'll ask.

Because the thought of it, the wonder of it, is hurtling through his veins, making him want to laugh, to dance, to *sing*.

'Gloria,' he'll say, and he'll be smiling, 'when are we going to meet our baby?'

Acknowledgements

Fairy Godmother: a female character in some fairy
stories who has magical powers and brings good
fortune to the hero or heroine.

I have two: Susan Armstrong, my ferociously effective and consistently kind, calm agent. Signing with her changed my life overnight. The other is Louisa Joyner at Faber, the editor every writer would love to have; whip-smart, intuitive and passionate. Thanks also to the wider team at C&W: Matilda Ayris, Kate Burton, Jake Smith-Bosanquet, Alexander Cochran and Katie Greenstreet, and at Faber: Pete Adlington, Hannah Marshall, Libby Marshall, Josephine Salverda and Josh Smith. Without exception, they have been enthusiastic and brilliant at their jobs. To Claire Gatzen, surely the most eagle-eyed of copy-editors.

To my writing teachers, starting with my English teacher at John Willmott Comprehensive, Lynne Jung, who told me I could be a writer. To Sally Cline, the late W. G. Sebald, Andrew Motion, Paul Magrs, Michèle Roberts and the class of 2001 at UEA.

To those who were gracious and helpful when they didn't need to be: Rachel Calder, Catherine Clarke, Anna Whitelock, Mary Nathan, Max Porter, Martin Wroe, Miranda Doyle, Jill Dawson and Isobel Abulhoul. To Kate Ahl and Andrew Hewitt, my intelligent, insightful first readers. To Gillian Stern, gifted editor and encourager. To Aki Schilz at TLC, Julia Forster, and the Bridport Prize.

From the dignified, dedicated world of undertaking, thanks to Billy Doggart, who coordinated the extraordinary volunteer effort at Aberfan, and fellow embalmer Peter Gaunt; two heroes who entrusted their stories to me right at the beginning. Thanks to James Skeates, for the window on to the inner life of an embalmer, and to Matthew King for letting me watch him at work. To Adrian Haler, for answering many questions about embalming in the 1960s (any mistakes are mine). To Huw Lewis, author of *To Hear the Skylark's Song* and child of Aberfan. To Tom Davies, reporter at the disaster and author of *The Reporter's Tale*, and to photographer Andrew Whittuck.

Thanks to Mark Tinkler, Alastair Roberts and Jonathan Hellyer Jones; all generous with their chorister stories. To Helen Robbins and Millie Cant for advice on all things musical, and to Tim Boniface, whom I watched at work with another unconventional choir. To Derek Rice from the Tate, for information on London galleries in the 1960s.

To Arun Midha, Barbara and Chris Matthews, my Swansea advisers. To Adrian Rees for a decisive conversation about the title. To Willie Williams and David Keleel, for the dream writer's retreat and without whom none of this would have been possible. To Jacki Parris, whose spare room was my study for a season and whose friendship has been for all seasons. To Miriam Ware for her wisdom.

Thanks to Carol Holliday and Steve Shaw, Julia and Martin Evans, for so many conversations and much laughter about life and the mysteries of the human condition. To festival companions Lesley Thompson and Kate Grunstein. To my Thursday morning writers and Friday lunchtime readers. To Isobel Maddison and the Lucy Cavendish community, and Cathy Moore and Cambridge Literary Festival friends; my nourishment over many years.

To my mum and sister, to Liam and Ada. To my magnificent, beloved daughters, Alice and Ruby, whom I'm so pleased to make proud.

And finally, my thanks start and end with John, my best friend for thirty-eight years, who frankly bordered on the ridiculous in his belief that this day would come.